1978

EARTH GIA

BY EDISON MARSHALL

GOTHIC ROMANCE

The Pagan King   A tale of fifth-century England
The Viking   A tale of the Sea Rovers of the ninth century
Castle in the Swamp   A tale of the Carolina Low Country in the nine-
    teenth century

BIOGRAPHICAL NOVELS

Earth Giant   A tale of Heracles (Hercules, as known in Roman myth)
Great Smith   A tale of Captain John Smith
Caravan to Xanadu   A tale of Marco Polo
The Infinite Woman   A tale inspired by the life of Lola Montez

REGIONAL NOVELS

Princess Sophia   A tale of Alaska in the period 1898–1918
The Inevitable Hour   A tale of Martinique in the period 1890–1902

HISTORICAL NOVELS

Yankee Pasha   The adventures of a young American frontiersman from
    Salem to Tartary after the Revolutionary War
The Gentleman   The adventures of a Charleston gambler at home, in
    the West Indies, and in South Africa, prior to the Civil War
Benjamin Blake   A tale of the bastard son of an English squire at home
    and in the South Sea Islands in the period of our Revolutionary War
American Captain   A tale of a young mariner in Maine, Malta, North
    Africa, East Africa, and England at the turn of the eighteenth century
The Upstart   A tale of strolling players in England about 1730
Gypsy Sixpence   A tale of a young Lancer on the Afghan frontier in
    India, his character and his story suggested by those of Richard
    Burton

BOOKS OF SHORT STORIES

Love Stories of India
The Heart of Little Shikara   Stories of animals of forest and jungle
The Elephant Remembers   A jungle book

MEMOIRS OF BIG-GAME HUNTING

The Heart of the Hunter   A looking-backward over hunting trails in
    Canada, Alaska, Africa, Indo-China, and India, and where they led
Shikar and Safari   A factual and objective account of various big-game
    hunts

EARTH GIANT

GIANT

BY

EDISON

MARSHALL

DOUBLEDAY & COMPANY, INC., GARDEN CITY, NEW YORK

1960

DEDICATION

To Their Majesties Paul and Frederika of Greece,
modern monarchs of the ancient land that
is the Mother-spring of Western greatness—

To these personages
I dedicate this book as a token of my gratitude
for their gracious reception of an American pilgrim
treading the hallowed paths.

AUTHOR'S FOREWORD

I searched a long time for a solid human being in the cloud of myth that enfolds Heracles, or Hercules according to the Roman corruption of his Greek name. Finally I believe I found him by imagination's light. Throughout the writing I never doubted that some such man lived in and about Thebes in the Heroic Age (circa 1000 B.C.). In the first place, there is almost always a true story behind a legend as far-flung and long-lived as this one. Place names, proper names, plays by hardheaded Greek dramatists, prose and poetry no more remote from his times than we are remote from the times of Columbus, pictures and statuary, and the impact of the legend on the skeptical Roman mind all lend support to the surmise.

The fact remains that this work is a novel, not fictionized biography. When details of the legend conflicted with my tale as I had conceived it, my tale had right of way. Fully half of the legend is preposterous, as every high school student knows. Whatever the original story, its myriad retelling by the folk long ago obliterated most of its resemblance to reality. My tale narrates labors, adventures, and exploits that were humanly possible and which seemed to me of a sort that might have given the legend birth. However, their being within human capability finds them a far cry from ordinary. If Heracles lived at all, he had supernormal strength in the inexplicable degree that has appeared in a very few human beings throughout recorded history. Also, I feel mystically about heroes, whether Heracles, Arthur, Roland, Ragnar Lothbrok the great Viking, Siegfried, Captain John Smith, John Paul Jones, and some living in the last century or even alive today. It seems to me that the Gods love them, that Olympian lightning plays about their heads, that Chance suspends her dull laws when one of the breed comes nigh, that Fate will meet them more than halfway, that event in ratio to their own greatness is their daily fare as long as their heroism lives.

E. M.

TABLE OF CONTENTS

LIST OF CHARACTERS

ACTAEON
ak-tē′ən

The great hunter, friend of Heracles

ALCMENE
alk-mē′ni

(Noble Lady), mother of Heracles and Iphicles

ALTHEA
al-thē′ə

Nurse of Heracles and his half-brother Iphicles (Right Doer)

AMPHITRYON
am-fit′ri-ən

(Wrathful Leader), in whose home Heracles was born

ANTAEUS
an-tē′əs

(Heart of Stone), a gigantic wrestler

DIAMENES
dī-ə-mē′nēz

A king in Stymphalus

DIOMEDES
dī-ə-mē′dēz

A king in Thrace

DYCTUS
dik′tus

A young drover

EURYTUS

King of Orchomenus

FOLD WATCHER

An old shepherd

HERACLES
her′ə-klēz

Who in Roman myth was Hercules

HIPPOLYTA

A queen in Krim

IOLE

Daughter of Eurytus and Priestess of Artemis

IPHICLES

(Right Doer), son of Amphitryon and Alcmene, Noble Lady, Heracles' mother

ISMENE

A shepherdess

LINUS

A player of the lyre

MEGARA
meg'ə-rə

Daughter of King Eurytus

NESSUS
nes'əs

The Horse Tamer, son of King Eurytus

NESTOR
nes'tər

A hero of the Trojan War

RHADAMANTHUS
rad-ə-man'thəs

Teacher to Heracles and Iphicles

SNAG TOOTH

An old drover

TIRESIAS
tə-res'i-əs

(Seer of Wonders), a prophet of Thebes

The following gods, goddesses, and supernatural beings were such a part of Greek life that, moving through the above characters, they become factors in the tale. Where these have been roughly identified with Roman deities, their Roman names are given in parentheses.

APHRODITE
afrə-dī'ti

(Venus), Goddess of Love and Beauty

APOLLO
ə-pol'ō

God of Truth and Prophecy, of Light, of the Lyre and Bow, and of Song

ARES
âr'ēz

(Mars), God of War

ARTEMIS
är'tə-mis

(Diana), Goddess of the Chase and pre-eminent in other fields

CERBERUS
sûr'bĕr-əs

A three-headed dog that guarded the gates of Hades

CLOTHO, LACHESIS, ATROPOS
klō'thō; lak'ə-sis; at'rə-pos

The three Fates

CENTAURS
sen'tôrs

Monsters, half man and half horse

DEMETER
di-mē'tĕr

(Ceres), Goddess of the Corn

DIONYSUS   (Bacchus), God of the Vine
dī′ə-nī′səs

HADES   (Pluto), God of the Underworld that also
hā′dēz   is named Hades

HEBE   Goddess of Youth
hē′bi

HECATE   Goddess of Darkness, one aspect of Ar-
hek′ə-ti   temis

HELIOS   God of the Sun
hē′li-os

HEPHAESTUS   (Vulcan), God of Smiths
hi-fes′təs

HERA   (Juno), wife and sister of Zeus, and
hê′rə   Queen of Heaven

HERMES   (Mercury), Messenger of the Gods, God
hūr′mēz   of Travelers, Traders, and Thieves

MUSES, MONSTERS, NYMPHS

PALLAS ATHENE   (Minerva), Goddess of Battle and pre-
                                  eminent in other fields

PAN   Goat-God of Herders and of Mountains,
                                  Woods, and Fields

POSEIDON   (Neptune), God of the Sea and of Horses
pō-sī′dn

PROSERPINE OR PERSEPHONE   Daughter of Demeter and Queen of
prō-sūr′pi-nē; pēr-sef′ə-ni   Hades

SILENUS   Drunken son (or brother) of Pan
sī-lē′nəs

ZEUS   (Jupiter, Jove), the Cloud Gatherer; head
                                  God of Olympus

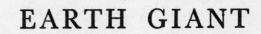

EARTH GIANT

CHAPTER ONE

THE GOOD SCHOOL

1

My name, Heracles, means "the glory of Hera." It may be that my tale will be told or sung to barbarian folk beyond our isles and the wine-dark seas of Greece, folk who worship trees or stones and know naught of our great Olympian Gods, so to these I make known that Hera is the Queen of Heaven, wife and sister of great Zeus. What of Zeus himself? Are there folk alive in some distant, darkened land that do not know the Thunderer, the Cloud Gatherer, he who hurls the dread and deadly lightning, he who overthrew his father, greatest of the Titans? It may be so. Even the mariners of Tyre who meet and trade with our far voyagers call him by another name.

My name was given me by my mother Alcmene, Noble Lady, whose beauty I beheld only with infant eyes, and yet which I half remember, as in a half-forgotten dream. She was a mirthful woman, or so my nurse has pictured her; and at whose expense was this merriest of jests? Was it for laughter behind the back of her husband, Amphitryon, whose name means Wrathful Leader? Or was it a taunt to that very Goddess, against whose jealous spite Zeus himself has been known to cringe?

No, I will not speak in riddles, as did the Sphinx. I will tell my tale simply, as bluntly as a Boeotian peasant tells of the matings of his plow beasts. It begins with an early, clear, compact memory of a real event. On a winter night I lay asleep in a house of sun-baked brick, neither palace nor hovel, about an hour's walk from the citadel of Thebes. It so chanced that two big sacks of dry cornstalks had been brought from the field to the stone court by one of our drovers—so I was told in later years, and the man believed he had been made the tool of my malevolent foe. I remember being wakened by some soft sound close at my side, or perhaps by a little movement under my sheepskins. I remember the flicker of a dying fire on the frescoed walls of the chamber. I was aware of cold, sharper than any I had ever known, as it bit my ears and nose, unprotected by my robe. I remember the happiness of knowing that my brother Iphicles, which means Right Doer, a year older than I, and almost a man, I thought, he being six, breathed quietly on a stalk-filled mattress next to mine.

Then I felt a different kind of cold near my waist on the right and left sides. It was not sharply cold, but dank, chill, and slippery, a little like a clam newly picked from its shell, and it was moving with a twisting motion in two narrow bands toward my warm belly. I cannot recall real terror at the visitation that I instantly knew was by living things; rather my body was filled with loathing and belligerence. Instantly I snatched at the top of each creeper, and each hand caught hold of something about the size of my palm, broader at the base than at the end, a thing horrid to the touch, and both fists closed with the strength of fury.

At once there came a violent threshing and writhing under and beyond the edges of my robe, and I think that I knew straightway that I had seized the heads of two big snakes.

I did not let go. I squeezed even harder. The only sound now was a scaly rustling and a thudding and thumping on the floor and against my mattress, and then the high-pitched yells of Right Doer, who had sprung to his feet in terror.

I too sprang up. Up with me came the thick and bloated bodies of the serpents, twisting and turning and wrapping their odious coils about my arms. I could see them plainly in the dim firelight, their mottled skins of strange design, and I would not let them go, and I did not yell, mainly because my teeth were locked as I exerted all my strength to squeeze. Then the head of the horrid visitor that I had grasped in my right hand slowly changed shape. Truly it became shapeless, and I heard a little crackle that might have been crushed bone, and a sticky fluid oozed up between my fingers, and the wildly writhing body hung like a loose rope. To kill the captive in my left hand seemed for long seconds beyond my strength, as indeed I could not until a renewed strength came, from whence I know not, except that it seemed born in my head rather than in my hand. For the first time in my life, I was summoning up something more than men call natural strength, and maybe it was a lending from some God that loved me, although such a thought could not then cross my infant mind. All I knew was it was there in my sore need. So my hand closed tighter, and I heard a distinct crack as the skull within the spade-shaped head was crushed flat upon itself.

Then at last I yelled with robust joy at my victory, and perhaps in mockery at Right Doer, standing pale and shrinking against the wall. I raised the dead snakes as high as I could, and the weight of each was as much as a peck of barley meal, and still a third of their length trailed on the earthen floor.

It was that second that my nurse, my beloved Althea, burst through the doorway in her nightdress. She looked first at Right Doer, because she loved him best, and then at me, and then her eyes fixed on what I held in my hands and her eyes rounded in a way I had not known possible for human eyes, and she gave forth a scream, piercing the ears like an arrow. I had started to run toward her, dragging the lower bodies of the snakes, to frighten her still more, only to stop when her yell rang on and on, to cease at last in a spasm of sobbing.

"Then it's true," she said quietly when the sobs died in her throat. "What Noble Lady guessed was true."

I did not know what she meant.

"Too well I know who sent those ministers of death, and for what cause, although I dare not say her name," Althea went on, speaking to herself; it seemed as though she had gone mad.

"Anyhow," I answered—soberly, for I had been torn by her sobbing —"the snakes are dead. See? Not one wiggle in their tails."

But on looking closer, I saw that their tails did wave a little, slowly and feebly, in the weird life that dead snakes retain awhile, and which would not end until sunrise. Althea stood staring into space. My brother, Right Doer, looked at me fearfully a long time, until the love I was used to seeing in his face slowly took fear's place. I yawned, and not liking the feel of the sticky crushed heads in my hands, I dragged the carcasses into the bitter cold of night, and threw them on the dung heap. Some large bird that I thought might be an eagle, but was more likely a great owl, saw me in the moonlight, hopped from his perch, and winged away in the gloom.

2

Althea loved Right Doer more than she did me. Still no ache of jealousy lodged ever in my breast, for somehow this division of love seemed fair. But years would pass before I understood, on the rare visits home of Wrathful Leader, why Right Doer could call him father, and sometimes climb his knees, while I was made to keep my distance and at his cold command address him only as Sir or Lord.

Even so, I was never begrudged my full portion of good meat and barley cakes, and with these, and with leavings that my brother, of less avid appetite, slipped into my hand, I thrived. Also when he was being schooled in the arts of war, usually by soldiers of the King's army that his father commanded, I took my turn at shooting arrows at marks, hurling a bronze spear, warding with shields the thrust and parry of swords. At the very first Right Doer was a better arrow shot than I at medium and close range, and as I improved at turtle pace, his gain was like a hare's in flight; and thick as my head might be, there got through it the solid fact that I could never overtake him. To console me somewhat, I could draw a far heavier bow, and cast an arrow twice or thrice as far as he with any bow, and hence at very long range I stood a chance at laying low that wariest of fowls, a wild gander, who at Right Doer's short-falling arrows did not deign a glance.

When I was twelve and he thirteen, I could wield a longer and much heavier blade, guarding my body with a fourfold shield of bronze plate such as weighed down and tired all but the strongest warriors. Yet behind his light shield, his skin was safer than mine from little cuts and scrapings, so lightning-quick he struck. Then, swift and agile as a ferret, he would dodge my counter.

It was a strange fact that many of our contests started with little vim, and for a strange reason. If, as usual, we had bared our breasts and arms, we felt a kind of shyness with each other because of my birthmark. Right Doer's very efforts to appear not to notice it made him flushed and awkward, and then my own mind became troubled and my attention wavered from the pursuit. This mark, close to the down-curve of my left shoulder, was of itself not disfiguring or even ugly. It was pink in hue and less than one finger long and two broad. In my early childhood I had thought it was the shape of a leaf of the hopvine which we grew for flavoring barley beer. Later I had perceived that a better likeness was the deeply lobed leaf of the giant oak. Maybe it only meant that I was fated to grow strong as an oak tree. Plainly my brother thought it meant something different, perhaps far more, an idea that I did not want to contend with yet and which sometimes, at the very brink of sleep, bore away my spirit into unearthly realms.

But both of us soon forgot the troublesome sign and went on with our game. Falling to with a right good will, we put each other to all kinds of trials, and in that way we developed our inborn powers. If I could lift twice or perhaps three times as great a weight, he beat me running and swimming. I could break with my hands a tree limb he could hardly bend, hurl a sharp spear through three inches of tough beech in which his point would stick, and throw down or yoke a raging ox that made him scamper. Our horses, which pranced and kicked and tried to bite him and run away and sometimes drag him in the dust when he had haltered them, soon yielded to my hand and the blows of my fist that I gave them at the tops of their shoulders, taming them much more quickly and better than the laying on of a whip. Then he was as proud of me as I was of him when he made a booby of me, jumping fences, racing over hurdles, vaulting with a pole, or leaping over brooks and bogs that I must wade.

Both of us took instruction from Rhadamanthus, that wise old man of Thebes, as to the nature and due of the high Gods, the long-ago lives of heroes, the lore of distant kingdoms and cities visited by our mariners, the mysteries of the stars and the tides, the science of battle, how to cast sums, how to care for slaves and beasts and cornland, and even how to deal justly with our fellows. And I reckon that for every pat on the back that Right Doer received for clear thinking and quick learning, I got a rap on the head from Rhadamanthus' gnarled stick.

Other differences between us became more plain as he came sixteen and I fifteen, until no one could guess that we were brothers of the womb. I was the more ordinary-looking—of little more than average height, about eight inches over five feet, thickly and solidly but not massively built, and plain of countenance. He stood only an inch short of six feet, of the slender build of Hermes, the swift messenger of the Gods, and his face was strikingly handsome, if not beautiful. He had large, flashing eyes; mine were small and triangular in shape because of close-fitting lids, and of a commonplace brown except when red with wrath. There was no indentation at the top of his nose; with his forehead it formed a bold, out-sweeping line as in the face, carved in marble, of an Olympian. My nose was big, good only for smelling and blowing, not for ornament; and my mouth did not look good for kissing or for singing songs.

So it came about that when we visited a fair or a holy festival, on him fell most of the smiles of jolly country wenches, as well as sideways glances from the daughters of chieftains.

All well-raised youths and maidens of good Greek families are taught to play the lyre. Right Doer could make it sing, and often he sang with it, ancient songs of Gods and heroes. But because my thick and powerful hands could not quickly learn to pluck melody from those seven little strings, I flew into a temper, gave my tutor Linus what I thought was a light thump on the head with the instrument, broke it into fragments, and came nigh to breaking the head of an accomplished and valuable slave. When Right Doer and I had brought him to, I begged his forgiveness and asked him to hit me as hard as he could on the jaw. This offer he declined—he did not wish to break his hand that he needed in the practice of his art. But, very properly, he refused to give me another lesson.

"You look like many other striplings," he told me quietly with that dignity of men, chieftains or slaves, who know their own powers. "Someday you'll look like many other men. But you'll never be a man. You'll be a monster."

I took the rebuke in good temper and face, but truly it cut deeper than he knew.

I hoped that was the end of it, and the report of what I had done would not leak to Wrathful Leader. This proved a vain hope—a female slave who was his spoil of a long-ago battle, jealous even now of the memory of my mother's beauty, had seen the little ruckus through an arch behind which she had sat spinning, and perhaps she had embellished the tale somewhat, to judge from the severity of my punishment.

"Heracles, you are not fit for the company of chieftains and their families," he told me, his face darkened with sudden rage. "I am going to banish you among my drovers and shepherds in the wilderness of Parnassus. There you will remain three years, eating the rough fare of the camps, sharing the labors of rude thralls, sleeping on the rocky ground under an oxhide, and there you will fight not with noblemen, but with wolves, lions, and bears."

"May I go with him?" Right Doer asked quickly, when I was struck dumb.

"No, you may not. You will come into your birthright as my son."

Whose son was I? How could I know? Perhaps the son of a burly slave performing some lowly task in my mother's chamber, while her husband was at war and her maids attended a holy feast. It was said that the arrows of passionate love often fly wildly through unfit bosoms, or the God who aims them is a jester.

Right Doer and I said our farewells behind a grove in the twilight, and his godlike face was wet with tears, and my pig's eyes were dimmed, as we kissed each other's heads and hands.

"You too must come into your birthright, Pride of Hera!" he told me with sudden force.

"What is my birthright? That of an ox to draw plows? No, I'll not let Linus' prophecy come true. I'll starve myself until my body's strength is no more than a jewelsmith's. I'll not grow another inch. I'll sleep in the sun, because if I work with the bulls, my muscles will swell like a bull's——"

"Be still, lest you waken the wrath of the Gods! Wrestle with the bulls. Eat mightily of their strong beef. Fight the centaurs that often drive off cattle, and impale the raiding lion on your spear! The Gods did not give you a giant's strength to cast away in sloth. What is the thread of your life that Clotho spins?"

I could not answer. Clotho was no slave girl spinning in our household; she was one of the three Fates. It is whispered among old friends, far from other ears, that Zeus himself cannot change that thread, or the lot that her sister casts for every human being, or the instant that the third sister lifts her shears to cut the thread; all these not Zeus the Thunderer can change in one jot or tittle.

"It is a wondrous thread of many colors," Right Doer went on, his eyes of hazel color now and shining. "It will be strong as the rope we use to picket our chariot horses, and the lot of your life is unlike any Greek's in song or story. Go from me in grief, but rejoice in your destiny."

3

Although I never ceased to be lonely for Right Doer, and his image haunted my thoughts and dreams, truly I did not grieve long. It was impossible in such a land—hills and valleys, forests and meadows, under Parnassus. With the rude drovers and shepherds by whose cook-

ing and watch fires I slept, I established fellowship. I had been told
to share their labors. This I did, fair weather or foul, and ere the moon
was out, I was loading the hardest and most dangerous on my unfrail
back.

With them I drove the flocks and herds from low to high ground,
following the grass. When they wandered off, I knew the bitter
anxiety of bringing in the strays, out of the paths of lurking wolves,
and knew the sweet relief of seeing every one bed down under our
close guard. With firebrands I helped chase away a raiding lion, and I
hurled my spear at him only to miss, and I heard him growl when my
long-cast arrow stung his tawny hide. I did not need Right Doer's
bidding to eat mightily of the half-baked beef and whole quarters of
mutton roasted on spits, and we did not fail to offer the bones, guts,
and some of the fat to the Gods, although I wondered what satisfaction
they took in the customary gift, the same that was offered at high
rites, and wondered if the great Olympians would not pay us off for
our stinginess, before man's course was run.

When I stopped to think of it, it was rather like us Greeks to cheat
even our Gods with offal, keeping the best meat for our own bellies.
We loved to dwell upon them, to hear tales of their wars, quarrels,
loves, and jealousies, to imagine their feasting while the Graces danced
in their wondrous halls behind walls of cloud, but we did not fear
them as terribly as the barbarians feared their dark and monstrous
deities, perhaps because they were so like ourselves on a grand scale.
The great difference was vast and unbridgeable: they were immortal;
they did not have to meet Death at any crossroad.

I went to look for them, in a way of speaking, on days when our
beasts grazed on open plains and I could be spared from the watch.
I would follow up brooks that fed our rivers until I found their birthplace in mountain springs, and always I expected to see beautiful
naiads, the nymphs of flowing waters.

Perhaps I did catch a glimpse of one now and then, as she disappeared in mist.

And how I loved the land itself, and rejoiced that it should be the
birthplace of Right Doer and me! It was the fit place for our habitation,
I thought, because it was somewhat like both of us—hardy and rough
like me, beautiful like my brother. And on some days its beauty gave
a great lift to my heart, and sometimes it made me sad, because I had
none of my own.

Once, in heavy forest above our pasturage, where the limbs of huge oaks embraced one another far from any habitation, I saw a dryad. All I had hoped for was a message in the rustling leaves, perhaps tidings from very Zeus, because his oracle is an oak tree, and instead I saw one of the lesser divinities, although immortal. It took the shape of a tall girl with red tresses, and she was gathering acorns, and her beauty flowed to me like waters in a brook flowing through a vale of dimness. She was at medium arrow cast when I saw her first, and she had not noticed me as yet, and if I had remained in the shadows perhaps she would have wandered toward me and perhaps spoken to me. Perhaps she would have done more than speak, even seen something in me missed by mortal maids, and taken me by the hand, and we would have wandered together until the grass grew soft and wondrous green, and there we would have lain and made divine love, and all my life would have been changed.

Fool that I was, I rushed toward her. She saw a stocky fellow with a big nose and an unruly shock of black hair running at her as though he meant to rape her, and she took to her heels. In an instant she had vanished in the vagueness of the forest, and I could no longer hear her light, running feet, and I stopped and covered my eyes with my hands, and only the Gods knew what things, vaguely seen, impossible to relate, that her flight from me foretold.

I was Heracles, perhaps a giant among men, perhaps a monster. In either case I was alone, listening to the rustle of oak leaves. And that, too, was a prophecy, though I knew not of what.

What fate awaited me, I would look in the face. That was my resolve, a thing harder than bronze, hard as the very iron which now and then was brought into our seaports from Babylon or from Egypt. Returning to our pasturage, the moon showed my shadow longer than before, for I had grown an inch or two in my stay under lofty Parnassus; and that night when a lurking lion dragged away a heifer I followed him alone, armed only with my bronze spear. He dropped the carcass that he had carried by the neck, and turned as though to attack me, and furiously he growled, and wickedly snarled, but when I advanced without changing pace, he skulked away.

I carried back his prize, unharmed except for the deep holes in her throat where first the lion's mighty fangs had set to kill, and in her neck where he had gotten a good grip to bear away his prey; and indeed these holes had bled the meat as well as could a butcher. Still my campmates balked at eating it at first, perhaps in fear of the lion's taking appropriate revenge. Laughing at them, I prepared a sacrifice. After wondering awhile what God to honor, I picked Hermes, greatly beloved in Greece, and my reason was twofold. In the first place, he was a mighty thief himself and the God of Thieves, and he should be pleased with a twice-stolen feast. In the second place, he had helped a beautiful ancestress of mine whom Zeus had changed to a white heifer to hide her from the wrath of his jealous wife. So while my fellows stared, pale in the face, I poured purple wine on some of the fat, bone, and guts, adding for good measure a succulent steak, then laid the lot on the high-leaping golden fire. After roasting the rest of the veal on a long spit, with what joy and appetite I fell to!

My chin had hardly begun to shine with grease when the watchers began to come up sheepishly, seeking a share of my feast. When we were through, our leavings would not have full-fed one of Zeus' eagles.

These little events occurred at the autumn equinox. Not long thereafter, there occurred a great event—the descent of Persephone, the daughter of our Goddess of the Corn, to the Underworld. For more than half a year she had stayed with us earthfolk, and the flowers had bloomed and the corn had greened and then yellowed, but now her mother mourned, and the flowers wilted from frostbite and the fields lay sear. The oak trees braved it out awhile, with multicolored banners on their boughs, only to stand at last bereft and naked in the blast of wintry wind.

And now we herders and drovers could not lie long abed, or sit long over our meat, for we must find pasturage for our flocks and herds somewhere, somehow; and my labors became almost equal to my desire. Besides taking my turn at watching and driving I searched hill and valley and half-frozen swamp for any herbage that the beasts would eat. The ever hungry lions waxed bolder, and the wolves, of whom in summer we saw little, returned from their wildernesses to harry our sheep and even to leap at the throats of our yearling cattle. It came to pass that I was ever driven, up mountains, down valleys, wading or swimming rivers icy cold, pelted by dismal rain, frostbit, chilled to the bone by raging blasts. Still I stuffed rich meat, was never sick or ailing a single hour, and grew another inch or so to eleven inches over five feet. Although my muscles did not increase notably in size, they changed shape, and their innate power steeped me in deepest wonder. There was one development I had not liked to look at, but it was my fate and I faced it with the rest. My arms appeared to grow somewhat long in proportion to the length of my body, and my wrists and forearms thickened until there remained very little tapering from elbow to hand. A manlike beast of some dank, rank-smelling, dimly lighted jungle at the headwaters of the Nile might have such arms, I thought.

The bleak winter, with brief, dark days, and long, chill nights of myriad jewel-bright stars, began to ebb. Warm spells took turns with the inclement; the turf turned grayish green; and suddenly, one morning, we found new-sprouted grass. If Persephone had not actually returned to the good earth out of the dim land of shades, she was here in spirit.

Having emptied a gallon measure of honey mead, the leavings of the whole camp from a huge batch we had made with our loot from a bee tree, I fell to thinking of Persephone's husband, Hades, on his golden throne, and of his feelings over her leaving his bed and board, and I could not help but laugh. Long ago, Zeus, Poseidon, and Hades, all sons of a Titan, had cast lots to see who would rule Heaven and Earth, the Oceans, and the Underworld of the dead. It must be that the Fates, or some dread power unknown, had fixed the lots to fall as they did fall, because Zeus was far the greatest of the three, Poseidon next great, and Hades the least great. Hades' realm was a sorry dole compared to either of the others—dismal rivers, dimness everywhere, unbreakable silence—and his subjects were the shadowy dead who could not speak unless given sacrificial blood from the Upper World. When he had kidnaped and raped Persephone and carried her to his bleak abode, he had not been strong enough to keep her the whole year. At her mother's mourning, whereupon the corn would not grow and turned sear and frostbit, Zeus had made the Death King yield her up for something nigh unto eight months, and for only four months could he have her in his kingdom. True, those four months had the longest nights in the whole year, and Hades and his bride could lie long abed. True, too, Hades owned a wondrous dog with three heads, Cerberus, to guard his black gate, but I proposed to fight him when the time came, and to break his back.

I know not to what other schemes and wonders my thoughts would have led me that night, if the strong brew had not prevailed over me somewhat. I fell into dreamless sleep.

4

Spring came into full flush, the incomparable Grecian spring, our flowers flamboyant, and lovelier to the sight because they bloomed amid rocks and brambles, every fertile spot adorned, and bleak hillsides radiant with blossom. By the waters, hyacinths of divine purple vied with violets, crocuses, iris, and wild roses for our glances of gratitude and praise. Eggs hatched; cubs suckled; voluptuous swans intertwined their necks. Lusty swains disappeared in leafy bowers where rosy milkmaids chanced upon them in astonishment. As for me, I made no loves except in dreams just before waking with wraiths of maidens I did not know, but perhaps fated to come into my waking life.

Even so, in the way of wonders I thought that I saw a centaur. These beings, half man, half horse, were known to come to lonely pastures to drive off cattle. We drovers had often discussed the likelihood of such a visit, and how to deal with it, yet when we appeared to see one making down a steep hill toward our herds, the hair on my head crept a little and I doubt not that the wintry scalp of our oldest shepherd did the like. In the first place, centaurs were reputed to be among the most belligerent of monsters, biting and stamping to death people who brooked their fierce desires. In the second place, all of us had met far more supernatural creatures in song and story than in everyday life.

" 'Tis a centaur, sure enough," the old shepherd said, in a shaking voice. "Ye can see the man part above the horse part."

"I think I see the top part of a man and all of a horse."

"Look at the beast run. He's swift as an arrow. We'd better lie low under this cliff"—we had been breaking our fast with our backs to the rock—"and let him drive off a few cows. He can't take many, and I don't want any dealings with his like."

Hoping this was truly a centaur, whom I would fight if need be, I must have looked more sharply than my fellows. Suddenly I perceived the truth that was hardly less wonderful than the visit of a monster—a man astride a horse as boys sometimes ride oxen. Many horses had been broken to draw chariots, but being half wild and savage-tempered, they could not abide the weight of a man on their backs, bucked him off by stiff-legged leaps, and often kicked him to death. Our visitor, whoever he might be, was a horse tamer indeed.

"I'm going to speak to him," I said, suddenly standing up.

"Heracles, you are a fool," a young drover told me. "But I'll go with you, if you want."

"No, I'll go alone, and I'll go unarmed." Going alone was merely a matter of propriety. I was the only man here belonging to a family of recent descent from the Gods, and I could not doubt that this rider was a scion of some royal house, if not a famous champion. Going unarmed was no feat, since our visitor bore no weapons but a leather whip, and anyway, I carried deadly weapons that had grown on me.

The horseman stopped his beast when he saw me approaching, and although it pranced and wheeled and snorted, not for one second did it escape from his control. Meanwhile I was taking a good look at him. An exceptionally tall man, at least four inches over six feet, he put me to shame with his beautifully proportioned body, darkly handsome face, and royal manner that our storytellers at religious festivals called godlike. Plainly he mistook me for a thrall of the cattle owner, but the thought came to me that his bearing would be lofty and aloof even with the sons of kings. There is no epithet more complimentary in all Greek lore than Horse Tamer. Charioteers, renowned for their haughty ways, only harnessed and drove horses with a bronze bit in their mouths. This stranger mastered his steed with his voice, pressure of his knees, a leather strap, and no doubt indomitable will.

"Sir, will you come down, and take such lowly food and drink as our camp offers?" I asked.

"Fellow, your speech doesn't match your garments and your occupation," he answered. "Nor, may I say, your coarse face and burly body?"

"You may say it because 'tis true."

"And if it were not true, what would you do?"

"Why, I take it, I'd upset your stallion with you on his back, and give you both a good bump."

Perhaps I would not have spoken so plain if I had not now noticed a peculiar detail of the horseman's garments, and had guessed at its reason. The stallion was a beautiful red bay; so were the baggy pants, rarely seen in Greece except on the legs of sailors from the shores of the Euxine Sea. The only cause I could conceive for the close match was that, at a distance, the rider's legs became almost invisible and he and his mount would seem one body, that of a centaur. By nature I was not a suspicious fellow, still the thought struck me, stirring my spleen no little, that perhaps a good many of the so-called centaurs whom frightened drovers had seen driving off their cattle had been mortal men astraddle horses. There might be a band of them in the employ of some greedy king. If so, why had a princely cattle thief let me draw this close? Perhaps he took me for a country lout with whom he could make game.

"Well, you're a fellow of spirit, and of some wit too, to perceive I'm a horse tamer and not half horse."

"A toddling child wouldn't mistake you for a centaur, sir, at close view."

"It was only my morning's sport."

"Why hide a greater marvel, complete mastery of a horse by a man, under a lesser marvel, the creation of a mere monster by the Gods?"

"A cattle drover aping a philosopher? Still, you may be better born than you appear—or else you've served some nobleman long enough to learn his tricks of speech. But I'll not take food and drink. I am Nessus, son of the King of Minyae."

I caught a quick breath, for Eurytus, my visitor's father, had of late become one of the most powerful kings of all Greece. Reaching out from his capital, Orchomenus, he had won overlordship of many towns, and our King of Thebes had paid him a yearly tribute of a hundred cattle. When the lion is away the wild dog barks. One great king lay dead by the hand of his wife's lover; another had never returned from the Trojan War; a third lingered on Pharos with his divinely beautiful wife, seeking to appease the Gods and regain his throne at Sparta.

"Royal Sir, I am Heracles, son of Noble Lady Alcmene; and if I'm not a bastard, my sire is Wrathful Leader Amphitryon."

"I've not heard of you, but my royal father honors yours by calling him his foe."

"I didn't know it."

"Is he not the Leader of the Host of Thebes? And this year Layius, the King, has failed to pay tribute to his overlord, my father, and they may be at each other's throats before the harvest. Bah! Whatever you were born, you are now a herder of cattle. To whom do they belong?"

"To Wrathful Leader."

"Then be sure you save one hundred of the best and fattest as a peace offering to Eurytus, King of the Minyae."

With that he touched his left knee to the horse's shoulder, which caused the beast to wheel to the right and dash away. I had got the small end of the horn in the encounter, it seemed to me, as I rejoined my fellows. But there would be other encounters, if the sullen glowings of my heart told truth. I might never master a horse, but I meant to master Nessus, and teach that arrogant prince to look up to me, not down on me.

5

The longest day of the year drew toward its lazy close. It was not a day of feasting among us Greeks, as was the shortest day in the year despite wintry weather. This last was celebrated with many a joyous festival, because we knew that the sun would straightway start back, and every night would grow shorter instead of longer, and that winter had broken his back, although he would hang about, shooting Parthian arrows at us, for three long and weary moons. Today's only event of note so far had occurred about noon, which was a thunderstorm of great violence and deep profundity, breaking over Parnassus and drenching the countryside with successive massive sheets of dark rain out of the black cloud close-pressing all. I believed it was some sort of sign, given to me alone. Zeus did not commonly waste his most dazzling and terrible bolts smiting the wild, unpeopled mountain or waste his breath in a continuous crashing roar. Was the coming event good or evil? I did not know until I saw a golden eagle, perching atop a tall dead pine like the skeleton of a Titan, fly safely away when the trunk was split asunder by one of the zigzag shafts. And his passage was from my left to my right, truly a sign of the good will of Zeus.

So I was not astonished, immediately after sundown, to see a mule cart advancing toward our camp, driven by a slave, while beside him stood a tall, lightly built man, the proud set of his head and his thrown-back shoulders remembrant of someone I knew and loved. I went to meet the visitors, and who should jump down and run toward me, his face like to Apollo's for light and beauty, but my best-beloved, my brother Iphicles, Right Doer, who in my sight could do no wrong?

When we had wrung and kissed each other's hands, he told me the news of our household in one burst. Red-haired Althea, nurse and foster mother to both Right Doer and me, had come to no ill. The fields had prospered well the succeeding year, our granaries were full, our thralls and our field beasts fat and content. But three weeks ago, Wrathful Leader, with his arms bearer and some slaves, had taken his war chariot and departed for Orchomenus, leading the host of Thebes to make war on Eurytus, King of the Minyae. The fortunes of that war Right Doer did not know. He had heard of one battle outside the earthen walls, when winged Victory would light on neither standard, although many young warriors, whose sires had died in glory before Troy, took off almost unnoticed for the Underworld, and thus families of great name came to an end.

"You must wonder that we two, nineteen and eighteen, in the flush of our young manhood, will eat meat tonight, instead of bite dust," Right Doer said gravely.

"Aye, I do wonder."

"We are both commanded by Wrathful Leader to stay with the flocks and herds until he summons us. Beyond this I know nothing, although Althea heard a roundabout tale that he had spoken to Tiresias, Seer of Wonders, before he marched."

Seer of Wonders was a gnarled old man dwelling in Thebes, a former slave and a shepherd of goats in the wilderness of Parnassus. Legend had it that he had once found the God Pan drunk and bogged in mud. After extricating and washing him, and restoring his lost pipes as well as what little dignity the Goat-God could muster, the lowly rescuer was frightened out of his wits by a blaze of light. Radiant in the dark forest stood Hermes, father of Pan, descended on his winged sandals from Olympus. To Tiresias he awarded the gift of prophecy, to come upon him only when tipsy with wine. Hence his auguries sounded hardly more credible in the ears of men than the wild outcries of Cassandra.

Still I could not dream what he had told Wrathful Leader to cause him to forbid Right Doer and me to follow him to war.

"We'll make the best of it," I told my brother. "It is a good life that we live here."

"As for me, I would rather kill wolves and bears to protect our droves than kill other tall young men in a test of might between two kings."

At first I was amazed at Right Doer, afeared that his remark might anger the Gods; then I thought of what good sense it made, of how it would please Demeter, Goddess of the Corn, Dionysus, God of the Vine, Hebe, the beautiful Goddess of Youth, and perhaps Apollo, who loved music more than the clash of arms and who was rarely known to kill people except the old and ill.

My fellow herdsmen were proud of me for having a brother as handsome and as royal-looking as Right Doer. At first they were loath to let him share our humble tasks; and when they saw how willingly and well he performed them, they idolized him. In the meantime, he and I rediscovered our happy brotherhood, if indeed it had ever dimmed in our sight. In our years of parting he had grown from striplinghood to full manhood.

He and I spoke little of the distant war in which we played no part. In the first place, we did not like to think about it, because it meant thinking of boyhood friends, boys we had wrestled and raced against, boys whose shouts had rung with ours, now pitched in bloody battle against the youth of the Minyae, and the Gods only knew how many of them had already found their dark way down into dim Hades. In the second place, our goats and herders did not like to hear about the conflict, because their lives were innocent and lovely, caring for cattle and sheep, calves and lambs, seeing that bulls of great scrotum covered the best cows and improved the breed, and making sure that lascivious rams were well fed and fat, ready for the breeding season, when they outdid very satyrs in the way of lechery; and they could not abide the vision of young men killing one another, some of whom had never begotten sons. Like Right Doer and me, they could only pray for the victory of Layius, King of Thebes, a just and generous king instead of a blood-smeared tyrant such as Eurytus, his enemy. Whenever we had slaughtered a young bull or ram for the spits, and set to one side the meat that we would eat, and prepared a sacrifice to some God, and given it to the fire, they would lie beside us two in a long row, uttering most heartfelt prayers.

"You are nearly twenty, I nearly nineteen," I told Right Doer on a hushed twilight after some months of exile. "By all thinking we are counted men, of age to make up our own minds as to what we owe our home lands and the Gods. Perhaps we should no longer obey Wrathful Leader's command, and make our way to the battle lines, and do what we can to win the victory for King Layius."

Right Doer gazed long into the fire, his fingers slowly working through his chestnut tresses. "Heracles," he answered at last, "I told you that my father talked with old, gnarled Seer of Wonders, the prophet of Thebes, before he came to this strange and harsh decision. Truly it was more difficult for Wrathful Leader to make than for us to obey. He dedicated himself to arms, kneeling before Ares, God of

War, when he was twelve years old. Why should he, when I am well grown and well schooled, withhold his own son from battle? Aye, he loves me deeply, but that love would have caused him to have me go and seek glory against the swords of the Minyae. There is only one possible answer to the riddle, strange as it may seem, and that is some prophecy made by Seer of Wonders, when, drunken with purple wine, he spoke the will of the Gods, the decree of the three Fates."

"That if you or both of us went to the war, you or both of us would not return?"

"That would not have restrained Wrathful Leader a single hour. It is the lot of warriors either to die in battle or to escape the carnage, hit or miss; when great Achilles sailed for Troy he knew he was fated for an early death. My father would have scorned to move his finger against such a prophecy; and he would only dwell upon it in his dark thoughts. The prophecy must have been that our great work is yet to come—no doubt after glorious victory or dire defeat has lighted on our King's head. This is a time of waiting, while our names are forgot, so when we are called no one knows that you are more than a great lubber of a cattle drover and I your brother, perhaps of greater wit, but still a poor weakling of a son to that great soldier, Wrathful Leader. Perhaps it is a time of training too. This is a wild and rocky wilderness, and here we stand closer to the immortal Gods than within the walls of Thebes. I cannot say that we better understand their being and their wishes, but at least all that we hear and see is true, my mind has more room to work, your muscles more opportunity to grow. We eat and sleep beside simple men. We hear the pipes of Pan; we see Zeus' lightnings on the mountains; Demeter, the Earth Goddess who loves all husbandry, comes close; and once when I was alone with a flock I thought I heard Apollo, the Friend of Men, the Truth Teller, half-brother of bloody Ares, but himself the hater of hideous war—I thought I heard him singing in the wood. Be of good cheer, Heracles. It comes to me you'll get your chance to use your great arms. If I may believe what is in my heart, our stay here is at the will of some God or Goddess who loves Thebes—perhaps very Hermes, who loves mankind."

No such consolation was in my heart. There was only a dismal feeling that all was going wrong, that the war was being lost, and while Right Doer belonged here in the wilderness, far from the crash of arms and the spurting blood, because of his gentleness and his beauty, and indeed his very name that fitted him so well, I, Heracles, strong as an ox, rough, uncouth, belonged in the line of battle, and if any God loved Thebes, he hated me for my dereliction.

I was thinking of this, dark of soul, as I was falling to sleep. And as the moon climbed, and the hours crept, and the pines wagged their tops in the fresh, cool air sliding off the mountain, and the beasts stirred a little, and one and one uttered low sounds, it seemed that a being came to my bedside and stood there with his gaze fixed on my face. Slowly I recognized the face and form of Linus, who had tried to teach me how to play the lyre. But he had changed in some utter and awesome way. He stood at the same height, it seemed, and he looked exactly the same except for his pallor and a bloodstain in his hair on the right side. Still he seemed unutterably distant from me.

"Linus?" I called.

"I am he who was Linus."

"Are you a shade?"

"Aye."

"Why have you come up?"

"I was sent up by one of great fame and of great power even in shadowy Hades, but I may not give his name."

"How could you pass through the gate guarded by the three-headed dog, foul Cerberus of the dragon tail?"

"At the word of him who sent me, Cerberus cowered down."

"Now that I cannot believe, unless he was an immortal God. Anyway, I am a herder of sheep and a drover of cattle, and have no dealings with Gods or, for that matter, with ghosts of great fame. I do not think you are the ghost of Linus. I think you are a dream in the night, that I dream even as I say so. If you are of the dead, how were you slain? What was the name of your slayer, and the day and hour, and in what battle? That at least can be verified by living men."

"Heracles, I was slain by you, when you struck me with the lyre. I did not die then—my skull was only cracked, not broken—but when, in battle, one of Wrathful Leader's chariot horses was felled with a spear, the pole swung around and dealt me a light knock, and the cracked bones gave way under my scalp and pressed against my brain, and my eyes were darkened. But I bear you no grudge. You are no more to blame for your hot temper than for your thick head."

And this last sounded just like our old slave Linus, who always spoke bluntly, yet who could pluck the most delicate and lovely notes from seven little strings.

"Have you brought me news of the war?"

"That you will learn soon enough. And then you will learn, too, why Wrathful Leader did not let you and Right Doer follow him there. But although you, Heracles, in your heart of hearts are ashamed, and the time may come that Wrathful Leader, too, will feel shame, I have been sent to tell you that he did well, and Right Doer's words as you sat together in the growing dusk were true words. Farewell!"

6

I did not tell Right Doer of the visitation, whether by a ghost or a strangely vivid dream. He would surely believe the former, for he was a man of darting imagination, as are most men of powerful mind; while I only wished to believe it, with a great wishing, and somehow I feared that in telling it I would reduce the chances of its being true. This much I knew. My heart was no longer troubled over my playing no part in the War of the Two Kings. In patience and peace I would await the outcome, certain that both of us would have our turn at great endeavors and at winning glory. And with what joy I sat beside him when we broke fast, both of us chewing away at the good meat, and air fresh in our nostrils, the hills about us looming in pride at the feet of great Parnassus, and a happy day of labor and loafing and little adventures long-stretched ahead of us!

Remembering Linus' bloody wound, I looked at Right Doer's head, and I thanked the Gods I had not broken it in rough play when we were boys. Truly I had rarely seen such a handsome edifice on the shoulders of a man. It was of good size, oblong in shape, and his hair grew in chestnut curls. His ears were low-set; and his brow being high and steep, with no indentation at the line of the eyes, formed one bold and handsome out-turned line with his high-bridged nose. An incurved line of some length separated the septum from his long full lips, and his chin was strong and cleft.

Still it was his head's interior, which no one could see or picture except as it was reflected in his speech and actions, that ever moved me to admiration and almost awe. And what this might mean to both of us, a stronger bond between us than we yet realized, was strangely shown in an incident of the chase.

My brother, armed with bow and arrow, and I, with a javelin, had tracked a magnificent stag in the foothills below Parnassus, famed as the grazing ground of the winged horse, Pegasus. Our quarry made for ever higher ground, with scant woods and many rocks, and then picked his way down a ravine falling sharply from a granite cliff. Fully a half mile away and far below us the late afternoon sunlight glinted on his antlers; then we made out his russet hide behind some thickets. But the descent was too steep for us to essay with reasonable safety, and twilight would fall before we could draw in arrow cast. And not even I, Heracles, could lug his carcass, more than twice my own weight, up the steep defile in the haunted darkness.

In fact the Olympian Goddess Artemis, daughter of Zeus and protector of stags so she could kill them at her pleasure, might be so incensed at our reckless chase of one of her charges that she would contrive to spill us both down the steep cliff to our early and inglorious deaths. Worse yet, in this forsaken spot our bones might never be found and buried, hence our shades must always linger, wailing, on this side of the River Styx, and never pass to the vague, dreamy, dismal realm of Hades.

"If we could scare him enough, he might return the way he came, and I could lie in wait for him at the top of the ravine," Right Doer said thoughtfully. "He would hardly try to climb out of the vale over yonder precipice."

"I could shout with all my breath——" And truly, my voice was strong as a bull's.

"He'd think it was thunder re-echoed from Olympus."

Right Doer half closed his eyes, in his way when his thoughts ranged far. Suddenly he spoke.

"When we were walking along the edge of the cliff, seeking a way down, I noticed a big stone."

"Well, so did I."

"Not two hundred steps from here—I think I can see it now. You couldn't have moved it when you left our homestead—it weighs as much as two grown steers—but you've fed on good meat here in the wilderness. It lies about five feet from the brink. Do you think you can roll it over?"

"If it doesn't weigh more than three grown steers, and isn't wedged in solid rock," I answered, my heart leaping with joy.

"My brother, it will be a sight worth seeing, and cause an uproar that will wake Echo from her sweet slumber. Put your shoulder to it, man, and I'll make for my hiding place."

I sped to the great piece of granite at the cliff brink. Its shape was more nearly round than I had hoped, and doubtless it had been hurled here by a Titan in the dim days before Zeus was born.

Perhaps it weighed as much as four big steers, but I cared naught, and truly my soul rejoiced because it was not lodged nor was there any obstacle in its five-foot path to the very brink.

At the first thrust of my shoulder it did not move. I stopped and drew a deep breath and thought upon the glory of the victory if I could win it, both to Right Doer and to myself, and how the palates of our fellows would relish the succulent venison. So I drew myself together, and at the second strong thrust the stone moved.

Now that I had moved it an inch, I could move it five feet. I knew that the power was in me and I need only call it forth by some great heaving of my heart and the steeling of my will. The stone moved again. It turned a little on its deeply curved side. I lifted and heaved in the same burst of strength, and suddenly it was poised on the very edge of the cliff. Careful that I would not hurl over in its wake, I gave it a light thrust.

As the great missile, almost an avalanche in one solid body, began first to roll and then to bound, I need hardly envy the Cloud Gatherer, Zeus, for his heaven-shaking blasts of thunder. . . . Echo wakened with a start, then called from every hillside, roared from every steep. In its cataclysmic fall, the stone struck the tops of other great stones deeply embedded in the rock or iron-hard ground, whereupon they screamed or bellowed like living things, and some leaped out of their age-old abode, and then roared down in the wild wake of their leader.

Finally it bounded high in the air, then fell to the valley floor with a shattering explosion. The tumult died away. Even Echo's voice was silenced at last, and the only sound was a low clatter of rocks as a great stag bounded up the ravine.

I did not hear the arrow's song or need to do so to heighten my joy. In a moment I came upon Right Doer, his bow and his lips in a big curve, and there lay the stag of Artemis, the shaft in his heart.

"Let it always be this way," Right Doer told me. "I'll do the thinking, you the heaving, and our deeds will win us fame and glory as long as we both live, and make us welcome in the Elysian Fields when Death darkens our eyes."

7

Right Doer and I had hunted and killed our stag in the last days of high summer, when green grapes swelled to juicy globes and the fields of barley yellowed. We spoke little of our pact, it being too solemn to voice freely, and we practiced it only rarely, one occasion being his smoking out of a truculent swarm of wild bees from a tall hollow stump, which now I pushed over with my shoulder to let us ravish their sweet hoard. Then, before the first frost gilded the aspen leaves, both of our lives were changed.

The change began with a runner making toward our camp. He was a fleet fellow, and our quick glance leaped to meet him, and at long arrow cast we recognized him as Scopas, body servant of Wrathful Leader; and it could not be but that he had come from the battle front with momentous tidings. He came and leaned against a tree, and one of our shepherds brought a horn of honey mead for his refreshment, then went quickly back to his fellows out of sound of our voices. Right Doer and I looked him in the face, but did not bid him speak. Straightly he returned our gaze and spoke manfully.

"Our King Layius has lost the war against King Eurytus, and half of our host is slain, and my master, Wrathful Leader, is direly wounded."

Right Doer bowed his head slightly and then I realized I had done the same.

"He has returned to his own place," Scopas went on. "Although he went forth in his war chariot, he returned on foot, limping with a crutch, and followed by only one slave. He has bade me tell you also to come home, not with such haste as to waste your strength, but with fair dispatch, because he doubts not that dark Death will overcome him before the leaves fall, and he has prayed to Apollo to withhold the arrow from his silver bow only until he may speak to you."

Scopas had given us the message just before sundown. At once I brought up a white bull without blemish, slew him, and prepared an offering to the Archer-God, that Wrathful Leader might be spared until we knew his tidings. When the sacrifice, purple-stained with wine and whitened with barley meal, had been consumed by the fiercely crackling fire, and we had feasted with our fellows in the darkening shadows that leaped upon us in between the upthrusting tongues of

flame, one by one the shepherds and drovers came up to kiss our hands
in farewell. Right Doer only clasped their toilworn hands in reply, for
he was the son of Amphitryon, Wrathful Leader of the Host, but I,
Heracles, knowing not my father, or whether I was high born or low,
kissed them as well. Only a moment thereafter I heard a sound not
unlike the plucking of a long string of a lyre, deep and resonant, and
while it might have been the outcry of some night creature, perhaps
a wakeful bird, or even a tree-frog or a locust, still I thought that our
offering had been well received.

Right Doer and I departed in the first light of dawn, and the long
leagues marched toward us, each with its hills and dales, or plains and
forests, or towns and houses and shrines, and late in the afternoon of
the second day we saw the smoke of the cooking fire of home.

Aging Althea had been on watch for us from our roof, and ran to
meet us as on the light limbs of youth, and her eyes were wide, although her lips were sealed. As I entered the arch I heard weeping
the very handmaid who had tattled to Wrathful Leader of my cracking
Linus' head, for which I had been banished, yet I took no joy in her
tears, and indeed pitied them and felt kindly toward her, and wished
that her master might lie with her once more before he descended to
the dim realm of Death, because that banishment had blessed me. Except for that, I might not now be mighty enough to honor the lot cast
for me, a most strange yet glorious foreboding in my soul.

Right Doer and I were taken to the chamber of Wrathful Leader;
and the grave dames who had waited on him, as well as the Priest
of Hermes, who had sought to ease his pain, departed quickly so that
we three were left alone. Although wan and wasted, his iron-gray eyes
were still those of a leader of men; and if his heart was failing it was
still capable of great rages. Did I wish I were his son, full brother of
Right Doer? I did not know. I only knew at last, by one glance into
his face, and before his pale lips opened, that I was not his son.

Right Doer brought an unwatered cup of purple wine, and held
it to his father's lips. He drank, and the Spirit of the Vine, Dionysus'
blessing and often curse upon men, flushed his gaunt cheeks.

"I will speak first of the war that is lost before the earthen walls of
Orchomenus. And I wish that our King had paid the tribute demanded
by King Eurytus, for what is a hundred cattle every year compared to
a thousand stalwart men in the flush of youth whose eyes have been

darkened by pitiless Death, and who now breathe not, speak not, and are shadows in shadowy Hades?"

He paused, and Right Doer spoke in low tones. "Perhaps some have gone to the Elysian Fields."

"One day of breathing is worth a thousand years of rest in the Elysian Fields. I, Amphitryon, a warrior by profession, declare it so. Yet it was not to spare you two, Iphicles and Heracles, from the common fortunes of war that I bade you abide with my shepherds and drovers. Aye, save for one thing I would have let you follow me, despite my knowing that King Layius could not muster forces from his sparse-peopled domain to match those of King Eurytus. Truly it was a much stranger thing than that. I had talked to Seer of Wonders before I left and he told me of a prophecy that Eurytus had heard from the oracle at Delphi. Heracles, bare your left shoulder."

I did so, my skin tingling.

"I behold a birthmark shaped like an oak leaf. According to the prophecy made to Eurytus by the Priestess at Delphi, he would be slain by a mighty man with the mark of Zeus on his left shoulder. What is the mark of Zeus? I knew not, nor did Seer of Wonders. But I knew what Eurytus would think when he learned of your birthmark and of your inhuman strength. He would surely send his minions to try to kill you, perhaps in fair strife, or by ambush or the poisoned cup. And if you died, so would Right Doer, and I needed no drunken prophet to tell me that. You might die quickly, or after a few hours of dire pain, but my son would take a year to die in agony of soul. Even his parting from you before had been a kind of death, so I would let neither of you come to cast the lot of battle."

Wrathful Leader had done this for my brother's sake, not mine. Somehow I was glad of this distinction.

"If we had won the war, I would have done wisely," Wrathful Leader went on in a low rumbling voice. "But we lost the war, and my shame at keeping you both from battle went to waste. Now Eurytus will demand a mighty tribute. How may I doubt that you, Iphicles, the son of the Leader of the Host of Thebes, will be punished in my stead? How may I doubt that you, Heracles, born of my wife, will be brought into Orchomenus before the King, and he will discover the mark you bear, and your mighty strength, and he will seek to circumvent the doom foretold at Delphi? Is there a curse on my house, even as upon the Royal House of Thebes? Me Eurytus cannot harm. I am

already halfway to the bank of the River of Forever Woe. But at my
departure I leave two hostages on earth."

"It may be we will follow you soon," Right Doer said quietly, "but
it may be that Eurytus will not find us easy prey."

"Thus speaks my son out of my wife, Alcmene, Noble Lady. Now,
Heracles, what do you say?"

"Nothing, until I know who I am. You call Iphicles your son. Whose
son am I?"

"Not mine. That much I know." And then, with his weak voice
gathering power, "I was far from home, fighting the Spartans, when
you were conceived. And when I returned and found my wife great
with child, she told me a tale of a visitation by someone—some being
—in my guise, and with whom she lay in innocence, mistaking him
for me. I called it a tale for children and the vulgar crowd. Yet the
nurse Althea swore to its truth, and I know that in old times various
amorous Olympians, lusting for the beautiful daughters of earth, have
taken the forms of their lovers or lawful husbands to visit and lie with
them. Also, there was the word of one who never before or since, as far
as I know, lied in his teeth when his eyes were upon mine. Does my
old shepherd, known as Fold Watcher, still live?"

"Sir, I kissed his wrinkled hands two nights ago."

"His testimony does not wholly support my wife's tale, yet lends
credence to it. He said he had risen in the night, awakened by the
snarl of a bear not far from the pen where lambs were being fattened
for the spit. The moon was in glorious full face. He saw no bear but,
at great distance, he saw what he took for a God. Thus he looked not
at all like me. He was tall and beautiful and walked with a godlike
stride, and the moon seemed to pour her light upon him in a copious
flood, and his bronze sword glinted at his side, and he laughed softly
to himself as he neared the arch. Always, it seems, in every tale that
the heart aches to believe there lies an imperfection. Doubt vanishes
only to return, like the red vulture that daily tore the liver of Prome-
theus. Fold Watcher confessed to me that, ere he slept, he had emptied a great horn of honey mead. It happened that at this time all
the kings of Greece and their liege men were assembling at the rendezvous to take ship for Troy, and the son of Fold Watcher followed
Agamemnon, and the shepherd visioned him slain in battle before
Troy's walls, and so had sought escape and comfort in deep draughts."

"Was the son killed?" Right Doer asked, breaking quietly into his father's anguished tale. And although I was standing breathless, hanging on every word the old warrior uttered, I did not blame my half-brother for the interruption, because it was inevitable, he being the man he was. Perhaps only the Gods knew whether the life or death of a shepherd's son was more important at long last than the paternity of Heracles.

"Aye. On the day that Hector, the Horse Tamer, drove the Greeks to their ships, the young man was killed."

"Will you go on?" I asked Wrathful Leader.

"Aye. So you see that my shepherd's vision of an immortal God as well as the snarl of the bear might have been no more than a drunken dream."

"Yes, so it might," I heard myself say.

"Yet another sign was given, late in the afternoon before the night you were conceived, and this was witnessed by no less than three of my household. A peacock from the woods lighted in a tree close to my wife's chamber, and an eagle hawked at her, and drove her away."

Now all men know that the peacock is the servant of Hera, Zeus' Queen, and the eagle is the servant of Zeus himself. The mark on my shoulder itched and burned.

"Heracles, what do you owe me for the good meat and the good drink that I provided you, and for shelter and care, and an upbringing like that given a chief's son?"

"Son of a lecherous slave or son of a God, I owe you all you ask."

"I ask only that you and Right Doer hold by your bond of brotherhood until Death parts you. You are mighty of body, he mighty of mind, and his boast that he spoke just now gives me hope that I will carry with me down to Hades. And now I am weary and will sleep."

"Before you sleep, I seek the answer to one question."

"Ask it."

"In your heart's belief, am I the son of a lecherous slave or the son of a God?"

"I do not believe you are the son of Zeus. I cannot think of him, the Thunderer, coming in any likeness to this house, that of a Leader of the Host, but far from the palace of a king. The birthmark on your shoulder might have been caused by an oak leaf blowing through the arch and lighting on the white and beauteous shoulder of Alcmene, as she lay with her lover in passionate embrace."

"Aye, that stands to reason."

"I have seen a birthmark on the face of a begger shaped like a lyre. Did that mean he was the son of Apollo?"

"No, it meant nothing."

"If it were a God that my shepherd saw, he was Dionysus, an Olympian, but an earth God too. He is tall and beautiful and lusty. But if I die tonight, I dare not go down to Hades leaving a supposition I do not believe still ringing in your ears. All men know that some women and wives of great beauty and refinement are drawn to coarseness. Heracles, I think your father was a brawny lecherous slave from some nearby household, reeking of sweat and lust."

Wrathful Leader turned on his side, his face to the wall.

CHAPTER TWO

THE SHRINE OF ARTEMIS

1

Wrathful Leader did not die that night, or on the next long, lingering day. Right Doer and I both knew that he wished to die, even tried to do so, if such a trial were possible without raising a hand against himself; and always when he wakened from his deep slumbers, more like an enchantment than natural sleep, he would glance about the room with wild hope in his eyes, which would quickly change to wild despair. No doubt he had hoped to find himself in the Elysian Fields, the abode of the shades of heroes, or even in the shadowy and silent realm of Hades; and instead he found himself in his own bedchamber, with breath in his nostrils and the light of life still in his eyes.

This longing for swift departure was readily explained by his shame over the defeat of the Host of Thebes and by the pain of his wound. Too, he did not wish to live to see the dark days ahead, when the conqueror exacted a mighty tribute from the conquered. But there was something more, Right Doer told me, another motive which he could not penetrate but which he thought must be connected with the indemnity Eurytus would demand.

"I have a feeling," my brother told me, "that it especially concerns me, and the danger to me would be somehow lessened if he is not alive."

We saw the face of danger which is sometimes Gorgon-like, turning men to stone; and sometimes, when its confronter is young and bold, that face is strangely beautiful. It was the habit of King Layius to appear on the battlements of the citadel at midday on the day of the moon's change, which was market day in the town, to speak to the people and make proclamations. The day of the new moon drew the largest crowd of all four market days in the month, and Right Doer and I had never failed to join the assembly if we were thereabout. The new moon would show her silver bow on the fourth day of our arrival home from the wilderness of Parnassus. We would, of course, attend, although with dread cramping our young hearts, because we thought it highly likely that Layius would declare the cruel cost of his defeat and Eurytus' victory.

My brother and I never took the busy market road. Instead, we wandered a lonely path we both liked, through a spinney of young aspen trees, over a hill, and across a meadow of rich grass on which stood, each alone and kingly, several tall, ancient sweetberry trees, black-looking from dense foliage. And it was no happenstance that to-day both of us had brought our bows and quivers. On every tramp into Thebes at least one of us had done so to shoot woodcocks or hares, succulent for supper; and we knew not, in these perilous times, what other need of the fleet shafts we both might have.

Still we were too trustful, and I reckon innocent, to expect any sort of brabble in the sweet-smelling, richly green, almost open meadow. The three Graces might like to come here in the moonlight and do a stately dance. So I was astonished when Right Doer, walking a few steps in my van, stopped, waited for me, and laid his hand lightly on my arm.

"Give no sign of alarm," he told me, "but there's an ambush laid for us two hundred steps ahead."

"I don't see it."

"Don't even look in that direction. Look to one side. Then make slowly for the watercourse that slants through the meadow. I'll be close behind you."

I did as he bade me. The watercourse had only a small flow, this time of year, although in freshet it had cut steep banks about six feet high. When we had dropped into it, as though to drink of its sparkling water, Right Doer turned to me with a faint smile.

"You know the very tall sweetberry tree that stands within thirty paces of the path. There are at least two men in it, and I think three. I saw a branch move and looked hard. They no doubt have bows and arrows, and only a tyro archer could miss at that range. Well, how will we teach them a lesson?"

"It's for you to say."

"And for you to do. Thank the Gods for your big bow and your mighty arm behind it. Can you send about six arrows in a row through the thick foliage?"

Perhaps because in my heart of hearts I loved strife and danger, I laughed at Right Doer.

"Very well," he said. "Here's a shelf on the bank that affords a good place to stand. Your head and shoulders will be in their sight, and when their perches get too hot for 'em, they'll let fly, but unless there's an Apollo—or another Heracles—in their band, their shafts will fall short or fly wild. I'll do the talking."

With an arrow ready on the string, I took my perch. When I had shot three times, a falling arrow lazied by me at five paces. At my fourth shot, two of their shafts were loosed, one widely, and the other well aimed from a strong bow, because it stabbed the ground ten feet in front of me. After my fifth, three arrows came flying at once, confirming Right Doer's guess as to the enemy number, but they were frightened now, perceiving that the trap they had set for us had shut its jaws on them, and all three darts hummed harmlessly and fell to earth. And I wanted to roar with laughter, thinking of the fools, how they could neither fight nor run, and lay helpless in the hands of Right Doer and me.

"Drop your bows and quivers," my brother yelled from far down the watercourse, where he had swiftly run. "If you don't, we'll stalk you under the bank and pick you off one by one like silly noddies."

"Will you spare our lives?" a percher answered in a shaking voice.

"Yes, if you instantly obey my command."

If it had been left to me, I would not have promised any sort of mercy. My blood was getting up, as I thought of the three skulkers plotting the murder of one or both of us, and my temper was on short, weak leash. It held because I held to the pact Right Doer and I had made, and truly he had been rightly named.

When the enemy still hesitated, I let fly an arrow in the part of the foliage from which the cry had come. And truly it must have well-nigh shaved the fellow, for he let fall his bow and quiver, which caught on leaves, only to tumble on.

"Let go, you others," Right Doer ordered. "Will it be your weapons or your own carcasses that bounce on the ground?"

There was a ring in his voice I had heard before, and I knew that he had clearly seen one of the enemy, and he had only to raise mid-height above the bank to ping him in the body. I was half hoping the men would still resist, and I would hear a great crashing of foliage, and then a heavy bump as the wretch hit. Instead I heard only a rustling of leaves as two bows and two quivers dropped lazily down.

"I think we can walk up now," Right Doer called to me. "I can see fairly well, and the enemy is disarmed."

So we came up, each with an arrow on his string, and presently we could mark all three of our fowls, two in danger of falling from their perches from tremulous fright, although the third man looked steady. Right Doer bade them climb down. Again he and I perceived the similarity of two of the knaves, and a mile-wide difference between them and the third. The former wore better cloth, clasped with gold pins. I thought they might be hangers-on of King Eurytus—not his Companions, of course, but lickspittles who had boasted of their skill at archery. They were in such haste to obey Right Doer that they almost fell down the tree, and were as clumsy as two cows blown into the top by a whirlwind. The third man wore no ornament but his grave demeanor as he made the descent nimbly and skillfully. Unless I missed my guess, the heavy bow lying under the tree with the two light ones had belonged to him, and he had shot at me the arrow that had fallen so narrowly short.

My brother lowered his bow. In respect to the stout fellow, I kept a shaft on my string.

"Well, what will we do with the prisoners?" Right Doer asked me, his face radiant with pleasure.

"You promised them their lives, and I'll stand by it," I answered. "So by your leave I'll cut off the noses and the ears of the whole batch, and send them back to their King."

"There's merit in your proposal. Nothing is to be gained by trying to appease Eurytus. I still don't know which of us two was their chief quarry, although they would have killed us both for good measure."

"I feel sure their main game was you, son of Wrathful Leader."

"And I would wager my sword that it was you, your father unknown, but bearing a birthmark shaped like an oak leaf on your shoulder. A leaf such as flutters down when frost bites and wind blows. And unless we go into exile from our native land, what we have seen today is barely a fair start."

"I would as soon go down into the halls of Death as into exile."

"I the like. Then what choice do we have but to live gloriously while we may? Remember that Eurytus will not want to kill either of us with naked power—he has his fame to look to, as well as the favor of the Gods, who in their usual illogical fashion punish open murder and often appear not to see it when it is committed in stealth. But Heracles, let us be content with lopping one ear from each man. Let them keep their noses and the other ear."

"If you think best. Will you do the cutting? You would do a cleaner job."

"On the contrary, I can't do it at all. Is your knife sharp?"

"As a serpent's tooth."

"Then get it over with, will you? And when you've cut 'em off, give them back to the owners to carry to their King."

Two of the prisoners started squealing at the first sight of my knife. One stood staunch and silent. I took by the back of the neck the loudest squealer, held him as in a vise, and clipped off his ear as neatly as the stem from a melon. This I caught in my left hand as it fell, deftly enough, and stuffed it into the fellow's loincloth. His companion yelled and pleaded when he saw the blood, and covered both ears with his hands. The third man, truly a man, as I had hitherto seen, different and apart as an oak from a willow, still made no motion or sound.

I had to put pressure on the back of the second scoundrel's neck to cause him to drop his hands. It was wise that he did so, since the bone had begun to bend. The appointed job well done, I turned to the brave fellow, who looked me straight in the eyes.

"What is your name?" I asked.

"Hermapollo."

"The names our mothers give us! I am named in honor of a Goddess, and you of two Gods, Hermes and Apollo. Are you a freeman or slave?"

"Sir, I am a slave."

"Yet with a certain valor. Right Doer, in honor of the two great Olympians of whom he is the namesake—perhaps his mother is so beautiful that both of them visited her on the same night—with your consent I'll let Hermapollo keep his ear."

"Heracles, you warm my heart with your contradictions. Now bid the three of them be gone."

I did so, and their departure was hasty enough.

"Right Doer, have we acted rashly?" I asked. "If so, I care not."

"We have signed our own death warrants, my brother—but on second thought, they were signed and sealed by the high Gods the instant we were conceived. Now let us go to the fair. With luck, we'll find two pretty country wenches who will go with us to pick berries. Then it may be that today we will honor the Goddess of Love, most beautiful golden Aphrodite, instead of bloody Ares, God of War, whom we must meet hereafter."

2

Our merriment and high spirits took a quick fall when we had gained the citadel of Thebes. The throng was one of the largest we had ever seen gathered here, but there was no jollity; rustics did not call rude jests, and in fact made almost no sound. The people were waiting with strained, anxious faces for Layius to appear on his porch. I could hardly doubt Right Doer's guess—that today the King would proclaim the tribute demanded by Eurytus, that some rumor of the terms had been whispered darkly through the city, and that these were more harsh than any gloom-steeped prophet had foretold.

Right Doer and I looked not at country wenches, nor did they gaze at us. The daughters of chieftains who had heard talk from their sires cast no sideways glances at my tall and princely brother, and their big and beauteous eyes filled with frightened forebodings hardly mitigated by reckless hope. A buffoon leading a polecat on a little chain and squirting water from his sandal with some small engine every time the scentless animal raised his tail did not cause the milkmaids and their bumpkin escorts to run away in noisy laughter. I thought that the clown's show was almost as sad as would be our King's.

Layius came presently to the porch, escorted by one herald. The King was a small, shapely man, who in his youth had been a wondrous archer and spear thrower, and was still a warrior not to be despised. His house was one of the noblest in all Greece, founded by great Cadmus, and this nobility abided in Layius and showed in his face, and perhaps it was more godlike because of the evil fate that had been brought upon his line by some unknown and implacably vengeful God. Men whispered that it was not done with yet, that the God's vengeance could never be satisfied except by some event too horrible for men's ears, and which would have to do with the return of Oedipus, Layius' infant son, who was said to have been carried off by an eagle.

There was a darkness on his eyes, related to Death's, as he addressed his subjects.

"As you know, the Gods did not befriend us in our war with Eurytus, and half our host were slain. But the haughty victor is not satisfied, and now my herald will recite his proclamation, dreadful to hear, declaring his wrath and the degree of his revenge upon us for my challenge to his power. I bid you listen well, even though your ears are stunned and your hearts broken. For unless the Gods intervene in our behalf, and somehow his fury is slaked or his power confined, what he swears to do he will do, for our host is routed and we lie in the hollow of his iron-hard hand. Woe unto Thebes! Yet if the vision beheld by Seer of Wonders, our old goatherd, who sometimes speaks with the deathless truth of the Oracle of Delphi, is a true vision, Thebes will yet live."

The King nodded to his herald, who, his face wet with tears, recited Eurytus' wrathful words that stilled our hearts.

> Now this do I, Eurytus, King of the Minyae, declare before the everlasting Gods.
>
> Layius, King of Thebes, having been inflamed with evil pride, in measureless treachery refused to pay tribute to me, his overlord, and made war against me. Whereupon I swore to the Gods that if they gave me a victory, I would inflict dire punishment upon Layius, upon Amphitryon, Leader of the Host, and upon all his subjects.
>
> This oath I will now keep. A mighty tribute must be paid me on the day following the autumn equinox in this, the twenty-first year of my reign. Every freeman of Thebes who has son or sons between the ages of nine and twenty-seven must yield his first-born son to me, to be sold in slavery or to do with what I will.
>
> Every freeman who has no sons but unmarried daughter or daughters between the ages of eight and twenty-five must yield his first-born daughter to me, to be sold in slavery or to do with what I will.

The master of every slave must yield to me the first-born of his slave, to do with what I will.

The owner of every mare, cow, sow, or ewe, must yield to me its first-born colt, calf, pig, or lamb, to do with what I will.

All beasts and human beings hereby forfeit must come or be brought before the walls of Orchomenus on the day before the autumn equinox, and if any Theban disobey this, my implacable command, his life as well as all his goods will be likewise forfeit.

If any attack is made upon my life by a Theban or an unknown, the leaders of my host have orders to reduce Thebes to dust and ashes, slaughtering all its inmates, annihilating the dwellers of its countryside, whereby the very name of Thebes will be forgotten and vanish from men's speech.

Eurytus Rex

The herald's voice ceased in the great silence, and soon that silence was strangely and terribly broken as his hearers began to wail. Many clasped their loved ones in their arms, mingling their tears, but a few stood staunch, proud, and pale. Right Doer took me by the hand and led me through the throng to a deserted court.

"There have been heavier punishments dealt to the vanquished by the victors," he reminded me. "We Greeks dealt less mercifully with our brave foemen of Troy. The great Gods must shudder in their high seats at the doings of pygmy men."

"Even so, we both will live to see Eurytus fall dead in his own palace," I answered, my hair rustling up and my eye jumping and the strange pain of prophecy in my bowels.

"Perhaps we will. But the mills of the Gods turn slowly and long before their final grinding. And now you see why Wrathful Leader ached to die before Eurytus' proclamation was made. If he had died, he could not be counted as a freeman of Thebes, instead, a dim shadow down in Hades, and he would have no first-born to be sold into slavery by the vengeful King. As far as this immediate matter goes, I would be safe."

"Then he must have foreseen what tribute Eurytus would demand."

"There are ways of knowing such things without going to the Delphic Oracle, or into the forests of Dodona where stands the Oak of Zeus, or even listening to the drunken babble of Seer of Wonders.

Perhaps Eurytus boasted to a minion, and Wrathful Leader captured that minion in battle, and the man bought his freedom with woeful tidings. Heracles, what will you do to save Thebes from unspeakable loss and shame?"

"I?" I asked in solemn wonder.

"If Perseus or the great hero Theseus were alive and loved Thebes, she would be saved."

"I am not Perseus, let alone Theseus."

"No, you are neither. You are Heracles, and who is Heracles? Only the Gods know. But you have the strength of a giant, and your brother Right Doer to whisper in your ear. Now let us put by the evil of this hour, and make good sport." His solemn tone abruptly changed and became almost gay.

"How can you, with those hateful words still ringing in your ears?"

"How may I refrain, with the equinox only seven days away, and the candle of both of our lives guttering in the winds of doom? Those candles are not yet blown out. Let us light them at both ends. I noticed two milkmaids standing near us who wept like Niobe as the proclamation was being read. Now I think the girls may be ready to be comforted. They are young and buxom and somehow beautiful, and they too know that the lovely flowers of life wilt quickly. Let us look now for a sign of good luck in the dreadful trials to come."

3

From Thebes to Orchomenus, the mule path most commonly used led through the Comais cornland on the west side of the mighty lake, and well back from the marshes. It was the shortest route, and the journey easily made in two days with heavy loads, or in a day and a half with empty bags, the beasts being made to trot before a running drover, shouting, cursing, and wielding his long-lashed whip. No doubt this way was thronged two days before the equinox by a sad throng. There would be hundreds of fathers bringing their first-born sons or daughters to feed the greed of terrible Eurytus; and some would be rich, and the most poor—a mighty difference in the world's eyes, although the ruin of their hopes and the darkening of their lives would be the same.

In and about that throng would be countless horses, cattle, sheep, and swine. From every homestead they would issue, in flocks and herds and droves from the broad pastures of the rich, one by one from the little pens of the poor; and they would raise a mighty dust, for no sweet rain had fallen lately; the equinoctial storms had been withheld from the whole land by some angry God. I thought he must be Zeus, the Cloud Gatherer, the Rain Giver. He loved not Thebes that I knew of, but it was said of him that as he gazed down from his seat of gold sometimes he took thought of human wrongs, and avenged them even, and that his dread name stood for right as well as might, and I wished I were his son.

The dim path that Right Doer and I took, along with two drovers, three youths and one maiden that were sons and daughters of some of our slaves, and the beasts that we must forfeit from our nearer pasturage, followed the eastern foothills of the Helicon Mountains. Considerably longer and far rougher than the trade route today, it had enough traffic to make lone eagles scream in fury and to frighten deer and other inmates of the woods and fields. Mainly our fellow travelers were shepherds from little cots away in the wilderness. They traveled in little bunches, always containing a youth or two or a wide-eyed maiden to go into slavery, along with kinfolk to bid them a last farewell, friends, and usually a bearded elder and sometimes an old woman on whose worn cheeks tears had newly dried. When I gazed upon them and their little offerings of calves and lambs and pigs, cared for and named and loved, sheltered from the storms in their own huts, I ceased to wish that I was the son of a God, and wished I were a God. Then I would bring Eurytus down to a cruel death, and lay a curse on all his line, and make a pact with King Hades whereby his torment there would be worse than that of Tantalus.

What good was wishing? I had no godhead and never would have, but at least I had the wrath of a God, bubbling and boiling in my soul, and a strange strength of body. It seemed to me that this strength was greater than ever before. I felt that it was, a dim and intangible intuition. And then I wanted to walk at a quicker pace, so that some battle, which no oracle had foretold me, and yet which cast prophetic shadows whose shape I could vaguely see in some distance beyond sight, as at the distant edge of moonlight between trees, could more quickly begin.

The long leagues lagged until, after nightfall of the second day, we came upon high ground in distant sight of the citadel of Orchomenus. From here we could see four lines of twinkling sparks forming a square, and we knew that they were braziers set on poles around the walls. Climbing higher, we could gaze down to the pasturage under the walls. Here were a thousand sparks, it seemed, bigger and brighter than the others, and what could they be but the watch fires and the cooking fires of the woeful pilgrims? Such they proved, on close view; and the whole distance between the citadel and the reeds of Lake Comais, a matter of two miles, was thronged with the new-gained booty of the King—slaves born of slaves at their rude camps, youths new to slavery born to freemen, and herds of donkeys, mules, cattle, sheep, and swine feeding on the luxuriant herbage. No doubt the King sat in his battlements, gazing in glory at the fine sight.

Close to the walls and to the lines of booths trading dried fish and fruit, corncakes, and meat to those with tiny ingots of tin or rolls of cloth brought from their looms, or watered wine, the camps stood so close to one another that the countless fires lighted the whole scene. Close to the flames fell a yellow glare; out a distance it dimmed to a golden haze; although every face and form in the multitude was distinguishable at twenty paces. But although visibility was good enough —too good for the heartbroken—hearing was bad; or at least it seemed so, for the ears strained for sound that did not come. When someone spoke it was under his breath. The fires crackled, although softly, and sometimes a colt, calf, or a lamb lately torn from the teat whinnied or mooed or bleated for its dam, and once a pig squealed shrilly and would not hush until its drover fed it from his hand.

The followers of Right Doer and I had scarcely laid our sheepskins when he came to me quickly, his face calm, his manner easy, but with a shine on his eyes, not cast by firelight, which I had seen before.

"Yonder, making this way, you see a man taller than I by two inches, finely dressed, and of fine appearance, followed by a giant of a man who overtowers him and would make two of his weight. The first fellow is Nessus, the great Horse Tamer, and the only son of King Eurytus."

"I recognize him," I answered Right Doer. "Truly he is of fine appearance."

In some lands far from Greece, folk might wonder that an illustrious prince would walk freely in any crowd, because there kings and princes are regarded as divine, and a brushing shoulder or the touch of a sweaty hand would defile them. But the Kings of Greece are not like those of barbarian lands, such as Phoenicia, Babylon, and Egypt.

All descend from Gods but do not count themselves Gods; they quarrel fiercely with their highborn companions over matters of policy; they harken to the voices of all the people; they will turn their hands to manual labor when the need comes, such as harnessing horses to their chariots of war.

Yet I marveled that even in Greece Eurytus would permit his only son to enter this throng, shamed by defeat and by the desertion of the Gods. Such woe is like a great weight of impounded waters in a cloud-burst; usually the dam holds, but sometimes it breaks. Even if Nessus was untouchable by pity, he could hardly fail to see some eyes black with hatred and no few steely bright with defiance, dangerous and explosive. A wise king would have taken thought on this, unless he was so puffed by his victory and his new-won power over Thebes that he had lost his wits. And perhaps Nessus had no wits to lose, because he walked with a proud strut and a mocking mien, although the strange idea struck me that he was trying to impress his gigantic companion more than the crowd. Possibly the giant was Nessus' bodyguard as well as his companion, and, in any case, the most formidable-looking man I had ever seen. He too walked with a princely mien, and mockingly before everyone, and, as far as visible might was concerned, he made me look like a rude swain of the fields.

"Who is the Titan who walks behind him?" I asked Right Doer.

"I can't say for certain, but I would wager my backbone, which now I need most fearfully and which has begun to tremble, that he is Antaeus the Wrestler."

My backbone jumped a little but did not tremble. It should have, perhaps, for I had heard o'ermuch of Antaeus, whose name meant Heart of Stone. Not two or three opponents at holy festivals had never gotten up after he had thrown them down and got a certain hold upon them. I reckoned his kill at at least six before he had come into the service of King Eurytus. Since then the list had strangely length-ened. No trifling number of the tyrant's enemies had fallen into quarrel with him suddenly, in the road or at a festival, and before the folk knew the cause or could hardly see what happened, a lifeless form with a crushed throat would drop out of the giant's hands. Nor did any Minyans of name and place inquire into the brabble, or charge either Eurytus or his giant before the Gods.

Yet in the death that had benefited most the King, ere he was king, when he was young and unknown and had little hope of the diadem,

Antaeus had no part. He had been an urchin when Eurytus' cousin
and best friend, Zetes the Well Beloved, son of the then King, was
crushed to death under his shattered chariot when he had gone forth
alone to tame a fiery team on the Thitherean Plain. No wonder the
folk whispered that some great God, most likely Ares the Bloody, loved
the covetous, vaulting grandson of a slave.

Darkly the people whispered of swift-ascending Antaeus; and far
away under Parnassus our drovers knew of him. Now it seemed that
I remembered every rumor they had heard and repeated in the secrecy
and safety of our watch-fire light. It was said that any boon he asked
of the King was straightway granted. Too, his wealth had increased
mightily of late, mainly in cattle. He appeared to be a kind of captain
of a band of high-born young men, all tall and lithe and godlike and
good charioteers, and the King's son, Nessus, was his boonfellow. He
was never known, at least for some years, to seek joy in woman, he
holding all women in contempt because they fell short of men in the
manly pursuits he loved. Lastly, he was beloved by the Goddess
Mother Earth, and when he was thrown down in any fight or game,
she restored his strength as soon as his body touched hers.

With none of these things I reckoned as he came nearer, and I got
a good sight of him. I was half expecting an ungainly man, awkward
of carriage and coarse of mien. Instead he was ten times more fit to
be Heracles than Heracles himself, indeed a stonecarver's notion of
Jason, whom the sorceress Medea loved, and who had yoked the
bronzed-hoofed bulls in the realm of the Golden Fleece. He stood
above six and a half feet. His head was covered with blond curls. His
face was truly godlike, not too massive, wonderfully proportionate of
feature; his profile of the Grecian type, but his eyes lighter than most
Greeks, his mouth large but refined, his neck a sinewy column like
that of the big pard that we called leopard, meaning lion-panther, that
readily killed full-grown steers.

His shoulders looked nearly as broad as the back of a horse is long,
and his arms and torso truly gigantic. But from thence his body
tapered gracefully to narrow hips, hardly larger than my own, and his
lower legs and feet were shapely.

As he came up close he looked at me with what seemed a respectful,
sober glance, and then I noticed in his left eye what we country people
called the mark of Pallas, which is a small section of the iris' being
of another color than the rest. It is rarely seen, and is usually of light

gray, and unless because the eyes of Pallas are known to be gray, I know no reason why the slight abnormality should be associated with her great name. In Heart of Stone's eyes the part was a fine dark blue, and the odd effect that the mark always conveys, beautiful but somehow unworldly, was even more apparent.

I could not give him further attention just now, because Nessus was addressing me; but the thought came to me I must give him the most close attention at some later time.

"By Poseidon, the God of Horsemen!" he broke out. "Aren't you the stocky fellow I met at the pasturage under Parnassus?"

"The very one," I answered, "and your prediction of war between our two Kings quickly came true."

"I trust you're not one of the——" and Nessus made a motion with his hand toward some young men, all with eyes cast down, ringed about a fire. They came from a village not far from Thebes and were all eldest sons of freemen.

"No, I'm not. Right Doer, my brother Iphicles, is forfeit to your royal father, by the cruel and wicked terms of the tribute he demands from Thebans."

"I won't quarrel with your language. The King himself used the expression 'dire punishment'—and of course you know the old saying, 'Hail the conqueror; let the conquered wail.'" Then, turning his head, "Antaeus, this bold speaker is named Heracles, and you have heard his brother's name, and both belong to the household of Amphitryon, Wrathful Leader."

"I have heard all three names before tonight," Heart of Stone answered in a soft and pleasant voice, strangely musical. "Especially that of Heracles. According to the talk of the countryside he is a stout fellow."

"Stout enough to threaten to upset my stallion, Earth Shaker, with me on him, unless I spoke civilly."

Heart of Stone made a puzzling comment, not odd of itself perhaps, but without apparent point.

"He would have had to stand close to you, to do that," the giant said, in the same soft, musical voice.

"Only a few feet." And then the expression on the face of the tall, graceful Nessus, son of the King, changed in a strange way. He changed color, a visible change in the bright firelight, flushing, then paling. I thought he would have given the jeweled clasp on his tunic to have held his tongue.

"I thought it was a rule of your order, the Sons of Poseidon, that except in an emergency, no member was to ride close enough to any person with good wit and clear eyes, and if he did so, he was to leave that person unable to tell what he had seen."

"Antaeus, this happened two suns ago, and I took Heracles for a country lout with whom I could make sport. Anyway, our game was even then about played out. Don't be vexed with me for a silly bit of horseplay."

"Of course not. You are my best friend, Nessus. Yet I remain puzzled over Heracles' staunch reply to your good jests. It takes something more than a stout fellow, as we know the term, to upset above half a ton of horse and rider. Could it be that the rumor we have heard of him was not exaggerated but understated?"

And if he were not playing a game, and his respect for my body's strength was growing, the like was my respect for his breeding and brains. No lubber could use such language as he employed.

"Truly, it was exaggerated. Heracles, could you have upset my horse?"

These present waters were deep. There was danger about, no greater than I had divined, but more than I had believed would show its face this soon. The encampment lay ominously silent. The crackle of the dying fires had become intermittent and startling, and their light ebbed and the stars brightened as the haze of smoke drifted away in the night wind off Mount Helicon, and they sparkled with an unnatural animation, as if excited by something. Still, I remembered Right Doer's good counsel, that there was no use trying to appease Eurytus, and that counsel had rejoiced my heart, and I followed it.

"Yes, Nessus, Prince of Horse Tamers. By seizing suddenly the right front leg and the right rear leg of a horse, and giving both a smart jerk, meanwhile throwing my weight against his body, I can usually upset him."

"Yet your arms do not compare in muscle with those of my friend Antaeus."

"Nessus, you cannot tell when we are both sleeved," Antaeus said. "Anyway, greater size doesn't mean greater strength. Have Heracles remove his tunic, and I'll take off mine. Then you can tell something."

"Heracles, will you do us this slight favor? I ask it not as a prince, but as one of four good fellows pursuing an interesting subject."

I had turned slightly, so I could see Right Doer's face. He gave me a slight nod.

"Certainly, if you wish it."

I bared my arms and shoulders, Heart of Stone the like. I knew where the eyes of both enemies locked, instantly and briefly—on my birthmark—then they began to speak of the giant's muscles compared to mine. And how glad I was that the Earth Goddess had made mine for work instead of show. Truly my own looked commonplace compared to the great growth, like that of a lion's, of the arms of Heart of Stone.

"But Heracles' muscles are different from those of most stocky, powerful men," Nessus said thoughtfully, "and I do not know why."

"They are unusually long," Heart of Stone observed, and there was great good cheer in his face. "Heracles, that birthmark on your shoulder—I have never seen its like. Have you, or had your mother, any notion why you were so marked?"

"I never cared," was my lying answer. "But my brother, Right Doer, remembers my mother more clearly than I do. Perhaps she told him the reason."

"She never did, but perhaps she told her husband, Wrathful Leader," Right Doer replied. "Anyway, I have heard him say that an oak leaf blew through the arch and lighted on her shoulder the instant Heracles was conceived."

"Now that is very likely," Nessus remarked. "Heracles, did you ever care for wrestling? I ask, because there will be a match of two at the games my royal father intends to hold at the equinox in honor of Artemis, and I thought you might like to compete."

"Prince, I'm not skilled at wrestling." The real reason I had neglected the sport so popular in Greece, a great feature at holy festivals, was that I feared to break legs and arms of good friends, youths from nearby homesteads, with whom I would compete.

"Do you know the holds?" Nessus asked.

"No, sir, I do not."

"Still, I think you would have a good chance against our champion —me, for instance. Isn't it likely that the Thebans will choose you for their champion?"

"It is possible."

"Then we will see what the day brings. Antaeus, do not forget that you have promised my sister Iole, Priestess of Artemis, to come to the shrine tonight, to help her prepare for the votive fire tomorrow."

"My good friend Nessus!" Heart of Stone replied, in wonderfully good spirits now, and it did not strike me that this was a too familiar address to a royal prince from a wrestler, said to be the son of a slave, his riches newly and secretly won. Perhaps the giant too was the son of a king, perhaps one greater than Eurytus, for he looked and walked and spoke like one. Perhaps he was more than that—the son of the God of Death.

4

In the early morning of the day preceding the equinox, our whole throng of Thebans and a multitude of the Minyans visited the shrine to the Huntress Goddess Artemis, patroness of Orchomenus. It stood in a clearing of an immense grove of cypress, tall and black and shapely but somehow bespeaking gloom, perhaps because this tree was so often seen in the place of graves. All fell silent as soon as they entered the forest; and I reckoned all their spines tingled, as did mine, as we came in sight of the shrine.

In the very center of the clearing stood an enormous cedar tree, unimaginably old. Its trunk was a good six feet in span and about twenty in girth, and this ran up without output of any branch for fully a hundred feet, so high that we must crane our necks to see the top, rather sparse to belong to such a giant, but towering fully fifty feet more. At one side of the trunk footholds were cut, making a kind of ladder in all twenty feet high. And part of the heartwood had been hollowed out to make a deep niche, three feet wide, fully as deep, and ten feet high. And in that niche stood the marble image of Artemis, a torch in one hand, her hunting bow in the other, the whole statue one of unimaginable beauty.

The hand that had carved the stone had been stilled longer than men could remember, but truly it had wielded more than mortal power, and how could I doubt that Artemis had revealed herself to this worshiper, in the fullness of her beauty—naked, perhaps, so he could behold her wondrous tapering limbs. Surely she had promised him some great reward if he could picture in stone what he had seen, and I did not question that now he abode in Elysian Fields, if he did not have a place among the stars. In the image she wore a sleeveless tunic, and her skirt was up-fastened not to impede her flight, as swift as a hawk's shadow over the ground. Folk said, with good reason, that there was no statue like it in all Greece. In most places Artemis was shown as fully clothed, even with sleeves on her arms sometimes, and usually the body was wooden-looking, stiff and unnatural, and often the lower limbs were no more than a half-worked block of stone. This was understandable, perhaps, for the other images had been worked in ineffably ancient times, before the art of stone-carving had been taught to us by her brother, the God Apollo; for Artemis had been worshiped in Greece, sometimes under the name of Cynthia, since the building of the pyramids of Egypt.

Thinking of those huge masses of stone that some Greek mariners had seen caused me to recall a rumor flying about the cooking fires of our assembly. And truly I confess that the rumor put an end to a good part of the glory flooding my heart and soul at the sight of the wondrous statue. It was that the present Pharaoh, thinking himself greater than the fabled Cheops, meant to build the greatest pyramid ever to loom over the desert, and it was to him that King Eurytus meant to sell his present great catch of male slaves. It could well be a false report. Our mariners had said that black slaves could be bought on the Nile for a fraction of the cost of white slaves imported over the wine-dark seas. But I fell to thinking, asking myself rather, whether, in case the story were true and Eurytus began the evil traffic, the beautiful Goddess would put a stop to it.

Artemis was the friend of all wild beasts, although she killed many of them with her own arrows to bring to the Gods on Olympus. Boys and girls were her care, and so were women with babies in their wombs. Scores of these were now moving through the crowds—some of them barely showing, others as big-bellied as Silenus, the boozy companion of Bacchus—in order to kneel at the shrine. Still this care of babies, children, and animals had not made her pitiful. I remembered all too well it was none other than Artemis, angry because proper sacrifice had not been made to her before the Greek Army assembled at the ships, who demanded the sacrifice of beautiful Iphigenia, daughter of King Agamemnon. And it was this same Goddess who, with her brother Apollo, shot arrow after arrow with deadly aim through the hearts of the seven daughters of boastful Niobe of Thebes. It came to me I had better not trust the Gods to rescue my brother and my countrymen from Eurytus' toils—not even trust Apollo, the true-speaker, who loved music more than war—and trust instead of the strength of my own hands. But I fondly hoped that these great divinities would not stoop to peek inside my head and find out what I was thinking.

The pregnant women knelt in semicircular rows before the shrine. All men knew that Greek women were the most beautiful in the world, and seeing this assembly, the plainest of them pretty enough to excite the procreative lust of a husband or lover, I was taking pleasure in deciding, which, to my eyes, was the most beautiful, the one whom I would be most happy and proud to have caused to have come here, when a young virgin put them all to shame.

She had come out of a small edifice, an arch and a little cell behind stone pillars almost out of sight behind cypress trees. Her long tunic of radiant white told me plainly that she was the Priestess of Artemis, and this I somehow guessed at first glance, although I had the impression that I had seen her before. At once I had to dismiss it as impossible; if my pig eyes had ever before lighted fully on that face, I would have remembered her in many a dream of day or night, and my past life would have been somehow different.

The mystical truth had now struck me that the face of the priestess resembled that of the Goddess she served. I had no doubt that a slight natural resemblance had been strangely heightened by a companionship of spirit and by her constant dwelling on that divine beauty. Both faces were the same oval shape to start with, but it was startling how the short, full mouth of one could be changed for the other's without hardly anyone's noticing the difference except of size. Both faces presented the same profile, wonderfully clean-cut, Greek of the highest class, and the Goddess and the priestess both looked tall, slender, and lithe; and I could almost believe that the sculptor who had shaped Artemis to the vision before his eyes had visited, as a shade, the mother of the priestess, about the third month, and whispered the secret of the babe's destiny, and together the fingers of their souls had shaped the formless being in the womb to this lovely form.

Of course her name was Iole. Nessus had spoken of his sister by that name as preparing a votive fire. Since Artemis was virginal, Iole would remain so, by implacable law, as long as she served the shrine. Still I need not feel a sharp pang in my heart, as though the Gods were reminding me that she was forever beyond my reach. More than one woman in the Kingdom of Thebes, now of fruitful and bountiful breast, had in her lithe girlhood served the shrines of the Huntress. When I searched Iole's face for signs of common humanity, absent in the image, I found more than one. In the first place her hair, although braided and bound about her head, looked fiery red. Even here in the deep shade it was red as polished bronze, as must have been the glancing helm of Hector that sent darts of light all over the plain of Troy. Many Goddesses, including Aphrodite, had hair like spun gold, but truly red hair was strictly human.

Her eyes, not large, were yet arresting because of their profound blue and the oddness of their setting, as if a cunning jewelsmith, fixing sapphires in ivory, had contrived to make visible the intensity of their blue fire. I had not enough of wit to guess the art employed—the hollow here, the slight protuberance there, the particular arch of the red eyebrows, the molding of the polished cheekbones—but I thought if I could wake up in the night and see her head on a pillow close to mine, the eyes opened as she saw whether mine were open, the whole face revealed from a brazier or by the moon looking through an arch, then every drop of blood in my veins would jump, and my hands would begin to wander, and my lips to search, and I would not envy lame, ugly Hephaestus on his couch with the Goddess of Love.

The image of Artemis was carved in marble, almost snow-white except for a glow in its depths that I thought was pink. The skin of Iole, when she lay in the cradle, must have had that marble whiteness, but she had lost it in the wind and sun. That could not have happened if most of the time she sat and spun or weaved wondrous webs; it must be that, like the Goddess she served, she went often to the woods and fields. Still, it looked like a smoother skin than I had ever touched—silk-smooth.

She had another feature never seen in a Goddess, in which I rejoiced. High on her left cheek was a tiny concentration of pigment, a perfect circle about half the size of her little fingernail, black as Erebus against her wonderfully glowing flesh. No doubt it had been put there by some divine being and had particular meaning which I could not hope to surmise, unless it represented Hecate, Goddess of Darkness, who is another aspect of glorious, bright Artemis. I hoped that she would consider it a blot on her beauty, for thus she might take a little more readily to a stocky, ungraceful, homely man. Of course it was no such thing; it accented all the rest.

Walking in long strides, as Artemis must walk, and with some of the sublimity of her office felt and apparent in her face and manner, she approached the great cedar tree, and with great sedateness climbed the ladder cut there until her ear could lie against the lips of the image. I did not see the lips move, as some spectators later swore they did, but I saw the flame-girt head nod now and then, and sometimes she turned it and cast her gaze over the crowd of tense, kneeling women, as though she were identifying one of them of whom the Goddess spoke. The imparting was not long drawn out. The supplicants, who could hardly breathe for excitement, many of whose faces were beaded with sweat, soon knew the divine disclosure. Iole descended the ladder and began to walk among them, bending every few seconds to kiss one of them on the cheek. At each kiss, the recipient heaved a sigh of happiness and sweet relief. She knew that by the assurance of the Goddess, who had care for the unborn and their bearers, she would have natural labor and give birth to a living, unblemished child.

But there were perhaps five women in the number totaling fifty who received no kiss, and their faces blanched, and they must bite their lips lest they wail in the hearing of the Goddess, and their eyes filled with stinging tears, and they were heartbroken.

5

In hardly a moment the mind of the crowd was taken off the lucky or the unlucky women by a royal visitation. Bearing his sword and shield, wearing a corona of what looked like foot-high feathers of beaten gold, into the clearing walked a massive and mighty man who I instantly surmised was King Eurytus. He passed within six feet of me. I had only to strike him in the head with my fist with all my might to kill him, but in the first place I wanted to live and fight a good while yet, to win glory and perhaps love, and not be cut into cat meat by the swords of his guard of honor. In the second place, his death at my hands would not save Right Doer and Thebes, but instead bring them and all I loved to soon and certain annihilation.

Yet my nearness to him was a lucky chance, because I got a good look at him. Truly, he was a splendid figure, tall, proud, strong-willed, handsome in a rugged way; and I did not know why I was a little encouraged instead of discouraged in regard to the future. Maybe he had a weakness that my soul confided but could not identify as yet, or would not name. I made the wild guess that it might be vanity. It might demand constant feeding on food for which he would risk too much. Truly there was something vain in the carriage of his nose and chin that caused him to have to look down to guide his footfall, instead of straight ahead.

At his side and a step behind him walked Queen Denira, known almost as widely for her good works as Eurytus was known for his bad; and behind them both strode tall and godlike Nessus, giving me a sideways smile as though we shared a joke. Next walked a girl of about twenty, surely the King's elder daughter Megara, and I could not decide whether she was beautiful or plain. She certainly was not pretty. Her eyes were too big and set too close together; above her nose her face seemed all eyes, also they were too dark—indeed, they looked soot-black—to fit the notions of beauty of the Greeks, who were a gray-eyed people. Her nose was delicate enough, although small and pointed and not full and noble-looking like the noses of our Goddesses, as visioned by our greatest sculptors. Her mouth and chin and throat constituted a complex of beauty, I thought, hard to put in words, felt rather than seen, the whole impossible to separate and delineate into its several parts. Of course the most ancient and reliable test of the beauty of a girl's mouth is that every swain wants to kiss it. Men too old to give thought to Aphrodite and her son Eros would want to kiss Megara's mouth, especially if they were great noblemen who had ofttimes cast the deadly lot of battle and seen and done and felt the best that life gives; and as for me, I would climb the steeps of Parnassus for one brief kiss. Her form was only fair for a Greek girl, long-legged and deep-bosomed; for the shaping of our girls has the studied care of our Golden Goddess as well as of Hera, Pallas Athene, and Artemis, for all love Greece more than any barbarian land, and wish our maidens worthy lovers, teeming wombs, and full-flowing breasts.

Still, Megara did not enchant me and cause my skin to tingle and my parts to throb as had her younger sister, Iole.

Behind Megara, and before the Companions of the King—great nobles, descended from the Gods, who had fought at his side in his dire and sanguine war with Thebes—stalked gigantic Antaeus in a robe of honor. And his manner was more kingly than the King's own, and a yokel might think the others were his cupbearers and the like, instead of men and women who, before Heart of Stone's sudden ascent, would not sit with him at meat; and that he, not Nessus, was the crown prince, if not the monarch. He passed close to me and pretended not to see me as if I, Heracles, were beneath his notice.

At once gilded chairs were brought for the King and Queen, Megara and Nessus and, to my great dismay and inexpressible rage, for Heart of Stone. He had sense enough to sit very lightly, lest the frail chair shatter under his bullock's weight; still, he sat with arrogance and, what was more infuriating, a truly godlike mien. At once began one of the most droll and charming ceremonies connected with the shrine of Artemis.

About eighteen little girls from about seven to ten years old entered the clearing from the woods, garbed as bears. All wore bearskins, with the skinned-out heads over their own heads, looking through the holes in the bears' eyes, above jutting muzzles and artificial fangs set along the lips. The meaning of the ceremony could not be told by the oldest man in the throng, because it was immeasurably older than he. Some said it had been brought from the region of the Euxine Sea in the days of the Titans. Still, the eyes of every beholder told his pleasure in it, even the eyes of a Theban child fated to gaze forevermore on distant scenes—the slavepen or the dungeon or the wooden toggle of slavery.

At first the little mock bears marched and did intricate figures to the music of flute and lute. Then they danced together, sometimes in a ring and sometimes two by two, and how wonderfully they imitated the shambling walk or awkward waddle of real bears! One little girl had the stomach of her robe stuffed with some light substance, and she made it swing back and forth exactly like the fat belly of a bear, and this child was the most charming and ingenious of the lot; and the word soon passed that her name was Arne, and she was the daughter of Bromius, a ship captain of the Minyae. Finally they played Bears in the Wood, in which skin-clad children hid behind trees and jumped out at Iole, who had joined in the game with all the grace and gusto and make-believe of its star performer, Arne, whose growls and snarls delighted all hearers.

Then the sunny day turned chill and hateful. The trouble began with Iole's suddenly quitting the game, running with wondrous lightness, and climbing the ladder of the Tree of the Holy Image. One man told me that one of the marble fingers of Artemis' hand had crooked, beckoning to her priestess—that he had seen it do so with his own eyes, and I could not call him a liar to his face, although I did not believe it in the least particle. All that I knew was a sudden great heaviness of heart, and a pain more severe than colic's in my bowels. Something horrible was about to happen, although I knew not what.

Iole put her ears to the cold lips of Artemis, nodded very slowly, then with a white face, yet still with the grace of a Goddess, made her way down the ladder. To the hushed assembly she spoke in grief-stricken tones.

"The Goddess has spoken. She so loves the child Arne that she wants her with her always. She has commanded that Arne be sent up to her on the votive fire."

An even deeper hush fell upon the throng, broken only by the deep and racking gasps of Arne's mother. Then up rose Eurytus, King of the Minyae.

"Priestess of Artemis."

"My sire!"

"This is a deathless honor that the Goddess has shown a daughter of the Minyae, yet we cannot wholly rejoice at it for missing the lovely little girl from our earthly scenes. Bid Arne remove her bear robe so we may look upon her."

Iole obeyed, spoke to the child, and in a moment she stood forth, naked, on the grass, sunny of hair, elfin of face, long-limbed and shapely for a child of ten, as lovely a little girl as I had ever seen, fit to be a daughter of Niobe, whom Artemis slew with an arrow in jealousy and hatred, after which she was no more lost to our world than if she had been offered as a sacrifice to walk forever in the Goddess' gleaming train.

"The command of the Goddess must be obeyed," Eurytus intoned. "All in sound of my voice know as much without my speaking my regal decree. But our hearts would be lighter, as the sacrifice is made, if both of Arne's parents perceive the boon that the Goddess has granted their daughter. Bromius, Master of a Tall Ship, voyager upon far waters, ever at the mercy of Poseidon, God of the Seas, and of Aeolus, King of the Winds, do you give your daughter in welcome and joy to the Patron-Goddess of the Minyae?"

Tears rolling down his cheeks, the wind-tanned captain nodded.

"And you, wife of Bromius?"

The woman sat motionless a moment, moaned a little, then shook her head.

"I myself will pray that no evil fortune comes upon your husband,

his ship, and your other children because of your defiance of the Goddess' command. Let the fire be laid."

At that instant the Princess Megara rose to her feet, and her eyes
were bigger than ever and more shining.

"My father Eurytus, may I speak?"

"If you speak wisely."

"I know not if I speak wisely, but I speak what is in my heart. Let
us defy the bloody wish of Artemis, who before now demanded and
received the sacrifice of beautiful Iphigenia, so that the Greek ships
might have a favorable wind to blow them to the plain of Troy that
they were soon to drench with blood. Let the Minyae be the first of
the Greeks to refuse to make human sacrifice to any God or Goddess.
What can they do in punishment? Kill us? yes, but we are fated to die
already. Punish us in the realms of the dead? perhaps, but let us defy
them still."

"Megara, I will hear no more. For this great sacrilege you must be
punished. By my crown and sword and shield——"

"Look, look," roared a great voice, and it was a second or two before
I saw that the crier-out was Nessus, as he was leaping to his feet. His
face aflame with feeling, he pointed at a kid that had come running
through the cypress wood, as though it had been frightened from his
dam's side by a prowling wolf. The animal stopped, bewildered by
the great assembly, and in an instant Nessus had caught it by the
neck.

"Iole, Priestess of Artemis," called forth Eurytus.

"My father, the King!"

"Again put your ear to Artemis' lips, and ask if it be her divine
will that this goat without horns or blemish be sacrificed to her in
Arne's place?"

Iole scrambled up the ladder fast as a monkey. Instantly the whole
throng knew by her happy expression that the sacrifice was acceptable.
I myself thought the marble lips had moved to give assent, that they
had almost smiled, and yet I could not quite get rid of a foolish regret,
an errant wish, that every man jack of us, Thebans and Minyans alike,
and every woman, and every child, had risen on our feet to stand beside Megara when she had implored the refusal of bloody human sacrifice to a great Olympian Goddess. If we had done so, the first great
assembly of Greeks to join heart and soul in such a glorious cause,
the memory of this day would never die.

CHAPTER THREE

TRIAL BEFORE BATTLE

1

The votive fire leaped high, and the kid, across the throat of which Iole had swiftly and mercifully drawn a knife, was offered whole to Artemis; and the aromas that rose were no doubt pleasing to her lovely nostrils. Many of the women wept at the ceremony, and we men were deeply moved. Iole's eyes were like stars for the brilliance of their shining, because the Huntress Goddess had shown mercy to one of our own, mercy not being a familiar sight in one of the Olympians when he or she had his heart set on something. Truly the people's offerings to the Patron-Goddess of the city would be greater than ever.

After this ceremony, the King's herald announced that games would be held in the big meadow fronting the cypress grove—foot racing, hurdle jumping, weight throwing, and, as a final treat, wrestling. For each event except wrestling, the Minyans would choose two contestants and the Thebans two. To winners and those who won second, the King would award prizes. In wrestling, only one champion of each host would be chosen, and no holds would be barred or no fouls called, so the contestant who knew the Gods had deserted him and he was losing had best lie quickly on his back in sign of defeat, because otherwise he might find himself on the dismal journey into the realm of Hades.

The first contest was in weight throwing, the weight being a bronze disk, thicker in the middle than on the edge. It had the first place because the hurling of the weight was not as exciting to Greek spectators as other games, they being an impatient, fiery people who became restless during the careful measurements of the casts. However, to make a winning throw was more a matter of skill than of brute strength, and I was not surprised, and in fact pleased, that I was not chosen one of the two champions of the Thebans. I preferred to husband my strength in case I should be called upon to wrestle the Minyan champion. If he should be the giant Antaeus—which somehow I doubted, because King Eurytus' subjects would not think it a fair match—I would need every ounce of pith in my muscles.

A stout Minyan won the discus throw, and King Eurytus bade him name his prize, to be awarded him if it were a suitable one in the King's sight. The winner asked that tomorrow, when something like a thousand daughters of Thebes would be forfeit to the King, he might choose one of the plainest to keep for his own. The King scratched his head, and then, after a whispered consultation with one of his Companions, he agreed.

The second-best cast was made by Biton, a country-born youth of Thebes, second in strength to me and well trained in games, and except for stumbling as he threw, I believe he would have won first place. For his prize, he asked that his little sister Batea be exempted from forfeit on the morrow and be allowed to return with him to the homestead.

"Is she in the throng?" Eurytus asked, a merry ring in his voice.

"Yes, my lord."

"Fetch her and let me see her."

And then the crowd laughed, for his "little" sister, standing about five feet, looked to weigh as much as a brood sow, and was a country wench with a pleasing, amiable, red face.

"Batea shall be forfeit to me, then returned to you to take home, and be sure you guard her well from a lusty satyr she might meet in the wood, who might covet her beauty," the King proclaimed.

The second event was the hurdle race, requiring both great swiftness of foot and agility in the running jump. Not to my surprise, Right Doer was chosen as our main champion, with a fleet Theban youth, said to be a bastard son of Wrathful Leader, as his companion. The race was close and wildly exciting, because my brother and a wonderful fleet and agile Minyan ran neck and neck; then at the very last my brother gave a kind of forward thrust of his body, the effect of it not unlike being kicked by a horse, and reached the goal a full stride ahead of his main competitor. I felt that he had won with his head and heart rather than his legs. Both had unguessed powers, as no one knew better than I.

"You have run exceedingly well, and deserve a rich prize," Eurytus remarked in a kingly voice. "What do you ask?"

It came to me, a dim glowworm of a hope, that Right Doer should ask that he himself be exempted from forfeit to the King. The throng had cheered the great race he had run, Thebans and Minyae alike, and although he was the son of Wrathful Leader, the King's enemy, Eurytus would find the request hard to refuse. Then the little glowing went out in my mind and heart, and I did not know what wind had quenched it; I only knew that Right Doer would seek some other boon.

"Sir," he answered, "in our host, to be forfeit to you tomorrow, is a nephew of Linus, the great lyrist, and he himself can play most wonderfully upon a flute and bring joy to saddened hearts and sweet sound to yearning ears. I ask that he be exempted from forfeit unto you, and be allowed to return home." And I had never seen as much beauty in my brother's face or heard it in his voice.

"I have no need of flutists," the King answered sulkily, "unless their music can make great stones move by themselves into place, as did the music of Amphion. Your request is granted." I thought Eurytus had expected Right Doer to ask for his own freedom, which request the King had looked forward to refusing with a fine speech.

The next event was a foot race, always one of the most popular at public games. The Greeks greatly admired and set much store on fleetness of foot, they being such lively folk, and the ability to get from one place to another in the briefest possible span of time seemed to them a godly gift. Besides that, good foot racers are almost always pleasant to look upon, a fact of unexpressible importance to the beauty-loving descendants of beautiful Gods and Goddesses. Such racers almost always have trim legs, with long muscles, deep chests, and proportionate, if slight, build. We Thebans had a hard time choosing our two champions, with the final choice of first place going to beautiful Actaeon, more famed as a huntsman than as an athlete, yet so swift on his feet that he had been known to run down and kill a marauding bear. Right Doer was chosen for second place, he being terribly swift in any kind of foot race, but more likely to win in various kinds of obstacle races that included leaping as well as running. Loyal Thebans, the two trim youths kissed each other's hands in solemn pledge to do their utmost to beat the Minyan champions, which one beating the other making not a grain of difference.

Then I, a country lout who had attended no games in these parts in my whole life, was given a pleasant start. Although it evoked no surprise among most of the Thebans, I had somehow never heard that the best foot racer among the Minyans was not a beautiful youth, but a most beautiful maiden. She was Iole, the King's daughter, and she had girt up her robe so that her wonderfully shimmering legs were bare except for sandals. I kept my mind off these legs long enough to admonish myself for my bumpkin astonishment. Artemis' greatest fame was as Huntress Goddess.

If she had been a contestant at the Judgment of Paris, and the contest had been to prove the most fleet of foot of the Goddesses instead of the most beautiful, Aphrodite would have come in last; the judge would have never received the bribe that brought on the war with Troy, Eurytus would not have waxed great, and we Thebans would not be in our present fix. Iole was Artemis' priestess. Of course she would emulate her in every way possible, and the mere looking like her, with the same build, was an index that she might be as fleet-footed as a barren doe. Then with great happiness and excitement my thoughts went back to her legs. By the Gods, I had never seen such beauties even on the statue of Artemis. I thought of her making love with them as ardently as with her arms, as well as with the ardor of a huntress when she has drawn blood from her quarry and is panting on its track—whereupon I became dizzied, and the race was almost ready to begin before I could steady myself.

The course was measured off—a hundred strides of gigantic Antaeus. A woolen string was stretched between two posts while the four contestants waited for the starter to launch an arrow from his bow, a reminder that the contest was in honor of Artemis. The shaft left the string, the runners left their line with what seemed the same light, swift thrust. And truly, now we spectators were given a sight to store in our memories and treasure always. The three males were naked except for loincloths; Iole wore a band from just below her exquisite maiden breasts to just below her shapely hips. My position was near the finish line, and in fact I had shouldered through some of the Minyan soldiers to gain it, so instead of drawing farther away from me, as usually it seemed the most beautiful of women did, I saw Iole coming closer, the flash of her limbs brighter, the white parts of her body, not tanned by wind and sun, ever more radiantly white, and the pink buds of her breasts taking on color as do roses as gray dawn changes to full, bright morning.

At the very start, the Minyans' second choice got behind his three opponents, and remained so. These three ran shoulder to shoulder most of the distance; and who here, nobles and poor alike, could look upon Iole causing both Theban runners to put forth their utmost and not think of Atalanta, who in infancy had been left on a mountain to die by her father, angered that he had not borne a son. Suckled by a she-bear, she became the best marksman and the swiftest runner in all Greece. It was said that she beat Peleus, father of Achilles, in a wrestling match.

Still I offered a quick prayer, first to Zeus and then to fleet Hermes, that one of the Thebans win, knowing it was not a particle of use to pray to Artemis. My reasons were mixed, one of them certainly that the pall of defeat and loss hanging over us be mitigated even briefly not only by the victory, but a prize that either Right Doer or Actaeon would be bold enough to ask. But it seemed that my thoughts had time to spurt a hundred miles while the runners dashed a hundred paces, and I knew that I wanted Iole to lose as fiercely as I wanted a Theban to win not because she was the daughter of Eurytus, but because she was so beautiful. Always winning, I thought, she would not look twice at a graceless hulk like me.

She won, just the same. She just stretched out a little more and seemed to pass Actaeon and Right Doer with serene ease. Atalanta had always won in the race with her wooers, until she encountered one who decoyed her off the course with golden apples. I had no golden apples to offer Iole. I could not melt her heart with music plucked out of the seven little strings; and being a virgin, she would stay out of holes and corners, not only in my company but with any man, lest a little accident befall, whereupon she must surrender her priestess-hood. This would arouse her father's ire. A head as thick as mine had no trouble perceiving that her office was of great use to him, a source of prestige, if not of revenue. There was one thing I might give her, a long time from now, and that was the name and trappings of queen. All that needed doing would be to slide Eurytus' throne out from under him and to sit myself down.

When the King, with great majesty, or so it seemed, asked Iole what she chose for her mead of honor, the maiden asked that the flame represented as issuing from Artemis' torch, now of burnished copper, be changed to burnished gold. And as she made the request, a beautiful expression came into her face—serene, yet a little sad, like the expression on the face of very Artemis, for truly the great Gods and Goddesses must know sadness, knowing that their temples perish at long last, and the world changes from what it was when they were newly born, and even their great power cannot turn back the shears of Atropos from some priestess as beautiful as Iole or from mortal lovers who have shared their couches.

Actaeon came in second, a hand's breadth ahead of Right Doer, and the mead of honor for which he asked was the deliverance from slavery of a grandson of old, gnarled Tiresias, Seer of Wonders, so feeble now he could scarcely hold the winecup to his own lips, and hence his true prophecies were told to us briefly and far between.

A stir now moved through the crowd, for despite its heavy heart it could not help but lift its eyes at the prospect of a good wrestling match. And then there came to pass a heart-warming thing that must please the Gods as well as the Greeks on both sides. As our elders conferred as to candidates to offer to our host for acceptance or refusal, we heard the Minyans, one voice after another, or often a chorus of voices, shouting to the King that they wished Nessus the Horse Tamer to be their champion in the coming match. Not one mother's son called the dread name of Antaeus, Heart of Stone. Everyone knew that he was a mighty wrestler, and a man of giant's strength, yet they knew too that he was the King's assassin, by contrivance and underhand, and despite his crescent fortunes, they did not want him to represent them in what was so dear to Greek hearts, the manly games played in honor of a God or Goddess. I was watching Iole's face, hardly damp with sweat after the exertion of the race, and dwelling on its forever-imprint on my soul and meaning in my life, when I saw the corner of her lips turn up in such a smile as Artemis herself might give when alone and apart from everyone, provided her beauteous marble lips could curl. I did not know exactly what it meant, for it was not a smile of joy or triumph. I wished Right Doer had seen it, so I could ask.

Meanwhile I was wondering whether the thunder was on my right or left, whether my fortunes would better or worsen since Nessus, and not Antaeus, had been chosen the champion of the Minyans, and pro-

vided I would be champion of the Thebans. The matter was compli-
cated in the extreme—I could not look all the way down one road, let
alone two—so I decided it was on the lap of the Gods and let it slide.

The leaders questioned Right Doer, then nominated me for the
crowd's first yea or nay. When the King's herald called out my name,
such a cheer arose that the nominators did not bother to submit any
more. Nessus scowled at me, as though he meant to break at least my
leg; and I looked forward in intense joy to teaching him a lesson. Today we would both stand on common ground, and he could not make
game of me from the back of a horse.

We stripped to our loincloths. Seeing my almost naked body,
staunch enough in appearance but in no way unusual-looking, many
Minyans continued to lay bets on Nessus and, from what I could
gather from their babble, three ingots of tin against two that Nessus
would win seemed to them a fair wager. In the first place, he was a
skilled wrestler, knowing all the age-old holds, while I must rely on
untutored strength. In the second place, he topped me by three inches,
and his magnificent body—so cleanly carved, big in the chest, narrow
in the waist—looked far more agile than mine, and, the Gods knew,
far more godlike.

In low ground between two long slopes that would give the throng
a good view, a circle was drawn by a sharp stake. If a finger or a toe
of either of us stuck outside of the circle, we must both rise, face each
other, and seek new holds. Then the referee spoke winged words to
my opponent.

"Nessus, you are the son of Eurytus, the King, and thus better born
than your opponent Heracles, whose mother was noble but whose father is unknown. And thus it is for you to say whether you two will
wrestle as a test of skill and strength in the ancient sport, or if you
choose pancratium."

This last word was the wrestler's term for a combination of boxing
and wrestling in which no fouls were called and the opponents could
bite, kick, or strike each other and try to break one another's bones.
I could hardly doubt that, considering my lack of skill, I would more
surely win at pancratium; still my heart leaped in a strange and puzzling way at Nessus' noble reply.

"I am not sure I am better born than Heracles. My royal father was
the grandson of a slave and my mother, although a lady, had no such
divine descent as had Alcmene, Heracles' mother. Anyway, today we

face each other as equals in the great tradition of the sport. Still, I will speak my preference. I have no desire to disfigure this stout opponent, who once offered me food and drink when I was far from home. But of course if he prefers pancratium, I will yield to his wishes."

"Sir, I do not prefer it, and would rather wrestle fairly."

And I was still so astonished by his courteous remarks that I let him get a strong hold on me, one hand at the back of my neck and the other above my right elbow, before I could realize that the contest had really begun.

But he took no immediate advantage of his superior position. Instead he gave me a surprise that dwarfed all the little surprises he had hitherto given me. With his lips close to my ear, he barely muttered a strange injunction.

"Don't throw me immediately. Make it last a good while. I have much to tell you of vital import."

When I had caught my breath I broke his hold on me, and the one I took on him looked dangerous enough to the crowd, but I put no force in it, and all we did was reel about the ring with neither of us falling.

"I do not understand," I murmured.

"Why should you? What does a cowherd know of courts? But you will have to wrestle Antaeus before the sun sets—the occasion will be nicely provided—and that means you either win or be done with sunlight forevermore."

A cold chill ran up and down my back and a kind of glory surged into my soul. These two feelings were a world apart, both of them strong, yet I had room for a third, which was a kind of humble agreement with Nessus over what he had called me. A cowherd I had been, and still was, and always would be. A pipe-voiced boy knew as much of courts and, likely enough, of courting.

"Whom can I trust?" I whispered, when he had me by the neck-hold, his hand on my thigh to brace against being thrown.

"Of all the Minyae, me alone."

"Not even your sisters?"

"Never trust any woman. She might fall in love with your enemy, and then all is lost."

"How may I trust you, when you came to our pasturage to steal our cattle?"

"I did so at Antaeus' bidding. We all bark or lie down at his word—

all except Eurytus himself, and he may join our number before this course is run. Now listen closely. Do you think you can beat Antaeus at wrestling?"

"Aye, I think so."

"I'd believe no word of it except for one report—and I've no time to repeat it now. If you've any great doubt of it, raise no hand against him. Take his insults—even a blow in the face—and beg his pardon. What is a mead of shame if thereby you can live awhile and perhaps take revenge when again the Gods love Thebes! There is still one other choice to make, and you must make it. The King believes you can down me, as I know it full well, and he wants that to happen so Antaeus' attack will look less like open murder. But if you wish, you can let me win. Then the King will be hard put to countenance open conflict between you and his bravo."

"I'll do my best to throw you and you do your best." What else could I say?

"You innocent fool! Why tire yourself out when this great trial awaits you? I tell you the Gods will leave their cups, and the Muses will stop their frolicking to gaze down."

"I've one more question, then we'll set to. If I win, what can I do to help Thebes?"

"Ask Right Doer. His head has twice the depth of mine. Tell him what I've told you, but no one else, or my loving father would have me fed to his dogs.—All right, you want a good match, I'll give it to you."

Truly we were a better match than I had ever dreamed. My opponent was not only a most skillful wrestler, whose cunning holds I could break only by great strength; he was also far stronger than any man my arms had ever encircled, and sure-footed and agile in the extreme. When the crowd had begun to cheer instead of jeer, thinking that at last we were taking each other's measure, and those who had bet on Nessus could almost count their gains. I took him quickly around the waist, heaved him off his feet, whirled him around, and flung him— not too roughly but giving him the good bump I had once promised him—full on his back. For a few seconds he could do nothing but lie supine, both shoulders on the ground, and the prize was mine.

After the loudest and longest cheers had begun to die away, and before the King, in whose mouth butter would not melt, made his announcement, I received glorious mead. Who should come up to me in her lithe stride, but beautiful Iole. Her eyes were strangely agleam, the deep blue irises like sapphires set in a silver ring.

"I cannot speak for the Goddess whom I love and serve," she told me. "Yet by meditating upon her and taking closest heed to the least change in her aspect, I dare to try to guess her thoughts even when she gives me no open sign. So I cannot doubt that she was pleased that you strove so well in the great contest with my brother, with which my father sought to do her honor."

"Now I need ask for no mead from the King."

"Ask it, anyway. You deserve it. And you deserve this—if you will regard it as part of your mead of honor."

She leaned toward me, as graceful as a tall reed on the shores of Comais, bending before Zephyr, the West Wind, and kissed me on the mouth. And not even the kiss of a Goddess, I thought, not even from the lingering lips of golden Aphrodite, could so stir me to my depths and exalt my soul. Truly I could almost believe that the burning, itching birthmark on my shoulder was no happenstance of a fallen leaf on my mother's beautiful shoulder when I was conceived, but a sign of some awful visitor to her couch, one who was enraptured by her beauty—the one whose name at this resounding moment I dared not let take shape within my thoughts.

2

When my sweat had been wiped off and my hands washed by one of the King's maidens and I had put on my tunic, a herald blew his trumpet. At once Eurytus stepped to the balustrade.

"Heracles, winner over my son Nessus in the wrestling ring."

"My lord!" I answered.

"What do you ask as a mead of victory? If it is within reason, I will grant it."

I had had a brief coaching from Right Doer, and although his instruction seemed to go against common sense, I decided to obey it.

"Sir, I ask that while you, conqueror of Thebes, keep all the animals my countrymen have brought as the price of our defeat, you liberate all our youths and maidens."

His face darkened slightly. "Heracles, your request is not within reason, nor is it seemly, coming from one whom the Gods gave victory in a mere game played in honor of our Goddess. I won my prize of victory—a great prize truly—in the red fields of war, amid the crash of arms, the neighing of maddened steeds, the moaning of the wounded and the dying, the shouts of the victors. And I would listen with greater patience to your presumption if you too, and your brother Iphicles, had fought beside the brave youth of Thebes, instead of lingering in safety in your father's distant pasturages, seeing no more blood than that spilled by a slaughtered bull. Even so, if you had so fought and won great glory and not dark death, I would not dream of releasing the youths and maidens I have declared forfeit. As for your prize, I myself will name it: one ingot of tin to harden a melting bowl of copper to make a bronze sword." He paused, and then added thoughtfully, in a less haughty and harsh tone, "Still, I now forgive the rash words that have escaped the door of your lips. You are yet young and untried, and your victory over Nessus puffed you up with conceit. And since you did so well in the game just played, perhaps I will let the throngs watch you attempt other feats of strength or agility which, if you perform well, will win you fair mead."

When, red in the face, I returned to Right Doer, I expected him to be abashed over the worst piece of advice he had ever given me. Instead, he appeared in good cheer and indeed gave me a little smile, the same as I knew and loved of yore.

"That was all right," he told me. "If the game of chess were within your mental scope—surely one of the greatest legacies inherited by us Greeks from the decadent Minoans—you would know that the first move by an accomplished player often appears useless or worse. Mark you, Heracles, the King does not like public attention called to his great catch of slaves. His subjects do not like to think of it—they want to forget, as we camp outside their walls and match them in manly games, that we are soon to go under the whip of some alien Pharaoh. You have suggested the possibility of our being liberated. It will remain in all minds, conquerors and conquered. Also it was a most bold proposal on your part, hardly to be expected from a country bumpkin, not even the son of a king. Whose son are you?"

"I do not know."

"Nor does Eurytus—but he greatly wonders. And therefore I think something that we both want to happen—the conqueror-King and I, merely Iphicles your brother—is more likely to happen."

"You can mean nothing other than a wrestling match between me and Antaeus, Heart of Stone."

"Of course I mean that. But before the Gods, Heracles, it must be by Antaeus' own challenge or by the open instigation of the King. That means you must not drink too many cups of mead." And at this last, I set down a cup that had been filled for me by a chief's daughter.

"They make you jolly sometimes," Right Doer went on, "but sometimes quarrelsome. I've seen you like an old bear with the toothache; today you must emulate the lamb. Don't walk into the woods even if Iole would walk with you, which she won't—stay in plain sight and hearing of the throng. If Antaeus insults you, give him a soft answer; let him start the quarrel, force it, and stick it between your teeth before you act."

"I don't see the sense of it. If I am fated to fight Antaeus—and that is what I hope—why should I submit to——"

"He is the King's killer. Everybody knows it. The more he forces the fight, the more the Minyans will rejoice if for once he meets his master, and the greater mead of victory you can ask and get. But Heracles, no test of your powers you have ever undergone will be as great as this, nor half as great. He will be a terrible antagonist—a champion wrestler, a man of terrific strength, and I think the favorite of some God or Goddess, perhaps the latter's lover. It is said that he renews his strength whenever his body touches Earth—I do not believe it, yet the way he rebounds lends credence to it in common ears. And now what is this?"

The trumpet of the herald had again ordered silence and the King rose to speak. The burden of his speech was that enough cattle and sheep were being slaughtered to feed both hosts; barley cakes in unreckoned numbers were being baked; and that vats of wine were being mixed with water to wet all throats. After this midday meal other contests, or feats of agility and strength, would be performed for the pleasure of both hosts.

"Eurytus is being unusually generous with his spoil of victory," Right Doer remarked. "It seems he seeks to put his people, as well as ours, in the best possible spirits. I think he is planning something that otherwise they might not stomach. You see, Heracles, the public spectacle of Artemis' demanding little Arne to be with her always and then the fortuitous appearance of the kid was not the great popular success that he had expected. His own daughter Megara spoiled the whole show."

"You don't mean that Iole was party——"

"Heracles, I love you; I delight in your forthrightness. I think all the more of Iole for her deceit—thereby she becomes a first-rate Priestess of Artemis instead of a sluggard or a dullard, like so many priests and priestesses. The position is a notorious sinecure, almost always obtained by royal influence. She works at it, schemes, and hence the shrine at Orchomenus is the most famous shrine of Artemis in all Greece. Also I do not doubt that she is devout."

"I fear that she is," I answered sadly, thinking of her long straight limbs, the whiteness of her belly, and, with the hardest ache in my loins and forehead, of the polish of sweat that had covered every inch of her visible body when she had finished her race.

"Now, as the poets are wont to put it, let us satisfy the desire for food and drink. That satisfaction at least, Heracles, is within your reach."

3

When all had eaten and drunk watered wine, the crowd surged or wandered back to the gaming grounds, hoping that Eurytus would presently order another contest. I thought he had done so already, the order given to his closest confidants, or perhaps he had told no one but Antaeus himself, leaving it to him to make the arrangements that would appear not even to brush the King. I confessed, in an even closer confiding, that I feared the soft-voiced giant as I had never feared any man. It would have done no good for Right Doer to suppress his suspicion that he was the favorite or even the lover of some Goddess. The same thought had struck me because, at times, he had a godlike air about him, impossible to mistake. I wondered if very Artemis had come down from Olympus, broken the injunction by her father or by fate, and had invited him to break her divine maidenhead. In a more practical part of my brain I feared Heart of Stone's skill at wrestling. If he had half my body's strength and ten times my skill at the ancient sport, he would surely win.

And it appeared quite true, to judge by report, that Earth loved him too, restoring his strength the instant that his body touched hers. At least he had always leaped up as though by some miraculous restoration.

The herald came to the balustrade. The crowd stilled. After the blast was blown, the King spoke in majesty.

"My fellow countrymen, and citizens of Thebes! It is not fitting that this day should pass without an exhibition that could not be seen anywhere in Greece save at the citadel of the Minyans, Orchomenus. Since time out of mind, the men of Troy, with whom some of the elders here and the sires of many of the young men and women fought ten grievous years, have been known as the Horse-Taming Trojans. And it is true they are charioteers without peer, save for great Achilles and a few other heroes. Yet even the King of Troy, in the days of her greatness and her insolent pride, could not have shown you what I, Eurytus, am about to show you." And then to the herald, "Blow three shrill blasts."

The herald did so, and out of the woods dashed a company of horseback riders, led by Nessus and numbering about fifty. I had no doubt that these were the Sons of Poseidon, the order of which Antaeus had spoken when he dared question Nessus about his revealing himself to me not as a centaur but as something more wonderful, the master of a horse without reins or harness. Dolt that I am so often, the idea had struck me then that many of these horsemen had pretended to be centaurs in the sight of country bumpkins, that this accounted for the unusual number lately seen, when actually real centaurs are among the rarest of monsters, and that the real business of the equine society had been cattle stealing. If this last was true, who had been the chief gainers? Certainly King Eurytus and his soft-voiced bully, Antaeus. Because of fright or something more strange, Nessus the King's son had become Antaeus' creature.

Yet he alone had mastered a great stallion. All the other Sons of Poseidon rode mares. Also, he was by far the greatest horseman of the lot, his movements to control the beast being almost invisible. When the whole band moved in ranks or cut figures, the mares seemed to be more guided by the stallion's leadership than by their own riders. At the conclusion of the exercise the mares formed a long line with the stallion in their van, fronting the King. Then, at Nessus' command, all reared up on their hind legs in salute.

Eurytus was so flattered by this homage, which no king west of the steppes of the Euxine Sea could command, worthy of payment to a God, that he was impelled to make another speech.

"Minyans and Thebans!" he began, and truly he had an impressive, rolling voice. "None of the horses you have seen in this parade had been broken when its rider undertook its training; none had been chariot horses. Still, not one will obey any rider but his own, or, for that matter, let him mount. I tell you in my pride that my son Nessus, some day to be your King, was the first to break a horse to ride—with the help and under the guidance of his good friend and my Companion Antaeus, who in no far future may lead my host astride his charger."

Only the more thoughtful Thebans, these mainly great noblemen, took special note of this last utterance. Perhaps I would not have given it much thought except for a sideways glance from Right Doer and a slight lifting of his eyebrows. On close scrutiny it was an utterance to stun any Greek. Eurytus had not only voiced the likelihood of a low-born wrestler's becoming his chief general—more than one slave of great military capabilities had won to a like place—but had called him his Companion, a title which in all other Greek states was reserved for the heads of great hereditary families of recent divine descent. Some of the leaders of the Minyan Host, standing near me drinking mead, looked at one another with sick, incredulous glances.

Perhaps Eurytus perceived he had spoken rashly and gone too far. Since he could not eat his words, he waxed jocular.

"Now some of you young men who live on farms have ridden oxen and donkeys," he remarked slyly. "It occurs to me that one or more of you might like to try riding a horse. I must warn you, though, that when the mare catches your smell, different from her master's, it were better you had tried to ride a raging lion. She will throw you off and then, if you are lucky, merely kick you. If the Gods are not with you, she will strike at your head with her forefeet."

"King Eurytus," I heard myself cry out, "I ask to ride Nessus' stallion."

No one in the throng could have been more astonished at my words than Heracles himself. I had not anticipated saying them—I had been thinking of something else, it seemed—and the instant they were out, my first thought was I had played into Eurytus' hands, and my second, almost as galling, was that I disarranged all of Right Doer's plans. And now, as the crowd and the King, too, seemed out of breath to speak, Right Doer spoke in low tones:

"You boastful fool! No, I take that back—it was no kind of a boast, vain or otherwise, but that cursed defiance of Gods and men and Fate itself that you can't help. But if you are thrown, you'll be kicked to death. If you stick on, the King may not give you a chance for life and power by fighting Antaeus; the idea will hit him that you might win;

and he'll see to it that the man bearing the mark of Zeus is ambushed in the dark." Then he fell silent, for Nessus had raised his voice.

"My father the King! Have I your leave to speak?"

"Aye, you may."

"I cannot permit Heracles to attempt to mount my stallion Earth Shaker. Even if he got up, a new smell and new pressures and voice other than mine would do damage to my stallion's training that would take months to undo. But if Heracles wants to show himself a horseman, I have another, unbroken stallion, new from the steppes, which he is free to try to ride. If he agrees—and by your royal will—I will send four stout fellows to fetch him here with blacksmith pincers in his nostrils and with throat ropes."

"I would thank you kindly," I told Nessus.

"If such is the young man's wish. . . ." Eurytus remarked complacently, rubbing his hands in the ancient gesture of washing them.

In a moment Nessus had dispatched four of his train, then he wove through the crowd to get to my side.

"Heracles, I think you are mad—although perhaps with a semidivine madness put upon you by Dionysus. How many cups have you had since you ate dinner?"

"Three."

"A mere thimbleful—comparatively speaking. My friend, you can't possibly ride Erebus. He will buck you off and then try to kick or strike you. He is the most savage-tempered stallion I have ever seen— also the most costly. I had intended to starve him for a week before I put my weight on his mighty back, and hobble him front and rear. You may be killed—but if so, it's the will of the Gods. But try to stay on long enough to make a good show for the people, in which case Antaeus may think twice about challenging you, whereby his reputation for omnipotence may falter a little, and some good may accrue from this wild and witless exploit."

"Will you tell me how to cling on, other than with my hand in his mane?"

"Grip with your knees and thighs. That is the only possible way. Grip with all your strength. Farewell! Theseus, who slew the Minotaur, will no doubt welcome you respectfully when you enter Hades."

I needed wait only a few minutes for Nessus' drovers to arrive with the plunging beast. Erebus was a good name for him, I thought, since his glossy black coat showed no white hair; his only other tint was his rather light-brown eyes, large, luminous, and fierce. He was led to the gaming ground and the crowd stood respectfully back.

"Shall I mount?" I asked Nessus.

"If such is your stubborn will."

"Then bid the men take off the ropes and release the pincers as soon as I seize his mane."

Right Doer stepped close to me, took my hand, and spoke confidingly, in his deeply lowered but wonderfully warm and exultant voice, in my ear.

"Remember, my brother, how you killed the big snakes before you could talk plainly."

"I will never forget."

At my signal, the men slipped three nooses from around Erebus' neck. I moved briskly up to him and got a good grip on his mane with my left hand, holding Nessus' leather whip with my other. The man holding the pincers opened and dropped them, and ran. In the same instant I swung on the monster's back.

For a few long seconds he stood motionless, as though he was astonished out of his wits. Then he bounded straight in the air and landed with stiff legs, jarring me to the last segment of my backbone. Thereafter I could not know what he did in the way of bounding, bucking, rearing, whirling, kicking, and striking—everything but turning his sleek neck to bite me, against which I would have had no defense. I did as Nessus had told me and gripped with my thighs and knees. Still, I could not have kept my seat except for my powerful grip at the base of his magnificent sable mane.

The fact remained that I was not taming him in the slightest measure, and his struggle to throw me became more frantic, and his eyes were rolled back and white. The truth came to me: I could not stand many more jouncings and heavings and sudden and violent whirlings, and my blows of the whip on his neck and sides only enraged him the more. So I slipped back a little farther, so that my knees as well as my legs were against the ribs of his mighty chest, and, once more securely seated, squeezed with all my might.

Did I say all? No, at first I applied only a great deal of the strength of my thighs, not their full strength. This would not win for me—the beast grew frenzied—so I summoned up my whole strength, from what store- or treasure house I knew not, knowing not whether it was given me by the Gods or by some strange lot cast by Lachesis, one of the three Dread Sisters, when I was conceived. I squeezed with enormous power. The horse began a great upward bound. But when he smote the earth, it was not with jolting force; instead, he lighted gently and crumpled down upon it. I got my leg free just in time to save it from being crushed.

The eyes were still rolled up, still looked white, but somehow they had a different look than before, and I looked in vain to see the beast pant. In that gaze I noticed that the skin on his uppermost and visible side had changed slightly in appearance. I could not doubt that he had bled inwardly, and when I ran my hand along his ribs where my legs had pressed, I felt sharp and broken bones.

The only souls to come near me were Right Doer and Nessus, both pale in the face. They gazed upon the dead steed and Nessus felt the glossy hide.

"Eurytus, my father the King!" Nessus called.

"Aye."

"My stallion Erebus has died of what I believe to be heart failure, caused by frantic exertion. And although I have never before seen an instance with my own eyes, I have heard of a good many similar cases, when the horse was of high mettle and in great wrath."

"Nessus, would you count it that Heracles won the victory?"

"How could anyone count it otherwise? He remained up until the horse fell."

"Since I promised no mead of victory for a yokel riding one of the mares, I will offer none to Heracles, who successfully rode a stallion. But I will make up the lack in case, as it may be, he takes part in some other contest, perhaps to be set later in the afternoon, when again he may test his strength and skill in the sight of the Gods."

Nessus spoke to me quickly in a low voice.

"Heracles, are you tired?"

"A little, but a mess of beef and barley bread will revive me."

In great haste, then, Nessus called up about fifteen of his troop, calling them by name, and asked them to drag the carcass of the dead stallion into a thick, brushy clump of woods.

"I wish to conceal it from the birds of death until he can be properly buried, with honors due a great steed." And this made good enough sense. Vultures were numerous in the desert stretches of Boeotia, and if one spied the carrion and came in his horrid haste, within an hour fifty or more would come, and they would find the skin and muscle weakened over the broken ribs, and there they would make their frantic entry to the dead beast's bowels. But folk told falsely that the gruesome fowls could find carrion by its smell. Right Doer and I had often covered with brushwood a newly slain stag, left it for the night, and found the carcass intact late on the following day.

Nessus at once set some of the household slaves to making fire, boiling meat, and baking barley bread, and shortly thereafter a wonderful thing must have happened, of which I knew nothing until its consequence. This was, when the meal was ready, the King's daughter Megara came to our little cooking fire in a bower-like clearing in the cypress woods to see to my comfort and well-being, in the way of Greek girls unto honored guests. And while her beauty was not as startling as her sister Iole's, still it was of plenteous measure, and my heart had warmed to her ever since she had asked the King to defy Artemis in defense of little Arne, the leader of the troop of mock bears, and my heart glowed at this mead of victory, and my soul exulted.

"You received no prize when you had ridden Erebus," she said in her deep voice, "and that shamed my father before the Gods, and shamed all the Minyans, so I asked that I might redeem the dereliction, as far as in my power, and I will wash your hands and face and anoint your skin before you eat; then I will serve you the meat with my own hands."

I could think of very little to say to her, since her defiance of the wrath of Artemis and mine of the rage of Erebus were uncomfortable topics of talk. As it happened, it did not much matter, because she hummed a song, a sweet one I had never heard, as she scrubbed my face and hands, and then for good measure washed the sweat from my big chest. Finally she poured into her palm sweet-scented oil from a little ewer and began rubbing it into my skin wherever it was naked, and it seemed to me her hands lingered a little longer than need demanded at the more sensitive places—the back of my neck, the region of my ears, the nipples that on a man are so minute and unnecessary and yet which respond to the lightest caress, the soles of my feet, and the backs and tops of my thighs. By now she and I were alone in a little dell. Right Doer had strolled away, and when stragglers from the throng looked through the leafage and caught sight of us, they quickly walked on. I realized I had done what Right Doer had forbidden—gone into a covert out of sight and sound of the multitude. Still, my common sense told me that the injunction was no longer valid. In the first place, a surprise attack or a crudely arranged quarrel with Antaeus was not to be feared today. In the second place, I had a strong feeling that I could not explain that the presence of Megara served me as a shield of as many folds of strength as the shield of Achilles.

"I saw Iole kiss you after your wrestling match with Nessus," the Princess remarked in an offhand way as she was oiling my armpits.

"Yes, she did kiss me, as a mead of honor."

"She has a wonderful gift for getting on the right side. Whether I like it or not, her head is longer than mine and her eyes much sharper, and she perceived before I did that you would become the hero of the day. You were much more pleased than if I had kissed you."

"I won't say that," I muttered, flushing a little.

"I'll say it. I know it too well by experience. I can't compete with Iole; always I am no more than second choice, and often not that. And you might as well be told, before you find it out for yourself, that her kisses are always political. There is only one passion in her life . . ." And then Megara's lovely caressing hands grew still and she remained several seconds in deep reverie.

"Well?"

"Heracles, I am not sure that what I started to say is true. Iole has depths I have never penetrated. There may be something more in her life than her priessthood of Artemis—it might even be that she believes she is Artemis herself, come to earth, her human incarnation. If so, she believes she has been sent here on some great mission. But to judge from her daily actions, by all her visible moves, she cares for nothing except the exaltation of the Goddess and this shrine. She pleased the people by kissing a victor over a brother, especially a man as plain-looking as you, whom they were naturally supporting. And they hadn't forgotten that mead of victory when you proved your prowess again by riding to death Erebus, one of the mightiest stallions ever bred on the steppes, that cost a talent of gold."

"Great Gods! I had expected to pay Nessus for his loss, but where would I get a talent of gold?"

"Nessus will not expect you to make up the loss. He is always honorable—except when in the power of Antaeus. And many of the strongest beasts have weak hearts. You, Heracles, might have a weak heart."

The words could mean that I would die of heart failure during some great exertion, but I thought that she meant more than that. Because she had glanced partly away, as folk often do when they mean more than they say, I studied her face with great care. The fact was no longer incredible to me that she had asked the throng to defy great Artemis, even if we were, every one, blasted in one burst of Zeus' wrath.

Her immense eyes appeared jet-black in this deep shade and unplumbably deep. I thought, "She is a maiden of deep feelings," and did not try to find any other clue to their meaning, and could not have if I had tried. And since they were too dark to meet the Greek ideals of beauty, and set too close together, why did their full gaze make me at first dizzy and then breathless with desire? If I were fool enough to fall in love with either of the King's two daughters, certainly it would be with splendid, goddess-like Iole. Then I kept looking at Megara's mouth—full and red, not pink and perfect like Iole's mouth, and somehow at odds with her nose, pointed, childlike, and charming—and I knew it for the mouth of a passionate young woman, whose hands could hardly keep from caressing my skin that was smooth enough to suit her, despite the roughness underneath. Then I heard myself gasp like a callow boy.

"Will you kiss me, Megara?"

"If you wish."

She did so, not a light touch but a wholehearted kiss, with some length to it, and soft pressure, and meaning beyond itself.

"I suppose that too was second best," she told me, turning pink and with a little heave of her bosom.

"No, we are alone here, and no one was watching, and maybe you put more heart in it somehow, so it was the best kiss anyone ever gave me in my remembered life."

"Even if you had said it was second to Iole's, still I would have given you my message," she went on, after a long silence.

It was on my tongue to ask if we could not hurry to some retreat, a bower deep in the forest, and seek what bliss might be waiting for us there; and I thought if we found it, her big eyes would pop out of her head, and even I, Heracles, come nigh to swooning. If a dryad who loved the soft grass there and the pale green light, strained through a canopy of tree leaves, and who sometimes led there by the hand some not ungainly yokel she had met on the path should chance upon us, she would watch us through the screens of vines in secret, agonized convulsion. But I did not make the proposal because of Megara's expression—intense, but having nothing to do with love.

"It is not a message, and instead it is a request. I have paid you the due of a guest, washing and serving you, and kissed you besides, and to ask some little boon is in accordance with ancient custom."

"Aye, it is."

"What I ask is a great boon, not to fall upon my head alone, but upon the heads of all Grecians. You will be invited or challenged to wrestle Antaeus, Heart of Stone, and by the rules of the pancratium, which means without rules. I, Megara, ask you to accept."

The sweet taste of her kiss ebbed away and perhaps there was wormwood in my mouth, for I made harsh reply.

"You differ greatly from beautiful Andromache, who pleaded with her husband Hector not to meet deadly Achilles on the plain, and to remain safely within the walls." And this was from a tale told by a blind poet who had it from soldiers returning from the war in Troy.

"She and I differ as day from night. I would have lain with Hector for the last time and then sped him on his way. There is a time for yielding and a time for defiance at any cost, or so the Goddess of the Corn, sweet Demeter, has confided to me."

"Perhaps Eurytus asked you to do this when you had washed, anointed, served, even kissed me. I am known as well for my thick head as for my strong muscles. I could be easily persuaded—so he might think—to accept battle that the whole host believes I will lose."

"Your head is not so thick as to believe the first part. As for the last part, three members of the host in the best position to know believe you will win. Those three are your brother Right Doer, my brother Nessus, and you yourself."

I kissed both her hands, and then knelt and kissed her toes under the strap of her sandals. And then my surging heart quieted a little, and my thick head stopped reeling as from a hard punch dealt me by a God, and I was able to speak with good sense.

"And you, Megara? Do you think I will win or lose? I will fight him anyway, so speak truth."

"Heracles, I believe you will win. At least I know it is the time to try, to risk all, although there is hardly more than an even chance that you will come forth alive and well. There is hardly less than an even chance that your eyes will not be darkened by unyielding Death, or else your body so broken that you will pray to the Gods for death. But remember there is no one else who would have any chance. If you are fated to die this young, with the mighty deeds that you seem born to do proven only a dream, only shadows that were never real, ere you cross the River Lethe and you yourself become a shadow, forgetting all that ever was or ever might have been, take comfort in what I tell you now, again, that there is no one else on whom the Greeks, Minyans and Thebans alike, can call in their awful need. Heracles, I believe you will win. Hereby I join the company of my brother Nessus, your brother Right Doer, and Heracles himself; and our common faith, our mighty bond, is that you will win. And that common faith and mighty bond has made us four companions always, for as long as we live on earth, and forevermore as speechless shadows, knowing not why we herd together, in the shadowy realm of Hades."

And her great eyes shone, and her face flamed so that it seemed to give forth light.

"And if you win," she went on, "it comes to me it will be a great winning. I told you you would be invited or challenged to fight Antaeus. That is true as far as it goes, but there is much more to it. In the first place, the King knows within his soul that you are his great adversary, and there is no other. He knows it not by this mark on your shoulder that I bend and kiss, hoping it means something but believing it means nothing. Rather he knows it by his great cunning, by what he has seen already with his own eyes, by the wit and cunning of his counselors, perhaps by the confiding of some God who loves not Thebes, the same that laid the curse on the house of Cadmus. And he is fully as sure of another thing—that if you accept the gauge of battle, Antaeus will win. But he cannot be sure that you will accept, and it is not my father's way to leave any stone unturned on which he might stumble. Thus I believe that he and his counselors have arranged a stratagem. Before I came here with you, I had seen him in talk with Antaeus and with a lowborn fellow called Cacus, who calls himself Eurytus' body servant but is truly the prime inventor of his plots." Then Megara hesitated, as though to weigh the effect, the good or ill to follow, of what she was about to tell me.

"Open your mouth," I told her, for she had pressed her lips together as she sat in reverie.

She did so, fully knowing what I intended, and our tongues spoke to each other in a silence as eloquent as were once Linus' strummings on his lute.

"Afterward the King's lips curled in a little smirk that I know too well," Megara went on, when she could again use her tongue for speech, and her voice was all the more lovely and warm because of the warm, lovely passage between us. "Wait, Heracles, I still can't guess what the stratagem may be . . . but I feel closer to you now . . . have greater care of you . . . and that quickens what brain I have . . . and I think—of course, that's it: some dreadful charge will be made against you, and you will be given trial by battle with Antaeus to prove your guilt or innocence, and if you should refuse the trial, he can have you killed by naked power. But if I am right, and you make the trial and win, and then ask a truly great prize of victory, Eurytus will be hard put not to pay it without losing the respect of his subjects and the Gods. And Heracles, the Gods themselves will be watching from the porches of their golden houses above Olympus. It is no longer merely the attempt of a King to prove false the Oracle of Delphi—that has been tried many times and has always failed. Great forces are being arrayed—for you, and against you—among them Pallas Athene, who cannot abjure a battlefield. Also will come ever-jealous, scheming Hera, choosing the side that has paid her the richer offering—and what of Zeus? Heracles, who is your father?"

"I do not know."

"I do not think it could be Zeus, despite the tale of the eagle hawking at Hera's peacock the night before you were conceived, a tale that has somehow reached the Palace of Eurytus. You do not look like the son of a God, unless it were lame but mighty Hephaestus, blacksmith of the Gods. But Antaeus may be Zeus' son. He looks the part."

"If so, I have lost the battle before it begins."

"No, Zeus may be away, paying court to another beautiful woman of earth, or some lovely nymph. If Antaeus is Zeus' son, Hera will be behind you in the battle, and she would serve you better than her forgetful, inattentive, henpecked husband. But I greatly fear that Artemis, before whose shrine you will battle, will try to help Antaeus. She is bursting with rage at my proposal of defiance, and she has listened to our talk out here in the wood, and she respects me even though she hates me, and would take Antaeus' side if only for spite against me."

"That is only too likely," I said. But I would not blanch one bit. I would fight with the weapons with which I was endowed, by whom I knew not. Still I wished that Iole, too, would be on my side, for that would temper the wrath of Artemis; and I thought she would be, to judge from the way she had kissed me when I had beaten Nessus. A better sign than that was the way she had looked at me, her beautiful red brows most curiously raised and a wild light in her blue eyes, when I had killed Erebus.

"My sweet Demeter will try to defend you," Megara went on, quickly summoning my wandering mind back to the present scene. "She loves Thebes and she loves me and she loves strength like yours, which is latent in the corn she blesses. Dionysus, God of the Vine, will also, and Pan, God of herdsmen and drovers. I fear Apollo the Far-Darter. Perhaps he is Antaeus' father—both are beautiful enough to be father and son. As Artemis' brother, he is always inclined to side with her. Hermes, I feel sure, will be on our side, although I cannot tell you why. Perhaps because he loves laughter, and common things of earth, and is the God of Thieves."

"I stole a dead heifer from a lion that had stolen her——"

"That is not your only theft. I won't tell you what the other is. But I tell you this, in farewell. If you win, I will give you anything you ask of me, and which I have the power to give."

As I stood dumfounded, Megara appeared to melt away into the greenery, as once did a fleeing dryad above our pasturage under Parnassus. It happened that I never had found the woodland nymph again. Perhaps I would never find Megara or ever find anything more of beauty and ardency and truth, not even great meals and horns of wine and sweet sleep thereafter, from which the dreamer rarely doubts that he will waken in good time to all that he knows and loves. I loved life so greatly—even more than before, it seemed—and I would be such an anomaly in silent, lonely, dismal Hades, the realm of shadows. Yet it might be I must stand my great trial, which Megara's tenderness to me had not concealed and instead revealed in the hard light of contrast, before the present winged hour had passed overhead.

CHAPTER FOUR

TRIAL OF BATTLE

1

I took a different path in leaving the bower than in coming here. It fetched me up still in the cypress wood not far from where a gang of slaves were burying the carcass of Erebus, and almost directly behind the great cedar of Artemis' shrine. Then it so chanced that I thought again of the dryad who had fled from me in the oak forest. Indeed, for one instant I had the feeling of seeing her anew, only to perceive that I was gazing upon Iole, who was standing, light on her feet and lovely, behind a screen of vines. And suddenly I knew why, on first laying eyes on Iole, I had had the fleeting impression of having seen her before. Truly she was very like the dryad, not only in slender and sinuous shape, but in her lineaments, and had the same flaming hair.

"Are you waiting for someone?" I asked, ill-mannered rustic that I was.

"For you," she answered. "I had begun to think your tryst with Megara would never end. But my message is short and will only take a moment to tell. And that's a good thing, because the King is about to make an announcement which you must hear."

"I'll listen well, both to you and to the King."

"Heracles, I beg that you do. And what I have to say is not news— that you know or have guessed already—but a petition. I have here some goat blood, also a stick that you might break off from a tree to use as a cane. I ask you to let me smear the blood on your leg and, as you join the throng, come limping on the stick. Also, I would like to scrape skin from your knee with the sacrificial knife, because it can never be put to use more pleasing to my Goddess. Then when the King invites you, as the conqueror of Erebus, to please the throng once more by fair wrestling with Antaeus, you can tell him that you have suffered a hard fall. It is easy to fall on the rocks when clambering down to the Spring of Good Fortune a little way back in the wood. Thus you may fairly ask that the match be postponed until your wounds are healed. Never fear that Artemis herself will not speak to restrain the King's anger and the disappointment of the throng. Indeed, I believe that her word alone, without the false show of a wound, would stop the contest, but this little dissembling will lend greater credence to it and give it more power."

Her low voice, scarcely above a murmur, was charged with intense feeling. I could not fail to see the feverish glitter in her beautiful eyes.

"Will you tell me, Iole, why you so dread a fair and manly contest between Antaeus and me?"

"Yes, I'll tell you, although I think you already know. Antaeus' fame is well won. When he gets into any kind of fight, a rage to kill comes upon him; I do not know why, unless he is the son of Ares, God of War, which some men whisper as truth. Not Apollo, as his beauty and his soft voice might hint. Not Poseidon, God of the Sea, but Ares the Ruthless. And Heracles, his strength and yours are so nearly equal that his far greater skill at the game will most certainly prevail. I make this petition only to save your life. I have never seen you before today, but I have kissed you, and even I, Priestess of Artemis, took delight in your wrestling with my brother and your battle with the great steed, and Artemis' spirit has imparted to me her own delight, as great as I have ever known her to take in contests held in her honor. And I greatly fear that if you refuse my request, the wish of my Goddess as well as my own, she will fly into her swift and deadly rage, the same as caused her to kill Niobe's children, and then she will support Antaeus in the battle instead of you."

"Iole, you do not know the whole truth. I have reasons to believe the contest will be forced on me, regardless of Artemis' wishes, and the lot has been cast; there can be no recall."

"No, you can avoid it with honor if you try."

"I cannot try. The spirit of my father, whether God or king or lusty slave, speaks to my spirit and tells me the battle must be joined. It does not promise victory. I am not sure it promises glorious death.

But of one thing I am sure, it threatens shame, and the name of traitor to all that I love, and a darkness on all my days on earth, if I turn my back. Iole, I do not believe that mighty Hector fled three times around the wall of Troy ere he took his stand against godlike Achilles. I believe that some vengeful Greek whose son or brother or father had felt the sword of Hector cleaving his body invented the tale and poured it into the ears of the blind poet, who now recounts it. But to you, not the first woman of great beauty who has implored a warrior to forego the battle—in this case a beauty like Artemis' own, and in this case a warrior plain to look upon, one without fame, one unworthy of your concern as far as my soul confides—to you I am ever indebted, your bonded servant. I see you standing there in the very likeness of the Goddess, except for the woe that I do not understand in your illustrious eyes. No glimpse of such beauty of form and face has ever been given me except once, behind our pasturage below Parnassus, in an ancient oak forest, for there I saw an immortal dryad. At your feet I lay my no small strength."

"Yet you still refuse my plea."

"Aye."

"What if I offered you my body, which you deem beautiful, as your prize?"

"If a priestess of the Virgin Goddess would give me her body—which I cannot believe, and the mere hint that she might is a madness brought upon her by some subtle enemy, divine or mortal—I would still refuse."

"Then I must turn to my great Mother."

She left me as an arrow leaves a bow, and Time had hardly bethought himself and resumed his creeping but remorseless pace when I saw her spring up the ladder as though taking wing, kiss Artemis' image on both cheeks and then, long and passionately, the marble lips. Presently she slowly descended and knelt before the shrine. And she had not moved her beautiful flaming head one jot from its deep obeisance when the herald of King Eurytus blew three shrill blasts.

2

The folk gathered under the palisade, their faces drawn with anxiety, their eyes strangely dark, and the little children came with their hands in their parents' hands, looking up into the beloved faces, and their own faces became troubled, although they uttered no sound of fear and woe. And when all had come, the two great hosts, and the heavy silence had hung, it seemed, for an endless time, the King stepped to the palisade, alone except for his herald, and just below him stood the Queen, his son Nessus, and the giant Antaeus.

"Heracles of Thebes!" the King intoned.

"Aye."

"It is commanded by the Gods, and by my own soul, and decided in council of my great Companions, that I make a charge against you grave and hateful to us all. When some of my slaves were burying the carcass of the stallion Erebus, who had died suddenly from what my son Nessus thought was heart failure when you were on his back, one of them chanced to see a small, thin object thrusting about an inch from the base of his neck, a little to the right of the neckbone, in the part of his mane that you had held in your left hand. He drew it forth, and it proved to be a kind of dagger made of flint, filed to a needle point and razor-sharp on both edges, about ten inches long, less than half an inch in breadth, and thin as a golden coin used in trade in Egypt. It has come to me and to my companions that you had this small but deadly knife in your possession, and when, after your rash request to ride Earth Shaker, you saw great Erebus led forth, unused to the weight of man, you repented your folly. Then, perceiving that you could not withdraw without shame to you and all Thebans, you determined to mount with the weapon hidden behind your hand, and if the contest began to go against you and you perceived you would be thrown and likely kicked to death, you would drive the blade into the stallion's neck so quickly and lightly that the act would not be seen, and its razor-sharp edge would surely sever an artery or a great nerve, and the horse fall dead. Heracles, are you innocent or guilty of this hideous crime? Speak so both hosts may hear."

I drew a deep breath, my short ribs sharply indrawn, to force a great, reverberant blast of air through my throat.

"Eurytus, King of the Minyae, I am innocent."

"That will presently be shown, or proven a loathsome lie. I decree that you stand trial in the sight of the Gods and of these throngs. Of three trials, I will permit you to make your choice. One is by fire. If you stand in its roaring flame with your skin and hair unburned, we will know that the Gods have moved to defend you, and you will be freed of arrest, and you may ask of me a boon of no small measure in

atonement for the wrong done you by a false charge. If you reject
trial by fire, you may choose trial by the hemlock cup, and if when
you have drained it, you do not vomit it up, and you remain well and
strong as you stand now, neither wan nor feeble, it will be the same
as though you had stood trial by fire. And if you reject trial by the
hemlock cup, your final choice is to stand trial by battle with my champion Antaeus, and it will take the form of wrestling that we call
pancratium, and if you emerge victorious, it will be the same as though
you had stood trial by fire or by the poisoned cup. But Heracles, if
you reject all three trials because you dare not undergo them, or for
any other reason, I will straightway call upon fifty spearmen to close
in upon you and to riddle your body with their burnished bronze
points, and you will be slain without mercy, and your corpse made
unrecognizable to your own brother, and you will go down to Hades.
Your name shall become accursed to all Greeks, and never be spoken
again in the hearing of men. Now, how will you have it, Heracles of
Thebes? Speak your choice."

I appeared to hesitate briefly, but that was only to make the crowd
hold its breath and the King and his counselors take thought of what
they had done and become uneasy as to what I would do. If I chose
either fire or the hemlock cup, they would be in a pickle, because neither throng would take kindly to my being burned or poisoned. Also,
I might choose to fight the fifty spearmen, and if they knew the fire
mounting and leaping in my heart, they would rue the choice more
than any open to me. I took it that a whole batch of Minyans would
have to walk in attendance upon one Theban, lugging their weapons
while I swung my big arms at my side, and with sheepish grins, as I
went down to shadowy Hades.

And while about it, I took time to think that Iole could not have
known beforehand of her father's charge against me, or she would have
saved her breath. I wondered if she were still kneeling before the lovely
statue of Artemis, praying—for what?

"King Eurytus, I choose to fight Antaeus," I bawled with all my
breath.

A great yell rose from the hosts, as vociferous from the throats of
Minyans as from Thebans. The King said something, but the shout
drowned him out. As he stepped back, a giant of a man came to the
edge of the palisade and, like a God from Olympus, looked down on
the suddenly silenced throng. As for me, my heart turned cold. Seren-

ity had always been marked in Gods—it is depicted in statues, the faces grave, unearthly beautiful, and ineffably serene—and in gravity and serenity, Antaeus' face was like theirs. In addition to these qualities, and perhaps partly because of them, it was markedly beautiful—not too massive, classically Grecian, lighted by large, pale-gray eyes, rosy-looking in contrast with his blond hair, a curly aura about his head and half hiding his lips and chin with a small, curled beard. Perhaps because he knew himself to be the son of a God he knew he would win the victory. Perhaps he knew because of knowledge of his own powers, and suddenly I feared this more than divine conception.

In a moment the ring where I had wrestled Nessus was redrawn. The throng was parting to let me through, and then making the path far wider to let Antaeus through. We did not glance at each other as some Theban girls came up to take charge of my sandals and tunic, and Iole and Megara, both big-eyed and white, did a like office for Antaeus. It was customary at most athletic encounters for the contestants to wear loincloths, or at least a thong at the waist with a small cloth in front. But when Antaeus stripped off the last thread, with a mien so quiet I could not call it boastful, I did the same. And if there was any Goddess who had not yet made her choice between us two contestants, she chose now.

Hera, Queen of Heaven, do not lend your terrible might to my enemy, do not strengthen his thews and weaken mine in jealous hatred! I am not the son of your husband Zeus; when my soul seemed to whisper that I was, it was caught up in pride over my body's strength that has never achieved more than heaving stones, lifting logs, toppling beasts, and winning contests of might over men of ordinary strength, and now may prove vain. Amphitryon, Wrathful Leader, spoke truth that darkling night. I am the son of a burly slave who came to Alcmene's chambers reeking from the field.

Pallas Athene, awful in battle, merciless avenger, you aided my ancestor, great Perseus, when he slew Medusa; will you aid my enemy now? I have never given you your due in sacrifice. You are the Goddess of the cities, and I loved not their stony walls but instead the fields, the forests, and the mountains beloved of Dionysus and of drunken Pan. So I dare not ask you to take my side; only to watch with your great gray eyes, your hands folded. Artemis, you too love fields, forests, and mountains, all wilderness where roam the deer and bear; but something stands between us, perhaps an offense of mine that I did not know I gave you, perhaps that you looked into my heart when Megara cried defiance against you. So I will not ask your help—somehow I know it is useless—and I hardly dare hope you will not aid Antaeus. Aphrodite, I knew where your eyes would turn the instant that Antaeus bared his body, more manly than that of your lover, Ares, God of War. It does not matter greatly because your hand is weak to strike, of power only to caress. Demeter, of you alone of all the Olympian Goddesses, I implore favor. Remember the corncakes I ate, along with the strong meat, and how I thrived. My strength, Megara told me, was of the corn that you bless, that the plowman must eat before he drives his beasts afield. Sweet Demeter, Goddess of the Corn, with hair the color of ripe corn! If I survive the battle, in due course I will build you a temple, and no beasts will be slaughtered there, let alone men, women, and little children; only the wine of Dionysus will be poured, and the barley meal strewn.

3

Now that my orisons were done, I stood in the center of the ring. Around me Antaeus walked in long and graceful strides, ineffably powerful as the strides of lion bearing off prey, and I moved only enough to keep my gaze on his. Then he walked up to me and, out of range of my right arm, his foot lashed up, swift as a mule's lashing backward, to kick me in the groin. But he had overreached himself a little, and I grasped him by the ankle, and except for his sideways wrench, I might have toppled him. As it was, he broke free, and we grappled hand to hand.

Then, in the while ere either of us could break the hold and we were perforce in close and terrible embrace, he spoke to me in a low voice such as Nessus had employed during our unequal contest, but its tone was vastly different, being lofty and contemptuous, and his tidings hateful in my ears.

"Heracles, who was your father?"

"I do not know," I answered, somehow proud to speak the truth in the hearing of the Gods.

"It was not Zeus. I do not believe that the mark on your shoulder was drawn by him or any other God. Eurytus believes it was, but today his folly will be cured, for within the hour he will see it on your cooling corpse, which will prove you are not his fated slayer of the

Delphic prophecy, and some other, still unknown to him, bears the fatal sign. Heracles, this is your last sweat, and it is in vain."

"Perhaps we will both die," I said in sudden wonder and awe at the whims of the Gods.

"No, because I am the son of Ares, by a mortal mother; and although I am fated to die, it will not be in battle, where my father will not let me die, because battle is his domain and passionate love. Do you doubt me? How can you look upon me and believe I was conceived by any other? You know how I show no mercy. You know how I always kill, those who fight well or those who fight weakly. How can the son of Ares spare his best friend, once we have grappled?"

"If you are so certain of the outcome, why do you waste breath to tell me of it?"

"I can spare a little breath. Also, with it, I can promise you one boon. My father watches with joy, no matter how certain the outcome, and always he speaks to the God of the Underworld of those of whom I have sent to him, and there they are given a little preference over the common dead. I do not mean you will go to the Elysian Fields. Only great heroes go there, and what heroic deeds have you performed? If there are any, I have not heard of them. But when blood from the sacrifice is poured into the pit, those whom I have slain are given a little of it, and for a brief while they can speak to one another, and they can remember, dimly and far off, glorious days on earth. So be happy that Atropos will bring her shears while we are in combat."

I could not answer, only strive to break his hold. And now, listening to his speech, somehow I could no longer doubt that he was indeed the son of the God of War.

"Except for the eternal ban against incest, Aphrodite herself would leave Ares' bed, sometimes, to come to mine," Antaeus went on; and who but a God or the son of a God would dare to say it?

In listening to what he said, I had to brush my mind across it hard and fast to grasp its meaning, because this was no time for meditation. The fight was slowly but surely speeding up. Antaeus gripped me again and again; always I broke his grip largely by main strength, always he laughed and almost instantly attempted to gain some other advantage. Again and again we were both down, he trying for some classic hold, I putting my trust in greater strength and endurance. Even so, if I should let him fully gain any position he sought, my strength would not prevail, for the reason that it did not surpass his in sufficient measure, and he knew how to apply his own strength to handicap mine, and then he would slowly creep from hold to hold until he had one upon me from which I could not escape, and only my spirit would issue weakly through my mouth or ooze out of me like sweat on its way to Hades.

He never missed a chance to strike or kick me, and since the reach of his arms and legs was so much greater than mine, he gave me much cruel pain. He did not succeed in crippling me only because I never gave him quite room enough—always, so far, I had knocked his fist or foot a little to one side, or balked it somehow. Nor was I ever able to land a full-strength blow or kick to any part of his body because of his swift, strong guard. Once he caught my fingers in a mighty grip and started to crush them and break the bones, but his brawny neck became exposed, and I dealt him a blow on it with my other hand, a very short and hence weakened blow, but it caused him to let go of my other hand and, I was glad to see, to open his large and lustrous eyes as though in astonishment.

After that he did not laugh when I broke his holds one by one, and his color heightened somewhat, and if I could catch the time to think about it, I could expect some of the more tender maids to swoon in ecstasy at his rosy face and body, and the sweat gleaming on his skin and the sun shining on it. So when wooers of these maids went forth again to some tryst, they might marvel at what had happened to them since last they paid court to them, so fiery they might have waxed, or cold they might have waned. As it was, I was kept so busy of mind and body trying to save my bones from his crushing grasp, seeking desperately to forestall him just a little by watching his eyes and the first deceptive movements of his arms and legs, that I forgot what a pleasant fancy was, let alone an earthy joke to smile over, and nigh forgot the sun was still in his place in the sky, and how in the name of the Gods I had got in this fix.

Even so, once when I was lying on my belly in the grass, Antaeus' arms in my good custody, but with his right leg around my belly, the foot braced under his left knee, in a position to squeeze my guts out unless I could break the hold, I found myself looking into the wild eyes of Iole, who stood in the van of the throng on the long slope. Their blue color was incredibly intense. The white corners and the rims above and below the iris glimmered like silver. Her face was so pale that the little circle of pigment high on her cheek looked unearthly black. She stood as tensely as a leopard before his deadly pounce.

I broke Antaeus' hold on me by getting a roundabout grip on one wrist. I was able to put only a little pressure on it, not enough to break the bone, but he broke loose and stood up and aimed a kick at my head, which I warded so well that he toppled. Still, I had no time to pursue the advantage, and soon we were again dancing about the ring, I as awkwardly as a bear, he with almost the grace of a nymph, each of us as far from victory or from defeat as when we started.

Not long after this, a similar set of circumstances fetched me up with my gaze full on Megara's, and her black eyes looked enormous and seemed to be glowing with pride that I had lived this long, and with hope that I would live on. As she caught my eyes she put her hands around her neck, as though to caution me against Antaeus' hands getting around my neck, and good sense the warning made, for he had choked to death more than one adversary, and he had never been known to let go until well after the blackness in the victim's face had turned blue and then to ghastly white.

Nessus towered beside Megara. He gave me a short, sharp wave of his hand that I knew was a salutation. In front of him the King breathed hard, for he had reckoned that the fight would have been finished long before now, and the birthmark on my shoulder need trouble his dreams no more. Instead, he saw me forging patiently on, somewhat like the turtle racing the hare in the tale that farmers tell— not even bleeding as yet, let alone with broken bones thrusting through my skin. And I saw the whites of his eyes that were usually hidden by close-fitting lids like mine, and his face was beaded with sweat, and I took pleasure in thinking those beads were cold as drops of spray from a mountain waterfall.

Then, when we were both so intertwined we could not hurt each other or hardly extricate ourselves, Antaeus spoke again in his cool, low voice.

"My father Ares must be absent from his throne today. Doubtless he is away courting some nymph who doesn't object to the smell of blood he always carries with him, and which golden Aphrodite finds so enchanting."

"Happily I do not know who my father was, so I don't expect his help," I answered, when I could catch and hold enough breath to speak.

"Heracles, you are the stoutest antagonist I have ever met. You deserve to live so that we can fight again, perhaps for a greater prize than may be won now. If you agree to lie on your back and yield, I will swear before Apollo, the God of Truth, I will not harm you."

"No, I want to finish what we've begun."

"Don't you perceive, you country lout, that the fight's going against you? So far you've broken all my holds, and more than once by the weight of a hair, and sooner or later I will get one that you cannot break. Meanwhile, I confess, I might give you an opening for a full-powered blow of your fist, from which I have taken only short and awkward blows, and in respect to it I have made you this offer."

"I thank you kindly, but decline."

"Consider this. Ares may have failed to come to my help so far only because he thought I had no need of it, as in my previous matches. But if you refuse to lose and live, you will surely lose and die. I know my mother. She has told me of the night that Ares visited her, and how his dog guarded the doorway, and a flock of vultures perched in the trees about the court croaking in ecstasy because they could foresee the fruit of that mating. At this moment she is in the throng of Minyans. I have only to give her a certain sign and she will signal her lover in a way she knows, and he will straightway leave his wooing, even the perfumed bed of Aphrodite, and make his way hither, invisible in a tenuous haze that men try to rub off their own eyes, and lend my thews the little extra strength they need to end the contest swiftly."

"Signal your mother, so she may call in the bloodstained God, and while she's about it, call in his sister Discord, and her son Strife, and his attendants Terror and Panic. I'll have a punch to spare for every one of them."

For some feeling, indescribable, but causing the back of my neck to tingle, was asurge in my heart and spreading out to my veins.

"What you ask, you shall receive."

And with a movement so quick my eyes could not follow it, Antaeus disengaged one arm and held it up as though brandishing a sword.

A second later he tried to jab me with it in the front of the neck to crush my larynx, and I warded it well; still, a man of sense might be sorry now he had spoken so defiantly of the most ruthless of Gods, for truly it seemed that Antaeus' strength had doubled. At least his attack doubled in fierceness. Still I was not sorry, perhaps because I lacked good sense, mainly because it was in my fate to answer Antaeus' threat in this same wise; and anyway, I hated Ares for having slain in blood and dust so many of my young companions in the war between Orchomenus and Thebes. Somehow I strengthened my defense so I still broke his holds, still kept him from getting any lock on me with his legs or arms that I could not disengage. And he was foiled, and a terrible wrath came into his light-gray eyes, and the little blue section in one iris gleamed like a jewel, and his rosy color darkened, and truly he seemed Ares himself, always furious and rabid, blood-hungry, yearning for the sound of breaking bones and the gasps and grunts of dying, or for the great sad and unbreakable stillness that is death.

4

The penalty I paid for stemming Antaeus' attack was great exertion, the like of which I could not remember, and it came to me that I could not endure it for long. The question, cold sober in my head, was whether Antaeus or I would give out first. This much I noticed to my good: Antaeus fought so hard that it caused brief openings in his ward. They closed too fast for me to turn them to good account, but if he proved tardy for the twinkling of an eye, I meant to strike like a thunderbolt and win glorious victory. And as I panted and puffed, again and again whenever the chance offered, I glanced at Right Doer, standing by the great hunter Actaeon of the royal house of Thebes, a little way back from the King. Never did my brother fail to catch my glance and give it back to me with a smile of praise and confidence.

Then Antaeus undertook what I did not doubt was his master stroke, for which he had waited his chance. If my wits had been sharper, I might have observed that he was making a series of maneuvers with some great end in view. It came to pass that we both stood, my back to his belly, and he had a weak hold on me that I had started to break. Then with a lightning-swift movement he hooked one foot about my ankle, at the same time giving me a powerful thrust. I toppled on my stomach and, like a young lion that cannot kill with one bite or bat a full-grown bull, but has knocked it down, he sprang on my back.

Before I knew it, he had one knee against my backbone and both arms linked about my neck, lifting my head back with all his strength. A wrestler of the dimmest wit knew what would happen next, unless somehow I broke the hold. He would continue to lift against the leverage of his knee until my neck could no longer stand the strain and the bones broke. The throngs, too, perceived that I was in the direst straits. A sudden, incredible silence fell, and every eye was fixed on my futile struggles, clawing at his hands and heaving at the torturing thrust of his knee. Then the silence was broken in a most strange way. It was only by Antaeus' voice, very low and soft, the voice of a demigod who has stooped to kill a mere mortal.

"I warned you, Heracles. I gave you a chance to save your life. You refused it, in your pride, and now your pride is cast down the Well of Shame, and in a few seconds your life will end, yielded up to me, your victor. I will not spare you, Heracles. You will never again see the stars come out, and fade in the rush of dawn, and the sun rise. You will hardly know what hits you, when the bones shatter. Even now they are strained to the utmost—if you hadn't the neck of a bull, you'd be dead already—and only I will hear them break, no great pop, a soft sound I have heard so many times before, lasting a bit longer than you would think as the shattered pieces brush each other, and then your eyes will be darkened. . . ."

I did not hear what else he said. Instead I listened to a ringing shout from someone in the crowd. It rose up and came to me, straight to my mind and heart, and it was clear as the call of a turtledove and as strong as the roar of a lion.

"Heracles! Remember the great stone you rolled from the rocky cliff under Parnassus!"

I did not try to answer Right Doer with words. I had not the breath or the time. And most of the answer I made him was within my heart and soul—a great upsurging, a revival of my utmost might, a rallying of my strength; aye, an upsurging like the seas in tempest, a revival like the sweet grass when Persephone comes back to earth, a rallying as of the dark clouds, each charged with wind and unvoiced thunder and bearing the dread shafts that will rend the mountains, each going about his business, then suddenly gathering in the sky at the command of Zeus. Instead of trying to break Antaeus' grasp around my back, I reached back and somehow caught him by the thigh, and with the strength that I had heaved the rock and sent it rolling and bounding down the steep, I heaved Antaeus clean over my back to shatter face-down on earth I thought was soft and yielding until I heard the thud of his big body.

Then with great awkwardness I piled on top of him, and, holding his body down with mine and his legs gripped by mine, I put my arms around his neck and locked my hands, fingers hooking fingers. I had no knee in his back to employ leverage, but I had something better, it seemed to me, which was a strangling grasp of his throat——

"I yield to you, Heracles," he gasped.

I answered with all the civility I could muster.

"That I cannot permit in the son of the God. The son of very Ares, yielding to a country lout who knows not his father's name? No, it is far better that you die in honor. And Ares will have care of you when you are in Hades, and will let seep down to you some of the blood that he loves to make flow on the battlefields of little mortals. This you will drink, and thus be able to converse with the other shades, and tell them that Heracles said you are the better wrestler of us two, and that I killed you only with a lout's strength, not handily as you sought to kill me. And if you see the hero Perseus there, tell him you were killed by the son of Alcmene, his granddaughter, and although it was not my godly lot to slay the like of a Medusa who turned men to stone, I slew the son of the God of War, whose father and he himself turned men into blobs of rotten meat. Go your way now, Antaeus. You are through with killing, and even breathing. Have you ceased to feel the pressure of my plowman's hands? It must be so, because you do not answer, let alone boast, and why has your beautiful face turned so dark, and you turn your head weakly this way and that? As it comes sideways to me, I see that your eyes have popped almost out of their sockets, and they are indeed like globes and the left eye has a blue streak in it, from the iris deep into the ball, looking more like a foreign object than part of the eye, and the outer end of it caused the little blue segment in the luminous gray iris.

"To look at you, one would think you were staring at some marvel never before seen by the eyes of man, one that turns your pale face into black stone. Instead you are gazing at what a myriad men have seen, and some looked staunchly at it, and some averted their eyes, and at what every man of us here, and every woman, and child, must look upon some day, soon or late."

I started to speak again to Antaeus, to see if he would give any sign of listening to me, when my words were drowned out, not by any shout of the throngs that watched in a heavy, brooding, unbelieving silence. Then I perceived it was the scream of a woman, more piercing and wild and higher-pitched than the scream my nurse Althea had uttered when I killed what might be two messengers of Death, sent by a Goddess, but more likely two big snakes who had come into the house in two great sacks of cornstalks. And then I glanced up from my work, and I saw that the screamer was beautiful Iole, and I believed the outcry was one of ecstasy too great to express by tears or any common utterance, and since she had tried to save my life by begging me to forego the fight, it must be that she had fallen in love with me, bumpkin though I was.

Still my thoughts lingered more briefly on this than on Althea and of that bitter cold night long ago, no doubt because to squeeze the life out of Antaeus with both hands reminded me of how I had squeezed the two evil heads. That night I had heard their skull bones crackle, and now I heard Antaeus' larynx crush with a soft sound under my thumb. And suddenly I knew I was wasting strength on a corpse.

I rose, leaving Antaeus dead at my feet. I did not like to look into his face, which was mottled red and black, and his protuberant eyes; still, I could not refrain from a glance of admiration at his godlike body. Not even Perseus or mighty Theseus, who slew the Minotaur, had had such noble form given to them by the Gods, I thought, and I could not imagine even great Achilles boasting its like, since he had been seen walking the earth by men now alive, one of whom had stood close to him, and this informant had told me he had been tall, but far from a giant, and the greatness that enfolded him like a mantle had been in his carriage, his haughty head, his eyes that darted fiercely left and right, and in the godlike chiseling of his face, and in every movement of his hand.

Amid a great silence, for Iole leaned swooning against Nessus, and the crowd could not yet believe its eyes, I was wondering whether the three great heroes might come to the gate of Hades to behold Antaeus' entrance, for they could not have helped but note how many dead he had dispatched to the dim realm, and now they must take thought of Hades himself, King of the Dead, Zeus' brother, who could never get enough guests under his roof to suit him, and who would be in a vile temper for a few days, to have such a furnisher himself furnished to him, and they needs must walk with care until he regained his good spirits.

And now a confused babble began to rise from the throng, and some asked questions and others answered them, and in that interval I looked into Megara's black eyes, and they were speaking to me, but I did not understand their message. And I looked at Right Doer and gave him the little wave he had given me. And lastly I looked at King Eurytus, who was hard put to it to retain his dignity and calm, let alone his good color, although he was still royal, still formidable. And such is the contradictory and perplexing nature of man that suddenly I was ashamed of my nakedness in the King's sight, and the sight of the throng. As though caught in a like fix in a lady's chamber with her husband beating on the door, in great and awkward haste I put on my clothes.

5

Sedately dressed once more, feeling far from sedate and instead wildly drunk on joy and triumph, still I had eyes and ears for what was going on about me. Truly it was worth noting. The King seemed in haste to make a speech, an announcement or a proclamation that would help retrieve his enormous loss, and to this end he was talking heatedly with some of his Companions, and his so-called body servant, really the hatcher of his plots, the rascally Cacus. The fact remained he could not essay it now, for the simple reason that his herald could blow his windpipe inside out without attracting the throng's attention. These were remarkably quiet as yet. A great many of the people looked stunned, many more incredulous; no few were flushed and wildly happy in the face, they spoke to one another in brief questions and answers; not one shouted. All had eyes for only one object, which it surely was, being no longer a man—the dark-faced corpse of Antaeus. It was quite like other corpses, except several sizes larger. The people seemed to be still waiting to see if he would revive, and come rushing at me and break my neck.

And then a young female, whether country wench or king's daughter I could not tell, uttered a piercing yell. It consisted of one word, "Heracles!" but for some reason it moved the throng more than a eulogy by the finest orator in Athens. It was answered by a great bay, open-mouthed, at the top of their voices, by two thousand or more

Thebans. Then they kept on yelling, and before long they were repeating my name with a kind of rhythm, "Heracles! Heracles! Heracles!" The Minyans listened uneasily for a few seconds, their impulse at odds with their notions of propriety; then the boldest of the lot, mainly country louts, began to join in the chorus, and from thence it spread through the Minyan host like the frenzies of Dionysus through a pack of women worshiping at his mountain shrine. Three of the King's Companions, white-haired nobles and heads of ancient, semidivine Minyan families, played catch with one another's helmets. I saw someone sneaking off the palisade, and it was the small foxy man Cacus, who had no doubt contrived the scheme and who had seen his bubble of eminence and fortune, with his pick of a slave girl from the King's catch, and menials bowing and scraping to him, burst with Antaeus' larynx bursting under my thumbs. Only the King's Guard, under the rigid discipline of the captains, kept their mouths shut, and every man jack of them tapped his foot in time with the shouting.

I caught a glimpse of Nessus, pale in the face and strangely wide of eye, walking about the ring gazing from every angle at the dead wrestler, and now and then shaking his head as though to clear it of fog. Iole had fled, fast as the deer that her Goddess hunted, toward the shrine, stumbled, and fell hard, got up dazedly, and then looked into the sky with terror in her face; and all this made sense somehow, if I could fathom it, which I could not, hence it seemed she was out of her mind. She stumbled on to the cedar tree, climbed the ladder, and then spoke long in Artemis' ear, and although her face was too far to see clearly I saw the strange tension in her body. Megara alone of the royal family spoke to me as yet. She seemed in great haste to tell me something of great import; as I stepped close to her, she poured it forth in one burst:

"Don't sit back, you fool. Don't think the victory is won. Ask the greatest possible prize, for the more you ask the more you'll get, and watch out for deadfalls. Don't do anything, even go forth at night at nature's call, without telling Right Doer so he will stand guard. Remember you wear the oak leaf and you still live. It is a combination of circumstances that the King cannot abide."

Soon now we saw the King's herald mount the parapet and put the trumpet to his lips. Perhaps those standing nearby heard the blast he blew, but the main of the hosts heard nothing but their own rhythmic happy yells, not a paean of praise to me as much as a chant of joy at the death of Antaeus. At the same time Eurytus knew it as an eloquent rebuke to tyranny, and he liked it not, and he hated me the more, and mayhap he trembled all the more at the dread words of the priestess on the tripod over the gaseous pit at the oracle at Delphi.

Then the King himself stood up, and waved his arms, once, twice, and a third time before the Minyans began to hush, and the leaders of the Thebans likewise implored silence. Still the faces of all had a shiny look I had never seen in a multitude of faces until now, and their eyes looked beady. Right Doer stepped close to my side to coach me in meeting what was to come.

Again the herald blew his horn and the sound rang true and far. The King came again to the parapet, with the Queen, Nessus, Iole, and Megara, backed by his Companions; but the throng saw nothing of Antaeus, overtowering all, quietly smiling like a God, and it was an odd and satisfying thing how countless eyes, so many that you could lump them off as the whole batch, shot a quick glance at the carcass stretched out, arms extended, dead hands grasping grass, dead teeth biting dirt, in the center of the wrestling ring. Thus his absence from the royal group was most satisfactorily accounted for.

"Minyans and Thebans!" the King proclaimed. "You have just seen a wrestling match worth watching by the Gods, worthy of their applause, if a mere mortal king may say so. And while it is a pity that one of the great contestants met dire death, it is the law of games that when both adversaries agree to the style of wrestling that we call pancratium, and one is gravely injured or slain, no claim can be made against the victor by the kinsman of the dead or wounded man; and hence I, King of the Minyans, make no charge of foul play against Heracles."

He paused, as though expecting the throngs to cheer. Not one callow boy raised his piping voice, as the King might have known full well. He could not buy their approbation as cheaply as that. The Greeks are born traders, as many a crafty huckster from Egypt or Phoenicia has found, but they will not pay something for nothing.

"Also, it is my great pleasure to announce that Heracles of Thebes has proved his innocence in the sight of the Gods of the charge I made against him before the trial by battle. And I, Eurytus, will seek no further as to who sped the little dagger into the neck of Erebus, the stallion. Doubtless it was some handler on the faraway steppes who hated the beast, and who introduced the narrow blade with Oriental cunning, knowing it would not kill at once, and thus his crime be known; but would only kill when the steed's blood was up, and he strove in great exertion. Moreover, it comes to me that I opened the door of my lips to make you, Heracles, a promise. It was that if you stood the trial of battle and won, I would undo the wrong I had done you in no small measure. What prize do you ask?"

"Eurytus, King of the Minyae, I ask that all the youths and maidens who are forfeit to you by the terms of your proclamation be set free and permitted to return to their homes. More, I ask that half of the number of beasts forfeit to you by every freeman or slave of Thebes be returned to their owners, the odd beast, in case of unequal division, being offered as sacrifice to the Gods, and that in those cases where a Theban freeman or slave had only one beast, whether colt, calf, pig, or lamb, to forfeit to you, he be permitted to keep it and take it home. And if you do this, I will count it that the wrongs that you have done me have been undone, and the name of the killer Antaeus that now beclouds the great name of Eurytus will be forgotten, and the Gods will again take pleasure in hearing your name; and an inkling has come to me, I know not from whence, that great Zeus, the Cloud Gatherer, King of Heaven, whose wrath you have invited, will be appeased, and he will cause your realm to prosper, and let other blessings fall upon your head."

And I could not help but take pleasure in the good speech, the roundings out of the hasty prompting Right Doer had given me. I could not help but glance into his calm, serene face—getting only a quick wink of his eye in return—before I studied the face of the King. Truly it was a study. He knew he was in a pickle which no mere explosion of royal rage would get him out of. And truly, as Right Doer told me later, and perhaps his own soul had told him, this was his opportunity for a truly royal gesture, almost godlike, whereby he would bind the Minyan people closer to him than ever, and likely cause the Thebans to be willing and loyal subjects to his overlordship.

Even so, I had not the slightest hope that he would award me so great a prize. Still, because I had asked so much, I think he found his hands more strongly tied against packing me off with a petty prize. He knew as well as I the spirit of both hosts, and that the Minyans stood in cold, stern judgment waiting his answer, and the Thebans in half-incredulous hope. Perhaps he thought that the Gods were like-wise alert and listening. Perhaps he knew that he, not I, was being tried, not by fire or the poison cup or by battle, but before the thrones of the great Olympians who now and then, when they could be diverted from their pleasures and their own hates and loves long enough to notice, have taken the side of good against evil.

"No, I will not give that much," said Eurytus in a resonant voice. "To every Theban freeman or slave who has brought me only one beast, I will return that beast, and he who has brought me two may retain one, and he who has brought me three or more, he may retain one third of those he brought. To the Theban youths and maidens forfeit to me, I will give one year's reprieve whereby they may return to their homes, and it may be that this reprieve will be extended if you, Heracles, their champion and hero, perform well the labors that I demand of you, the nature of which I do not yet know. You shall remain hostage to me, the King, as long as I see fit to let the Theban youth and maiden walk not in chains, but free. And this is the judgment of Eurytus, King of the Minyae, not to be questioned on pain of death. And now all of the Minyans and Thebans who earn their bread by commerce on the land or on the sea, and hence have no fat animals to give our Goddess, and hence have brought ingots of silver, lead, and tin, and bolts of cloth, may form a line, and lay their gifts on the grass at the feet of the holy image."

Artemis had no direct power, that I knew of, over ships, winds, and waves. Her realm was the wild woods and fields, and all fastnesses, the beasts that dwelt there, the care of pregnant women and of children, and of earth and Heaven when neither the sun nor the moon was shining. In this last office she was known as Hecate, and was prone to linger at crossroads, when, strangely, she had an ominous and even sinister aspect to travelers, and wakened inarticulate fear in their hearts. Since merchants of all sorts used the roads in their pursuit of gain, it was no wonder that many of them, well-fed fellows rarely muscular and beautiful, joined the line of gift bringers. Almost always the giver spoke in an undertone to the priestess Iole, asking, no doubt, that he get the better of some pending deal.

But Artemis' role as the Goddess of Dark Night did not explain the presence of numerous seafarers, invariably wind- and sun-tanned, active, limber, self-assured, robust, and good to look upon. None would be here, living men instead of food for fishes, were it not for the tolerance of Poseidon, God of the Sea, and Aeolus, God of the Winds, but since they rarely sailed out of sight of land, almost always in daylight, I did not see why they made such a to-do over the Goddess of the Chase—some said she was also Goddess of the Moon, although Phoebe and Selene were the moon's more ancient mistresses—and to be giving her such a store of precious tin, lead, copper, and even iron . . . well, it was not my business. And the mere thinking of it might indicate that my relations with Artemis were not as warm and friendly as with, say, Hermes, Demeter, Dionysus, and Pan. Perhaps in my heart of hearts, into which I had a hard time looking, I was jealous of the service to her by the beautiful, lithe, long-legged, virgin Iole.

In this interval I expected to encounter Right Doer, and no doubt receive a few hints as to what would likely happen next and how to deport myself, but evidently he was away at the edge of the throng or had slipped away into the woods, on what business I knew not.

The offerings having been made, the herald blew a blast. Once more King Eurytus came to the parapet to speak.

"Great hosts!" he called. "In a brief time we will say farewell. Indeed there remains, that I know of, no matter to bring before you of bearing on the King's welfare and your own. And after suitable observance of one royal custom, ancient in Orchomenus, honored in our fathers' time, and in many other lands, I will dismiss this assembly, order a funeral pyre for the Wrestler, Antaeus, and you may go your ways."

He turned to his herald, who blew one long pure note, echoing and re-echoing through the cypress wood.

"The ancient custom of which I speak is to ask if any person here, under my overlordship, knows of some wrong that should be righted, some calamity that I may be able to mitigate or avert. If so, he may raise his voice, and I, the King, will promise what redress I can, by the will of the Gods. But take mind that the wrong you wish righted must be a public wrong, affecting many people, not some mere evil done against the petitioner, which must be dealt with by the elders of every village. Does anyone wish to speak?"

The same custom was observed by our own King, and the great Rhadamanthus, who had taught Right Doer and me, had told me that it had been fetched long ago from some eastern land, perhaps Egypt or Phoenicia. Since news of public calamities sped swiftly through the little Grecian states, and often kings did not take kindly to complaints made at their assemblies, usually such a question as Eurytus had asked went unanswered.

Greatly to my surprise, a poorly dressed fellow who had come to our cooking fire to ask Right Doer for a firebrand spoke in his brisk and manly voice.

"O King, I am Dyctus, slave of Belus, who is confined to his bed with illness. Our pasturage is in Nemea, above the plain, and there many other chieftains pasture cattle, horses, sheep, goats, and swine, and all are afflicted with the same calamity, which is known as the Nemean Lion, which many say has been sent by the Goddess Hera to afflict us."

Dyctus had been speaking rapidly, anxious about taking the King's time and trying his patience, and yet with typical Greek determination to present his case. Indeed Eurytus was in no humor to hear tales of marauding lions, all too common in the Greek hills and deserts, and a cloud as dark as some of Zeus' was in his face, and I knew what had caused it, and my heart rejoiced. But now his interest in the tale abruptly quickened. He interrupted the herder's discourse, not to bid him shorten it, but to ask a question.

"Fellow, do you yourself believe that saying?"

"I am of two minds about the matter, O King. You know that Hera's temple stands above the Nemean Plain, and in May she is worshiped there in the Festival of Flowers, and five years ago one of our maidens, who served as Flower Bearer, gave offense to Hera, whereupon she fled from her wrath to the island of Melos, where she became a priestess to Aphrodite, whom Hera hates. Also, it was five years ago that the lion was first seen."

"Now that is evidence of the truth of the tale, but it is not proof."

"Nay, it is not. Nor is the great size of the lion, or his great fierceness, and a certain viciousness that I have never before seen. Mark you, when he comes on a mare or a bull strayed from the drove, or when he comes upon a drove that is not guarded, he will rush and kill the same as any other lion. But when he comes on a drove over which a poor herder such as I stands on guard, he will stalk and kill the herder before he lays claw on any beast, and then lets the corpse grow cold while he takes his pick of the drove and makes his leisured meal, not in the fashion of a common beast, but as the king of beasts. Also, sometimes when he has killed the herder, breaking his head into little pieces with one tap of his paw, he will make sport with the herd, driving them thither and yon, putting them in a frenzy of terror, finally to make his choice and go his way."

"Now that is most strange," Eurytus said thoughtfully. "But speak your petition, and I will reply."

"O King, whether or not this lion is the scourge of a Goddess, of a certainty he is most terrible and most cunning. All our devices fail against him, and there is no relief for us, or no safety until he is slain. So I pray to you, Eurytus, that you send some mighty hunter, of such skill with arms and of such felicity at wile that he may stand a fighting chance against this fierce and deadly beast. But I pray you, send no weakling or novice, because at best the hunter's life will dangle as from the thread of Admetus, and if her sister Atropos does not cut it with the dread shears, all may thank the Gods, and I myself will offer to this shrine the sleek heifer that my master gave me for my own."

Then I had the strange impression of a light shining on Eurytus' face. It was the effect of a wonderful idea's striking his brain and flooding his heart with joy. Then a very studious look came into his face, as though he were pondering some great project, but he did not take me in with his furled brow and false solemnity—he had decided the matter at first flush. Then he spoke with pompous mien and voice.

"Heracles of Thebes!"

"Aye, Eurytus, King of the Minyae."

"King, and also the master of your body and soul as long as you remain hostage to me, as long as I grant reprieve to the Theban youth and maiden forfeit to me. I have heard the words of the herdsman Dyctus at a fortunate moment. I do not know how great a hunter you are, but you must have a fair skill in the chase, since you and your brother Iphicles spent a great part of your youth at Wrathful Leader's distant pasturages—distant, I may say, from the walls of Orchomenus, where most of the Theban youths battled bravely against the youth of the Minyae. Also, you have shown us your great agility and strength, good traits in a lion hunter. Thus it comes to me to appoint you the labor of slaying the Nemean Lion, which, if told true, is worthy of your powers. Your brother Right Doer may go with you if you both choose, and one or two other Thebans, all without arms, to help you keep camp, but you may take the customary Theban weapons, bow and arrow, spear with bronze point and shield. I will not set a period of time in which you may complete your task or acknowledge your failure. Now the leaves fall; when they are again in the flush of greenery I hope to hear good news from you. Farewell."

CHAPTER FIVE

THE CHALLENGE

1

Megara had not spoken to me since my victory over Antaeus; but her blunt words of warning before it had already begun to have a prophetic ring. And all my dealings with her were somehow tied in, or involved with, my dealings with her sister, Iole—why, I had no notion; and I ached to speak to her too, before I set forth for Nemea on a great adventure.

Iole had tried to do me a service—no less than saving my neck from the rending force of the giant's hands. The device she had proposed had been desperate and strangely clumsy, likely to have been penetrated by Eurytus and his crafty counselors, in which case his rage against both of us would have known no bounds. But that her heart was in it, a full and fiery heart whose depths I doubted that even Right Doer's dagger-sharp wits could ever plumb or great Rhadamanthus' wisdom encompass, had been told me truly by her burning eyes and passionate low tones.

I found her not far from her Goddess, directing the storing away by slaves of the offerings of ingots and cloth from the merchants and mariners. Out of the throng of Thebans, laughing and weeping in delirious joy in one another's arms, she saw me pass almost unnoticed and at once ran to me in that free-limbed, deerlike, lovely swiftness I had previously seen. She caught me by the hand and led me to the pillared sanctuary, a miniature temple from which she had emerged that morning to conduct the ancient rites. It contained a stone bench on which lay a flat stone such as the Spartans used long ago for pillows, and I visioned Iole sleeping here on warm afternoons, her garments in disarray and her beautiful limbs agleam and her face rosy with dreams. In one corner lay the rubble of what once was a life-sized stone image which I thought might have represented Artemis as perceived by some alien tribe who, in the mists of history, had captured this region, only to be overthrown by its native sons and flung into the sea.

Part of the torso remained, revealing not two, but fully a score of teats, horrid to contemplate. Lions and other animals climbed up her arms, and the images of goats, deer, and cattle formed bands about her thighs. Indeed her aspect was so ugly that I would gladly have gathered up the fragments and hurled them into the deep mire of Lake Comais. But evidently the Goddess, as well as her countless priestesses throughout the centuries, had wanted them preserved and venerated.

It was a joy to take my eyes from the broken image to lay them on the beautiful maiden just sitting down on the bench and laying there her hand, palm up, a sign that I was to sit beside her. There was more beauty in her hand alone than in all the palaces of all the kings, and again the thought struck me that she might truly be the avatar of the Huntress Goddess, Artemis herself, dwelling awhile on earth, serving her own shrine. Not that I wanted it so. Artemis was forever chaste; no lust for a lover could ever flush her pure pale cheeks, darken her azure eyes, and furrow and bead with sweat her serene brow. When I had the chance to study Iole's face, I saw more woman and less Goddess than I had seen before. Indeed I had a startled sense of its having changed in some most subtle way since I had spoken to her on the path. Her present tranquillity did not appear very deep and I was not sure it was quite real. Deep down in her sea-blue eyes shone lights I had not noticed until now, and she breathed so deeply that her breasts heaved up under her robe, and I could imagine their buds, deep red as the climbing roses of late spring. I was in no hurry for her to speak to me. Just to gaze at her made me warmly dizzy, as from the first deep draft of mead. But she did speak.

"Heracles, I did not entreat Artemis to forbid the battle between Antaeus and you, because she guessed my thoughts before I could speak, and she gave me a whispered message."

"Now, that was good." I meant that it was good fortune, because Eurytus would have been hard put to it to disobey his patron Goddess' command, and Antaeus might still be walking the earth with his kingly, if not godlike, stride, and the dreadful fight would be before instead of behind me.

"Artemis told me that you, not Antaeus, would win, that famous Antaeus, not unknown Heracles, would be killed. For once I could hardly believe the tidings, and would not if they had held the least ambiguity; instead they were as blunt as a cowherd's speech, and a child of six summers could not have misunderstood. And for one of the few times in all our concourse, her whispering was gusty enough that an eavesdropper ten feet away could have overheard."

"Did she mean that I would win because she would help me win?"

"Heracles, I do not believe that she meant that. I am far from sure that she took your side, or either side. I believe she was simply stating fact, one that she had been told by her brother Apollo, who, of all the Gods and Goddesses, always tells the truth. And do not forget that Apollo has some bond with the three Fates—how else could the prophecies of his priestess at Delphi be never known to fail? It must be that Atropos confided in him that when she brought the dread shears to the dreadful battle in the little ring, it would be the thread of Antaeus' life, not yours, which she would cut."

As Iole spoke, she looked deeply and intensely into my eyes. The back of my neck prickled as though I were overhearing the talk of Gods and Goddesses and their great affairs, of which side would win in some grievous war, of what great hero was fated soon to fall, of what mighty king must soon become a silent, gliding shadow in dismal Hades.

"But Heracles, my Goddess is not as certain of the outcome of the coming battle between you and the Nemean Lion. I have spoken to her just now, since your appointment to the labor, and the snowy marble in which she stands to our sight did not glow faintly pink, as from mortal blood under the skin, and her eyes did not light up and her lips remained cold and still. I am not even sure of her favoring you at the battle. Look at the carved lions on the dismembered arm of the image older than these hills—full proof that lions, the same as deer and bears, are in her special care. So those that love you must await the fortunes of this coming fray with deep misgivings."

Was Iole one who loved me? Surely she felt some lively passion for me, a flame kindled in one day, but such a kindling had been most uncommon to my experience, and I wondered if hate of Antaeus, rather than love of Heracles, had not caused her to champion me today and to wish to safeguard me in future wars. I was more worried about this than whether Artemis would take the beast's side against me. This last would be the issue of some tomorrow not yet pressing close; while today Iole's beautiful round breast was in easy reach of my hand if I dared raise it. Still, her warning was so passionately breathed that I could not let it pass without risking her anger.

"What do you advise me to do, Iole, Priestess of Artemis?" I asked.

"Sacrifice a sleek bull, preferably white without blemish, at her shrine in Nemea. But there are other ways to please her. Remember that I know her well, better than any other mortal in Greece. When you pursue your tawny and fierce foe, and finally bring him to bay in some mountain defile from which only one of you may escape alive, why not go unarmed except for your bow and arrow, weapons of my beloved Goddess, indeed sacred to her; and if your arrow misses the mark, or does not inflict a mortal wound, you can still slay him as you slew Antaeus. Surely no lion is of Antaeus' might that only this morning's sun shone down upon and beheld like to a God's."

"It is too soon to talk of the weapons I will bear, when I have not yet laid eyes on the foe. I only know I will not give him any advantage that I can withhold, for Artemis is the sister of Apollo, and so can love not fools. And what heavenly pleasure it would give Antaeus, almost enough to console him for his defeat, if I would come trailing after him across the River of Woe, through the awful gate guarded by horrid Cerberus, into the dim halls that would be my prison, world without end—coming to join him not when I am old and weary of war, but before the leaves bud again, mayhap before all are sear and fallen, and before the snow flies on Parnassus. Take thought of that, Iole."

"I have taken thought of it already. It is the thought uppermost in my mind, and it will be the theme of my dreams. In respect to it, I may go up to your encampment in Nemea and do what I can. My hands are stronger than you know."

"I know their beauty, and I kiss them, but your mouth is more beautiful still, and if it kisses mine, my soul will so exult that I will have no fear of the Nemean Lion, come what may."

"Those are sweet words. The mouth that uttered them will be sweet upon mine."

She leaned toward me with a kind of fierceness, her eyes glimmering, and after long pressure of her soft lips, her tongue intertwined with mine and made little darting movements, more delicious in my mouth than the nectar of the Gods. And then, as my whole being thrilled with a godlike rapture and my big hands were reaching awkwardly but unafraid, it must be that she was carried out of herself by passion, or some storm broke within her breast, for her teeth closed on my upper lip, and instead of a little nip that was ever a part of love-making, she bit harder than she knew, and the warm salt taste of blood was in my mouth and a trickle on my chin, which she quickly wiped away with the palm of her hand.

"If I can bite that keenly with my little white teeth," she told me in dreamy tones, "take thought of the great rending fangs of a lion. Even so, go forth unafraid. I am sure now that my Goddess will heed my prayer."

2

Right Doer set much store on closing sheepfold gates before the wolf got in. Indeed he was forever closing gates that I had not realized were open, the act that differentiated a long-headed man like him from a short-headed man like me. He put no trust in circumstances, none whatever in friendly Gods, and very little in lots falling to his advantage. He liked to prepare beforehand for possible twists and turns of fortune. He would take long chances because he must, sometimes because it offered great sport; but by and large he did not like to gamble when, with a little forethought, he could make his gain in safety. Just as at present he was concerned with my free and easy roaming of the ground about the citadel, and getting into holes and corners in the woods. If he were Eurytus, he considered he would not wait in patience for the Nemean Lion to put an end to my distasteful presence on the earth, but would try to achieve the same soul-satisfying goal in a field fertile for accidents caused by the disorderly, surging throngs.

Even so, Right Doer knew of no safer fort than the pale glare of countless fires and the gaze of the Argus-eyed throng protecting our little camp outside the wall. There we had two visitors, one of whom was Dyctus, the herder who had asked the boon from the King, and whom Right Doer had invited here, and the other Actaeon, the great hunter of the godly house of Cadmus, who had come at his own whim.

In our store were wine, mead, and baked meat enough to befuddle and begorge ten times our number. An hour could hardly pass without some wind-tanned herdsman or husbandman coming to our fire or, more frequently, sending his small son or his big-eyed little daughter with a horn of his best brew or a spitted carving from the loin of his choicest veal.

Obviously Right Doer had summoned Dyctus to learn more about the Nemean Lion, and hence of the work cut out for himself and me. Happily, Dyctus was a keen fellow with no habit of silence caught from the hills and cliffs and forests of his native heath, a close and intelligent observer, who told us what we should know, not what he thought we would most like to hear.

"We have a name for him," he told us, "that fits him better than you yet know. At first we called him 'The Lion,' but it did not suit him, or suit us. There were other lions. Often in their wanderings from one wilderness to another they would hang at our pasturages long enough to kill a cow or two, or a colt, then wander on. Then for a time we called him 'Hera's Lion,' but soon we dropped the name, perhaps because most of us doubted that Hera had sent him to ravage our herds, when we had no more to do with Zeus' tumbling the Flower-Bearing Maiden than our own newborn lambs; and while Hera is vengeful as a leopard bearing a festering wound, jealous as a she-eagle, and spiteful as a snake, still it is not her way to make the innocent suffer in lieu of the guilty."

"I am not so sure of that," Right Doer answered thoughtfully. "Her great fury when Paris awarded the beauty prize to Aphrodite was hot against them both, the briber and the bribed, and against the bribe itself, incomparable Helen. Even so, the golden Goddess still rules the ruler of earth and heaven, and wears not even a black eye. Paris has the pick of the loveliest women that breathe air—and why not, when he, called wife stealer, coward, and carpet knight, laid low the greatest warrior of our own and our fathers' times, Hera's one-time favorite, great Achilles? The wronged husband of Helen has forgiven her; once more she rules his roost; and truly she waxes more beautiful year by year. And meanwhile Troy lies in rubble and ashes, her innocent wives and children wail in slavery, and a myriad of young men who had no more to do with the affront to Hera's vanity than Dyctus' newborn lambs, and who only valiantly defended their native city, roam in hushed, purposeless droves through the halls of Hades."

Since Dyctus could not answer Right Doer, and I knew of no one who could, even wise Rhadamanthus, when this poetic fire blazed in his eyes, I spoke quickly, so the business of the evening could go forward.

"Dyctus, you say that the Nemean folk no longer call the marauder Hera's Lion. What do they call him?"

"I will tell you, Heracles. There is an old drover among us, known as Snag Tooth, who followed his master to Troy and, like all who fought there, was forever changed—kings turning almost into Gods, chiefs speaking with the tongues of kings, even unlettered minions such as Snag Tooth taking on the mien of heroes. The Marauder stalked and slew Snag Tooth's nephew. Snag Tooth frightened him away, only the Gods know how, and reclaimed the youth's body and burned it on a funeral pyre before the birds of death could sink their beaks into his flesh. By that fire Snag Tooth spoke unto the lion, lurking somewhere in the thickets in range of his voice.

"'Doer of Iniquity,' Snag Tooth called to him, and his voice rang like a trumpet of battle in the dusk, and his aged face became beautiful in our sight. 'You will harass us a long time yet. You will ravage our land, and lay low our brethren, and eat countless of our sleek beasts. But the day will come when iniquity will have its reward. We will see your tawny hide stretched by our fires, and your green glaring eyes will be darkened, and your gleaming dog-fangs, as long as my forefinger, will flash no more. Your name is Iniquity. By that name you shall live, and by that name you shall die.' So it came to pass that thereafter we never called him by any other."

The hunter Actaeon, who had said almost nothing until now, stirred a little in his place, sat motionless, and then stirred again. Then he leaned forward, his burning eyes upon the eyes of Dyctus.

"Is he truly the King of Beasts?" Actaeon asked.

"My lord, so I believe."

"Now I have seen many lions, and killed eight, five toms and three tabbies. None were inconsiderable, all were doughty foes, all had strong lives they did not readily yield up—all were lions, no more, no less. Yet it has begun to come to me that this Nemean Lion, Iniquity, is as great among lions as Achilles was great among men. Tell me, does he weigh twice the weight of Heracles—or perhaps a little more?"

"To look at him, Heracles will tip the scales against four bushels of barley. If so, Iniquity weighs about three times as much."

"Is his mane black or tawny, and is it well grown or sparse?"

"Sir, it is well grown, and fiery red."

"Now that I have never seen. And tell me, Dyctus, when he rushes and kills a herder or a bull, does he invariably charge against the wind?"

"Aye, so his victim may not smell his rank smell."

"When he has killed a bull and made his meal, does he return to the carcass the next day?"

"Aye, he returns, but he does not come up into spear range until he inspects it from all sides, and if the scene is even slightly changed, grass beaten down or a shrub broken off, he goes his way to kill again, leaving the carcass to the birds of death. And so it comes that when we lie in wait with weapons, willing that one or more of us be slain to rid the land of its oppressor, we wait in vain."

"Has he well-worn paths? I mean, are his comings and his goings according to the hours of the day, the seasons of the year, or the changes of the moon? Does he lie many afternoons in the same den? Does he drink from the same water hole as long as he is in a particular region? I pray you, Dyctus, be patient with me, for I do not waste breath in idle questions."

"That I perceive. Great Hunter, the comings and goings of Iniquity cannot be charted beforehand. They may be of any hour of day or night; half a season may pass without our catching sight of him, then he comes and sits himself down in our pasturage as though he owned it. He has no den. He sleeps in the sun amid the rocks of the hills. Sometimes he drinks at dawn, sometimes at sunset, at any pool or pond that takes his fancy. He has the body of a beast, but the soul of a frivolous woman."

"I will put you one more question of great import. You told the King that often he will run and chase an unguarded herd to make sport. But you also said that if he comes upon a bull or mare strayed from the drove, he will rush and kill it like any other lion. Does he do so at once, or does he sometimes play with it awhile, chasing it here and there before he attacks?"

And to my mild astonishment, Actaeon's eyes were burning under his heavy brows, and he seemed to hold his breath while he awaited Dyctus' reply.

"My lord," the herder answered, "if he is full fed he does not look twice at a stray cow. But if he is hungry, he never makes sport with his victim, as with a herd. He stalks quickly and with great skill until he is in easy dashing distance, say forty of his great strides; then he comes in a mighty rush, and then, as if Zeus had hurled his deadly shaft, the animal falls with a broken neck, the great fangs already closed in its throat."

"Dyctus, the hunt for Iniquity will be a great hunt, and perhaps a long one, but do not despair." Then Actaeon rose from his place and took a seat at my fore. "Heracles, will you take my hand?"

"In pride and honor," I answered, for old Rhadamanthus had taught me proper speech by dint of many raps on my head with his gnarled cane, though I could never equal Right Doer in quiet and grave courtesy.

"You and I have never met before your coming to Orchomenus," Actaeon went on. "And it comes to me that our meeting here was provided by a God who loves me. Let us press hands. Do you feel friendship in mine?"

"Aye, and strength."

"Do you think it is the hand of one who breaks faith?"

"That I cannot believe."

"Now mark you, Heracles, the proclamation of Eurytus. He said that when you went forth to hunt the lion that afflicts Nemea, Right Doer could go with you and—his very words—one or two Thebans to help you with the camps. Did you know I am uncommon handy about camps? I can bake meat and barley cakes, run up shelters against the rain, chop and carry wood for watch fires, and can skin and butcher deer for the spit."

I would have known all this by looking at him closely. All that becomes a man he could do cheerfully and well. Of slightly heavier build than Right Doer, he had the like open countenance, something of the same free and easy ways, and lustrous, steadfast eyes. My heart warmed to him and to his words. Yet I heard myself stammer in reply.

"The King——"

"Eurytus can have no objection to my offering myself as body serv-ant to Right Doer and you. I will bring no weapons. I will touch none throughout the hunt. Do not speak the harsh word no, my new friend, if your heart cries yes."

"Now that is a wonderful thing, and it comes to me we will be friends as long as we both live, and I do not accept your offer, but make one on my own behalf—that you come with Right Doer and me, and, I hope, with Dyctus, and we remain welded in one band until the marauder Iniquity lies dead under my hand, and the birds of death turn at last upon him who has provided them so much good meat."

Actaeon's face lighted as though the long-sunken sun had shot up and shone upon it, and he kissed my hand, and I kissed his in troth. Then I turned to Dyctus.

"Can you too abide in my camp, or must you return to your master's flocks and herds?"

"My master lets me come and go as I see fit," the fellow answered in a ringing voice, "and since I have been involved in this matter from the start, I will remain so until the end."

"Now those are happy tidings, for you must know Nemea like the palm of your own hand."

"Like my wife's bottom," Dyctus assured me in deep earnestness.

"Some great God has befriended me, Dyctus, that you did not appeal to the King before now, for in that case I would have never been appointed to the office, the labor, as he called it, but in my mind a mighty boon. But tell me, since Iniquity began his raids five years ago, and has never rested from them, how does it happen that you or your master or some other sufferer from his maraudings has not sought the King's help before this?"

"I will answer you, Heracles," my brother said in his bland voice. "It is well known that Eurytus does not relish a reply from any of his subjects when he performs the ancient ceremony—he does not like to have unpleasant truths regarding his realm brought to the attention of the multitude. So while many a dweller of Nemea has often considered asking help of the King, none ever did so, in respect to his wrath."

"Then what emboldened Dyctus——?"

"Not a God. Only I. I assured him, after your victory over Antaeus and the King's loss of booty, that he would be overjoyed to hear the heartfelt appeal, that it would turn him from his angry thoughts, and I would wager a cask of purple wine against a horn of honey that he would grant the petition. It so chanced that the Gods were listening, and eager to watch a contest of such lively promise. I won my bet."

"I should have guessed it. My head is as thick as a plow beast's. But I still do not fathom your motive. . . ."

"Heracles, I did not want you staying at Eurytus' court."

And the quiet intensity of his words shook my backbone.

3

The Plain of Nemea had been blessed by the Goddess Demeter and produced barley golden as her hair, wine grapes, figs of surpassing flavor, and olives big with meat and fat with oil. Here tillers of the soil kept plow beasts, but these were fed in stalls and shut in byres at night, and Iniquity was never known to raid the peaceful countryside. Hence the dwellers of the region took little interest in him, and rarely spoke of him lest they call him. Yet from their little fields they could look up without craning their necks to the foothills above the plain, to ragged patches of forest, to dense thickets, and to green hillsides where droves of cattle, sheep, and a few mares showed as dark patches that moved a little under close watch, and even changed shape a little, and here the marauder made his fatal forays; and the whole wild track, far more beautiful than the staid plain, was accursed.

On the day following our arrival, Actaeon, Right Doer, Dyctus, and I joined hands to make a snug camp on a shelf of a hill that Iniquity could not raid without a steep climb or a sharp descent across open ground. Here we raised a shelter against rain, thatching it well, and laid stones for a cooking place, and saw to making four good beds by leveling the ground, casting out stones, and spreading sheepskins. Our plan was to occupy only three of them at any particular time. The four of us would take turns keeping a two-hour watch, also keeping the fires well fed so they would cast their gleams afar. By this arrangement each of us would sleep six hours every night, all that young men need in the flush of youth. While our camp had a good deal of natural protection, it was by no means a citadel, and Actaeon had joined with Right Doer in insisting on this vigilance when the treacherous moon leagued with our foe, or in that dark and awesome time when Hecate reigned.

For the rest, we had a cozy camp where we could cook in comfort, eat hearty meals of meat and barley cakes, stay warm and dry when the Cloud Gatherer flung down his chill rains, and give little thought to his bolts of lightning smiting ancient trees and clefting iron-hard rocks. Indeed we felt a curious safety from the blinding-bright shafts taking their instantaneous zigzag course from the black clouds to the storm-darkened earth, perhaps because of our inability to raise the lightest shields against them. Hence we might as well sleep on, keep

on eating, continue with any pursuit in which we happened to be engaged, and hardly bother to look up, since if one of us were hit, he
would never know it on this earth, and if one of us were narrowly
missed, it was as good a miss as a league's length.

On the following day we began making the rounds of the pasturages
on the grass slopes and amid the brushwood and thorn. There the
drovers gave their hands to Dyctus, and their faces became beautified
by the small, quiet smiles of men who have known one another long,
and are free of spite. Their faces grew swiftly grave when Dyctus told
them of my mission, and invariably they gave me great startled glances,
then many little glances that asked and answered questions.

When I had clasped the rough hands of one of them, I invariably
asked when he had last laid eyes on Iniquity. Before the fellow answered, he could not help but make a quick scan of the immediate
scene, eyes sharp, narrowed and vigilant, lest the Gods play a trick on
him and the Beast be with us even now. Then in every case I was told
that no hide or hair had been seen of him, by the witness or any other
drover whom he knew, since the first or second day of the young moon.

I was not satisfied until I talked to Snag Tooth, he who had given
the Nemean Lion his fit name, and who was still hale and hardy, and
whose utterances as repeated by Dyctus had struck my mind as those
of a peculiar, exact mind. We found him in the loftiest pasturage, one
of three under the mountain, and true enough he was well named, for
when he opened his old, grim mouth, like to a wolfhound's, the single
snag of a tooth gleamed through his beard. He was a tall, lean, proud,
lonely man who reminded me of Fold Watcher, the ancient shepherd
whom I had known and loved under Parnassus.

"Where do you think Iniquity has gone?" I asked, when he knew the
names of all of us three newcomers, and had sounded them in his ears
to tell when or where, if ever, he had heard any of them before, and
had corroborated the report of the Beast's absence since the young
moon.

Snag Tooth made no immediate reply. He felt the weight of the
question, which I felt in the air, and he considered with great force,
for he was not a man to speak lightly, although I noticed that he spoke
softly.

"Sir, I think he's gone over the mountain."

"Have you any notion when he'll be back?"

"He has overstayed his usual time already. The cattle are leaner over there, and the naked hills do not suit him for his slumbers in the sunlight. I expected him in the last days of the wasting moon. Now it is dark, and he will make the journey in the late afternoon today, or at latest tomorrow, or else a bull blessed by Dionysus has driven his horn deep into the tawny hide even as he fell dead. In that case Iniquity has followed him, spouting blood through the horn hole, and he will be given some dreadful office in dim Hades, perhaps to claw out and devour every day the new-grown guts of Aegisthus, who killed King Agamemnon for love of his lecherous queen. But the bull that killed Iniquity will be pastured in the Elysian Fields, along with his pick of all the cows slaughtered this year, and he need do naught but graze, sleep in the sun, and increase his herd."

"A fit reward," I said. "I hope that mine, if I kill Iniquity, will be as glorious. Friend, if he returns from over the mountain this afternoon or tomorrow afternoon, at what pasture will he make his first kill?"

"It will be one of three, depending on which of the three paths down the mountain he will make his prideful way. One is this pasture you gaze upon. If he is hungry enough to take the shortest, roughest path, he will come here first, and here he will kill, almost as certain as that yon pine will wag in the hard north wind. If he takes one of the two longer, smoother paths, he will visit first the pastures of Aturis or the pastures of Charnides, lying eastward behind the Hill of Olives. But word has come to me that the herds over the mountain are skin and bone this fall because of scant rainfall, and hence weak grass, by the neglect or pettish anger of great Zeus. I will lay you a bowl of honey mead, fresh and sweet and warming, enough that the four of you will join in joyous song, against one of your well-made arrows with fang-sharp point, that Iniquity, lusting with a mighty lust for a sleek, fat cow, will first come here."

"What use can you make of one of my arrows? You have no bow."

"Nay, I have no bow worth speaking of, and my ill-made, blunt-headed spear will not scare away a stag in heat, but if I win one of your arrows, I will keep it ever at my side. Then when the day comes, as it will come, when Iniquity takes me by surprise and seizes me in his great arms, I will thrust its sharp point as deep as I can into his evil breast ere the light goes out, and thus I will put my mark on him, to rankle in his beast soul as long as the Gods let him live and kill, and to bear in hidden shame as he swaggers down to Hades, when the Gods suffer him to die."

"Then the wager is fair. And what will you do, old man, if he comes today?"

"What can I do but be gone? What but watch the barren crest of the lowest ridge of the mountain where he must show himself, sharp and black, if he takes the path hither, and when I catch sight of him, take to my heels? My master has not set me here as bait for lions. True, Iniquity will pick the sleekest bull or the most winsome cow in my herd, but that is the tribute I must pay for my wardship, and by that wardship I see that the cows are well covered in season, and have good care and rich eating while they carry calves, and, when born, the calves flourish. Thus patiently, with much wracking of my soul, I maintain the herd as is right, and may cause it to increase a little, in favorable years."

"By your leave, old man, I will kiss you on the white head that holds such good sense, and give your heart that beats so staunchly and so true the blessing of my heart."

"I give my leave, and ask your leave to kiss your hand, great chieftain."

We exchanged the courtesies, then I asked him a question for which I could hardly summon breath, so anxious I was for a happy answer.

"Do you know of any place with a good view of the pasture where we four might lie in wait, my spear at hand and an arrow nocked on my string, where there is a likely chance—or at least a dim hope—that I may hurl the spear or launch the shaft at the marauder?"

"Heracles, you are but lately come to Nemea. Your coming with your allies has caused my soul to flutter in its mortal cage, and fetched a weak but yet real hope within my heart that some God or Goddess has befriended us at last, and that in some fashion, I know not how, you may live on and Iniquity will be slain. But I will not put you in his path until you have seen him work and kill, until you know his flagitious ways, until the odds against you are a little more even, and the balance is not weighed so heavily against your life. You must take time to choose the battleground to your advantage, and to plan it as old Nestor and great Odysseus planned battle against the Trojans, and then to risk all in one great foray. Even so, I will tell you where you may lie to view the pasturage and behold the Beast in his glory and, it may be, if some Goddess loved your sire or some God your lady-mother, launch an arrow that may not fall so short he will not hear it sing.

"It will be a song he has not heard these many years," Snag Tooth went on. "Thereby he may take thought of his mortality and have evil dreams as he lies sleeping in the sun. Aye, he may know at last that a hand of puny man dare raise against him, and he may wax more cunning but less bold; thus some herders' lives may be spared, for it is his awful boldness against which we have no defense. Behold the low rock hill under the oakwood. It is a short climb but surprisingly steep, and Iniquity will not attack you there unless he is direly wounded, in which case you will stand above him while he labors up, and you will have a warrior's chance to impale him on your spear before he can claw or bite."

"Why, it's a good plan, to start with."

"And pray you, do not leave your citadel until Iniquity has killed and eaten, after which he will pay no heed to any beast or man that comes or goes, but will seek a place of slumber."

So the four of our party made off, and with a deal of grunting and panting, and hanging with our fingernails to holds of the rock, we climbed to the crest of the knoll. Truly the site offered a view of the pasture far and wide, as well as of the naked ridge Iniquity must surmount if he took the path to Snag Tooth's pasturage. We could have counted every head of his cattle, and such small portions of the main that we could not survey, being obscured by thickets or rough ground, seemed too small to hide a skulking fox, let alone a lion. At about four hundred paces rose a taller knoll, perhaps offering an even better lookout, and I did not know why Snag Tooth had not sent us there instead of here, except that its slope was not nearly so steep, and he must have feared that Iniquity might get the notion of attacking us, and one or more of us would be killed before the great hunt had well begun.

Even so, the more I looked about me, the more pleased I was with our perch. If the lion took his regular path, plainly visible as a narrow, curved, pale-brown streak in the grayish brown of the hillside, he would pass within two hundred and fifty paces; a fairly long cast even from a Turkish bow with the weight of mine, still it was one I had often made, and which occasionally, although not very commonly, had sped true. To make such a cast, the crescent of horn and wood had to be more than half drawn. To cast three hundred paces it must be three fourths drawn, which demanded all the ready power of my right shoulder. Even so, I had always known I could launch a shaft perhaps fifty yards farther if I gritted my teeth and summoned that

almost magical might with which I had once rolled a boulder down a
hill and had tossed Antaeus over my back to fall farther than any valley
below any mountain ever raised by the turbulence of giants imprisoned
under the earth.

Truly this was a great bow, and many folk said its like was to be
seen hanging in the palace of Odysseus, awaiting his return from
Troy, whence he had sailed twenty years ago. It had come into my
possession in a curious fashion. At the games played in honor of
Dionysus, who was born at Thebes, I had once made the farthest cast
of any contestant in the trial, this with an old bow left among the
gear of Wrathful Leader. I did not win the laurel wreath because my
shaft missed the mark, and had stabbed savagely at a tree fifty paces
beyond it. Even so, I had somehow won a greater prize.

A young man whom I did not know, dressed as a herder and with
the weathered skin of a defier of wind and cold, emerged from the
throng of spectators and put in my hands the bow and a quiver of
long, bronze-tipped arrows beautifully worked in ash, each flanged
with falcon feathers. I had eyes for nothing but these, such a bow and
shafts as I had never seen, and I had gaped at them like a lout. When
at last I glanced up, prepared with an aching heart to give them back
after their having been shown to me, their owner was nowhere to be
seen. He had somehow vanished in the throng, and for the first time
I saw him clearly with the eyes of my mind, calling back his lineaments.
Truly he had been tanned brown as any drover, and had been arrayed
like one, but he had worn his dark hair long on his shoulders. The
only man I had ever seen of something like equal beauty had been
Antaeus, since it had not been in my fate to lay eyes on Achilles,
whose own dire fate had sent him down to death in my urchinhood.

I had turned to Right Doer then, himself a beautiful human being,
and the whites of his eyes had showed, and he was trembling.

So I have never known who gave me the great bow, but I have never
really doubted that it was Dionysus, the nearest to us mortals of all
the great Gods, and, with Demeter, the most beloved. I believe that
he had come down to watch the games, and had been pleased with
my long cast, and had given me a mighty prize. Where had he gotten
it? Like as not he had stolen it from his half-sister Artemis, perhaps
her favorite weapon for killing her enemies and mighty stags, boars
and bears, for she would not need such a heavy bow to kill old and
sick people, tired of pain and life. And I could not forget that Dionysus

was the God of Thieves; and ever since his childhood, when he had made off with Apollo's cattle, himself a famous thief.

Well, if the bow had indeed belonged once to Artemis, I could only hope that she had so many others that she did not miss it, or else she had forgotten about its loss, for the memory of the Gods seems very like man's own, sometimes harboring a trifle for an endless time, sometimes letting affairs of great moment slip out of their minds. Heaven knew I did not want her enmity, now that the merest thought of Iniquity stirred my short hairs.

We kept watch of the barren ridge, and when we had crouched here nearly an hour and the fourth hour of the afternoon was being ushered in, Right Doer said "Um" very softly. I might have known he would be the first to spy the enemy, because his watch had been so intent, never wavering a moment, and his gray eyes were so clear. At once all of us saw him, minute as yet, black, and curiously sharp. His gait was steady, purposeful rather than fast, his head carried on one side and tilted. Still, I thought it the gait of a hungry lion, and there would be but little beating about the bushes before he went to dinner.

Snag Tooth's eyes had looked old. They had appeared dim and watery. But when we tossed him a quick glance, intending to warn him of Iniquity's approach, he was already taking off, not at a run that would tire him, but at a quick walk. In a moment he had disappeared over the hill, sad of heart, no doubt, over the coming loss of one of his most beautiful beasts, but remembering that man is man, and beast is beast, and he had work to do yet, and the only pleasure to be taken by anyone at his death between Iniquity's fangs would lie in Iniquity's iniquitous heart.

When we looked again at the beast, he seemed to be growing like one of Jason's dragons, when he had sowed their teeth. Although he did not look anything like life-size at this half-mile distance, I could distinguish his red mane from his tawny sides, and the glorious shape of him, and perceive something of grandeur in his stride, and have an inkling of his godlike pride. If he will only keep to the path, I thought, I will have a clean go at him at two hundred and fifty yards, and perhaps give him the surprise of his life, which would remain in him, startling him anew every now and then throughout the eternity of Hades. And if the battle I had meant to wage should end before it was well begun, I could gladly spare the great adventure of prolonged conflict for the sake of the light that would break in a hundred wind-tanned faces at the news—faces of ilk of mine own, for I had been a drover before I had been a champion wrestler, and it was still my calling in the sight of the Gods. Also, it would give me secret mirth to cheat King Hades of Hades of the quick arrival of some souls he had already numbered in his book. Also, it would be great sport if, with modest mien, I could lay Iniquity's skin at Eurytus' feet before he had hardly taken notice of my departure.

Man proposes, the Gods dispose. When the Beast was about five hundred yards he suddenly made a light bound and disappeared. Obviously he had jumped down into a dry watercourse or some other depression close to the path. Then no four men were ever busier, using no tools but their eyes, than Right Doer, Actaeon, Dyctus, and I. We looked high and low, near and far, aching for a glimpse of that great tawny, red-maned shape, but not a leaf stirred or a grass blade bent, except where the herd grazed peacefully.

"Do you think he saw us and has gone back?" Right Doer whispered.

"Not he," Dyctus answered quietly.

"I agree with Dyctus," Actaeon said. "He's drawing up to the herd right now. In a moment you'll see something swift as an arrow, but it won't be an arrow, it will be Iniquity in his charge. It will come from downwind. Beyond that——"

"Look," Dyctus whispered.

The wind was blowing fitfully from the cool valley toward the sun-baked hill, but there must have been little eddies reversing the flow, or Iniquity had got in a crosscurrent, because suddenly the whole herd was alert, every head up, all ears cocked. Perhaps they knew—a soundless message passed from one beast soul unto another, swift as lightning—that one of their number was about to die, and every one must wonder if he were the one, and if so, it was useless to ask those Goddesses who have care of cattle, Hera and Demeter, to save his brute life. Hera would be too busy at her great affairs, or at tormenting some hapless mortal maid whom Zeus had tupped, and Demeter's great love was the fields with their golden grain, and she was a gentle Goddess who could not fight with lions or hardly with Zeus' wolves.

And then we four spectators beheld a wonderful thing. The cows with yearling calves began to draw back, and with them went bullocks and half- and full-grown steers, and then the young bulls, and then a few bulls that looked mature. But the oldest and greatest bull, snow-white, fit for sacrifice at eve of mighty battle, thick of neck, broad of horn, with a scrotum worthy of Zeus when, in the guise of a bull, he wooed Europa, moved slowly forward with his head lowered. I felt the magnificence of his advance; I thought of how great life was, how godly, not only in men and women and heroic children, but in many beasts, such as horses that will fall dead with broken hearts rather than lose a race, or in dogs faithful to the charge. And I wished to the high Gods that the bull had made his stand two hundred yards from me instead of five hundred, for I would have sent a messenger to meet Iniquity even as he rushed; and Apollo—who loved all greatness, and who himself sang of heroes in the Olympian halls, and who especially loved the crescent bow that bent so deeply at the backward sweep of the shoulder of a powerful archer, and who loved the song that the darting arrow sang—great Apollo, the Truth Teller, might have sped my messenger on a straight course.

Then came the charge. It burst from grass that had looked empty. One instant there was nothing there, and at the next, out shot the living missile, great Iniquity, a king among lions, running low to the ground, his feet scuttling and throwing turf, his tail outstretched and stiff, and his speed unbelievable. The bull gave a sideways sweep of his horn, once forth, once back. A tiny drop of warming hope hid in my heart that he might catch the Beast in the side just as he leaped, and a great wave of joy tingled every drop of my blood as he bellowed in defiance. That was his last outcry. Never again would he summon a cow by his deep-throated call when his loins ached and he knew the godly need of procreation. The lion swerved in his charge, clearing the sweeping horns, and then from the side leaped on the bull's broad back and crushed him to earth. Then he turned a little, and the next we knew, he had closed his fangs in the throat of his prey.

The bull made no motion after his fall, and I had never seen a more instant death. Then Iniquity stretched his great body and stolidly began to make his meal. With his great fangs he ripped open the bull's belly, and with his huge forearms he clawed out meat, no doubt the heart and liver, and bracing against the carcass with his foot, he tore off slabs from the sides. Some parts he swallowed whole, some he chewed like a tomcat, and his head and neck and forelegs became smeared with blood. Suddenly, then, his feast was interrupted, and I never knew its cause. Actaeon had told me that lions have a weak sense of smell, so it was not likely that an eddy of wind brought him a hateful scent. On the other hand, the lion's power of vision is one of the greatest ever given by the Gods to living creatures, and it might be a little movement had caught his eye. He stopped eating and stood tense, gazing in our direction.

I stood tall and waved my arms. I could not forebear from hoping that his rage would come on him, and he would attempt to storm our citadel, and I would have a close shot at him as he made his first upward spring, and my spear would be waiting for him, the odds of battle leaning on my side, as he labored within its reach. Instead he dashed away, snarling and yowling, and at once began to climb the less steep knoll I had observed before. With ease he bounded up its easy slope, and took his stand on what I now observed was a flat rock on its very crest. Then, looking straight at us, he gave forth his full-throated roar.

It was such a cry as a Titan might have uttered when he lay dying on the battlefield of the great war with Zeus. It rang against the rock of the hills, and echoed and re-echoed, and filled every inch of the air, until it seemed an element of nature rather than a beast-made sound. And now I thought to make him the best answer that I could. The Gods knew I could not launch an arrow such a distance with my shoulder and arms, because thus I could not fully bend the bow to its perfect round. Then a God that loved cattle and the men who herded them, perhaps great Pan, new wakened from drunken slumber, brought to my mind a thing I had considered and with which I had toyed sometimes, but of which I had never made full trial for fear of breaking my bow. Cocking my longest arrow on the string, I lay on my back and put my two feet on the bow's belly, one on each side of the protruding shaft. Then pulling back the cord with my right hand, I pushed powerfully with my feet. The bow bent, deeper and deeper the harder I thrust, and still it did not break. Soon it was more rounded than ever in my use, and still it bent, until at last the base of the bronze point touched the horn, and it was round as the full moon.

Then, taking such aim as I could, I let fly. The horn of the bow cried out, and the string hummed, and the arrow darted, faster than any shaft of mine had ever sped. It climbed in a lovely arc, with the late sun shining on it and burnishing its highly polished point, and at three hundred yards, when it had begun its dip, it was still darting forward as might a Harpy in her dread attack. Still I thought it would fall to earth a little short of the mark, and no doubt to one side, because I hardly dared hope that my rough-and-ready aim could be true.

But some God who loved cattle and cattle drovers, and perchance loved me a little—for I had tended the herds well when I had been given the appointment—not only sped the arrow the necessary distance, but let no puff of wind molest its aim. Down it dipped, weakly but still flying, to the red mane; and through the skin at least, and perhaps into the outer muscles, the burnished point stabbed its way. Then for the first time in his life of rampage, Iniquity knew pain at the hand of man, the little forked creature that he so scorned, and he gave a great brief growl of astonishment and thwarted fury.

Instantly he bit at the arrow, breaking off the shaft. Then he dashed down the hill, and without stopping to resume his feast, rushed on and soon disappeared among the rocks and thickets. And tonight, I thought, he would lie and brood over the bronze dagger sticking in his side, and even if he drew it forth with his teeth, or left it to fester and fall out, tonight his dreams would be most evil, and a little shadow of doom that now and then he seemed to see in the dimness of distance would appear to grow and blacken.

4

It came to pass in Nemea that the life of the great lion Iniquity was noticeably and sharply changed for a matter of eight weeks following his being hit by a falling arrow from my bow. To this every drover of the pasturages overlooking the plain would bear earnest witness. As to the deeper reasons therefor, why a mere flesh wound in his shoulder would affect the monster in this fashion, hardly any two drovers agreed. Almost all thought that one or another of the Gods had a hand in it, since it was manifestly impossible for my shaft to have flown so far, four hundred clean strides between the two knolls, without Aeolus' blowing on it, or Hermes' catching it and carrying it on one of his invisible aerial journeys, or great Pan, who loved cattle almost as well as his bottle, pronouncing a tipsy incantation as he saw it fly, or Apollo singing it on its way.

Even so, not one of the drovers who came and gaped at the places of the shaft departure and arrival believed for a moment that the great change in Iniquity would last long.

It remained for Actaeon, the great hunter, to give me the most likely solution of the mystery.

"I think that Iniquity was unable to pull out the bronze point with his teeth and it festered and ultimately fell out. That festering poisoned his blood as a like wound sometimes poisons the blood of a man, and he developed a stiffness, a great soreness, and a lameness in his left front leg. I have noticed that a mere thorn in the foot of a leopard, hurting when he walks or runs, changes his habits greatly. He no longer pursues deer—he cannot catch them—and kills sheep and tame goats that have lost their mountain swiftness. The same must hold true of a lion. Observe that of twelve cattle Iniquity has killed since he took his wound four were themselves lame, five were so old and infirm that their drovers had neither the heart to slaughter them or the teeth to chew their gristle, two were bogged in mud, and one was apparently trapped in a defile in the hills. Because Iniquity no longer trusts himself to make lightning rushes from ambush or to dodge a swift javelin, he no longer lurks near the camps, rarely shows himself, has forsaken his favorite lairs, and has attacked and killed no drover. Heracles, we will not again behold him in his swaggering glory until his wound has healed."

Worse than that, we did not see him at all. When we hunted for him, ever he was elsewhere. He was employing his great cunning not to oppress and terrify the countryside, which was his pride and glory, but to lie low. It might be that we had passed within fifty steps of him with no inkling of his nearness. Once I thought I heard his limping step in a dense thicket of thorn, and once Actaeon was almost certain that he had caught a whiff of him, a smell like that of tomcat urine ten times multiplied, mixed with musk, and so rank and heavy that it hangs in the air, defying the winds to waft it away, and seems to drip from the trees.

But despite the lion's fading from the sight of man, no drover failed to note that he managed to kill often enough to keep his maw well filled and his strength replete.

The weeks crawled, and the drovers dozed longer and watched less beside their watch fires. Sometimes they slept in the midday sun, although doubtless they always wakened with a start, sprang up, seized their weapons, and gazed wildly about them before they sighed in content. Meanwhile, as my companions and I hatched sterile plots and made fruitless journeys up and over the hills, down into woods, and across deserts to remote pools where Iniquity had been known to drink, the Wolf of Winter made ever bolder forays. Thunder roared less often over the hills, great bursts of rain no longer wetted us on late afternoons, clouds became gray and cold-looking instead of black and angry, the wind was less violent than in early autumn storms, but blew hours on end and bit bones.

Two moons past the autumnal equinox, the nights seemed endless. The aspen trees had been the first to change color, this a pale sweet golden, and then for a week or so every wooded vale and hillside rioted in red and russet and lovely brown. Then Boreas came over the mountain puffing and threatening, and then he appeared to grow angry, raving and shouting and sometimes howling. All night the trees creaked and their branches moaned, and in the morning only a scattering of their painted leaves clung to their boughs, and their parents that had stood so proud looked old, sear, and sad.

And on the following midday, Iniquity raided the pastures of Aturis and caught and killed a fleet heifer, and dragged it into the thorn to devour it. Aturis himself, being asleep in the sun, did not know what had happened until he was wakened by the bellowing of his bulls. Then I reckoned he thanked the Gods that he had not died in his slumbers from a little bat on the head from Iniquity's mailed paw, knowing nothing but the pale foreboding of a dreadful nightmare that never came to pass. The evidence presented was that the marauder could run as fast or almost as fast as ever, that his festering wound had healed, but his great wickedness had not returned to him in its full force, and that his heart still lacked an iota of its boldness.

Thereafter he went over the mountain, and Aturis saw him cross the naked ridge, his head cocked as usual, the great fluff of his foremane causing his head to look twice its natural size, with not a sign of a limp. Thereafter there was naught in the way of hunting that our party could do until our quarry again yearned for his home pastures and the sleek beasts that he no doubt believed were herded there for his express benefit. Actaeon, Right Doer, and Dyctus went cheerfully to work fortifying our camp against the onslaught of winter, soon to befall. But it so happened I did not share their labors at the outset.

Late on a raw, windy afternoon, Actaeon, with the ever watchful gaze of the born huntsman, and Right Doer, who kept watch of everything as a natural process of his being, spied at the same instant a cheerful sight—no less than a cart, drawn by two mules, winding up a rough track not impassable for narrow-wheeled wagons that led from the Plain of Nemea. We dismissed completely the possibility that the luck it brought was bad, for all of us were young, of high heart; and if Eurytus had sent us evil tidings, they would have been brought by a horseback rider, to hasten their delivery and to impress the people with his power. It could be that a great Nemean aristocrat was sending greetings to highborn Actaeon, to Right Doer, and while about it, to the foster son of Wrathful Leader and the slayer of Antaeus, Heracles.

Presumably a white-bearded slave, with bared lower legs, drove the mules. But the hairdress and fashion of the tunic of the person who stood behind him took my eye and caused a pleasant quickening of my heart. I watched and hoped but did not pray, for I was never a great prayer, saving my orisons for emergencies. The fact remained that I had made a wild guess at the visitor's identity, and as the distance shortened, as when a snail watched by an idle loafer makes his tortuous way toward him, compared to which a turtle moves with the winged sandals of Hermes, that guess became a creditable possibility, then a probability, and then a surety. Megara, of the big black eyes and raven-black hair, was paying me a visit.

Soon the track leveled and the driver goaded his mules to a brisk trot. The cart rattled up to my camp, and while my three companions stood a little back, I held out my arms and bade Megara jump. This she did, like a fox for ease, and I caught her lightly, then held her closer than was any need, and reluctantly put her down. Then Actaeon and Right Doer paid her courteous due, although Dyctus still hung back. So she came up to him and took his rough hand and wished him the favor of the Gods.

"I bring no evil tidings," she told us, which we knew already from the pleasant flush of her face and the gay tilt of her nose and the ever-changing lights in her dark eyes. "It chanced that, three nights past, the King put down his winecup to wonder how the hunt was going, for he had suddenly recalled a dream of the night before that Iniquity had killed someone, so rending the body of his prey that Eurytus' wandering spirit could not recognize it, although the inkling came to him that it was you, Heracles, whose eyes were darkened, or else someone dear to you."

"The Gods forbid!" I cried.

"Then the King complained that he could not send my brother Nessus to bring him the unvarnished truth, for Nessus was away in Ithaca, bearing royal greetings to Ulysses, who at last came safely home and regained his kingdom. The tales that old men will tell! I doubt not that he has slain a dozen monsters, a score of giants, been captive to a sorceress more beautiful than Medea, and weathered such gales as would drown Proteus' seals. But if the truth were known, I would wager he has been living at ease with some fisherman's buxom daughter, dreading the lash of Penelope's tongue."

"Megara, you should not speak so lightly of so great a hero of the Trojan War," I said sternly.

"Ajax, who defied Zeus' lightning, was my hero, and he was slain. Besides, Heracles, I have met Penelope, and there is more to her than meets the eye, and I do not believe for one moment that she could not have gotten rid of her horde of suitors, if she had the mind. The old soldiers say that Odysseus would cheat an Arcadian shepherd out of his ewe lamb! And now, by your leave, I will continue my account of the King's dilemma. He could not send a slave to bring him the news, for the fellow would rather hang than come nigh Iniquity, and the King's Companions are busy storing the harvests of their great domains. So who should speak up but Iole?"

"Iole?" I echoed stupidly, a quiver racing down my spine.

"None other. She said that she wished to visit Nemea, to build a shrine to Artemis in these very hills where the Goddess had once killed a man-eating centaur—a tale I had never heard before. In the same visit, she could hear news of the hunt."

"I dare say the King would not permit her to go, fearing she would be ravished by a rude drover."

"Such a thought could not cross the King's mind, no more than mine. Iole has a great capacity to care for herself in all places and situations. It was I who threw, as the country folk say, the dead cat in the soup kettle. I merely told her I would like to go with her, for I wished to drink from the Pool of Truth not far from here, which gives immunity from lying, and permits the drinker to penetrate all lies, for one day and one night. Thereupon she remembered some religious duties that had slipped her mind, and told the King, with sorrow in her lovely face, that she could not go at all."

At this moment Dyctus again turned the spit on which a yearling doe was being roasted whole, and such a delectable smell arose that Megara must wipe her mouth. The sun was like Hector's far-glancing helm when we began our feast, dipping through heavy clouds at the summit of the hills, and occasionally shooting his golden ray through a rift to pick up for our view some lovely feature of the distant landscape, or a gnarled tree splendid in decay, or a white heron's solitary

flight, or a crag on a faraway mountain with the face of a God. Before
we were half finished, for we Greeks eat slowly, savoring our food
when we are in good company, you could not tell hill from plain in
the gathering gloom, and the great planet Hesper followed down his
lord in sublime attendance. There was enough meat for all, including
the mule-driving slave, and enough left to eat cold in the morning for
our breakfast.

"Megara, when you heard the King's dream that I, or someone close
to me, had been killed by Iniquity, did you believe it?" I asked, the
six of us making a circle about the fiercely leaping fire.

Foremost it was a festive fire, but a watch fire as well. Although
Iniquity had gone over the mountain, his herds on the other side
might be scrawnier than ever because of the late dry weather there,
and he might take one look at them, roar mightily in wrath, then turn
straight homeward. In joy we watched the red-gold flame ever pounc-
ing upward, ever falling back, and saw its ring of firelight brighten or
dim, and the shadows advance or retreat.

"I knew you were not dead," Megara answered. "If you were, I too
would have dreamed of it, and would have seen you lying white and
still in death. If you had suffered great loss, I might not have dreamed
of it, but would have wakened just before sunrise with an aching heart.
Let us speak not of it. Instead I will tell you of a dream of old Tiresias,
Seer of Wonders, whom the King summoned to prophesy on what
matter you may guess. But the wine would not make him drunk, and
his lips would not open for soothsaying. Horn after horn he downed,
dizzying him no more than so much water, and truly I believe that
great Dionysus gave him immunity, to spite the King whom the laughing God of the Vine could never love. But in my bower on the following afternoon I knelt before the seer and offered him a single cup of
honey mead, which straightway flushed the old gray crag of his face,
and although he spoke no prophecy of direct concern with you, he
muttered about Iniquity in a strange, wild fashion, as though he had
seen a vision."

The eyes of Actaeon, forever the hunter, lighted up as always when
he heard the marauder's name. Although Right Doer's eyes never
dimmed, unless it were in sleep imitating death, they narrowed a little,
betraying the utter fascination that Iniquity held for him.

"Seer of Wonders does not believe that Iniquity was sent to ravage
Nemea by a spiteful Goddess," Megara went on. "Rather he thinks

he is a precursor of some conqueror yet unborn, who will some day ravage not a little wilderness of stone and thorn, but all the world within the encircling seas. Iniquity was born near the market town of Pella in Macedonia only six years ago. When only a yearling, he fought his father, a mighty lion, the terror of the countryside, and killed him, and then began his roamings. I asked Seer of Wonders the name of the conqueror to come. He did not know. I asked if he would make himself known within my lifetime. The old man answered that oak tree after oak tree would grow old and die before the conqueror was born, that the shores of oceans would change to shapes undreamed, that the palaces of the Pharaohs would lie forgotten under rubble deeper than a well, and only the songs of a blind poet would still be sung and be as beautiful as Hebe. But he said also that when the conqueror came, he would carry his head as does Iniquity, a little on one side, and that the hair above his forehead would grow in a thick mat. Finally, he said that the conqueror and his precursor will have suffered from the same infirmity—that they dreamed that they were Gods and not of mortal cast. That is all the tale, to take or leave."

All of us hearers were sobered a little by it, I know not why, unless men find it pleasant to contemplate times long ago, because they know that the seed of that day gave seed, generation after generation, until the seed of which they themselves had sprung was duly planted. Thus they themselves had been fated, even then, to emerge from the blind Unknown and breathe and speak. But they cannot with such complacency imagine the far future, when no track or trace of them remains on earth, and no man knows their names or where lie the vestiges of their bones.

So we had best make merry while we may, and take such happiness as might come to hand. And I gazed upon Megara, and I stopped wishing that she had not interfered with Iole's visit here, and the wisdom came to me that no man who is a man will trade solid reality that he may grasp for a tenuous dream that ever slips through his fingers. And I looked upon her mouth that I had kissed, and I beheld her beauty, not at all like that of a Goddess, but real and warm; her skin was warm instead of cold, as was the marble of the image of Artemis. Then I visioned her soon retiring from the firelight to undress and lie down, although it would follow her to her retreat and sometimes its far-sped beams would gloss her limbs and glimmer on her breast. And if I conquered Iniquity and did not die between his fangs, it was within reason that I might have that beauty for my own, close and warm within my arms, and mayhap I would lie awake and listen to her even breathing, and mayhap she too would waken, and we would woo each other, and her needs would be as great as mine, and she would not hide them from me, and their fulfillment as blissful to her as to me.

And it might be that this reward would come to me, my mead of honor, merely for challenging the marauder, before we met in splendid trial of battle. If so, my thews would be greater than ever, and my sinewy hands more strong, and my heart would be like iron for strength, and my chance of victory enhanced.

CHAPTER SIX

THE POOL OF TRUTH

1

Before Megara had finished her hearty breakfast, Right Doer had recounted our first and only meeting with Iniquity. Careful to employ no fulsome praise, and with laughter, some of which seemed at my expense, still he gave me my due, if not a little more. The account of the great flight of my arrow, the bow bent with my feet instead of arms, my brother acted out, lying flat on his back and pretending to push and pull, his brow furrowed and his mouth pouted as he swore mine always were when aiming a shaft. But his having me bit by ants was pure invention.

The recital caused even Megara's mule driver to break into hearty guffaws, all the pleasanter to hear because of his usual solemn mien. This last I reckoned he had acquired by serving King Eurytus, before whom jovial, fat Silenus, Pan's son or Pan's brother—he was always too deep in drink to remember which—would not dare crack a smile.

Actaeon and I contributed to the account of Iniquity's later actions, the nursing of his wound, and his disappearance over the mountain, whereupon Megara was as well versed in the story as ourselves.

"All you have told me I shall report dutifully to the King," Megara said.

Actaeon looked distressed, and Right Doer spoke out.

"Megara, will you please forget to tell him that one tender of Heracles' camp is Actaeon, the most famous huntsman in Greece?" he asked. "I pray that you remember the King's secret that every child who has cast his milk teeth has guessed—that the royal design is not that

Heracles kill Iniquity, but that Iniquity kill Heracles. Even at best it is an even chance." And Right Doer's gay tone had faded away like a shaft of sunlight through clouds when they thicken and join to give full scope to the rain.

"Is it really as close as that?" Megara asked. "You needn't tell me; I know too well. No, I will not mention Actaeon to the King: Actaeon, I do not know you by sight. I agree with you, Right Doer, that Eurytus would not take kindly to any guidance he might give Heracles, even though he walks unarmed. I shall carry home a cheering account that Hera has taken Iniquity's side—which of course she would do if Zeus had gone frolicking twenty years ago in the likeness of Noble Lady's husband. It is a tale that the King more than half believes since his favorite, Antaeus, lost the wrestling match, along with the loss of wagers placed by every courtier and the half talent of gold risked by the King in his bet with—but I had better not speak of that." She turned to me with great earnestness, almost in entreaty. "Heracles, you yourself do not believe the story—do you?"

I had to think briefly but hard. There was still a little string running between the dream and my heart. I broke it with a little tug of my will.

"No, I do not."

"Thank the Gods! And in justice to you, you have never given word or sign that you believed it. If you had, I would not have jolted these long miles in a mule cart; why should I trouble my head or my heart about a son of Zeus? Antaeus never doubted that he was the son of the God of War. It is hard to tell about Iole—I only know she believes something quite wonderful about herself. Heracles, you are the son of man, but perhaps no ordinary man, perhaps a Persian who called himself Atlas, and who performed at festivals about the time you were conceived. Because he was not a Greek, he could not compete at the games. But there is no doubt that he could lie on the ground with a platform made of boards supporting two stalls across his chest, let two oxen be fastened in the stalls, then lift it to the full height of his upraised arms. I tell you with my heart's truth that your hope of returning from Nemea with the hide of Iniquity about your shoulders may burn twice as bright since you do not believe yourself begotten by a God. Not that you will be less bold. You cannot win without great boldness—and the wit of your three companions. But you will be fighting for men, your brothers, not for Olympians whose only care is their own amusement; and that is the only road to godhead. I have not yet drunk from the Pool of Truth, but I know that much."

"I will take you today to drink of that pool," I told her. "I know where it is—only a short walk." And obviously I had not drunk of it either, or I would not have told her this whopping lie. In truth, I had not even heard of the pool until she had spoken of it.

"I'll go with you gladly, and since the effect wears off in one day and one night, I will be able to tell Eurytus of your arrow's flying wild, and of your spear breaking its point against rock. He will make offering to Hera, trusting her to score over Zeus as she almost always does. Heracles, can we leave at once so I may gain the plain before nightfall? I dare not leave Iole alone with the King for very long."

We did depart at once, but I went by way of Snag Tooth's pasturage; and by leaving Megara to admire an unseasonably born russet-colored calf, pretty as a fawn, I seized a moment or two alone with the old man.

"The Pool of Truth," he pondered, scratching his white pow. "I wonder if she means the Pool of Apollo, where it is said he once bathed? Apollo is the God of Truth; and when I think of it, I believe I have heard the tale of his leaving some of his essence in the pool. If so, it can be no other than below two springs that flow from between cracks in the wall of a grotto under the Hill of Olives that separates the eastern end of my pasturage from the western end of the pasturage of Charnides. Both springs mingle their flow into the pool, or neither would be good for anything. One is so cold that it would crack my last lingering tooth, my pride and joy; the other so scalding hot you could use it to pluck fowls. But Heracles, the Princess was mistaken in thinking you need merely drink from the pool in order to be absolved from telling lies, or from being taken in by lies, for one day and one night. Visitors to the shrine must bathe in the pool to obtain this dubious blessing."

His old eyes had a shine which aroused my usually dormant suspicions.

"Snag Tooth, didn't you make that up?"

"I swear I did not—by the pretty Godling Eros!"

"The most notorious liar south of Hyperbore."

"Besides, Heracles, the mixed water in which Apollo bathed and washed off his divine sweat is still too hot for good drinking, although it is perfect for soaking out the chill of winter weather, and infusing a pleasant glow of heat."

"In that case, I beg forgiveness for doubting your venerable word."

"Also, Heracles, I advise you to take one of my sheepskin robes. The lady should wrap herself in it well, and perhaps slumber a short while, lest she catch cold. I can only hope she does not carry away on her lovely person some of my favorite fleas."

"She can scratch them as well as you or I."

Meanwhile I was gaping at the gaffer, almost unable to believe he was the same man who had spoken with such dignity of his enemy Iniquity. Suddenly it came to me that fifty years ago he had been a Dionysus among men, tall, lithe, agile as a mountain goat, with great beauty of countenance. Then I found myself readily believing the stories told at the camps of how a dryad, beautiful beyond a poet's power to tell, had once visited him the whole of a long summer night. In the following season, not one heifer in his flock remained barren; and on the second anniversary of that night, the nymph had come again, and showed him what looked like a Godling toddling behind her, with flaxen hair and a single baby tooth gleaming pearl-bright when the babe gave forth its chuckling laugh. And this last had been a sign, so said a shepherdess with eyes wild as Cassandra's, that while its mother could not give immortality to her lover, he would never lose all of his handsome gleaming teeth; even if, at long last, only one snag remained.

I took the robe that he offered so solemnly, and folded it to carry under my arm as inconspicuously as possible. Even so, it seemed as eye-catching as the round belly of a gravid woman, the robe being a foreshadowing, as it were, the round belly an unmistakable consequence. Happily, Megara did not appear to notice it—the acme of good manners, I thought, since she could not be certain of the hopes I had for it, although she could no doubt make a likely guess. No doubt, too, she did not know her own mind. She followed me cheerfully up the dim path that Snag Tooth showed us winding safely between jagged rock and thorny briar; and from the look of it, Iniquity might have paced it from time to time, and deer, foxes, and other free folk, and perhaps bold young bullocks eager to see the world, but pilgrims to the Pool of Truth had been few and far apart.

Yet when we came to the grotto under the hill from which a baby brook, warm to the touch, rippled into the deeper valley, Megara told me that the crypt at Delphi, the site of the most famous oracle in the wide world, was not more impressive from outer view.

"I did not go in the crypt," she explained. "I did not want to know what the future held. If it held happiness for me, I wished to be pleasantly surprised. If it held great loss and sadness, I could not change it. I think that for once I acted wisely. The King went in, panting with hope of the bounty of the Gods, and came out trembling with fear of their soon disfavor. And that persuaded me, Heracles, never to put much trust in the Gods or to fear them either. Iole is giving her whole life—or what she has made people think is her whole life—to the service of Artemis, yet when she comes to some crossroads and needs her help, the Goddess need be only hot in the chase of a deer, or sniffing up the aroma of some distant sacrifice, or maybe shooting arrows at the children of another Niobe, to pay her not an iota of attention."

"Megara, I don't think you should say that about any of the Olympians." But my protest was aroused mainly by a creepy feeling got from gazing into the shadowy depths of the grotto. And I forgot how my heart had leaped when Megara had cast defiance into the teeth of this same Goddess before her shrine.

"Well, I will say it—of every Olympian except Demeter, who lives most of her days on earth amid the growing corn, and Dionysus, God of the Vine. And perhaps Apollo too, a gentleman among Gods—most of the time. If you want me to be still, you'll have to cut off my tongue."

I thought of her sweet, warm tongue, and decided quickly that her dealings with Gods and Goddesses were in no way my affair. As for myself, I had rarely felt more awe of them than in this wild scene. A few tall pines stood like enchanted Titans, silent and somber, and piled about lay mighty boulders and slabs of granite as if thrown there in their last great battle with the Gods. A black wolf that might be Zeus' own bared his teeth and skulked out of sight, and there was no sound anywhere but the soft purling of the tiny brook. Standing in the maw of the grotto, as my eyes were being adjusted to the dim light, I saw it was a fitting place for the birth of a monster, by the mating of a Sphinx with a captive hero, or of the Cretan Bull with Pasiphaë, Queen to Minos. Then my mind took a little turn, and instead of awesome, the wild spot became beautiful. It lay not in the deeps of some green sea but instead at the end of a little footpath easily followed, yet you would think we were the first mortals to have visited it in a hundred years.

I could see the outflow of both springs, and the steam from the hot spring condensed at the touch of the cold, and caused drops to be-jewel the walls like diamonds. Light, sifting in the maw, played over the pool and changed with every cloud drifting across the sun, al-though part of the pool, back under the wall, remained soot-black, and part golden, and part pearl. The springs themselves were a joy to my sight, flowing shrouded in mist to fill the mysterious pool.

Anyway, I was Heracles, who had fought Antaeus, who must yet fight Iniquity, so I strode deep into the grotto, reveling in its cozy warmth this chill winter day, in my native warmth quickened by its solitude, and thinking that, instead of the fit setting for monsters to copulate, it was a perfect scene for youth and maiden to make love.

2

"Megara, you were wrong in thinking that drinking of the water would make you speak truth and see truth for one day and one night," I told her when she had tagged me, as though afraid to let me out of her sight, into the cavern's depths. "According to Snag Tooth, who knows the legend well, you must bathe in it."

She bent and carefully dipped her hand in the pool. "Well, a bath won't hurt me after the dusty ride."

"By your leave, I too will bathe, since the streams near our camp are so cold that they freeze my innards, and our pots for heating water are small, and we must use sponges. I have not been truly clean all over since I left Thebes."

"Then get truly clean, Heracles. I will take the cooler, lower end of the pool, while you take the hotter, upper end, for you have been starved for hot water, and I have not."

She moved a little deeper into the shadows. Like most Greek girls, she had none of the demon-driven prudery of some barbarians, and had no shame of the lovely, long-limbed body which was her birth gift from the Gods. But like our very best girls, she was skilled at disrobing with a kind of modest deftness, whereby an avid watcher caught only glimpses of beauties usually hidden, and these so brief and fleeting that he could hardly make himself believe the event had occurred. The mists swirled around her as she emerged from her retreat and dived into the translucent, far from transparent, water. Meanwhile I was shedding my winter garb; not ashamed of my stocky form, but not proud of it either, and instead keeping in mind that this was the Pool of Truth. With outward boldness but inward trepidity, I too immersed myself.

For a while we were busy bathing, standing in water breast-deep on me, almost neck-deep on Megara, and taking turns with a rough cloth she had with her, which we handed back and forth. When we were well washed, she spoke to me in that deeply earnest, rich voice that emerged from her slim throat when she was moved, and which always moved me in response.

"Heracles, it may be only a story that is told about this pool, but let's pretend it's true."

I could not help, unless she rebuked me strictly, from walking up to her and putting my arms about her waist, and linking my hands at her back. Still, I did not draw her close to me.

I felt against my lower chest only the tips of those two lovely projections of the female body, at once so meaningful and so mysterious to man, which brushed my skin and even pressed it a little as she breathed. And this stirred me beyond measure, whereby a projection of my body, not soft and yielding like these, made a little dent midway of her belly. And this stirred her to faster, deeper breathings, and thus each of us forged alternate links in an interlooping magic chain. My dizzied mind wandered from what she had said, and her black pupils grew until they swallowed the sable darkness of the iris, but still her gaze was full on mine, steadfast, demanding the answer to her questions, and she would not be swept off her feet by passion until I gave it.

"I will believe it, if you will," I said, knowing not what else to say, sensing her complete earnestness, although still unable to grasp its cause, or what truth she was taking this way to seek.

"Will you promise that you will not lie to me, even in one word, the rest of the time we are together here? If you will, I will make you the same promise."

"I will."

"You were disappointed that Iole did not come instead of me. I saw it in your face."

"Yes, for a moment."

"Why? She is in love with a Goddess—and perhaps with a God that visited her once, if they ever really do it, and it too isn't a story."

"I do not know why."

"I think I do know. She is far more beautiful of face and body than I, and woman's beauty is the complement of man's bravery and strength. That is only part of it. She has served a Goddess so long that she is like a Goddess. How I burn with envy when I see her run, or leap, or shoot arrows. But I was still very young when I found out I would always be people's second choice. The only exception was when gnarled, old Seer of Wonders who, for some reason I can't guess, loved me and did not love Iole, and for that I love him, and I kissed him as Eos kissed aged Tithonus, and gazed upon him with divine compassion, and made him as happy as I could.

"And as people's second choice," Megara went on, "I have used my head and heart, and have cast forth stinging bitter pride, and usually have come out well. Have I come out well today? Remember your vow, and tell me if you are still sorry that it is not Iole, instead of me, whom you now embrace, both of us burning with love's fire? Think of her again before you speak. It could be her nipples instead of mine, more beautiful than mine, that now no longer brush your chest but press it with love's insistence. It could be her belly that you thrust against in lust and barely controllable strength. Now speak."

"No, I am glad it is you, Megara, and that is the truth of my heart."

"Do you know why?"

"How can I know, unless I know also that she would escape me at the last and forever escape me? I do not wish to know it, or even believe it, yet it must be that I do."

"And it must be that the magic of the Pool of Apollo is true magic, not a myth, or you could not have said that."

"Knowing it does not mean that I will not again succumb to her spell. It will come upon me with brookless power, and likely I will welcome it, and my heart will tremble and yearn; and that is why I cannot plight you my forever troth."

"I do not ask it now. She will beckon, and you will still pursue. Yet I think she will remain uncapturable, and you will turn back to me."

"Would you take me back?" I marveled.

"For a while, yes, because I think that, too, was part of a bargain I made with a Goddess. I know not who she is, although I believe it was sweet Demeter, who loves me as she loves the yellow corn that will nourish people. If she came to me in a dream, or when I was

delirious with fever, I know not when or where. So I think she came
ere I was conceived. I was one of a host of souls, more shadowy than
the Dead in Hades, that was fated never to be incarnate, never to be
beautiful or ugly either. Never to sorrow or rejoice, never to love or
hate. I was like a seed of corn planted in the ground, fated to wither
instead of burst forth in a green shoot and wear leaves and flower and
itself bear seed. She told me what price I must pay to be born and
breathe, and I agreed to it. I agreed to take second place behind Iole.
I agreed to take as my true and lifelong lover a man whom no other
woman would want. Heracles, are you he? Have you ever had a sweet-
heart?"

"No."

"Why not? You are not a beautiful man such as Right Doer, but
not an ungainly or ugly man, so there can be no reason but your inhuman strength. Well, I can see how every other woman would turn
away from it, because her own frailty would be laid bare. But it so
chances—or it was so given—that I am less frail than other women.
What other would have defied Artemis?"

"None."

"Heracles, do you believe you will live long?"

"I think I will live gloriously, but not long."

"Achilles lived gloriously, but not long. He had maidens that were
his prize of battle, but no woman ever loved him of whom I have
heard. Heracles, why did you bring the sheepskin robe?"

"Because old Snag Tooth suggested that I bring it, and I did so,
hoping that his old eyes saw farther than mine, and that you would
lie with me, here in the warmth after we had bathed."

"We have bathed in the Pool of Truth. Do you love me, Heracles,
even though you are more enchanted with Iole? If you do, I will lie
with you here in this grotto of the Gods."

"By my soul's truth, I love you, but do you love me, monster though
I may be, or are you only keeping a bargain that you made with an
unknown Goddess? No woman has ever loved me except my nurse
Althea, and she loved Right Doer more. If you do not love me, by
your heart's urge, I will abjure my longing, defy my aching loins and
tempestuous hunger. Other maidens I will have, for their pleasure and
for mine ere we go our ways. From you, Megara, I must have true
love, or I would be ashamed."

"I love you, Heracles, I have loved you in a sadness ever since you wrestled with my brother, Nessus, and won so gently. Ever since you killed great Erebus, trying to keep your seat on his back with your impressed knees, I have loved you passionately as well."

"Is the sadness still there?"

"Yes. It will never pass away. Now hold me close."

CHAPTER SEVEN

THE GREAT HUNT

1

When Megara and I left the grotto and started back to camp, both of us had little to say to each other. Still bound by our pledge of truth, I found myself tongue-tied, not by a temptation to lie, but by a limitation of power to tell the whole truth, it being too large for me to grasp. The main state I was in was exaltation. All that I tried to say came forth in excited and exulted tones as in the first flush of the spirit of the vine. Also, my senses seemed preternaturally sharp. There was more and lovelier color in the hills, rocks, trees, dead grass, and wind-stripped trees than when I had come hence. There was more beauty in Megara's face than before, and partly this was because of my sharper seeing, but partly because it had increased beyond question in the past hour. I wished to walk hand in hand with her, a wanting and, I believe, a heartfelt need, but for the time we must walk in file in the dim, narrow and, to me, forever lovely path.

When we came to Snag Tooth's pasture, the old drover had marked our approach and hastened to meet us. It had come to pass that Megara was carrying the sheepskin robe, I knew not exactly how or why, except that she had folded it neatly and picked it up and shook her head when I had offered to relieve her of its weight and bulk, and I felt it had something to do with her being a woman and her responsibility as such, and perhaps her superstitions. She put it in Snag Tooth's wrinkled, unweakened hands with a little, somewhat ceremonial bow of her head.

"Did you roll up in it and take a nice nap?" he asked, trying, I suppose, to be polite, and overdoing it, I thought.

"No, but we made other good use of it, thank you," she answered, looking him straight in the eyes. For she had pledged truth today and tonight, and anyway she was true Greek if one was ever born.

"It is nearly noon. Will you both stay and share my midday meal? I have a rich broth, barley cakes, and the sweetbread of a bullock that broke his neck in a stump hole."

"I cannot, grandsire, to my sorrow, for I must take the road, but I will ask sweet Demeter to bless the good food, for your long sustenance, and Dionysus to bless your cup." And the thought came to me that she might have mentioned Aphrodite, had she wished, for her mind was always equal to pleasant invention. The truth was, Megara seemed to lack respect for the golden Goddess of Beauty and of Love, despite the world-wide and timeless greatness of her realm. I think she disliked her personally, although I do not know why.

"Then farewell and a safe journey, and return soon to these hills, whom you gladdened to their rocky core by your visit here."

"For that I give you this," and gravely she kissed the wrinkled old hand, then the lean, white head.

We went on to our camp, where my companions treated her like a queen, and before I knew it, she was in the loaded cart with her driver urging his team. As the wheels started to turn I could not forbear from jumping in and riding with her till we got behind a little spinney where, out of sight of my friends, and with her slave's gaze fixed ahead, I could take her in my arms for a farewell kiss. The little token did me more good than I could tell.

I leaped down, and watched the cart out of sight. Then, at the camp, while Dyctus prepared the midday meal, I sat down with Right Doer and Actaeon, who were engaged in grave talk.

"Is there news of Iniquity?" I asked.

"No," my brother answered, "but no news is too often bad news where the marauder is concerned, and Actaeon and I have been discussing ways and means to make the news good."

I did not want to think about Iniquity today. I wanted to daydream about Megara, with Iole stealing into the dream whether I invited her or not. But I had to come to it.

"He will not return until the new moon," I said. "Meanwhile I thought of asking the shepherd Telemon, who knows smithery, to cast longer and heavier arrowheads out of our store of metal, while

I shape shafts to carry them. The bow can do its part. That has been shown."

"It is a good notion, Heracles, and at least we may start the job, but it may be—with wonderful luck—we need not finish it."

"Then you have thought of another plan of attack."

"We have been studying the brute's ways, to find out if he is a brute, and not a werelion, or the son of a God. If he's only flesh and blood, he has at least one weakness, one loop in his armor, for the Gods never created man or beast that had none. Well, we hit upon it. It comes into play when, going over the mountain or coming back, he invariably takes one of three paths. All offer opportunities for well-laid ambush. Actaeon believes that now, while his wound still smarts and is fresh in his memory, he will take the path that leads either to Aturis' pastures or to Charnides' pastures and he will avoid for a long time yet, perhaps forever, the more westward path to Snag Tooth's pastures, where he was wounded and forsook his kill. This is the way of lions, Actaeon says, and when all is said and done, Iniquity is a lion. Well, how may we know his choice in time to gain either of the two ambushes that we will prepare beforehand, there to lie in wait for him, close to his course, with your spear in hand, and your bow ready if he should become suspicious and forsake the path or turn back?"

"Heracles, we will lay an ambush on all three paths," Actaeon broke in. "Ninety-nine out of a hundred of my grains of knowledge of wild beasts insist that he will take one of the two more eastward paths. But the hundredth grain—small, withered, and unworthy to associate with its fellows—warns that all signs fail in dry weather, and the weather over the mountain has been uncommonly dry."

"Aye, we will heed the warning. And Right Doer, I have surmised your plan, and I was thickheaded as a plow beast not to have thought of it sooner, and both of your heads need a little dusting to have taken so long about it. The drovers over the mountain herd only scrawny cattle, yet no doubt love them dearly. Although Iniquity visits their pastures but rarely, still they hate him with a mighty hate. We will visit them, and ask them to post a watch, which they will gladly do. When Iniquity sets forth to return to his own—his flocks and herds that are his main support—they can signal with smoke which of the three paths Iniquity has taken." I stopped and scratched my head, then went on, with no great dearth of wit. "Smoke will not rise on a day of heavy air, before a rain. In that case they can spread sheepskin robes on the crest of yon Cliff of the Eagles, one, two, or three groups of ten robes each, all plainly visible from our camp."

"You have caught up with us, and surpassed us," Right Doer told me with his wonderful smile. "We had thought of spreading green pine boughs on the black rock, but white sheepskins are better. Now let us set to the baked ham of the wild shoat which some satyr, hating Iniquity for the goats he has eaten, offered up to us with a belched blessing. At least the beast appeared in a stone's throw of our camp, where Actaeon shot him with Dyctus' bow. If Eurytus hears of it, he might quibble you are receiving armed assistance in your campaign, but I will swear by Apollo that Zeus himself felled the pig with the mightiest thunderbolt in his bag."

2

We ate, and then we talked with Telemon about arrowheads fit for shafts as long as a pygmy's spear, and he promised to make them, and to file them dagger-sharp, from our ingots of tin and copper. In the late afternoon and evening I shaped an arrow of stout ash to replace the one I had lost, while Right Doer and Actaeon explored the paths that our enemy took, to seek a good site for an ambush. On the following morning we three made over the mountain, only I bearing arms, all of us thrilling pleasantly over the dim chance of coming face to face with Iniquity at some blind bend, as he made homeward aforetime. It did not occur, but we thrilled in another fashion at the welcome given us by the drovers below the steep. They had heard of Actaeon, and of course they knew of the labor assigned me by the King, and they could not help but see the soundness of our tactics. Only one old man, no fool by the look of him, hard-bitten, tough as yew wood, and sour as green plums, declined to put the least faith in our undertaking.

"No mortal will ever lay low Iniquity," he predicted, "now that Achilles, conquering great Hector, then felled by the arrow of a fop, has gone down to Hades. Not that the beast is Hera's scourge. Such tales are for children. But ordinary lions are not only far stronger than men, but have better minds. Iniquity is greater than any man alive in strength and in cunning. So I'll not lend my sheepskin robe, to be wetted with rain or befouled by the droppings of mountain ravens, nor will I waste my well-hoarded strength cutting wood for signal fires."

The other drovers appeared ashamed of the caustic gaffer, and in great haste promised all that we asked.

We shared their midday meal, the toughest and leanest beef I had ever eaten, then returned to our camp. And since the old moon had wasted to a wondrous similarity to the young moon—causing Snag Tooth, who visited us to hear the news, to wish that old men could return to the shape, and resume the functions of, young men—the test of our stratagem was not far off.

We spent the days of the moon's last quarter laying two ambushes beside each of the three trails, one farther up the mountain than the other, a kind of two strings for a bow. Also, we fitted on the heavy heads Telemon had cast for my new-shaped arrows. Meanwhile we rejoiced to think of our fellows over the mountain, risking their necks to keep track of Iniquity, spying on his comings and goings and his sleeping in his thorn, where ever he dreamed of gushing blood. Right Doer counted the marks we had cut in a nearby tree trunk to mark the days. The day came that was the last of the waning moon, she was done for, the glory of her fullness was long gone, she showed not her wraithlike shape from sundown to sunrise, and tomorrow night a new-born Queen of Heaven would receive the obeisance of the stars.

Every moment of that day one of us four had his gaze on the Cliff of the Eagles, or in the nearby sky, watching for a signal. The watch was resumed, with higher hope, the next day, but still no white patch showed on the black rock, and no dimming trail of smoke curled into the sky. The weather, which was mainly the affair of Zeus, befriended us still, not plaguing us with mist or rain, and the air was clear as water in a limpid pool. On the following morning Actaeon, who was facing the cliff as he broke fast, said quietly, "Look." We did so, and we saw both a solitary white spot on the black rock, and, not far distant, one thin, blue, upstreaming smoke. We waited a few minutes thinking another spot might appear, and a second column of blue-gray smoke, but neither did so. Both signals broke the same news—that Iniquity had started up what we called path number one, the most eastward of the three, that led to the pastures of Aturis.

I slung my bow and quiver over my left shoulder. In my hand I grasped my spear, and I loved the feel of it. Its weight was perfectly attuned to my easy handling, and I could not help but admire its burnished head, bright bronze as Hector's glancing helm, and sharp-pointed as a snake's fang, with edges whetted to cut a hair. I took the lead, as was my right, Actaeon behind me bearing his skinning knife, which if Eurytus called a weapon against Iniquity, he would make his own Companions crack their ribs with laughter. Behind him strode Right Doer, his great eyes shining, bearing only a rope with which to tie, and carry handily, a mighty, tawny pelt with a red mane. In silence we made to Aturis' camp, and began to ascend the mountain.

Since the signal had been sent so early, and since Iniquity was never known to cross or recross except in daylight, I passed by the lower ambush to gain the upper and better ambush, feeling sure we had plenty of time. Also, the higher on the path that we awaited the marauder's haughty approach, the better the chance that he would not change his mind, remember a bull that had taken his eye in Charnides' pasture, and cross to the number two path. As we crouched in our hiding place, Right Doer calculated the time since clear dawn, the distance from the nearest of Iniquity's over-the-mountain lairs, and the speed of his walk.

"We can expect him in a third part of an hour," he told Actaeon and me in low tones.

In half an hour Right Doer caught the first glimpse of him. He uttered a little grunt, and Actaeon and I knew its cause before it had passed the channels of our ears, and then the three of us grinned at one another, that our forethought seemed to be proving sound. Iniquity strode along, his head on one side, about a half mile distant. The Sun God, Helios, not long awake, appeared to see him too, and rubbed his golden eye in astonishment, and the light appeared to grow where the beast walked, as though the God had cast a special beam to see him better. We saw his red mane, fire-bright, although his tawny sides still looked dark brown. And we saw the power of his stride, the pride of his carriage, and his glory in his own wickedness, so far unbrookable by man. And I looked to my bow which I had unslung and lay ready, and I grasped with a passionate love my great spear.

Iniquity's long and steady stride quickly cut in half the distance between us. We three waiters breathed in unison, deep, silent breaths, and my heart thudded, and I knew my comrades' hearts did the like; their faces were set like flint, and their gaze fixed implacably on the oncoming foe. But suddenly the heavens threatened to fall. At about five hundred paces, Iniquity stopped still, gazing in our direction.

He could not see our crouched forms, but the thought struck me, like the first cold chill of a fatal sickness striking the heart, that in my

pride I had polished too well the head of my spear, and in this outpouring of brilliant sunlight it had glanced into Iniquity's eyes.

He stood still, motionless, his head straight now, and lifted, while
my heart thumped ten times more, and it ached with an awful ache
for him to be reassured and continue on his way. Instead, he turned
and made a powerful bound to the right, which was westward of his
position, and then vanished in what must be a rift in the rock. And
only then we heard his angry growl, which he had uttered at his first
leap, reaching us like the rumble of distant thunder.

"Make for the lower ambush on the middle path," I commanded,
the same command that Actaeon would have given were he the leader.
"We've still time to gain it and wait his coming."

So we sprang forth and ran, and it so happened that a grove of
mountain laurel hid us from his hawk-sharp eyes, even as it hid him
from our frantic eyes. The middle path was hardly a half mile away.
The ground was rough and rocky, and we dared not try to run, for
we would thus be spent and helpless at the meeting that I prayed to
Pan, lover of drovers and cattle, might be fated still. Instead we walked
as fast as we could. Iniquity too would walk, not run, over this rough
ground and sharp rock, for it was not possible that he had been frightened into panic by a mere glitter of light.

"I think he might have seen the flash of your point before, when
we lay on the mound above Snag Tooth's pasturage, just before he
felt the sting of your arrow," Actaeon said, controlling his breath well.
"Even then it was too bright. I wish to the High Gods I had thought
of it sooner. Still, I think we will be given another chance."

In the matter of a sixth part of an hour, we came on the ambush
with Iniquity not yet in sight. Swiftly we dipped into the hiding place,
and I laid the spear low from where it could not glance again. A bend
of the path far above us was screened with rock and thorn, and again
we resumed our desperate watch.

But it grew strangely long. My yearning for a glimpse of his swaggering form grew aching and then sick. Where in the name of the Gods
are you lurking, mighty foeman? What are you doing, that you loiter
so? Here lies the path to Charnides' pastures. Do you not lust for
one of his sleek bulls, after blunting your claws and tiring your jaw
muscles on the stringy gristle of over-the-mountain cattle? Unless you
have grown old and feeble and gone to sleep in the sun, make haste

to your appointment. And walk with a last great pride, for it is with
death.

Then up spoke Right Doer, not looking at me, instead his glance
frozen to the upward winding path, and in a low, halting voice, as if
he could hardly bring himself to speak.

"Heracles, Iniquity might have stopped to reconnoiter. But if he
had chosen to come this way, he would be in sight by now."

"Do you think he has returned to the path we watched?"

"Perhaps so. I will sacrifice to very Ares, whom I hate, if it is so. For
there is still another path he could take. That is the westward path to
Snag Tooth's pasturage. In that case we are too late to intercept him."

I looked in wild entreaty to Actaeon.

"I do not believe it, Heracles," the great hunter told me, terrible
strain in his face. "If he fled from the other path because of the flash
of your spearhead, it would be because it reminded him of his wound.
Then surely he would walk wide of the scene of that wounding. Is it
not so?"

"Don't ask me. Tell me."

"I can only say it would be so with every other lion I have ever
known."

"Great Zeus. All the drovers have tried to tell us—and my soul
told me too—that Iniquity is half God, like the Chimaera and the
Medusa. If he is idling, he might still come this way, but I cannot
wait for him. Although it is too late to intercept him on the westward
path, provided his mind is made up, still I must go in all haste over
rock and through briar. Will you two follow me as fast as you can?"

"We will keep even with you, Heracles," Actaeon answered. "And
even if he has taken that path, Snag Tooth will see him and yield
him the field. Anyway, I still believe he will walk wide of man for a
long while yet. So bid your blood come back to your pale cheeks,
and the light of hope to your eyes."

"You too are pale, Actaeon, and you, Right Doer, and your eyes,
although vigilant, are like stones," I told them as I slung my bow over
my shoulder and hauled out of our retreat.

3

So we climbed the ridge to the westward of this second path, and
when we reached its crest, where the East Wind could again bite us

to the bone, it brought news to our ears along with chill to our most inward and sheltered hearts. The news was that Iniquity had not paused at the middle path, nor had he loitered for anything, and he had already come down to Snag Tooth's pasture and wrought havoc there; and was there even now, or had gone his vaunting way. This news was told by a low medley of sounds, its components indistinguishable at this distance, but itself unmistakably the outcry of a herd of cattle in terror and dismay.

We hastened on, although taking care not to suffer a bone-breaking fall on the rocky and rough descent, for we were minded more than ever of a day yet to come, when we would need our full powers more than we had dreamed. And now we could distinguish the bellowing of the bulls, not without a rumble of defiance in their massive throats, for no matter the terror in their hearts, they remembered they were the grandsires of the herd, broad of horn, burly of neck, mighty of loin, and that bravery was forever interlocked with virility. Soon we could mark the mooing chorus of the cows, and if I would let myself believe it, the outcry was of sadness as much as of fear; and not one cow in the herd could restrain from mooing at short intervals without surcease. It might be that very young calves hovered silent under their dam's bellies, but we plainly heard the immature voices of heifers and the lowing of steers whom Great Pan had not saved from the geld, maiming body and soul. We heard, too, not yet rumbling blasts of bullocks, who had played at love with their young and pretty opposites, and had not yet tupped them, but who yearned for the day of their triumph.

Now we struck the westernmost path, and we looked down at its dirt and gravel, here and there revealed between patches of sparse dead grass, ere we looked out and down to the pasturage. And here, deep printed, showed the pug marks of Iniquity as he advanced full stride, never pausing, a great purposefulness somehow revealed in this mere echo of his passing.

And then we looked at the herd, to find it closely bunched but not milling, and indeed almost motionless. In its van stood the bulls, identifiable by their greater size and sweep of horns, and behind them the steers, cows, bullocks, and heifers. And there was no eye in our three heads that did not search its environs, then the whole of the wide pasture, in aching and vain search. And how useless felt the great spear in my hand and the bow and quiver on my shoulder, and the muscles of my thighs and calves and the sway and swing of my shoulders and arms, since I had come so late. But whatever happened, the sun would set at his due time and in the morning he would rise again.

We came down to the pasture, and our first impulse was to look in little gullies and behind rocks and beat through the thorn. Walking in a line to cover the ground well, we soon collected at Actaeon's call, where he had found the still warm carcass of a bull, the blood spilled at his killing not yet congealed, and one thigh torn away and missing, plainly carried off by the killer. As again we parted, Right Doer called Actaeon and me, not to show us something, but to tell or ask us something, for his face was lit with thought, and his eyes were burning.

"Heracles, which of these buttes would Snag Tooth climb, hoping to watch your battle with Iniquity, or at least to catch the first glimpse of your return? The one from which you shot, the one where Iniquity roared his challenge, or the one farthest east?"

"Surely the last, called the Hill of Olives. It affords a fine view of the eastern flank of the mountain."

"Then let us go there together, and find what is there, and confront it together."

So we started up the same steep which Megara and I had mounted about ten days ago, days that had dropped so fast into an Abyss of Dead Days that I could scarcely see them flash, then dim, darken, and disappear forever. And here in the dusty path we found the tracks of Snag Tooth, stepping long and lightly as he climbed, showing unmistakably the patched sole of one of his sandals which he had shown me proudly. Descending prints there were none, and this was an eerie thing to contemplate. Nor did we see the deep-pressed pugs of Iniquity, a fact none of us mentioned, being too proud to think of it as hopeful, because if the great beast should for any reason wish to climb the hill, he would do so from any point in ferocious bounds.

There was no sight of Snag Tooth, nor did we hear his yet manly voice hallooing to us.

We gained the crest and started our brief search amid the rocks and thickets. Then in the silence, Actaeon uttered a grunt, as though he had suffered a stunning blow, and he looked up at us with a still face, one that would not give anguished sign of a thing settled, and then down again at something behind a ledge of rock. We walked to his side and gazed at the ruin of what was, in the hour just sped, a mighty drover of cattle, skillful, forsworn to duty, long-seasoned and tough, suffering Time's attack but defiant of it. And because I must not spare my eyes or my heart, because both must remember always the full scene, I gazed at the wound. No doubt Iniquity had struck him high on the head with the whole power of his mailed maul, for nothing remained of it but the lower jaw, which showed his snag tooth that was his mark before Gods, men, and beasts; and the little fragments of his skull must have flown in a red shower, for none lay close at hand.

Plainly Snag Tooth had taken his stand at the highest point of the hill, and from thence he had not run in hopeless flight. Near his feet lay the feathered end of the arrow I had given him, broken off near the head, which was nowhere nigh, as I made sure with unrelenting search. Then the awful strain of my heartbeat eased a little, because I knew that the old man had jabbed with it as he had promised, and thrust it deep into the tawny side ere his soul sped, and he had made his mark on Iniquity that would never be erased.

We three had been silent a long time now, except for Actaeon's grunt, and I was a little startled by the sound of my own voice.

"Actaeon, I think you were right in saying that Iniquity saw the flash of my spear, and it caused him to remember having seen it before, when we lay atop the hill, and to remember the pain and shame of his flesh wound," I told the mighty hunter. "But instead of causing him to avoid the pastures of Snag Tooth, it impelled him to turn from the eastward path, and seek revenge."

"Aye, I have not done justice in my thinking or my speech to this Beast of beasts."

"On the crest of this hill, where Snag Tooth died, I mean to burn the body of the hero on a funeral pyre, and here also I will burn the carcass of the bull he had slain. It is not quite whole, but still a fit offering to the Gods, in which if they are truly Gods, and not impostors, they will take pride and pleasure."

"We will help you bear the carcass to this place," Right Doer said.

"Nay, one of you gather brushwood and the other go speedily to our camp for the sharp ax of bronze, whereby he may cut stouter fuel to make the fire blaze high. I will make fast the front feet of the bull to the remaining rear foot, and tie the neck to these, and heave the whole upon my back, and bring it here."

There came a strange light in the eyes into which I gazed, but they spoke no more and went about their tasks. I began my task for which I would have never before believed I had the strength, but now no doubt of it could cross my mind. When I had fastened the stout thongs and was heaving up the carcass, the thought struck me that whole, he would have weighed four times my own weight, and he was now above three times my weight, but I made off with him, easily enough on level ground, and when I came to the hill, I drove one leg after another, took stride after stride, and although I panted and puffed, I never stopped to rest. When the burden grew most great, I remembered the performer at festivals of whom Megara had told me, no Theban, not even a Greek, who had lifted two full-grown oxen and their floored stalls as well, the full length of his arms. Then I strode on without faltering, and I thought that at least one God who loved or hated me put down his cup of nectar to watch my battle, somehow a preparation for a greater battle yet to come.

I gained the crest, lay down my load, and sat down on a stone to pant my fill. And all the day and well into the night, Actaeon and Right Doer and Dyctus, who had joined them, cut and piled wild olive wood, not permitting that I help them, until the pile was great enough that our offerings could be utterly consumed in flame. I then lifted the stiffening body of Snag Tooth onto the pyre, and heaved up the carcass of the bull, and there I carried flame from the little bonfire Dyctus had made with a torch brought from our camp. And this little flame slowly grew, and the intermittent crackle became continuous, louder and louder, and under it and through ran the song of the flame itself, a great humming and strumming, and the fire leaped high, and somewhere in the dark it shone on the eyes of Iniquity, and it may be that a cold chill ran down his tawny back.

And when the fire had begun to burn down, and there was no longer the smell of burning meat, I spoke to my three companions.

"It is my desire to call upon the Gods to bear witness to an oath," I told them.

"Do so, Heracles," Right Doer answered, and I looked at the other two tall, young men, and both of them nodded.

"Gods of Olympus!" I called, not in a great voice but ringing and deep. "Gods of Earth who are nearer to us, Demeter of the Corn, Dionysus of the Vine, Pan of the Wild Wood, Silenus of the Flowing Horn. And Apollo, God of Truth, if your high companions will not look down from their golden seats, I entreat you, most of all, to hear my pledge. I will seek Iniquity in the pastures, here and over the mountain, amid the rocks, in the dark thorn, deep in the forest, and

if he flees Nemea I will follow wherever his track leads. And this I
will do not as a labor appointed me by a king, but at the command of
my will, the entreaty of my heart. And when at last we meet, Iniquity
and Heracles, one or both of us shall be slain, but both shall never
leave that final field of battle. I do not ask your help, O Great Ones,
to strengthen my thews, or to guide my arrow to the mark, or to sustain on its true course my spear with its shining head of bronze. All
I ask is that you remember the vow I hearby take, and let fly your
Furies to me if I fail to keep it. But if I keep it and yet live, I entreat
that you send the least of your messengers across the River of Woe,
down into the dim realms of Hades to find the shade of Snag Tooth,
and tell him the news. And in case you know me not, or regard me as
beneath your notice, know that I am Heracles, who in my infancy
slew the Messengers of Death, and who lately slew Antaeus, who I
believe was the son of very Ares the Bloody. And these I slew in my
own defense, but I will slay Iniquity in revenge of those whose bodies
we have offered up in flame, and of many innocent ones he had slain
before now. And as the flames die down, the moon shows her glimmering shoulder over the hills, and now she rises in glory and beauty, and
that I take as a sign that you have heard me, and that you will heed."

And then Dyctus filled four wooden cups with purple wine that he
had brought from camp. When we had poured a little on the dying
embers, we stood in a ring and drank.

4

When I had got to bed, my sadness over Snag Tooth's death soon
passed away. He had died in battle, dauntless to the last, against the
foe of those within his love and care, the flocks and herds. Also, his life,
lived far from the citadels and the assemblies of men, the life of an
aged man whose given name was long forgotten—poor, obscure, whose
craggy head had never worn a laurel wreath—such a life could not,
short of forceful intervention by the Gods, have ended with more
flaming splendor. Truly his dispatch must have caught the attention
of King Hades and his subjects, for in the very buff of death he had
made his mark upon his titanic adversary. I could not help but think
pleasantly that his arrival on those shadowy shores would make some
little stir, whereupon a myriad of dim and hollow eyes would be fixed

on him, and that even on the Elysian Fields the heroes would rise up
from their beds to take brief note.

Even so, when I fell to sleep my dreams were troubled. They kept
wandering around and about something that had been told me ere
my labor had well begun, a thing that had great bearing on the war
between Iniquity and me. I kept stumbling over it, and sometimes I
almost grasped it, only to have it dim away. Then, as once more ever
young and beautiful Eos rose from the bed of wasted Tithonus, and
had started to put on her rosy robes, I sprang awake with the memory
hard and fast in my mind.

I pondered it a few minutes, then sat with shivering Right Doer,
Actaeon, and Dyctus about the fire where they were warming yesterday's broken meats, but I did not speak to them yet, for men are rarely
open-minded, and often their minds are muddled, before the cramping of their empty bellies is relieved. But when we had all broken fast,
I bade them give ear.

"Cast back, Dyctus," I said, "to your recital of Iniquity's ways before
we came to Nemea. You told that when the marauder came on a bull
or a tender heifer that had strayed from the herd, he would rush and
kill like a common lion."

Right Doer threw me a quick, narrow glance. Countless times he
had guessed my thought before I gave it words, as though his gaze
could penetrate my skull. This was not one of those occasions; I saw
in his face an intense, ill-hidden alertness.

"Aye, so I did," Dyctus murmured.

"Do any of you know if there is a large, well-preserved, unfaded
bullhide, with legs and tail unsevered, at any of these pastures?"

"I can answer that," Dyctus said after brief reflection. "A herder
whom we call Long Bones—I know not his cognomen—has such a
hide. A very large and venerable bull, the sire and grandsire and the
great grandsire of his best begetters and sleekest cows, he fell on a
greasy grass slope while answering a young and lovely heifer's call,
and broke his forelegs. Long Bones slaughtered him and made an
offering to Zeus, and ere we fellow drovers feasted richly, we had games
in Zeus' honor. And since the season following was notable for sturdy
calves and overflowing udders, it must be Zeus did not laugh at our
awkward jumping and weight throwing and loutish wrestling, perhaps
because our foot racing would not have shamed the runners at Olympia,
we having been well taught by Iniquity to show clean heels."

"Would Long Bones lend it to us, although it may be ripped to ribbons, for the stratagem I have in mind?"

"If you mean to use in the war, he will lend it as cheerfully as Long Bones' wife would lend her bounteous teat to a hungry babe."

"Heracles, it is my turn to speak," Actaeon said with dignity. "If you mean to stuff the skin and stand it in some lonely place that Iniquity frequents and lie in wait, I can tell you now the scheme won't work. No lion born this season, his mane a mere fuzz, would be taken in by a stiff dummy of a bull that does not walk, or lower his head to graze, or switch his tail."

"The bull I have in mind will be partly stuffed, but he will walk, lower his head and switch his tail."

"What in the name of the Gods do you mean?"

"Did not the wooden horse that destroyed Troy have armed men in his innards? Our bull will contain one armed man, with a short spear, razor-sharp, and a stick of wood running from the head through the stuffed neck, with a joint for raising and lowering it. Behind me will be my fellow, to help propel the dummy and switch its tail. You have told me repeatedly that lions do not hunt by scent, but by sight. You say, too, that they recognize life mainly by movement, only a small part by outline, and a man standing still in thin thicket or even on an open plain has often escaped attack."

"My words in my teeth!" Actaeon muttered, his jaw dropping.

"Has the trick a good chance to work?" I asked. "Speak plain."

"As Apollo is my judge, it has! A young lion, his might untried, his youthful caution still upon him, might stop and stare and become suspicious, but Iniquity is monarch of all these pastures, and never doubts his godhead. What I meant was, Heracles, I believe the trick will work as far as drawing the Beast's charge. Then what?"

"The bull will be looking downwind, from whence all lions charge. My companion and I will be watching through loopholes. As Iniquity attacks, I will attack, for I will have some kind of door through which I can pass the last instant."

"Again I cry upon the Gods! Heracles, no man of wit, or no fool, indeed no man that ever lived, as far as song and story tells us, ever set himself up as a target for a charging lion, and this lion is Iniquity! Still, I can think of no better trick. If Atropos' shears do not go snip, snip—perhaps snip, snip, snip, for a clean job—I will go back to school!

Now whom do you choose, Right Doer or me, to play the rear parts of the bull?"

"Actaeon, great hunter, I must invite Right Doer first. We have a pact made when we were striplings. Speak, my brother. Will you come with me?"

"My brother, I cannot. To do so would be beyond the last wrench of my will, and my blood would turn to water, such as trickles down from the snows of Parnassus. Pit me against a mortal man and I will do my utmost, but to wait about in a bull's hide, flicking his tail with some sort of handle, while very Iniquity crouches to attack and then rushes at us in demonical fury—Heaven above and Hell below, I would rather defy the Gorgon, who turns men to stone! Remember how I stood and shrieked while you killed the two big snakes. I was only a little child, but a child is father to the man, as far as wild beasts go."

Then up spoke Dyctus, in his quiet, forceful way.

"Heracles, you will now invite great Actaeon to be your companion. If he should decline, I pray you let not your heart be sad. I will go with you in joy and pride. And mark you, neither Actaeon nor your brother owes the debt of hate to Iniquity that cankers my heart, and hence they do not lust for this consummation. How many of my master's cattle, that I knew by name, that lapped barley from my hand, have been torn by his shining fangs and devoured? And, mark you, Snag Tooth was my grandsire's brother, and I am the only living heir of the feud of blood."

"Then you shall go in my place if Heracles agrees," Actaeon cried in a great voice. "Heracles, I was prepared to stand this gaff, for I killed a lion in the thorn before I ever breached a maiden in a haycock, and I can still remember that Iniquity is yet a lion by nature, and a monster only by attainment. Dyctus can play the part better than I. He knows the mien and habits of a bull as he grazes, how fast he moves, how often he snatches grass. And now name your choice, to ease our troubled hearts."

"Either of you would be stout companions, but since he has volunteered, I choose Dyctus."

"And thereby wanes my hope of ever lolling in Elysian Fields," Actaeon told us with a wry laugh. "Still, I believe you have chosen wisely."

Then we four pressed one another's hands, and straightway began to prepare for our great stratagem.

5

Right Doer had pledged me long ago that he would do the thinking while I did the main of the heaving. This was a different kettle of fish from rolling great boulders down a cliffside, but the principle remained the same. It was Actaeon, Dyctus, and I who busied our hands and feet, while Right Doer thought of ways and means to obtain our goals, ever insisting on as near perfection as we could attain. Since we would set our trap in knee-high grass, we need not concern ourself with the images' lower legs and hoofs. On the other hand, the remainder must be light, easy to propel, and bear enough resemblance to a bull to loose the raging arrow of Iniquity's charge. Our main difficulty was to obtain all these, yet have good loopholes, room for me to carry a four-foot spear, and some kind of door through which I could pass.

Since time out of mind, we Greeks have been famed as ingenious craftsmen. Mainly our hands are sinewy and delicate; our handicraft, traded in Phoenicia, Persia, Egypt, and the outer islands, reaps us a greater profit than the scanty olive oil and wine that we can spare from our boards. Other drovers lent us their skills, and what seemed at first almost a hopeless undertaking began to take fair shape. By the jerk of one string the head and the neck of the image fell free, through which opening I could spring with a short, stout spear that was dagger-sharp.

True, on one thrust the lives of both Dyctus and me appeared to hang. The fact remained that a frontal attack on a hornless beast was a common act of Iniquity; we meant to invite it, maneuver to meet it, and pray to great Pan to bring it about. And since this God of Herdsmen was the most manifest of any in this wilderness, hardly a night passed without our hearing his wondrous pipes, we promised him—no other God, who might have other irons in the fire—a sacrifice if we lived to make it, with a light dinner but a great outpouring of heart-warming wine.

In these weeks a wondrous, hopeful fact became apparent. It did not seem likely we would have to set our trap day after weary day to attract the enemy's notice. His habits had changed markedly since he had slain Snag Tooth, and the only cause that our common sense would accept was the most thrilling imaginable: that the old man's dying thrust with the dagger-pointed arrow had dealt his slayer a shallow, yet somewhat disabling, wound. Before, he had walked lame on his left foot; now he favored the right. This was apparent only when he paced the pastures, not when he charged; we supposed he forgot the pain in his surging ferocity, then recalled it full well after his bloody feast. No longer he chased the herds in sport. He killed no more herdsmen, a sport that had let bloom his iniquitous pride. And he confined his cattle killing almost entirely to three pastures below those immediately under the mountain, where the soil was richer, the grass softer, and there were fewer stones to afflict his wounded foot. Finally, he almost invariably killed in deep twilight, picking a cow from the flank of the herd—and in this grayness our ruse had a better chance to win.

Invariably he slept at midday in a great thicket of thorn, thirty or more acres in extent, as bleak as it was black; why he eschewed the weak, welcome sunlight on the rocky hilltops we could not satisfactorily explain. True, he knew that no bright pointed thing, harder than stone and fastened on a stick, could sting him there, and that he could attack from ambush—one leap and kill any enemy that came nigh his lair. Perhaps he sought rest in his war with his frail, forked foes until his new wound would heal, then he would come forth with his red mane ablaze, and once more become a name for wanton slaughter.

We four Thebans in deadly pact against him could not help but take not great, but warming comfort in his debility, believing without much base that it increased Dyctus' and my chances to survive our grappling with him on an evening not far off. Even this tepid comfort cooled somewhat when a stallion of fearful stature, long teeth, and knife-sharp front hoofs escaped from some horse breeder on the plain and wandered by moonlight into the pasture below the thorn, was set upon by Iniquity, and died instantly with a broken neck from Iniquity's stroke.

That same moon waxed round and dazzling bright in the frosty nights. On the day before she was to rise in full girth and glory, Dyctus and I went into our stuffed bull, a curious diminutive kinsman of the wooden horse of forever fame, walked him about, learned to turn or wheel with ease and swiftness, practiced signals, and made sure that the mechanism that freed me for battle worked without fail. We had long forsaken the notion of having him stand five feet, the height of the bull who, unknowingly, had bequeathed us his handsome hide. This would have made us crouch where there was little room, and too, this would be dreadfully tiring to our backs and limbs. Instead, we stood straight, the disguise reaching only to our knees, which would not matter since we intended to make our trial in two-foot grass. That such tall prey would intimidate the great Iniquity, neither Actaeon or the drovers believed for an instant. Indeed it was more likely to attract his attention. But thus too, the uneasiness of Dyctus or myself over his swift and easy killing of the great stallion had a good side to it as far as Iniquity's courage was concerned, since the quarry had stood fully eighteen hands.

Iniquity was rarely known to emerge from the thorn until the winter sun was dipping over the low westward hills. We took our stand an hour before then, prepared for a four-hour wait if heavy clouds did not hide the soon-rising moon and a black sea of night drive us to firelight. The total weight of our costume was not more than fifty pounds, roughly divided between us. That my companion would become tired, either of body or brain, I had no thought. He was of somewhat slighter build than I, not quite so tall, seasoned to long labor and long vigils. Without great pride and a buoyant soul he would not have volunteered for the perilous office. If I were appointed to choose a typical Greek for some great sculptor to carve in imperishable marble, I would well take Dyctus.

The shadows lengthened swiftly. Drovers were gathering in their distant herds to lay them down close and compact in the glimmer of watch fires; and now and then a calf cried or an old cow mooed, although mainly they moved in silence. I wondered if some of them caught an occasional whiff of their enemy, brought on the shifting breeze; if so, they were used to it and could do naught about it, so they quietly did what they were told. Dyctus and I kept close watch on the dark edge of the thorn forest down the wind and about two hundred paces from us, for this was the side from which Iniquity usually emerged. The fact remained that he did not always take this way, though we took comfort in the fact that no matter which way he came, he would attack against the wind.

One moment it was late afternoon. The next, it was early evening, the clear sky turned sallow, the grass dark gray instead of sear; the pine trees, of such dark and lonesome green when other greenery had died, looked raven-black. And then Dyctus nudged me happily in my back with his elbow. Over the boldly rugged summit of an eastern hill, the merest glint of silver had caught his quick eye. I too saw it, the topmost arc of the round moon, and swiftly it increased, and then a whole section showed itself, and then with what seemed great swiftness, the whole heaved up, gloriously shining on the world, and the dying daylight appeared to revive like winter's half-dead herbage at Persephone's return. Whatever happened now, Dyctus and I would have light to fight by, and not perish in the dark.

And then I saw something against the thorn, a little less dark than its background. Dyctus drew a sharp breath and held it, for the object had not yet moved, and we could not be sure. Then suddenly it had moved ten feet, perhaps in a playful pounce, so happy the thing was to be rid of sleep, the weak brother of strong death, and to have the whole luminous night to range, hunt, kill, and feast.

"Move forward to catch his eye," I whispered, for we had stopped our slow, grazing pace at sight of the newcomer to the scene. I suppose it was in wonder and surprise, perhaps because we had feared that this evening of all evenings he would change his ways and we would catch no glimpse of him, and after a heart-heavy wait we would return alive, but desolate, to our camp.

And only an instant later both Dyctus and I knew full well that Iniquity had seen us.

His head had been turning as he stood and stretched, and suddenly it stopped. His tail made a quick sideways lash, left and right, and then began to straighten and stiffen. He walked a distance at a rapid pace, and then disappeared behind a little thicket of aspen trees. He did not emerge, and then I thanked the Gods that Dyctus and I had explored this whole area with sore care, for that saved us a great falling of our hearts. Well we knew where he had gone, and our hopes did not wane and instead waxed until they cramped our bosoms. Behind that copse was the head of a dry watercourse, and it was unthinkable that he had not entered it to walk down its graveled bed to fetch him nearer to us. This would lead him to a region of scattered thickets which he could enter unseen, and through this he would surely creep until he had us in close survey, after which he would either attack or turn away.

"Watch to the left of the lone cedar tree," I told Dyctus. "If he charged from the right of it he would have to cross the wind." For Actaeon had insisted I must never lose sight of one verity of lion conduct, which was that no lion ever rushed to kill except where the wind would blow back his rank scent, instead of into the nostrils of his chosen prey.

Then my companion and I began what my mind told me was a wait of some minutes, although my heart felt no great strain, for it never doubted now that the beast was moving nearer, creeping through the brushwood, to some place where he would make a last, brief pause. Then, if his beast brain gave the command to his tense and quivering muscles, something like a flash of fire would dart to them, and they would hurl him forward, and he would be committed to the attack. That place would not be farther than a hundred paces from us. It was the way of the lion to make his rush to kill short and incredibly swift, advancing either in ferocious bounds or in a scuttling run close to the ground, depending on whether the terrain was rough or smooth.

Night deepened in those moments, but Dyctus and I cared naught, for Hecate could not stop the moon from shining, and indeed, as she climbed higher her effulgence grew, and her silver sheen lay out and far, and brought sharply to our eyes all the features of the nearby land- scape. And we loved her, Selene, sister of Helios, and would make her an offering at this very spot, perhaps build her a temple here, and here travelers that she had befriended could pay her due. And now Dyctus stiffened, for he caught a glimpse of something a little way behind a bed of tall, dry reeds that had grown on ground swampy in wet weather, but now sun-baked and iron-hard.

"Did you see Iniquity?"

"I think so."

What he had seen was well to the left of the cedar tree, in brushy ground on the near side of the watercourse, and if it were Iniquity he had followed the pebbly path only about thirty yards ere his ferocity had overcome him and he had sprung out. And I thought to turn a little to the left, to face the spot more squarely, only to be afraid that the movement would be awkward and raise a ghostly doubt in Iniq- uity's mind, and he would snarl and make off. So I led on very slowly on the same course, intending to make the turn when the charge had been well launched, as might a brave bull who knows death rushes upon him, but defies it still.

Dyctus and I waited a moment more, almost unable to breathe, so taut and full were our breasts, and with hearts pounding. Then we heard a sound unlike any I had ever heard before, although I think it was like that described by sailors who have weathered great storms, and which is the sound of stout sails being torn apart by the wind. Instantly I knew its only possible cause was the rush of a great beast through the beds of reeds. We turned a little toward him. I gripped my four-foot spear, sharp as a viper's tooth, and then Iniquity cleared the bed in one beauteous, awful bound. Now we saw him in his dread magnificence, an enormous lion, appearing black as Erebus under the startled moon, as he rushed on to kill.

Perhaps he was fifteen paces distant when I pulled the cord, perhaps ten paces. No God who hated me made the mechanism fail; the front of the image fell to the ground and I stepped forth to meet my terrible enemy, my spear leveling and whipping back, and a great power rushing into my right shoulder and arm. And as Iniquity lunged, rising on his rear legs, the weapon drove forward in a full-powered thrust, its bronze head glittering in the moonlight, and its point touched the taut, iron-hard muscles, at the base of his neck, at the thrust's end.

I had struck an instant too soon, but it mattered not, because the beast's surging weight hurled him forward till the whole head was buried deep, and my arm stood the prodigious strain. And thereby Iniquity came upon his death, although it was not instantaneous, and he fell only to try to rise again, and then spun in wild circles, biting the air and mightily roaring until his gushing blood choked back the sound. And then again he fell, belly down, and still he had strength to raise his head and gaze upon us in implacable hatred, deathless in all the eons that Hades would endure and Time would turn. And, as the great green jewels of his eyes slowly dimmed their light, I could not taunt him for his death at my hands, and indeed must praise him.

"Go down, Iniquity; cross the river and enter the adamant gate, and again Cerberus who guards it will crouch down and perhaps whimper; and in those dim halls, walk with your proud stride to the throne of King Hades. For I pledge you that he will receive you with honor, for surely you were the greatest lion that ever trod the turf, greater than the monstrous Chimaera, breathing fire. Go with my hate because you slew Snag Tooth, yet go with my love which I cannot withhold from so mighty an adversary. And some day not far off, as Time is measured, when we are both shadows, mute and bereft of memory, we will both drink of blood poured into a pit as a sacrifice to the departed, and then we will recall this moment of dire battle, and you shall have due praise from Dyctus, Right Doer, and the mighty hunter Actaeon. And now the glare in your eyes dies swiftly. Only a spark remains. When it dies, only a great carcass will lie in the bloody grass. But the birds of death that hopped wildly and took wing at your softest growl shall not strip your bones of their massive muscles, or tear your great guts, or peck your iron-hard heart. I, Heracles, will take your hide as my mead of victory, and perhaps wear it ever as a robe of honor, but what else remains will be deep buried, and some of the blood of the sacrifice we will make to the Gods and Goddess that I invoked will be poured on your grave.

"Now the last glimmer of light goes out. You have gone hence, never to return. And the cattle begin to low as they lie listening, for they smell fresh blood, and the watchmen feed their fires, knowing not whose blood it is, yours or mine. And the moon, still low in the sky on this night of nights, peers down to take note of your great corpse, and the Olympians who perforce gazed down upon your death go back to their golden bowls, and once more the Graces dance before them, and the night is serene."

And then I put my arm about Dyctus' shoulders, for he was weeping in happiness and from overstrain, and then we heard yells. Looking across the pasture, we saw Right Doer and Actaeon running to us, out of the covert where I had bade them wait; and a great happiness came upon me, not unmixed with sadness I could not understand, and I too wept.

CHAPTER EIGHT

LASCIVIOUS INTERLUDE

1

Dyctus borrowed fire from the camp of Aturis, a curious article in which to trade, I was thinking, since it had no weight over and above the stick of wood it fed upon, it lost its value and identity as soon as it ignited the fuel that the borrower had cut and laid, and yet it would be worth a ton of gold, diamonds, and rubies to a drover lost on a windy mountainside on a night of bitter cold.

Truly we had little need of it for the watch my three friends and I would keep tonight, since the weather was mild and the moonlight fell unstinted in a silver flood. Still, we would like to glance now and then at the small dancing bonfire as we went about our tasks, taking pleasure in its small brisk leapings and its soft pops, as though it were a little puppy fire compared to the great hound of a fire that billowed up and roared. Also, Aturis, who came on the run with Dyctus, had brought a shoulder of veal, which we might have occasion to spit and bake in the hungry midnight hour, for none of us four had supped, and it would be no light work peeling off Iniquity's great pelt, fleshing it, then digging a deep grave and burying his carcass as I had promised.

And very presently we perceived that we could make good use not of a shoulder of veal, but of a whole beef. I know not how the word passed, unless some of the drovers in nearby pastures had heard the marauder's mighty roaring ere he cast his soul. If so, they had visited one another's camps to ask its meaning, and some had deemed that it heralded new calamity, and a few bold fellows had dared guess the truth. But all had marked the strange peace of the night; the moon rising in glory in a cloudless sky; the biting winds muzzled and silent. So when their flocks and herds had become quiet, dozing in a strange serenity, then one by one, or in little groups, they ventured to leave their fires and make their way, keeping to open land as far as possible, yet braving thickets and stony hillsides, to our bivouac.

When they arrived not one shouted, called on the name of a God, danced about, or laughed wildly. All stood and stared, half doubting their own eyes, and moved a little closer for a better view, and now and then shot quick glances into my face. When my party started skinning, and must turn the carcass or roll it over, they must have ached to help us with the labor, but none did so but one old hard-bitten shepherd. He was the father of the wild-eyed woman Ismene, whose husband of one year had been killed by Iniquity. Since then, some God, perhaps Dionysus, had given her the gift of prophecy, to come upon her in certain seasons. I suppose that the other men thought it would bring ill fortune to lay hands on the mighty corpse after the Beast had prevailed over them in life, and since a stranger and an alien had fetched him his death.

We had good reasons for the skinning and burying tonight instead of waiting for sunrise. The pelt was easier to peel from the unstiffened carcass, and we did not want a jackal or a fox to tear or to snatch the flesh of their fallen king. When, with final strokes, we skinned the forelegs, and when they too showed fish-belly white in the moonlight while the pelt lay in a glossy heap, I must gape with the other yokels at the muscular growth revealed. A very Atlas, I thought, must pay due to the mighty biceps, and it was no wonder that he could break any bull's neck with a tap of his forepaw. And now we set to fleshing the skin, cutting away every vestige of white fat, and skinning out all four paws, a task which would take us half the night, since we were resolved that no slackness on our part would cause its ruin.

And now Dyctus spoke quietly to his neighbor, and the latter to his friends, and some of the men went back to their camps to get bronze-headed picks and shovels. With these, abundant hands fell to, to dig the grave that must be deep and wide to hold its mighty occupant. At this task our fellows felt no fear, for they knew that the dread ghost of Iniquity would rejoice that his carcass was not left as a feast for the birds of death. And now others vanished on an errand I did not know, until I saw them returning with stores of meat and drink, so that all here could feast ere we departed hence. And I deemed that in the five years that Iniquity had ravaged the pastures above the Nemean Plain there was never a night of so much roaming back and forth from camp to camp.

We cleaned the skull inside and out, removing by bronze knives or tongues of flame any part that would spoil; and with this task finished, we were ready to roll the great corpse into the dug pit. It fell with a thud, but I reckoned the ghost of Iniquity barely heard the sound, so far had it sped; but mayhap it felt the first shovels of dirt drum against the flesh—lately so hot, now so swiftly chilling; lately so terribly living, now so inert. When the grave had been filled in, we fixed the skull on a stout stick and planted the stick deep at the head of the grave, and it would become a landmark mentioned in men's speech perhaps for a hundred years. Truly, few remnants of dead folk are more durable than their skulls; and I reckoned that foxes and jackals, and perhaps human wayfarers traveling late would walk wide of the haunted spot.

Now our visitors began to put on spits, and set to baking the meat they had brought for a parting feast. Some put portions of their offering directly into the flame so it would be consumed, and the delectable smells would waft upward to various Gods and Goddesses to whom they owed thanks, or who might owe them punishment for derelictions. My own head was feeling empty, not wanting to confront as yet the unknown future, and I found myself dwelling on the woman Ismene, who sat quietly gazing into the fire. At first I merely wondered what she was thinking. She had married at thirteen, Dyctus had told me, the year before the coming of Iniquity to these pasturages, and for her this arrival had been most dread, for she had dreamed that he would slay her husband within twelve months, which had duly come to pass. She had never remarried, and furthermore, a thing strange and almost unnatural in a fiery young woman of the camps, had never lain with a lover, passing or permanent. Instead, she dwelt with her sire, eating the rough food and doing the hard work of a drover and shepherd, standing long vigils, braving danger, performing these duties as proudly and as well as would the run of men.

Eying her with pleasure, I took the notion that in some ways she resembled Iole. Although my eyes had a hard time convincing my common sense, the fact remained. The two were not at all alike in feature or closely alike in structure. Iole's hair was a red flame like Iniquity's mane; Ismene's hair was so pale yellow that, except for its gloss and other signs of youth, it might be taken for the snowy tresses, faintly discolored by the smoke of the cooking fires, of an old woman. I hardly noticed her pretty nose because of staring at her mouth, with its fully rounded lips and brooding, sulky look. Her most remarkable feature was her eyes, which the word "wild" fitted well, the outer points being raised like a wolf's, their color a brilliant green, as are the eyes of prowling beasts when a torch beam strikes them, and their whole effect more lupine than human. The first guess that some rude beholders would make was that her sire had been a wolf or leopard, or that even a young lion had couched her mother. Tales of such matings are common in Greek lore, perhaps the best known being that of the Queen of Minos' passion for the Cretan Bull, and of their child, the dread Minotaur, whom Theseus slew. Also, it was told that a leopard had sought to console Oenone on Mount Ida when her lover Paris deserted her for peerless Helen. Even so, I could never believe in such abnormal birth, from noting that even sheep and goats, so alike in general aspect, never interbred, nor horses and cattle, and in fact no species farther apart than mares and asses.

Why, then, did Ismene make me think of Iole? I found the answer at last—that both girls had the wondrous limbs and supple bodies caused by much running, leaping, and other exercise in open air. When our meal was cooked, I found myself watching her with great pleasure as she made away with half a shoulder of young mutton. Her bites were darting and wonderfully incisive; she chewed the meat very little, swallowing it in hunks that made her slim throat work. Grease on her face was as pleasing to see as on a pretty child, the pleasure arising, I thought, from seeing such a charming person put down food so good, so utterly necessary, and on which the greatest folk set the greatest store.

I moved to where I could speak in an undertone to Ismene's sire.

"Pray tell me, father, if Ismene will prophesy tonight."

"It is not very likely, Heracles—at least before this great company. The gift of prophecy did not begin to come upon her until her marriage, or be of much count until her husband was slain, and it becomes manifest only when she is in high passion of anger, sorrow, happiness, or the like."

"I would think that her passion would be high now that her husband's slayer lies dead."

"Perhaps it would be so, if it had come as a surprise, but only last night she saw it in a dream. And it might still be high, without her giving much sign. I note that her face is composed, and she trembles not, but on several previous occasions when a spell was coming on her, she ate as she is eating now, with great fierceness. It may be that on such occasions she feels the need of storing strength for some great trial."

And then our speaking of passion in general made my mind wander to one passion in particular. Perhaps it was only a wish being father to the thought, possibly it was true divination; in either case I could not deny an inkling that in making love she would be as a summer storm breaking on Parnassus' summit—with thunder and lightning of her own making, great gales blowing through her, black clouds lowering, and rain as from a sea turned upside down. Although I had not pledged troth to Megara, the magic of her tender yielding bound me still, and I had thought to remain continent until we met again or until, should the impossible come to pass, Iole should give herself to me, a gift I could no more refuse than the gift of air I breathed. For Iole had the touch of a Goddess, almost the ways of one, and somehow a like power over mortals.

Ismene had reminded me of Iole. A priestess and a prophetess were strongly akin. In a measure Iole held both offices, and Ismene, too, held both, as she was surely the priestess of great Pan, God of the Herds and of their wild grazing grounds, and I reckoned she had talked with nymphs, and had been chased by many an ugly satyr. And even as I daydreamed of Iole, I could not summon up the faith that she would ever, even when she had quit the shrine, lie in big, blunt arms like mine. So if Ismene would consent for our mutual pleasure, why should I not invite her to come with me, away in the moonlight, to a bed of grass?

Desire rose in me like a fever caught from the poisonous air of marshes, but no chill rattled my bones, and instead a delicious warmth infused my veins as my gaze wandered first to her open and disclosed charms, a generous array since she had removed work clothes and all others except her tunic in her sensible accord with the mild weather and the glow of the cooking fire. Her skin looked as though it had been polished by the wind, and the rosy gleams cast there by the leaping flame in ever lovely change would cause old Tithonus to mistake her for Eos and to remember his great passion, now so dim and cold, and to call it back, and between the first glimmer of dawn and the bold sun's upheaving, he would wax young again.

Some nymph had told Apollo that a slave-born shepherdess of Nemea had prophetic powers, given to her perhaps by the Earth Goddess, who knew so well the print of her light foot. Although these powers were not great and rarely employed, he took note of her, for prophecy was his own province, and I thought he had come to her as she lay asleep under the summer moon, had scanned from all points of vantage her tranquil face and unclothed form, and he had touched her here and there with fingers light as the moon's own, at which she dreamed unearthly dreams in gorgeous color. When she rose at dawn, her sire had perceived that she looked not the same, although he could not find words to tell the difference and could only make haste away, lest his blundering questions anger one of the Gods.

She was still not as beautiful as Iole, who dwelt with a Goddess, or as lovely as dark-eyed Megara. But the beauty that she had was strangely vivid, and the firelight caressed it in sensuous joy. For a while I was spellbound by little things, such as the softness behind her knees that her crossed legs revealed, and the hollows under her arms as she clasped hands behind her head, and the yielding flesh under her collarbones at the base of her straight, proud neck. I could well afford to give a year of my life, I thought, if I could give it all to dalliance with Ismene; and truly I would choose this humbly born girl over any chieftain's daughter I had ever seen, except two, or any latter-day Helen whom Aphrodite might award me as my mead of honor.

It happened she was sitting a little apart from her nearest companions, her father and another old drover who this minute were breaking bones to suck out marrow. Now was my chance, and a chill of fear sped through me as I rose to seize it; and in the few steps I took to cross the firelit grass to gain her side, a bashfulness came upon me, a shamefacedness as the country people say, and I feared to my wits' end that she would refuse my invitation. Aye, I had meant to invite her to come with me, speaking easily and confidently, but my throat tightened and I stammered the proposal with the suavity and courtliness not of Paris, Helen's lover, but of a country lout.

"Will you walk with me in the moonlight, Ismene?"

"Into the grass, you mean, away from fire and shelter from the growing chill of the night?"

Still I did not feel as balked as I would have expected, perhaps because of her dim smile, which served to continue our intercourse, and which somehow suggested triumph.

"Well, where could we go?" I blurted out.

"Why not to my father's camp? I have a hut there of my own, with a fireplace, and creature comforts, and a bowl of mulled wine."

"Gladly. Will you go now? Or do you wish to wait till the feast is over?"

"I have waited too long already, Heracles, for this moment. I knew it would come at last—but I did not know when. Let us go now."

She raised her arm in a gesture of farewell to her companions. All the faces that turned to us, mainly well-weathered faces, showed bright with pleasure over my going with her, and the eyes gazing at us looked beady with imagination's light. I marked only one of the company who did not give us the favor of his glance. He was a tall young drover, one of the best of all these pastures, who continued to stare into the fire, yet I saw no sign of ill feeling in his manly countenance. Rather his expression seemed one of relief after long strain. The cords of his sinewy neck stood out.

2

Ismene seemed to have nothing to say to me as she walked in my fore, with a carriage as light and free as Iole's. Deeply perplexed by what she had said, still I dared not question her yet, lest I break some sort of a trance into which she had passed, and she might change her mind. The danger of this appeared to recede when we had crossed the nearer pastures and came nigh her sire's. Then besides its lightness and freedom, there seemed to be a lilt in her walk; also her head was high, her hair luminous under the moon, her back wonderfully straight. When now and then I caught up with her I saw in her face something I could not read. It was not pride, which, by thinking backward, I supposed would be natural enough over a camp girl's capture of the killer of Iniquity. Rather it seemed to me a deep, secretive exultation.

We came to her hut of baked brick with a thatched roof. It seemed snug enough for weathering the most bitter winter gale. We went in to find a few coals, red as a king's rubies, buried in the ashes, and on these Ismene lay dry leaves and grass, and blew upon them until they blazed; then to the little fire she fed fuel, carefully, as a mother feeds her babe lest it choke. Before I knew it a blithe little fire was leaping from the stone hearth in the center of the room.

Then she spread sheepskin robes, a fair heap of them, and with a little motion of her hand, she bade me seat myself. Then she swiftly heated an ewer of water, and with a woolen cloth she washed my hands and face and neck, and rubbed a pleasant-scented oil, that I guessed had been made with civet, into the skin. But she did not bathe my big chest, nor did her hands linger at my nipples and in my armpits as Megara's had once done. Still I was in no way discouraged and thought she was waiting for me to break the silence.

"Ismene, what did you mean when you said you had waited long for me to seek your company? Could it be that you had seen it in a vision?"

"Heracles, I had no vision, ever, of your seeking my company. But for five years I have had a vision of my seeking yours—although then you were a faceless figure that was fated to kill Iniquity. I could not marry, I could not make love, I could only wait. That was the command of my husband, whom I married when I was thirteen, who was slain by Iniquity when I was fourteen. Late in that same month his ghost came to me in a dream and told me when at last vengeance was his and mine, and Iniquity lay cold in death, I must give my first favor to his slayer. You are his slayer, and you asked me to come with you, saving me the shame of first asking you to come with me. So all the terms are met save one. If that one too is met, I am free of the bond of the dead."

"What term is not met? I pray you tell me, because my head is thick. I think I know what you mean but I cannot be sure."

"Will you lie with me tonight, Heracles, Slayer of Iniquity?"

When I hesitated, deeply wounded that her favor would not be free, that she would give it only at the command of her husband returning to her bedside from dim Hades, she misunderstood my feelings, and thought I did not crave her warm and vital body for my mead of honor. At once she sprang up and with fox-quick motions of her hands, loosed and let fall her tunic. And now she stood naked in the searching gleam of the fire, more beautifully shaped than I had divined, long of limb, narrow of thighs, with the deep high bosoms that we called Minoan, although I knew not why. Her waist was small and tightly bound by its elastic skin. With a deft movement, she let her braided hair fall low, and instantly its plaits came out and let it flow free, wondrously gold, although of a paler hue than a sea monster guarding treasure had ever seen, and if he would see it he would leave his ancient post in the green depths, and his adamant heart would break in unrequited love.

"See, I am not ill graced," Ismene cried out, her eyes gleaming with tears. "I am no king's daughter, nor yet a peerless priestess of Artemis; I am a slave and a daughter of a slave. I cannot strum the harp or ply the needle in making wondrous robes of silk. I have never in my whole life seen silk, let alone felt its smoothness. Yet some God or Goddess—perhaps great Pan, who frequents this wilderness, possibly straw-haired Demeter, who has care of the folk and hence of their cattle and sheep—more likely a mere satyr, who saw me from his covert and who knew my story, begged consent of his master to make me please the eyes of Iniquity's killer, whereby I might find freedom from the shadowy dead. Heracles, do I not please your eyes? If so, why are they dark with sadness? In these five years I have become again as a virgin. You will hardly know you are not untying my maiden knot. Yet well I remember all the play of love, all the feats of muscle, made possible by my young strength, that my husband relished. I will be no supine compliant, but a fit mate, this one and only night, for great Heracles. So we will spend these hours wooing and being wooed; and when you drift to sleep, I will suffer in patience only a few minutes, then rewaken you. Now give me your hand."

"Before that, give me an answer to one more question. What caused you to speak of the King's daughter and of a priestess of Artemis, both of whom are in my life?"

"Heracles, I saw the dark-eyed girl—Megara is her name—when she came here. I saw the priestess when my father and I went down to Orchomenus at the autumn equinox to deliver forty of our master's cattle and eighty of his sheep unto King Eurytus, which were forfeit because our master is a Theban and hence must pay the mighty tribute. I knew then that you loved Megara more, but lay deeper under the spell of Iole. Nay, it was no prophetic vision. It was only the seeing of my eyes as you yearned for the long-legged priestess who runs like a barren doe—even so, I would like to race with her over rough ground—and as you ached for your beautiful visitor and then went with her to bathe in the Pool of Truth. I too ached that day, and fiercely itched, not for my betrothed who has waited so long in patience, but for you. I had seen you slay Antaeus. It had come to me even then, before Dyctus entreated the King, that you would be ap-

pointed to slay Iniquity, and so become my couchmate for one night,
and so set me free. Now, I pray you, look not into the past, but into
the onrushing hours that will speed so fast away whether to my profit
or my loss, for your good sport or for swinish sleep. I pray you speak
no more with words except a few gasped out, or softly whispered, for
words are the enemies of love. They are like rain that drenches and
puts out a small, orange-colored, new-kindled fire. Again I ask you—
take my hand."

I did so, and she led it over her whole body, pausing now and then
to let me feel a band of muscle under pearly skin, the stout but-
tresses of her bosom, which no babe's hungry nuzzling or the head of
a sleeping lover could indent, the lovely soft round of their summits
with dugs erect and rose-red, in contrast with her snow-white chest.
And she led my hand from her tender throat down the upper side of
her arm, then up the inside to the hollow, moist and warm.

And now I perceived a ceremonious aspect in her actions, and that
she was guiding my hand in a fixed route according to some ancient
rite. Of all the folkways in Greece, those of shepherds and drovers
were the oldest. Rhadamanthus had taught Right Doer and me that
these antedated the very ancient rituals of corn- and winegrowers, logically enough since, while many barbarian people planted no seed, he
knew of none without flocks and herds. And then my hazed brain
stirred a little and I was almost certain the present ceremony was
called the Passage of Hands, of which Fold Watcher, the old shepherd
I had known in the pasturage under Parnassus, had told me. He had
said that ages ago it had been performed in public, a bride's sign to
the groom that he possessed her wholely; and it was practiced even
yet when the newly wedded lovers had partaken of nuptial meats and
repaired to their lodging.

She led my hand up the back of her neck, over her scalp, across her
ears, and down her face, lingering a little at her eyes and nose, with a
decided pause at her mouth when she lapped my palm. Then she
brought it down both sides in turn, across the curve of her belly that
is ever a joy to lovers, picture painters, and sculptors, and up the
slightly curved indenture of her spine. At this point she deftly unfas-
tened my tunic with her left hand, let it fall, and as she continued
to guide my hand in what became the most sensual and lusty part of
the ritual, her own hand imitated mine in every movement.

If I had needed being won over to her proposal, I would have become her passionate captive before the final passages of the ceremony were half complete. Half kneeling, she brought my hand to her naked foot, led it up the outside of one leg and across the top of her buttocks to the outside of the other. Then she caused it to wander, very slowly, up the inside, down the same path, and up the other to a nesting place, after which she well knew by my scant breath and dizzy tremblings she could trust it to find its own way to all other pillage.

Then she hung about my neck, and despite her slight strength compared to mine, she bore me down on the sheepskin bed; and then there followed a night of love such as I had never pictured in my most passionate dreams. What she had told me proved true; if she had not said otherwise, I would never have doubted that I broke through her maiden gate. Five years of yearning, crammed with hungry, lonely wakings in the night, of daydreaming in the summer sun, of savage itchings as she watched the rams and ewes in concourse and, more acute, great surging bulls with their compliant cows, and, what she could hardly stand to witness, screaming stallions with mettlesome mares in nearby pastures—five years of aching restraint she relieved in four hours of night and three more hours after morning broke. We knew of its breaking by fresh airs and pleasant smells, and enough chill to make us love still more the warmed skins of our bedmates, but very little light sifted through the smoke vents in the roof.

I reckoned that I fell to sleep six times, and was five times wakened by her, never to her disappointment, and from my sixth nap I summoned myself, to find her snuggled against my back in heavy sleep, and from this I called her. I had been afraid she might strike me or claw me with her nails, for I had heard that was the way of girls living arduous lives in the wilderness when molested in sound slumber, doing so not from any natural viciousness, but to drive away the thief of their precious, life-giving rest. Instead, she wooed me more ardently than before, perhaps because she knew that this would be our last joining ere she must rise and go to the field, but more likely because a spell was on her that I had not seen.

In our whisperings in the dark, she had told me that she was one of the leaders of a band of some hundred women who at certain seasons forgot their duties to homestead and field and went into the mountains to worship Dionysus. They went forth wildly arrayed, bearing flowers and greenery and jugs of wine, and often he presented himself to them as a beautiful youth with dark hair flowing; and they shouted and danced and sang in wild abandon and, it was feared, sometimes they caught goats, and tore them to pieces with their naked hands, and devoured the raw meat. In these moments of ecstasy Ismene often prophesied, in wild and rambling speech but with perfect truth. When I saw her eyes ablaze with green light and the wild expression on her face, I thought she might prophesy now.

And when we were locked in lecherous embrace, and the rhythm of our strong, slow thrusts were fetching us with delicious protraction toward the certain goal, indeed toward victory over Time and Fate and even Death, because for one moment we would have an eternity of life more violent and explosive than the life of a lion as it fells its prey, a change came over Ismene. Even now our lives were strong as an immortal God's, intensely realized; each knew the other and himself as only Gods may know such things; and it must be that Ismene knew even more, that which is beyond the natural for folk to know, which is the winding path of the future. Her eyes had rolled up so that I saw only a narrow crescent of the whites, gleaming like polished silver. Her moanings gave way to half-breathed words, disordered, yet of surmisable meaning.

"Labors, labors," she murmured. "Only the beginning has been made. Deep waters flooding, a secret of the Gods disclose. Mares that eat not grass, but where falls the vengeance? Not on unknowing beasts but on a king. Is it Eurytus? Not yet. He will live long, yet. The stag with golden horns. So men tell, and for what use is one prong broken from the branch? But that is only a drop added to a cup already flowing full. And death comes to a dear companion. It will be told that he gazed upon naked divinity, and so he was slain. And ere the leaves have fallen thrice you too will go down to Hades."

"Three times? Is that all? Look well, Goddess who speaks with Ismene's lips, yet speak plain."

"You will return thence. There you will see your mighty sire, but know him not. Fire sweeping and raging, and the ground heaving up, but it settles again, and the folk have been served. The little birds that kill men in the swampy woods cannot make their nests, and so they die, and again the folk have been served. Another journey is long. I hear the crackle of long-fed fires, and the red rock is melted, and I hear the sound of hammers, and again the folk have been served. Because of these and other servings unto the folk, you will never die. If your body is burned, and that I cannot see, for I will not see, your name will live forever on men's tongues, while the hills crumble away to a level plain. I can speak no more. Torture me no more, Spirit who gazes through the black curtains of Time, and who has seized my tongue and lips. Aye, I did the Passage of Hands to my night's lover; up out of the lost lore of love I called it back, but it was only to make him lie with me, so I might be free from the dead for my remaining days, and I did not mean to call you up from your mossy grave. Heracles, make haste! The dead stand thick about our bedside, and she who precoursed Isis bends and whispers in my ear, and she will not go until this bliss and pain have passed. Make haste, I beg you."

"Answer one question and you may have peace. Am I fated to wed Megara of the great eyes, or Iole of the clean limbs, of whom you ever remind me, and whose passion, yet inert, would be as great as yours?"

"It is a great passion truly, devouring and relentless. But she seeks to gain what I seek to lose, to bind fast what I would unbind. The wound on your arm, it is only a scratch. Why, there is more blood on my own lips where I have bit them. I will not look at it, hear me, Heracles. I will not, and to you, Spirit, I close my ears. Go from me, Spirit. In the name of sweet Demeter of the Corn, ever greater than you, forever your enemy, I bid you go. And now you begin to fade. Dimming too are the troupe of the dead who follow you. Heracles! The sun is high and shining, and we must soon arise. Yield me my desire, slayer of Iniquity. Hold me fast in your great arms in this last moment of our union. Oh, that is the way, payment is made, come to me, make me your own once more to break the last strand of the dark rope that has bound me unto Death. Demeter, Dionysus, Pan—all the Gods of earth—take heed as I break free to follow you into the sweet fields, to run upon the mountain with no cramped heart, to dance to the pipes. *Heracles, I am saved!*"

And at the end of that wild cry Ismene uttered a shriek of unmitigated ecstasy, which rang from the walls of the little room, and it must be that it echoed and re-echoed about the pasture, while the beasts listened with forward-pointed ears. I knew part of what it meant, but not all. And under that, it seemed that I knew my own fate, ever to be passing through the door of exit, not of entrance, to find a solitary path to the mountaintop.

CHAPTER NINE

DEATH OF THE HYDRA

1

With the lionskin bound by withes across my back, and our camp gear loaded aboard a mule, Right Doer, Actaeon, and I set out on foot for the King's citadel, Orchomenus. To our sorrow, Dyctus could not come with us, for he had left his master's flocks and herds too long already; and autumn-born calves did not know his smell, and the yearlings had half forgotten it, and if he did not return to them now, he would lose his control over them.

We made due sacrifice to Pan, as we had pledged, and to Selene, Sister of the Sun, who had shed her light whereby I had killed Iniquity.

Also, I had seen Ismene walking with her lover in the twilight, and both bowed deeply and passed quickly. A cankerous jealousy devoured me when, looking at their steadfast faces, I thought that she had already performed with him the ritual of the Passage of Hands, or that she would do so this very night. Then some God who wished to comfort me even with a lie, or more likely a Goddess who knew woman as I could never know her, brought me the strange inkling that this was not true, that she never had, and never would, share this plighting with her husband, and that it was mine alone forever.

We had planned to arrive at the campgrounds outside the wall on the eve before the winter solstice, which was ever a feast day in Greece. Thereby we gave thanks to the sun for reversing his southward course out of our realms, and starting his journey back to us with ever lengthening stays in our broad and happy skies, meanwhile pluck-

ing Hecate's raven plumes like tail feathers of a rooster. We journeyers had picked this day for our return so that a good crowd would
witness my presentation of Iniquity's pelt and, even more important,
hear the King's reply, for thus he could scarcely afford to be niggardly
with one who had rid Nemea of its scourge. No games were to be
held, but the best poets, lyrists, flutists, and orators would receive
wreaths of olive. Also, it was the custom on this day for great nobles
to make presents to the King of mares, cattle, goats, sheep, swine,
and ingots of metal. It had been Right Doer's guess that Eurytus
would give them quittance on this occasion, in respect to their having
fought beside him in his victorious war with Thebes, but my brother
had failed to appraise the King's cupidity in its true measure and
completely missed the mark. When we came to the campground, we
could hardly believe this was still not the autumn equinox, the day
of shame and ignominy to all Thebans, so many beasts grazed or
bedded down under the care of drovers and herders. Actually, of
course, this tribute to the King was probably not a tenth of the great
forfeit the Thebans had been forced to pay.

And I could not forget, while chills of terror chased one another
down my spine, that only a moiety of the prize demanded had yet
been seized, and its seizure nine months from now, or twelve months,
or perhaps never, might hang on today's events.

Right Doer coached me as well as he could, Actaeon fully agreeing
with his counsel. It was decided that I not hang with the crowd of
spectators in whose midst these two would remain, but join the gift
bringers immediately under the parapet, although the big pelt, fastened with withes and concealed by a woolen cloth on my back, could
hardly be reckoned as a free gift as much as the fruit of the labor of a
slave. I had taken my stand early, from where I could readily attract
the King's notice, and had at least an hour to wait for his appearance,
when a minion of some sort came to me with a message. I was to come
at once to the sanctuary of the shrine of Artemis, because the priestess,
at present holding service, wished to speak to me.

I did as I was told, and on coming nigh the wondrous image I saw
nearly a hundred women, some of them stately matrons, most of them
maidens, only a few great with child but all wearing rich robes indicat-
ing they were the wives and daughters of noblemen, kneeling before
it. I slipped into the cypress wood and quickly gained the small, pillared retreat. And I had had hardly time to glance with repugnance

at the ancient broken image of the Goddess with its multiple teats when Iole dashed in, and slipped her hand into mine.

I caught my breath, and had trouble drawing it with ease, as ever in the presence of Iole. Her oval face, perfectly Grecian, was slightly flushed from the excitement of the ceremony, or perhaps from some tidings whispered her by the cold marble lips of the image, and this caused an increased light in her dark blue eyes. How could it be, I marveled, that she could so resemble the Huntress-Goddess, and at the same moment an unlettered shepherdess of the plateau above the Nemean Plain? I thought that essentially the resemblance must lie in litheness of bone and muscle, which conveys an aspect of serenity and yet hints of high inherent passion. Why had the Gods given her the little circle of black pigment on her cheekbone? It was a beauty mark truly, yet a sign as meaningful as the oak leaf stained on my left shoulder.

"I have only a moment," she told me, half out of breath. "I wanted to see you alive and unharmed, after your battle with Iniquity. I knew you killed him—my Goddess told me so—but the outcome hung by a hair. You see, I could not come to Nemea and on the very scene ask Artemis to intervene in your behalf. Megara stopped me."

"How could she stop you?"

"By declaring her intention to go with me. In that case, Artemis would see her there, see you making love to her, and her anger at her would flame again, and my prayer would have gone unanswered. If Megara had not gone to Nemea, against my Goddess' wishes, you would have slain Iniquity a month or more before, and the old drover would not have been killed."

"How do you know that, Iole?"

"How could I know? Because Artemis told me with her own lips. Wisely I had stayed here, at the shrine, and every day I implored her not to vent her wrath against Megara upon me of the same blood, and at last I won her over, and you have conquered, and the scourge of Nemea lies impotent and dead. Heracles, did you win this victory with your own hand? That was the labor imposed upon you by my father Eurytus."

"Right Doer was with me, and two others who called themselves camp helpers, but I smote Iniquity with my own hand."

"Yet Actaeon, the great hunter and a Theban, arrived here last night about the same time that you did. If he was one of your helpers, it would be well not to tell the King."

"Now that is good counsel."

"If you will accept my kiss as part of your mead of victory, I would be proud, but I would not blame you if you declined, since the last time we kissed I thought of Megara's countless kisses given you in the bower, and I bit your lip."

"You may bite it again, if you wish. For me it was pleasure and pain both."

"I hate Megara. She is the profaner of my Goddess. But I will not think of her now, if——"

Iole thought of naught, in the lightning-laced moment that ensued, and surrendered herself to passion. It came to me that in this respect Iole was akin to green-eyed Ismene, paying off the blood debt of her husband. And again I found the comparison between them troubling to my mind, which seemed a kind of transience in their wild embraces. Their fire was by no means feigned. The gusty breathing of both girls, and the splash of color in each cheek, and the line of fine sweat over the eyebrows, and the immense expansion of the pupils were signs well known to every lecher and related in striplinghood to every youth. Still I felt that these were not the joyous giving of either maiden to a beloved, and instead might be a reward, heart-prompted, and the utmost that she could give, for a mighty service done.

Had I solved the mystery? In the case of Ismene, aching for the embraces of her herdsman lover, she had loved me greatly for one night for making it possible. Iole adored Artemis, perhaps loved her with unnatural love, and it might have been that gigantic Antaeus had lain with the Huntress-Goddess, whereby Iole had held him in deathless jealousy and hatred. Him I had slain in her plain sight. She had deemed it would never happen, that no mortal strength could prevail upon him, then suddenly she was rid of her godlike rival. As she coiled her tongue around mine, one hand tugging fiercely at the nape of my neck, the other groping deeply under my tunic, was she listening in fancy to the last gasps of his crushed windpipe?

It could be so with Greek maidens, for their like was not found elsewhere within the encircling seas. Mariners plying those seas had sworn it. If so, the reason was their close kinship and resemblance to our Goddesses. There was hardly one so basely born that she did not have a little of remorseless Pallas Athene in her heart and soul, or chasm-leaping Artemis, or fiercely jealous Hera. All were Furies without wings when their blood was up. All were half-sisters to great Electra.

But when I lifted the fold of her tunic and pressed my body against Iole's, my spine in spasm, she slipped away.

2

Regally King Eurytus stood on his parapet, his stately Queen, his big-eyed daughter Megara, and Iole of matchless beauty and his tall son Nessus in attendance. He had scarcely begun to call the names of his chieftains to find out the munificence or the paltriness of their gifts, and to utter hearty praise or veiled reproof, when his spy whispered in his ear. Eurytus could not restrain his gaze from darting in my direction. He had not noticed me until now, or at least had not identified me, for my hair was long and wild for lack of a good shearing and oiling, my face was wind-burned, and my tunic was of the kind worn by drovers. He recovered himself instantly except for a slight rounding of his eyes. Then he spoke in his most royal manner.

"One of my servants has just called my attention to a visitor here, a Theban I believe, with a large bundle under his arm. If by any happy chance he has brought me a gift, however humble, the ancient code of courtesy to strangers, the law of mighty Zeus, demands that I address him before my great Companions, to ask what is his mission here, and if I may in any way assist it, and most of all to bid him welcome."

"O King, I am indeed a Theban but not a stranger," I answered, putting enough power into my voice that all could hear. "In truth, I am Heracles, your bondsman, newly returned from the wilderness of Nemea where I was sent to perform a labor. To my sorrow, I have no gift to offer, only the fruit of that labor which is your due."

A thrill of excitement passed through the throng in the few seconds of Eurytus' silence. It moved in a kind of wave from the foremost ranks to the rear, and children gazed up at their mothers, and the great lords glanced at one another, and a great hush fell. As for the King, he had expected some such reply as I had made, for he could hardly fail to guess what was in my bundle, but perhaps he had hoped to the last I would make some other. He was a vain man. As such he

took for granted that all his ventures would turn out well, and the
deities of Olympus would go out of their way to coddle him.

"This fruit you speak of. I wish to see it, to find out if it compensates
me for your long absence from my fields. Please hand it to one of my
slaves."

"By your leave, King Eurytus, pray you appoint two minions, one
to take the left side, and the other the right, so all may properly see
what I have brought you, in its full expanse."

He did so, and in the meantime I ripped off the cloth that had
covered the trophy. Then I handed the left paw to one of the men
bending down, and the right to the other, so when they heaved, the
whole pelt came into view of the people, its size causing their eyes
to start, and the red mane ablaze in the winter sunlight. Eurytus must
have listened by now to many accounts of the great lion Iniquity, but
if he had believed them, certainly he had not believed of the Beast's
death at my hands.

"Has anyone here, especially one of you old mariners who have
touched the Egyptian deserts, ever seen as great a skin?" the King
asked.

"Eurytus, this was a God among lions," a bold fellow answered.

"Heracles, the labor appointed you was to slay Iniquity with the
help of no armed helper. Did you do so, or not?"

"Aye."

"Was there no lion hunter, of great fame, in your camp?"

I remembered Iole's warning, but in the same thought Right Doer's
counsel, and always at last I must depend on him, no other.

"Eurytus, in my camp was the great hunter Actaeon, who volunteered to do its common labor. Also he taught me the ways of lions,
although he bore no weapons, as he will attest. And since your prayers
joined with mine that Nemea be rid of its scourge, I knew that you
would be as grateful for his lore and guidance as I was."

This did not rest well on Eurytus' stomach, as his face revealed;
still he forced himself to smile.

"Heracles, you have done well. Did you slay him with an arrow
from your great bow?"

"No, with a thrusting spear four feet long, in open battle."

The people cheered, even if they knew this was not good news for
their King. And I thanked their good Greek hearts for the outcry, so
indicative of their love of adventure and battle against long odds, for

if the King still intended to be stingy with me, his hands were tied.

"Heracles, you are entitled to ask a boon. You may do so."

"Eurytus, as my reward for victory over Antaeus you gave a year of freedom to the first-born of Theban youth whom you claimed as your mead of victory. I ask that you extend the time by two years."

"That I cannot do, at present, but I will parole them for six months added to their year of grace, which will expire on the spring equinox fifteen months from now. And in your absence, Heracles, I have pondered what other labor I might give you worthy of your strength, in case you returned safely from the first, and I have arrived at the answer. By killing Iniquity, you have well served the good folk of Nemea, whose King is my kinsman and vassal.

"In Lernaea, close to the sea, dwells a many-headed monster known as the Lernaean Hydra. Her lair is an expanse of marsh, through which flows many waterways, and fishermen and sailors going down to the sea often traverse these ways in their boats, and many are poisoned by the Hydra's venomous heads, and many become too ill to set forth in ships, and some go down to Hades. We are told that if one head is cut off, nine others grow in its place, so the monster must be killed outright. To this labor I appoint you; and if you encompass it, the folk there will be most grateful to myself and to you, and you shall receive a mead of victory. And if you fail—but of that, time will tell." And the King smiled blandly in his short curly beard.

Eurytus knew perfectly well that the so-called Hydra was no sort of many-headed monster but a rank and malign swamp. Up from its bogs bubbled scores of springs, and these gave off some sort of effluvia, unpleasant to smell and poisonous to breathe. Sometimes boatmen could cross it with only a little headache and belly sickness, but on certain other days, when the vapors were confined by still, heavy, humid air, some of the boatmen fell in a swoon and, quite true, some never breathed again. Few who heard the King's pronouncement did not know this much, or not know the seeming mortal impossibility of stopping the poisonous springs and redeeming the foul fen for human use. So bright-faced a moment ago, now the throng looked sorrowful.

"How many companions and helpers may I take with me?" I asked.

"As many as you can find who will enter the Hydra's lair."

"How much time may I have?"

"Until the summer solstice, but the sooner you slay the monster and save the people, the greater your mead of victory."

"Then I ask your leave to go."

The King granted it, and I hastened to join my great companions, Right Doer and Actaeon. I thought that the latter felt at as great a loss as myself, for he too was a man of action, fitted mainly for hunting and fighting and labor with his hands, but Right Doer's wondrous head was still well screwed on his shoulders, and I could not help but feel a lift of hope at sight of his face. Its expression was of a troubled mind but far from that of despair. And as we were weaving our slow way out of the throng, a tall man, beautiful to see, hurried to join us.

"Nessus!" I cried. "Don't you know better than to follow those forsaken by the Gods?" But I would not have said this had I not seen his shining eyes.

"Heracles, I am a fool. So why should I not seek the company of fools?"

No more was said until we had gained our little bivouac; then, trusting Nessus utterly, Right Doer began to recall all he had ever heard of the Lernaean Hydra. I put a word in now and then, for I remembered the wise Rhadamanthus' telling us about the deadly region, with its noxious vapors, that bore this name. The old savant had said it might have been the bed of an estuary, since filled with silt. The vapors given off by the bubbling springs, each rising from a kind of dimple in the muck beside the winding waters, were heavier than air, inflammable, and had a faint or strong smell of rotten eggs, although our teacher doubted greatly that this malodor had anything to do with the poison. Its creeks wound down to the sea from a lake or slough, lying so close to a steep bank that some of its waters appeared to be swallowed up by the mouth of a gaping cave.

"Is the Hydra an old affliction in Lernaea, or had it come into being in the memory of living men?" I asked.

"I recall Rhadamanthus' saying that when he was a boy, the fen had a bad name. He said it has become more dangerous with the passing years. In any case, Heracles, you have your work cut out for you. The labors Eurytus assigns you can be expected to increase in difficulty until you meet with abject failure, for only then can he move directly against a public hero who slew Antaeus and Iniquity. You must realize that the latter feat has more than ever convinced him that you bear the mark of Zeus—that you are the man of the prophecy which he still hopes and believes he can forestall. Of course, if you are killed in the performing of a labor, all is well—or so the fool will believe. He has not the wit to perceive that such an event will only prove you are not the man, that he still cannot dream peacefully at night in the arms of a favorite slave girl, and that implacable Fate still wings toward him. He will not remember how many times in Greek history kings and captains have tried to balk a foretelling by Apollo, and how they always failed."

"Right Doer, do you think that trying to destroy the Hydra is more dangerous than hunting Iniquity? If so, I wish to take a maiden—make love—drink deep—feast—live to the full for a full moon before setting forth."

"Not more dangerous, I believe, but more difficult. The source of the poisonous vapors may lie far underground; how are you to reach it? We cannot burrow like moles. We cannot send word to great Achilles to come up out of Hades and cut it off with his flashing sword."

"Achilles would be no more use than I," Actaeon broke in, "on an enterprise such as this. The blind poet has never sung of his doing feats of the mind, even adding two and two, only of him sulking in his tent, quarreling with Agamemnon over a wench, raging forth like a lion into battle, mutilating brave Hector's body, at last being killed by the arrow of a craven. Still I want to go with you, Heracles, and do what I can. Your teacher said the vapors were inflammable. Perhaps I can cut wood to destroy them with fire."

"Actaeon, I would rather flee from Greece and spend the rest of my days in dark Egypt than go without you."

"Destroy them with fire," Right Doer echoed, his eyes glazed. "But how could you bring fire into as deep a pit as the crater of Etna in the Hesperides? And a fire hotter than Hephaestus' forge burns there already."

It came to me then that Nessus too was itching to speak. Often Right Doer, his brain turning over like a cart wheel, did not notice such little things. Nessus was shy by nature—his arrogance at our first meeting had been a cloak of some kind, Megara told me, perhaps for that very shyness—so I gave him a steadfast glance.

"Nessus, do you know anything about the Lernaean Hydra?"

"More than you might think. You see, my royal father has had it on his mind a good deal lately, as his spies in Nemea reported you not yet torn to pieces by Iniquity and might win out. The folk who live thereabouts are fishermen by trade. They have little else to eat but fish, and a kind of root from the fen which smells a little like rotten eggs but yet which they pound and use as corn. Once a Persian came to their set-tlement and promised to rid them of the Hydra if they would give him half their catch for the following year. When he confessed that he had failed utterly, and the Hydra seemed to grow worse, as if en-raged, the fishermen tied the poor wretch to one of their stone anchors and cast him overside for sea lice to eat. Of course they wouldn't have done it if he had been a Greek. Still, I doubt if they'll be helpful in your effort, or even take it in good part."

"I doubt it too," Right Doer said.

"Well, what are you three going to do for food and drink? The peo-ple will give you an occasional mess of fish, but such will get tiresome. What you'll need is ingots of tin and copper to trade with farmers up the valley for meat and corn. Have you any?"

Actaeon, Right Doer, and I glanced at one another. "I'm afraid we've spent all we had," my brother answered. "I can get more from home, but they are very scarce in all Thebes, because of the heavy tax. Will the King's treasurer allow us some?"

"Right Doer, you have not yet come to a full realization of my royal father's stinginess. He is not in the least agreeable to letting the great Delphic prophecy come true—indeed he puts his own inglorious ex-istence before the oracle of an Olympic God—and I assure you he won't give you a scrap of tin to smooth your road. Your needs will be extensive. It will be bad enough to smell rotten eggs day and night without eking out a miserable living on fish and swamproot. And it just happens that I am bountifully supplied with ingots not only of copper and tin but of lead, greatly prized by fishermen to weight their nets, and no few of silver and gold."

"I listen attentively," Right Doer remarked, with his wonderful smile.

"When Antaeus deserved a laurel wreath for a great public service —I refer to his rather sudden departure to other realms—I could not prevent Eurytus, the King, from seizing his great droves of mares and cattle. However, I got to his chest well ahead of the King's treasurer, not to mention Megara, close behind me, and wonder of wonders, ahead of Iole, whose long legs and fingers were for once unaccount-ably remiss, as though she were dazed. I could lend you all you want. And if you didn't mind—I mean if it would be agreeable to all of you" —and to my amazement Nessus' voice faltered and he swallowed pain-fully, and his eyes looked dark and strange—"I could go with you."

While Nessus was gazing elsewhere—anywhere to avoid our gaze—Right Doer threw me a glance of inquiry. I nodded; my brother beamed.

"Nessus, good friend, Heracles would have invited you long before now, except that he thought you might come as an act of friendship and pass out of favor with the King. Remember you are an illustrious prince, I am the son of a captain lately defeated, Actaeon belongs only to the cadet branch of the great house of Cadmus. We could not take liberties with you. But I want you to know that all three of us would rejoice—and make an offering to Dionysus, who alone of our great Gods seems to understand friendship, no doubt because one of his parents was mortal—in gratitude for your joining of our company."

"I care naught for Eurytus' favor," Nessus told us, again in good control of his emotions. "He is a skinflint king, treacherous, cowardly except when he fights with what he thinks is a charmed sword forged by Hephaestus. I wanted to go with you to Nemea, so I got myself sent on a royal errand to avoid the sting of not being invited. Then if it is settled, may I borrow a two-gallon bowl of unwatered wine from the stores of the great lord of Chaeronea, whose camp is nearby, and who seeks preferment with the King?"

"An excellent notion," Actaeon remarked succinctly.

So the wine was brought, and poured, and a libation given to Earth, because we might have to delve in her before long, and certainly she would decide whether we would be allowed to stop up one of her most poisonous fountains. Then we drank, and kissed one another's hands and heads, and as we sat in silence, I felt a bond being forged among us four, of deathless friendship and inviolable troth. We were all young men. As yet we had not begun to worry about living long. We still could give without asking a munificent return; we had strength to spare; we had not learned how to haggle with life; our hearts had not grown cramped with aching age. And I felt something else, each his own, which was audacity in the face of frowning fortune, a thrill of being alive briefly or long, the determination never to submit.

And suddenly I rejoiced that Fate had chosen me for this strange part—the doer of mighty labors for a king who sought my life, yet which, if I succeeded and did not fail, would free a host of my countrymen. He would not dare appoint me one manifestly impossible. His own subjects, who knew, if they did not always practice, the Greek ideal of fair play, would cast him from his throne. Also, to win the people's sanction, so far he had appointed me tasks of great dignity and importance, the performance of which would benefit the folk.

If I proved equal to two, or three, or four, let alone all that came into his well-scratched and aching head, I would have no quarrel with Atropos and her shears of Death. I would have lived greatly, in my time, and won wide fame, and would be long remembered. And the gift of my great thews would be justified before all the Gods.

Who had made the gift? I had all but forsaken the notion that it could be Zeus, and there had been no lie in Wrathful Leader's eyes when he had disclaimed me as his son. Yet it was no puny fellow who visited my mother's chamber in her husband's absence, thrice seven years ago. Some great gift of his had come down to me, although perhaps in an unrecognizable form. I wondered who he might be. I could not deny the possibility that he was an Olympian; yet for my own part I would rather he had been a mortal man.

My unknown sire, whether hero or slave, whether living or dead, your son Heracles salutes you!

3

I did not want to depart from Orchomenus without speaking to Megara. At the same time I shied a little at the prospect, for no reason that I knew other than my escapades since we had bathed together in the Pool of Truth. True, I had broken no pledge. We had plighted no troth with words at the beautiful rite we had performed, or in whisperings while snugly wrapped in Snag Tooth's sheepskin robe. I had told her of Iole's irresistible fascination for me; as for Ismene, surely the staunchest celibate—a very rare creature on this earth, and utterly unknown in our whole galaxy of Gods, unless he were Pan, whose goat feet enforced the condition—would not have thwarted her husband's command that she give a mead of honor to his avenger. So I settled it with my conscience. Why did it need settling when Megara, Iole, Ismene, and myself were all good unwedded Greeks?

On the day following the winter solstice, Right Doer, Actaeon, and I were shaved, shorn, scented, bathed, and attired in new, clean garments. On the next day my brother and I discussed a quick journey and a brief stay at our home in Thebes, to visit Wrathful Leader, ailing but yet living, and to hug our nurse Althea to our heart's content.

This sweet return we were forced to postpone until we had destroyed the Lernaean Hydra; and if she destroyed us instead we could not come at all, except as whispering ghosts on our hurried way to shadowy Hades. The point was, a boat that could land us three miles from the fishermen's village above the poison fen would sail on the following day, and we knew not how long we must wait to catch another.

On the afternoon before we were to set forth, I sent word to Megara by Nessus to implore her to come and eat a rough supper with me at our bivouac. She sent back a cheerful assent, and when she arrived, I was prepared for her hearty appetite and lively thirst with a wild goose spitted and roasting over the cozy fire, barley cakes to soak up the bird's surplus fat, and a horn of honey mead, hard to come by this time of year, since it was always brewed in summer or fall, and almost always down someone's throat before midwinter. Of course Right Doer, Actaeon, and Nessus had business elsewhere, and had taken themselves off.

When Megara and I were having supper, I observed another difference, no doubt of trifling moment, between her and Iole. Or, I should say, a difference in my feeling toward them over a mundane matter. I rejoiced to see Megara eat. Few sights could please me more than to see her take in both hands the whole leg of our ten-pound fowl, bite off big mouthfuls, and stow them quickly away, her pretty face agleam with grease in the firelight. I had felt the same sort of pleasure in Ismene at Iniquity's funeral feast, and no doubt I liked to see almost everyone partake heartily of the good, life-sustaining food, perhaps because I was a sound trencherman myself. Then I tried to picture Iole in Megara's place, and I could not. It seemed to me her fare should be not meat, dropping red juice, and grease-soaked barley cakes, but ambrosia and nectar, the food and drink of our divinities, which also I could not picture, let alone desire for my own rough innards. I took it that these dainties need not be digested, but were completely absorbed without the aid of stomach juices. Still I did not want any for myself or to serve Megara. My being a man, and she being a woman, ethereal in a small part, earthy in the main, suited me well tonight.

"You could always be happy with me, Heracles—happy as you are tonight—if Iole did not exist," Megara said, as though she had peeped into my cranium.

"What did you say?" For I had the common habit of pretending not to understand a question, to gain a little time to think of an answer.

"You heard me. We both know it is true. Still, I won't kill Iole to rescue you from your quandary. Sometimes I long to, and then I always wonder if anybody ever will, or could if he tried. If you told me it was your solemn belief that Iole is immortal, I wouldn't think you are mad. At times it seems unthinkable that she will ever die or even grow old. At least she won't go down to Hades with the rest of common humans. She will be turned into a star—a brilliant and beautiful one—or become the torchbearer of Artemis or be given some other splendid office. But Heracles, don't ever get the idea that she is infallible. She makes mistakes the same as any woman—or any Goddess, for that matter."

"Does she?"

"Who should know better than you? For instance, she advised you not to wrestle Antaeus—I know she did, because a slave girl, my confidante, saw the goat blood she brought to you in the wood; and what use could you have for it but to smear yourself with it and beg off on the ground of an injury? Well, despite his almost equal strength and far greater skill, you won."

"She had good reason to think he would win."

"Yes, but some of us knew better. Also, she thought Iniquity would win—unless she directed the hunt under the auspices of Artemis."

"If she had come to Nemea, I might have saved Snag Tooth."

"I am sure she told you so. But she didn't tell you to make the clean breast about the great hunter Actaeon's being in your camp. Her mind wouldn't work that way." And then Megara neatly detached an especially succulent tidbit of the fowl, being the part that we call the Nose of Silenus, its being shaped like a big nose and, like the tipsy God, very fat.

"No, Right Doer told me to say what I did," I answered.

"Did not Iole advise you to conceal the fact from the King?"

"The truth charm we both found in the pool has worn off, still I have to say she did."

"You know, Heracles, sometimes I believe Iole has no common sense. In that, too, she is like so many Gods and Goddesses on many occasions. A greater mystery is what seems her passionate love of Thebes and Thebans. Nessus and I detest our sire—we would both rejoice if he had been cuckolded by his meanest slave—but although Iole has always been his favorite, she tried to bring about his death in the last days of our war with Thebes, for no conceivable reason other than to save Thebans from Eurytus' vengeance. Their hero, Sirenes, grandson of Rhadamanthus, had just been slain by Antaeus; the Theban cause was lost. In the middle of the night, with the moon straight overhead, Iole sacrificed to Artemis a pet lamb she had saved from an immolation, with a wild prayer that Eurytus die—Nessus had followed her and heard her. Is she in love with some Theban? If so, whom? Let me ask you a foolish question. Are you sure that neither you nor Right Doer never had an encounter with Iole before you met her at Orchomenus? She has been absent on many journeys, some of them of a month or more—always, she said, to do honor, and bring offering, to her Goddess."

I raised my hand intending to scratch my head, but quickly let it fall. I was quite sure Right Doer had never encountered Iole before then, but I might possibly have done so. I was thinking of one I had thought was a dryad, with flaming hair, whom I had seen in the forest above our pasturage at Parnassus, and of her fleeing from me. If it had been Iole, she could have had a little bivouac with one attendant, shot a deer now and then, and lingered in those dark woods a good part of the summer. But I could make no sense of it and reluctantly let it pass.

"By all the Owls of Athena!" Megara burst out angrily. "Why should our talk always turn back to Iole? Pour me a cup from your bowl."

While I was doing so, Megara washed and wiped her face and hands, as I did mine. When we had wet our lips with the sweet drink, I had every right to hope that we could share the Kiss of Honey Mead, a pleasant rite of young folk at harvest festivals. With these youth and maiden the innocent experiment often leads to kisses for kissing's sake, and then to other pleasant passages, and then to breathless couples' stealing off to the corners of stone fences where the corn stands tall. But when I bent toward my lovely companion, she gave me a strange smile that balked me.

"Heracles, you went to visit Iole even before you brought your offering to the King."

"You knew that. You guessed what she told me."

"You did more than talk in that snug little sanctuary with the vine-draped entrance. But I have no right to protest. What I gave you in Nemea was my free gift. However, I do have the right to ask you to choose between us, not to make an immediate choice—that would be unwise, if not impossible . . . at least you must wait until you return from Lernaea, perhaps until the leaves not yet in the bud shuffle under our feet. Still, you must do so, in good time, if you want anything more of me. And to help you choose, to find out how little or how much you prize me—I'll speak plainly and say prize my love, for I have not been able to hide it from anyone—there will be no more sweet passages between us until, if ever, we are betrothed."

Her immense dark eyes had fixed on mine. The firelight played in them, and her hair looked raven-black, and great beauty was upon her, a special beauty born of her proud stand. She had always been chosen second to Iole, she had told me, and she had learned to expect and accept it, but now I perceived she had rejected the whole concept. She was only Megara, setting no store on being the daughter of a feudal king, still well aware that she was the less beautiful of two sisters, and lacking the strange demidivinity that every one sensed in Iole. Yet she suddenly knew herself as a prize fit for such a hero as Jason, or Perseus, or Theseus. Had I anything to do with it? I believed so, but my head was too thick to know what.

"I don't believe there is any answer I can make to that," I said, "except that I believe you are doing right."

"And Heracles, you must understand that my terms apply only to Iole, yourself, and me. I don't ask or expect you to be true to me where other maidens are concerned. I cannot help but think of you as a force of nature incarnate, one which I need not try to name or of which I do not know the essence, yet more than truly human, and in some ways less."

"Linus, whose skull I cracked with a lyre because I could not learn to play it, told me I would never be a man and instead be a monster."

"I fear he was right. I fear that all women, except me, will at last turn away from you, and I will too if you whore too long after Iole. That is my term for it. Whoring after a demigoddess. Perhaps I can foresee that if she would quit her office and marry you, your children too would be monsters, not good ones like you, putting your gift to great works, but monstrous in another sense. The children I would bear you would be people. You would found a race of people through me. But my head is turning; I see visions; they are vague but fearful, and I do not want to look at them. I will go now. When you go to Lernaea, my heart goes with you; but remember, you must not fail! You must save Thebes as again and again Theseus saved Athens. And more than a Theban, remember that you strive and fight first of all as a Greek, one aspect of Greece's greatness that some day will be honored in all the realms of the barbarians.

"Heracles, lift your eyes not to Olympus, from where the Gods and Goddesses gaze down on toiling men, but to Parnassus, to whose summit you gazed when you were a drover, and who lent you avalanchal strength, and the endurance of great stones. By these you can destroy the Lernaean Hydra. Then come back to me."

Then the moon was darkened, perhaps by great wings or by only a little cloud; and when the chill, gray light poured down again, Megara had gone.

4

What was called the lair of the Lernaean Hydra was a black bog running about a mile back into the hills, as if a giant had dug himself an enormous grave, half a mile wide, which had then half filled with silt from the fronting sea.

Its main features Right Doer, Actaeon, Nessus, and I perceived in one day's inspection. Indeed, from high ground we glimpsed its whole expanse in a single glance. It was flanked on both sides by low, but extremely steep and barren, uninhabitable hills. Right Doer ventured at once that these hills, arresting all light winds except those that Poseidon suffered to blow from the limitless ocean, had a great deal to do with imprisoning the noxious vapors which the Hydra's thousand mouths gave forth. Almost none of the bog was traversable by people on foot. Once a boat had floundered on a kind of lake, or slough, that lapped at the knees of less-steep hills immediately behind it. Five of the ten boatmen were unable to swim, and, fearful of being swept into what was called the Sink Hole, had attempted to reach solid ground by wading through the muck. They had started forth bravely, to sink at first to their knees, then to their waists, then to their necks; and their cries' still going unanswered by helpless people watching from the housetops of the village and unheeded by the Gods, they spouted mud from their mouths and noses and sank from sight.

The other five, being good swimmers, kept well out and to one side of the Sink Hole, until they could enter the creeks winding through the slough to a sandy beach where the fishermen kept their craft and some of their gear. So these lived to draw many a net more, and harvest many a basket of shimmering fish, and to be honored as elders in the little town, and their counsel sought, until in the fullness of years, the arrows of mercy of Apollo laid them low, and they went down into Hades.

These creeks took the main of the overflow of the big slough, and they glimmered blue in summer, gray under winter clouds, and there was no mystery about them, and they bore such good and homely names as Mullet Creek, Crab Creek, and Dead Man's Creek, this last name given because of a drowned sailor, whose name and country no one knew, being washed into it at high tide by a landward breeze. These were the fishermen's routes from their village, perched high enough on the hillside that only the smell of the Hydra's poisonous breath ever blew in their doorways, and the miasma itself lay thick and ominous below them. But before they could enter the creeks they must traverse the lake, and on still days, especially those that were chill and dark with cloud, the poison came and went over the waters, and the men rowed into it unwarned, even by a stronger smell of rotten eggs.

Of course what most stirred our fancies and moved us to solemn thought was the phenomenon called the Sink Hole. In the steepest hill on one side of the fen, near the seaward end of the slough and on the opposite side from the outlet to the creeks, was a black cave, the part above water at the present season high and wide enough to admit a big fishing boat with a man standing erect at the tiller. Below the surface the vent in the wall was of unknown depth, for no one in the memory of man had ever dared approach near enough to plumb the water there. Certainly some water flowed through the gap, although at no great pace, since there were no ripples or turmoil in the lake thereabout, nor was there any roar of falling waters at normal times, although when the landward wind backed in an especially heavy tide, and the gap above the surface was lower than usual, a low-pitched humming sound could be heard all over the lake, as though by a hundred swarms of bees. However, there was no doubt of suction at the opening, because now and then a lost paddle was sucked in at a snail's pace, or an empty boat not properly secured to the graveled shore of the lake just under the village.

We four had made our bivouac close by, and in the morning we talked to the headman. He told us that while many fishermen traversing the slough to get into the creeks caught heavy headaches and attacks of vomiting from breathing the malodorous vapors, and no few fell into a trance, almost always they made a quick recovery on drawing near the sea. However, he named a few who, in his own lifetime, dozed away into death, these being mainly aged men, or men subject to severe chest pains or great debility. Even so, we could not help but wonder that people continued to occupy the village, making a lean living exposed to constant peril. When we asked the stout fellow why his people did not quit the region, and go to some other fishing ground of our endless leagues of seashore, he made an eloquent reply.

"My lords, our grandsires lived and died in the little houses in which we dwell. They made offerings to Poseidon, as do we, and at the same little shrines, and to the Gods of the Winds, and once every year we propitiate the Hydra by giving her our day's catch, thrown in the Lake of her Stinking Breath, and then it usually happens that the vapors are less for a moon or so, although to this I cannot swear, because my heart longs for respite, and sometimes I believe it from wishing rather than by seeing and smelling. And before our grandsire's time I doubt not that their grandsires lived here also, for we find weights not of lead like ours, but of stone, and harpoons with heads of flint, and fishhooks made of shell instead of bronze. And sometimes for a period of one, two, or even three moons no man sickens, and the smell is no more than a faint whiff. In any case we are rooted here like the oak trees in the vale over the hill."

"Tell me," Right Doer asked thoughtfully, "when you give an offering of fish to the Hydra do you find them floating, bloated and stinking, on the surface of the slough, or are they devoured?"

"Some drift out to sea in the tidal creeks. The rest go into the Sink Hole, or so we believe, hence if the Hydra is indeed a monster greater than any Titan, it must be that she dwells, and takes her food, in a house far underground."

"So I believe," Right Doer said, and his eyes lighted briefly.

But after our day's survey, we four found that we had little to say to each other. To slay the Hydra seemed a labor beyond any power of man.

For a full moon we hunted, without any real directing by our minds, for an avenue of attack. We went with the fishermen in the boats, across the lake, through one or other of the creeks, down the beach. On these journeys the Gods did not give us a single sign of their favor, let alone show us any vulnerability of our enemy. Then we took to a dangerous experiment, which was to wade a short distance into the fen, close to the reeds at its edge, and touch firebrands to the nearest dimples in muck. More than once one or other of us stepped into what seemed a bottomless bog and had to be hauled out, plastered with mud, by our fellows. However, in every case that water bubbled from the dimple, or if we could hear it bubbling deep underground, the touch of the brand brought a brief flame, green, dancing, and thin as air, above the vent. After which we could pass fire over it without result for a matter of minutes, if not longer.

If we could ignite all the dimples at once, we told each other, we might destroy the Hydra. But that would be the work of a thousand men with a thousand firebrands, and anyhow, the bog was impassable.

Toward the end of the first moon after the winter solstice, when the days lengthened swiftly, we four sat late about our little fire for no reason that we knew other than we did not wish to separate and have our souls wander in the infinite solitude of sleep. Perhaps there was another reason. Retreating winter had made another savage sally, and for five nights frost had bitten deep, and the cold, gray clouds had never lifted or seemed to stir on the cold, windless days, and the vapors hung heavy over the slough. Yesterday an old man, seventy or more, had swooned on the boat journey to the creeks, and when he had been brought to the beach the salt air had not revived him, and he had been taken without struggle by implacable Death. We had barely known him by sight, yet he had been a good fisherman, a man of pith and wit, and a good counselor to the young; and his passing had dealt all four of us a sharp blow, or at least had given us a sound shaking of heart and mind, for it was the first proof since our coming of the deadliness of our so strongly barricaded foe.

"Let us go back to what the headman told us the first day," Right Doer said. "He told us that if the Hydra had a den, it is down the Sink Hole. That seems to me altogether likely; a solid truth might lie under the headman's flight of fancy. Well, if we could bring fire to her den, we might destroy her in one great burst of flame."

"I think so too," Nessus said. "But Right Doer, for us to go down the Sink Hole, in a boat, carrying torches, would mean—what?"

"The end of us all. The water must ultimately emerge into the sea, perhaps from a spring in its bottom, or out of a rift in the walls of some undersea cliff. But we would not be alive to see it. If we destroyed the Hydra by fire, the same flame would destroy us. Long

before we reached the Hydra's den we would be smothered by its
fumes. I do not wish to give Eurytus the satisfaction of all of us being
wiped out, even if thereby we can destroy the Hydra. We must strike
at her some other way."

My head had begun to ache and my temples throb and to my own
surprise, greater than that of my fellows, I spoke.

"I've thought of something we might try."

"In the name of the Gods, what?"

"Right Doer, you remember the little brook at the foot of the
meadow where we waded, and sometimes dropped fishhooks, when
we were boys?"

"Perfectly well."

"Do you remember too that we made little boats and set them to
drift? And once, when Althea had cooked a picnic supper in the
meadow, and we stayed till after dark, we laid burning firebrands on
the board that we played was our boat, and let it float down the current, and watched it with pleasure as long as we could see the flame."

"I remember that too! By the Gods, Heracles! I was to do the thinking, you the heaving, but perhaps our positions are reversed."

"I must still heave. I would not have thought of this if you had not
put it in my head. Well, we will build a boat—the smaller the better—
and line its bottom with sod, and on that sod we will build a fire,
feeding it enough fuel to burn half an hour, and guide it through the
Sink Hole, and await the pleasure of the Gods!"

"Pleasure! Perhaps their wrath. Pray that the flow is slow into the
Hydra's lair, for it may be we should be far from the Sink Hole when
—whatever happens, happens. Heracles, I am the faster swimmer of
us two. Can you not designate me——"

"You are the faster, but I am the stronger, and I can lay my labor
on no back but my own, as you know well."

"Aye, as I know full well."

Presently we went to bed, and my heart was greatly lighter than
before, and to judge from my friends' faces, theirs the like. We were
all up in the cold dawn, eager to discuss ways and means, and the next
sign of a turn in the tide of fortune was the headman's telling us we
need build no boat, that on the beach was kept a little skiff perfect
for our needs, owned by the son of the latest victim of the Hydra,
and he would give it to us with a glowing heart. Then I made the
decision that I would man it alone. The others could not help me at

the final trial and would incur a needless risk of their lives, all of which I greatly treasured. I meant to quit the boat and swim into one of the creeks when it had drifted near enough to the Sink Hole that it would certainly be sucked in. Meanwhile I could not help but grin at the uniqueness of the enterprise. Rhadamanthus had told Right Doer and me of fireboats' being used in a great sea battle between the Fleet of Tyre and that of a dark-skinned, hook-nosed people from the Euxine Sea, and of flaming crafts drifting with the wind to ignite the invaders' sails, but surely none had ever been employed to burn up a mighty monster with a thousand venomous mouths!

Preparations took only three more days. Then, as another good sign, the cold spell of weather passed, the cold clouds dispersed, the sun beamed down as though spring had come, the vapors on the lake were largely dispelled by a breeze from the sea. On the morning that I chose for the adventure, my three companions, at my request, took their stands on the bank of Crab Creek, the one nearest to the Sink Hole and the one I intended to swim when the fireboat had been safely launched on its sail into darkness.

A fire of long-burning alder wood was kindled amidship of the dinghy on the thick turf; then I rowed her within a stone's throw of the Sink Hole. Not the slightest pull of the water in that direction was manifest as yet; however, I slipped overside, so I could feel the first undertow and escape from its clutches before these became unbreakable, meanwhile swimming alongside the boat and propelling her with an occasional shove. Truly I had to advance almost to the shadow of the cliff before I could convince myself that the boat would enter the arch and not drift off into one of the creeks. The water in front of and obviously for a considerable distance within the opening was almost stagnant.

Presently I saw that the boat was making toward it, although at a snail's pace, without help from me. I lay out a distance, watching it; its speed did not increase, but its direction was now certain. Since I thought that some kind of explosion might occur soon after its entry, blasting fire through the black maw, I withdrew toward the head of Crab Creek. Watching over my shoulder as I swam, I saw the little skiff with her cargo of fire drift stern-foremost into the maw and its dark knife slowly cut away her little hull. When she was clean out of sight I swam rapidly.

This labor is too easy, I thought, to win me any prize or any thrill of triumph. King Eurytus will be chagrined that he assigned it to me. That any Olympian God would take the least interest in it, glancing down from his golden porch, was beyond my wildest imaginings.

There might be something else wrong with the scheme, I began to think—its final and utter damnation. As the moments passed, I was more and more oppressed by the idea that it was not going to work. Quite possibly the hole in the cliffside was the mouth of a limestone cave that came to a dead end except for faults in the rock where the slight inward flow of water was dissipated. My only hope now was that the current, instead of quickening, remained almost dormant for a considerable distance, and hence the fireboat was taking a long time to reach what we had fondly termed the gaseous lair of the Hydra. By now I was well down Crab Creek, in deepening water, only two hundred paces or so from its little cut through the beach, and on its banks I could see my three friends, their eyes fixed on the cliff but their hearts no doubt sinking.

I was about to shout something to them, a jest of some sort, when the sleeping Hydra wakened with great force. Looking over my shoulder as I swam, my gaze was fixed on the grotto in the cliff. Then out of its visible arc, below which the waters passed, leaped something I had never seen or expected to see on earth—a tongue of pale blue flame lashing out half the length of the lake. In the next instant the waters about the outlet heaved up, black streaked with snowy white, and some of them flew high, but these were instantly obscured by what looked like a black snowstorm upside down, which was flying muck.

I saw all this a full second, perhaps two, before I heard a great WHUSH that must have been made by the darting column of flame, instantly followed by the shattering roar of an explosion. It echoed and re-echoed from the hills, and was a wondrous sound, truly the roar of a Titan. Although I saw the upflung chunks of muck, mixed with a few great stones, reach their full height, stop in the air, then tumble to earth, ever the stones rising and falling faster than the thrown muck, I hardly heard the fall of either because of the still-resounding crash of the explosion.

Yet somehow I had hoped for more than this. The upheaval had been confined to the outlet of the lake and the immediately surrounding area, by no means to the whole fen, and through my mind darted the remembrance that the holes in the muck giving forth the fatal vapors were far more widespread. Indeed they were everywhere in the basin up to the headwaters of the creek, although now I had swum where they were few, if any, the bed of the watercourse being sand, perhaps washed in from the beach, instead of black mud, and the ground firming on both sides as I approached its outlet in the sea. What could I believe, then, but that while we had dealt the Hydra a severe and perhaps a crippling blow, we had not killed her?

I had noticed a few seconds before, perhaps only one deep swimmer's breath before, an old snag on my left hand, perhaps washed in by a gale of long ago, and a thing never seen in the basin itself, although a few were found on the lower waters of all the creeks flowing from the lake, and on the beach itself. I happened to glance in that direction again, and to my unutterable amazement it was still directly opposite me on my right hand—it had not begun to drop behind me. I stroked harder, only to find our relative positions still unchanged; it was as though it were traveling beside me, as in a fantastic dream. I stroked again, a full stroke of great power, only to perceive that it was no longer opposite me but ahead of me.

I rallied my scattering faculties with all the power of my will. My common sense grasped instantly that the waters of the creek had reversed their direction—that instead of moving lazily toward the sea with the outgoing tide, they were flowing into the Sink with rapidly increasing speed and power. I flung against them with all my strength, to find that I could make no headway swimming. Then some instinct made me drop my feet, which found firm bottom. I could hardly believe the evidences of my senses, for usually at this stage of the tide this region of the creek was deep enough to drown me. There could be no answer to the mystery other than that the water level was falling with incredible rapidity. The notion struck me that the explosion had torn a great rent in the ground or, more likely, broken the floor of the underground passage, and the lake water was pouring in in tremendous volume.

All this thinking and doing had occurred in not more than three minutes, perhaps two, since the explosion. Now it was followed by another explosion, compared to which the first was no more than the popping of a wind-inflated cow gut by an urchin.

Almost at the instant there was a blinding flash of deep-blue light, in which every distant feature of the landscape stood forth in marvelous clarity and those at hand looked pitch-black in contrast, and then the remaining waters of the creek struck against me with such force that I was hurled forward and knocked breathless. Truly it was a wonder that my bones were not crushed.

Then in wild terror I glanced over my shoulder and saw the whole fen in the most violent turmoil. Close to the cliff rose a mighty geyser of water, great as a waterspout seen at sea, amidst which huge rocks were hurled, and from there outward the great expanse of black muck, bearing what remained of the lake and the headwaters of the creek, heaved as might a monster, magnitudinous beyond imagination, rising from her bed. It rolled like the sea in tempest, with waves of black mud, and the creekbed under my feet was seized with heavy tremors.

These slowly lessened. The heaving fen began to settle into its ancient hollow in the hills, and its fearful waves abated, and slowly it grew still. I thrust through the waist-deep water toward the beach, and presently it was knee-deep, and then once more it began to deepen, I suppose from lake water, which had poured into an abyss, being spewed up by the second explosion. But the bank was firm now and I climbed out and ran toward my friends, one of whom had gotten to his feet; the two others were trying to rise, after being stunned by the cataclysm.

"It is my studied opinion," Right Doer told me with great manner as he stood erect and calm beside me, meanwhile wiping with the back of his hand a bloody nose, "that the Lernaean Hydra is as dead as Hector."

"She was some manner of dragon, and hence a serpent," Nessus said. "Although she may still shake her head and her tail, like a scotched snake, you've broken her back." And he sniffed deeply and in vain for the smell of rotten eggs.

Actaeon took my hand and kissed it, a salutation I answered in kind. Then we made our way to the village, all of its houses damaged and a few of them shaken down, but with its whole people out to meet us with jubilant, shining eyes.

CHAPTER TEN

TAMING OF THE BOAR

1

Ere we returned to Orchomenus, where I would report the outcome of my labor to King Eurytus, Right Doer and I went to Thebes
for a brief visit to his father Amphitryon, Wrathful Leader, and to
Althea, and to field hands and household slaves whom we both loved.
Truly we arrived none too soon, if we were to see the old soldier before
he took off in Charon's ferry across the River Styx. He was not greatly
wasted, despite his eating neither meat nor corn for many a week,
subsisting in a dim way on wine and a few dried figs. But the flesh
still cleaving to his bones was the direct result of what I took for a
certain symptom of his early departure—his sleeping in a deep, trance-
like sleep about twenty-two or even twenty-three of the twenty-four
turnings of the sandglass and hence his vital processes' making little
call on his store of flesh. He usually wakened five or six times in the
course of the day and night, at which times his natural needs were
served, and he talked intelligently, although feebly, with members of
the household.

These wakings had come at longer intervals and had been more
brief in the weeks preceding Right Doer's and my arrival. On waking
two hours before midnight to find us crouched before his sheepskin
bed, he recognized us instantly, his dim eyes lighted palely, and on
calling for wine, he also called for a little vial of the concentrated juice
of nightshade berries, which was known to apothecaries as a stimulant
to failing hearts. A little of this he poured in his winecup. At once a
trace of color appeared in his gaunt cheeks and his voice became less
feeble and more manly.

"I rejoice that you have come," he told us. "Not always, as I lay half in slumber, did my soul wander in dreams; sometimes it sped forward and backward in time, and I bethought myself of what I had done that I wished were undone, and of what I had failed to do that I wished were done. I have little to tell you, Right Doer, my true and valiant son, other than my joy in you and of my great satisfaction that I feel now, and of which a dim reflection may flush my face in Hades. If you live, you are to inherit my broad lands. Cherish them well, and cherish all who served me in the fields and at the loom and cooking fires. Truly the great Gods blessed me on the night that my seed was planted in Alcmene's womb, and there took root, and thereby she swelled, and in season gave birth to you, Iphicles, my only son born in wedlock, my heir, and my honor before the Gods."

Iphicles could not answer because he was in tears.

"And to you, Heracles, I owe a debt which my soul has yearned to pay ere I departed," Wrathful Leader went on, when a slave had held the cup long to his pale lips. "The last time I spoke to you it was in bitterness. My vanity had been hurt, and perhaps something more than vanity, my rightful pride, that my beautiful Alcmene had entertained a lover while I was far from home, fighting in dire battle, and that you were the fruit of that union. I told you that I thought you were the son of a burly slave of the fields, to whom she had yielded in abandonment to base lust. Those words I withdraw. I uttered them because of signs that I misread, such as your plain appearance compared to that of godlike Iphicles, and your tardiness to him in matters of the mind, and of what I thought was your brute strength. Since then I have heard of your slaying the giant Antaeus, the abominable, whereby you wrung from the tyrant Eurytus a year's parole from exile in dark Egypt for a thousand freemen of Thebes, and a thousand and more slaves. Also I heard of your dispatch of the great lion of Nemea, whereby the parole was lengthened by half a year. Also I heard of his sending you to Lernaea, to slay the Hydra that oppresses and slays the folk, and I doubt not that you, with your friends' help, have won this victory, too, for I perceived its light lingering in your eyes and those of Iphicles when I saw you, as in a dream, enter my chamber. Thus I this declare before the Gods. The blessings of the Gods when Alcmene conceived you and gave you birth, by some seed unknown, was greater than when she conceived and gave birth to my lawful son, Iphicles."

"Sir, you are wrong," I burst out in a choked voice.

"No, he is not," Iphicles broke in, gazing at me with burning eyes. "I have known it always."

"Nay, I am not wrong. The high Gods, or the very Fates, moved in mysterious ways to bring you into being, out of a woman of parts, a dame worthy to mother and give suck to the savior of Thebes in days to come—days already fated by the Remorseless Sisters, days even then like unto an army marching far off, shadows as yet in the polished mirror of Time, but their destination certain. For that was provided a fit sire. I know not who he was, but I know that his seed was a mighty seed, and it comes to me as in a dream that you, and you alone, were the issue of his loins, and that he was a mighty man. . . . Now I ask that you both kiss my head and hands, for my heart has beat wildly from the spirit of the wine and the elixir, and suddenly it is tired, and I must sleep, and I believe—I hope—it will be the sleep of death."

"Stay awhile longer, Amphitryon, Wrathful Leader," I bade him.

"Nay, I cannot. My soul has lingered until now only because it could not pass until we had said our farewells, and I eased my troubled heart by confession. Farewell, Iphicles. Farewell, my foster son."

So my brother and I kissed his head and hands, and sat beside him as he drifted off to sleep. Throughout that long night he slept, ever more deeply, sinking, it seemed, in an abyss of sleep at whose bottom waited patient, implacable Death, and we could not believe he would ever wake again. Yet, as the East was lighting and Eos rose in robes all the more gorgeous to our eyes because of the cold, bleak dawn, and her effulgence came through the arch into the room, Wrathful Leader did waken, and then rose on one elbow, and then he spoke.

"I did not speak urgently enough, when I advised our King to pay tribute to Eurytus and not risk the fortunes of war," he told us. "I loved him, and it was against my heart to see him appease an upstart tyrant; and I held my tongue against my better judgment. Now countless of my country have precoursed me into Hades. But partly through you, Iphicles, my son, and mainly through you, Heracles, some of the wrong done will be undone. Now my soul goes forth, lightly and with joy. I depart the sorry clay that has been my prison ever since my wound. Far away I hear the ripple of waters, and what can they be but the dark waters of the River of Woe, which straightway I will cross? Nay, I will not go to the Elysian Fields. I betrayed my trust as

Captain of the Host when I did not speak my true mind to my King. Still, in Hades I will behold many of my old comrades of battle, and although we shall know not each other, and cannot tell old tales, or speak, still a little start of remembrance will thrill through the dim shadow I am become. And there I will see many who fought and fell before the walls of Troy, which glory Fate had forbidden me, and I wish with all my heart I might lay eyes on the greatest hero of them all, Achilles, son of Peleus, the Greek without peer. Perchance some day I will wander from the cold halls of Tartarus, where gather the common dead, and stray unto the outskirts of the Elysian Fields, and there I may behold him at a distance, and the light of his countenance will glance into my eyes like unto the beams from the burnished helm of Hector. Sons of my soul, my breath fails, and my heart is overwhelmed. Hale unto Thebes! Glory unto Greece! Atropos comes with her shears; and she has lost her fearful guise and is beautiful in my sight. Now she is about to cut the thread, and in an instant more——"

I thought I heard a little snipping sound, whereupon Amphitryon toppled down; and when we gazed into his face, the strange, magical light of life was gone from it utterly, along with almost all likeness to the living man, and his open eyes were dark.

2

Iphicles, the field hands, and I brought wood and raised it in a great heap, and laid thereon the body of Amphitryon, and set the fire. This blazed high, and was plain to see from afar, whereby the King came from his citadel, as well as many lesser folk, to pour a little wine upon the flame. No few of his old comrades, maimed or scarred by battle, and husbandmen from nearby fields came to pay the Leader their last respects.

And among the visitors to the pyre was a gaunt old man with burning eyes, and white hair that ever stirred a little as though in an unfelt wind, and his face was one which, once seen, could never be forgotten, for he was Tiresias, Seer of Wonders, once a cattle drover in a distant pasturage, now the pride of Thebes.

When the corpse of Wrathful Leader was utterly consumed, and the fire had begun to sink, I came upon the old man sitting under a tree where some payer of respect to the dead had left a small skin of wine,

now nearly empty. Perhaps Seer of Wonders had sat down there only
to wet his lips, but one draught had called for another, and his face
looked flushed in the firelight and his eyes were so wildly bright that
I thought that he had drunk enough to addle his head and thicken
his speech, and hence the power to prophesy might be on his tongue.
For well I remembered the terms of Dionysus' gift unto a young
drover who had fished drunken Pan out of a mudhole, washed him,
and restored to him his lost pipes.

Seer of Wonders was muttering to himself and hardly noticed me
when I laid my hand on his shoulder. Yet in an instant he looked
into my face and recognized me.

"Heracles!" he said. "Your next labor will be one of the lesser of
many you may perform, and Right Doer's part in it will be greater
than yours, yet I hear great rocks falling, and the sound of rushing
waters."

"Tell me what lies beyond."

"The night is bitter cold, and the wind bites to the bone," the old
man went on, not answering my plea, and instead still intent on the
same vision. "You and your friends will be bivouacked just under the
snow, and that night the dying winter seizes the whole mountaintop
in an icy grasp, which is what you have been waiting for. And for this
labor you will be cheated of your just due and mead of honor by the
miser King, but despair not, for Atropos has not brought her shears,
nor have you yet caught her merciless eye. But beware the next labor.
I see you returning alive, and you walk staunchly, and bear no visible
wound, yet I think that your soul is wounded by some stroke I cannot
see. Nay, I will not drink more of the good wine. Already I repent
my many draughts, for I will lie sick all day tomorrow with an aching
head. Heracles, will you offend a Goddess? All is confusion in my mind;
the visions start to come, then fade away. Beware the labor following
the next, because its peril, if unseen, is still great. How many are
there in all? I cannot count them on my fingers and my head is too
thick to do sums. And after the last, what then? What is this light
that throws shadows on the ground?"

"It is the dying funeral pyre of Amphitryon, Wrathful Leader."

"I told him he would lose the war, and a mighty tribute would be
demanded. This last you will alleviate, but at what price? Heracles, it
is not good to be great. Greatness is never given by the Gods free of
cost to man. There is great loneliness, and often great sorrow, and

often untimely death, as Achilles died by the arrow of a craven. Another arrow flies. It all but misses, and frees but a few drops of blood. Yet a great storm breaks, and the Gods rouse up from their pleasure and their repose."

"Seer of Wonders, who is my father?"

"That I know not. I behold a vision, and it is shining and beautiful, but it makes no sense to my addled mind. Some day you will know, fear not. Now go from me, because my head splits with pain, and I am an old man, past four score, and I have no longer strength for these excesses, and I must sleep."

He turned from me and lay down and I had no choice but to turn away.

3

For my reward and mead of honor for destroying the Lernaean Hydra, and because he could not get out of it, public feeling being what it was, King Eurytus postponed the surrender to him of Theban manhood for an additional six months.

As my next labor, he appointed the capture alive of the Erymanthian Boar. Again a fanciful name was being used for an inanimate force of nature, in this case the Erymanthus River, which in flood times tore its banks and ruined fields with what seemed the ferocity of a gigantic beast. The river poured from a ravine in the heights of Mount Erymanthus north of Arcadia, fed by heavy rains and especially by the melting of winter snows. The King's command that it be "captured alive" meant of course the controlling of its freshets, but how in the name of the Gods my three companions and I could go about it, I had no glimmer of an idea.

When I searched Right Doer's face, my spirits rebounded. He did not seem in the least depressed by the appointment. At the first chance he reminded me that although the lowlands had been planted to corn, vineyards, and olive orchards since time out of mind, only in the lifetime of living men had the river been destructive and the Erymanthian Boar become a common term in Greek speech. Something had happened half a century ago, some sudden event of nature, that had changed the ways of the waters. But until we knew what it was our hands were tied.

This inquiry proved an easy one—indeed we discovered the answer on our first day's visit to the region of the floods. An old grape grower told us that in his own boyhood the Erymanthus River had occupied a different bed from the present one—much broader, and with higher banks, a bed that now carried only a minor brook. So the four of us climbed the lofty mountain, one of the most beautiful in Greece, and the mystery of the river's change of course was readily solved.

The river was born of the overflow of a beautiful lofty lake, no doubt originally formed by a landslide. A later landslide had choked a wide, steep ravine into which it had poured, whereby the waters had flowed over its rims and scoured out a passage to a smaller ravine that led to the bed of what had been no more than a large mountain brook. This had captured, and become what was now the inadequate bed of, the Erymanthus River.

Our problem, a weighty one to be sure, the answer to which I could not dream, was somehow to clear the original ravine of a great slab of shale, perhaps once part of a cliff, weighing a hundred or more tons, broken, or at least cracked into innumerable segments. Only then could the river resume its flow and recover its ancient bed.

"A tenth of the vapors that we exploded in the lair of the Lernaean Hydra would do the trick," Nessus said, "if we had them handy."

"But we haven't," Right Doer answered, "and it would take the labor of a thousand men and two thousand oxen, for the Gods know how long, to remove that heap of rock by brute force."

In his drunken babblings, Seer of Wonders had prophesied that the present labor would be one of the lightest I would undertake. I wished I could see some sign of it—to me it appeared difficult almost to the point of the impossible. Yet Right Doer pointed out a fact that I could not yet call hopeful, yet which lightened my heart. The great slab of shale in the ravine was precariously poised. It lay on a steep pitch of the ravine and jutted out over a precipice, and here a waterfall must have glimmered in the sunlight, flung up rainbow spray, and in flood roared like a lion. One thrust of a Titan would hurl the whole obstruction into the glen below. But most of the Titans were dead, slain in the great war with Zeus, and the few that still lived, such as Atlas and Ocean, did not concern themselves with doing chores for pygmy human beings.

"If we had long enough poles, I think we could push over some of the sections, and then maybe the whole mass would topple," remarked Actaeon, who had been probing with sticks the rifts in the shale.

"I think the laws of leverage would be against us," Right Doer answered, whose high, round dome had never spilled a scrap of what Rhadamanthus had taught him. "How deep are those cracks?"

"They appear to go clear to the ground."

"What becomes of the rainwater that must fall into them?"

"I noticed a little seepage under the rocks which you can see trickle onto the precipice and down into the chasm."

A biting wind out of the north had come up—sharp-fanged Boreas, who forgot that this was the end of the second month since the winter solstice, when Zephyr, the mild west wind, should have her turn. We left the cold heights and soon were taking comfort in a crackling campfire that knew no seasons, which we had built at our bivouac below the great steep of the mountain. On the following morning Right Doer was inclined to hurry us through our breakfast and back to the scene we had left, with gravely troubled minds, the afternoon before.

Once there, he went straight to look at an earthen jug of copiously watered wine which Actaeon had lugged up and left close to the pile of shale. It had begun its journey, I recalled, half wine, half water, but yet warming, for Actaeon loved his creature comforts. After we four thirsty, sweating climbers had taken generous draughts, he had always refilled the jug at every spring or brooklet. As a consequence, it had barely tasted of wine when we had begun our cold descent.

Now the jug held not even water, for it was shattered into fragments.

"The freeze last night on these heights must have been severe," Right Doer remarked with a lilt in his voice I had heard before.

"We could have expected that," Nessus answered, "because of the biting wind."

"Nessus, you once wished for a power as great as the exploding fumes in the lair of the Hydra. You have seen such a power in operation. A vessel of solid iron would have broken as surely, as the water turned to ice. Also, I wish to point out to you that the God who hurled this rock into the ravine was good to us in three respects. First, that it fell on a steep slope, second, that one end actually overhangs the chasm, and third, it has many deep cracks and faults. The difficulties in setting our trap will be great but far from insurmountable. The great question is, will Boreas return with his icy breath? Spring is waxing fast."

"I think he will return," Nessus answered. "He will come, and bring hard frost. Until after the spring equinox, shepherds who graze their sheep on such mountainsides never venture up without their fire sticks and sheepskin robes. Although I was never a sheep stealer, only a redoubtable cattle thief under Antaeus' sway, I know that much!"

"By great Zeus, we will make an offering to Boreas," Right Doer cried, his eyes sparkling. "No one ever has, that I know of, unless it be sailors becalmed in the seas of Hyperbore—most Greeks detest the icy-fingered, unconvivial wretch. Heracles, you have your bow? Can you provide a stag—a mere yearling buck will do—while we continue Nessus' experiment of probing the cracks in the shale? And this afternoon we will organize our corps of water-bearers."

I had no trouble shooting a two-year-old red deer and lugging his carcass to the scene of our endeavors. Actaeon, skilled at butchering, prepared the offal, the bones, a good deal of fat to warm Boreas' cramped belly on cold nights, and some succulent steaks as a surprise, for a sacrifice. We had no barley meal with which to dress it, but poured on a libation of wine from the wooden flask that the great hunter invariably carried on a shoulder strap before we laid the offering on a small, especially built fire. Boreas would not like a large, high-leaping, crackling fire, Right Doer told us solemnly. His element, his domain was the great cold.

After our party had feasted on one quarter, I lugged the other three down the mountainside to a village of woodcutters and charcoal burners on the banks of what was now the Erymanthus River. We soon learned that their elders or their now departed sires had been greatly upset at having to move here from their former village, now left to decay on the bank of what was now almost a dry river bed. The "old river," as it was called, had flowed to their convenience; they could set timber adrift, and it did not jam at the bends and narrows; it welcomed all they could cut, and carried it safely to the towns on the plain. The present course gave them no end of trouble, and in periods of flood their logs were often cast ashore, from whence wicked lowlanders made off with them. Obviously these people would be eager helpers of our enterprise.

They had never heard of Heracles; anyway I had no gift for dissimulation. This mattered not at all, since Right Doer easily persuaded them that he had been instructed by an oracle to pour water by the hundreds of gallons into all the cracks of the shale blocking the old bed of the Erymanthus on a night of heavy frost, whereupon the river would resume its former course. Truly a shiver ran down my spine when Right Doer told them in deep solemnity that the Dodona Oak, the oracle of great Zeus himself, had so prophesied, for even such a free spirit as Megara, or as free a thinker as white-headed Rhadamanthus, would have hesitated to take in vain names of such import. Right Doer went on to explain that all water originally fell from Heaven, of which Zeus was king. Hence it was quite natural that it should be the agent of redressing a wrong done the folk by a giant, one of the sons of Gaea and Ouranos, imprisoned under the earth nearby.

Winning the villagers' hearty agreement, Right Doer asked to speak to the best weather prophet of the settlement. This old woodsman told us that without doubt cold would strike once more, a few days before or a few days after the equinox, bringing chilly weather and bitter wind to the lowlands and severe frost to the uplands. Could he predict two days, or at least one, in advance? Surely he could—by the look of the sky, the flight and call of birds, the actions of flies and especially of wild bees. Then at noon of the day he named, forty stout fellows were to gather at the scene of the rockslide, each with the largest utensil for water carrying that he owned. This agreed upon, I gave them the three quarters of venison I had lugged downhill for their night's supper. Then my companions and I went happily to our camp.

Three days before the equinox, a dismal day of cold white clouds and the low moanings of Boreas filling all the air, and with the new-budded trees creaking and groaning softly, our crew of water carriers gathered at the appointed hour. We fed them well, and bade them sit long over their meat, for the reason that the water we sprinkled on the grass had not yet turned white and sparkling, and if water were poured now into the clefts of the rocks it would only drain out. About two hours after noon, the deep frost began to strike, and our breaths smoked, and the men poured a little water in every crack. Seepage slowly ceased, and when the bottom of every rift was plugged with ice, the men began their slow filling with ice-cold water from the small pool of impounded water above the rockslide.

As the cold deepened, the men's pouring became more bold, and before long their busy scurryings to the pool and back to the rocks would have suggested a gang of fire fighters in full hustle. What amazed us all was the amount of water required to fill the many rifts—instead of hundreds of gallons, we poured in a full three thousand. Then, as the sun set behind darkling clouds and the wind died away and the cold deepened, the men came to the fires to warm their red and aching hands, for every rift was full filled with half-frozen slush.

Then there was nothing to do but wait, a harder trial on Right Doer than on me, for he was of more nervous and impatient disposition. I suppose it was nine o'clock when a great piece of shale, weighing perhaps two tons and jutting out from the main crag that overhung the fall, broke off and fell with a crashing roar into the ravine. The water-bearers looked at Right Doer with rounding eyes, for although they had hoped fervently that their curious and seeming senseless labor would fetch results, being human they had only half believed it. Then another smaller piece broke off, quickly followed by a third.

Then, as we gaped, the frontmost crag began to lean forward and down, and I looked and saw the whole rock pile stirring as though it were alive. It was trying to break into fragments, I thought, but it could not, because so much of it was interbound, and surely it was originally one great cliff fallen from the nearby height. My heart had time for five or more great, painful beats before the black mass began to fall. We could barely see it in the thickening dark, and it looked ominous in the extreme, and I found myself remembering a world I had never seen, could not possibly have known, but which perhaps I had visited in dreams—the world before men came to abide here, or any beasts, or any trees raised their proud tops, or any oceans beat upon the strands, when the face of the earth was naked rock, to be torn and broken and heaped up in unspeakable violence.

Down into the chasm tumbled that mighty mass with frightful roarings that deafened all of us for a space, which stunned our brains, and which aroused folk from their sleep unmeasured leagues away. Behind it poured the waters of the pool, glimmering a little even in the half-dark, and in wild tempest, and although this fall was reduced awhile, it never ceased altogether, for the waters that fed the pool likewise careened down. After a while the flow began to increase, as some of the waters feeding the ravine of the present river retraced old steps, because an ancient way, long closed, was again open.

Days were to pass before the old bed fully reclaimed its own, and the old river had fully recaptured the new, but tonight the villagers saw the unmistakable signs of the conquest, and they sat about our fires until dawn in wondrous communion with one another, too awed to say very much, but joyous to be alive. And we four knew we had captured alive the Erymanthian Boar, and no more would he ravage the lowland fields and vineyards, and that the hand of man was a strong and able hand when put to thoughtful use, and at long last it would do more to make the world better for the folk than all the Gods and Goddesses of Olympus.

CHAPTER ELEVEN

THE STAG AND THE HUNTRESS

1

Eurytus awarded me no mead of honor for my part in slaying the Erymanthian Boar. A meaner deprivation in the sight of the Gods was his giving none to Right Doer, who we four companions perceived perfectly clearly was the true destroyer. The King sought to justify his niggardliness before his court by relating that I had help not only from my friends but from forty charcoal burners and fuel cutters of the hamlet.

Actually he was in a truculent and ignoble mood. Time rolled on, bringing him closer to his own destruction, from which his wealth and high place could not save him. He had not yet laid low the man who he thought bore the mark of Zeus, and still he dared not by naked power. It occurred to me that his refusing me my due was in the way of practice for some more overt and harder stroke. He knew it would rankle with his subjects, great and lowly, for all were Greeks, who are often rapacious and bloody but never small, but perhaps he wanted to test his own popularity and power.

"Your next labor," he told in pompous tones before his assembled court, "will be to capture alive the Cerynean Stag, the greatest of all stags, with golden horns, sacred to Artemis. And on this enterprise not my son Nessus, nor your brother Iphicles, nor the great hunter Actaeon may go with you. Nessus must go as my ambassador to the King of Thessaly on an urgent matter of state. Iphicles is out of favor with Artemis for making a sacrifice to Pan, whom she loves not, whose pipes often scare the deer that she most loves to chase on moonlit nights, this sacrifice being made in gratitude for your slaying Iniquity, one of her charges. With you, Heracles, she is most incensed for slaying a young stag, without mark or blemish, that she had picked for her own quarry, and which was to have been a fit feast for the Olympians. Instead, you slew him with an arrow to make a sacrifice to bitter Boreas, and as a bribe to loutish woodsmen to carry and pour water. Thus it would be useless for you to pursue the Cerynean Stag without help from Artemis. You would utterly fail if you did not tumble to your death down the mountainside. But I will send with you someone greatly beloved by the Goddess, who will implore her forgiveness and her favor upon your venture."

"For that I thank you, King Eurytus," I replied, all I could think of to say to his specious speech.

"The one I mean is no other than Iole, my daughter," the King went on. "And while it is not necessary that she have an escort, her office protecting her from any violence even from a lust-mad centaur, still she was a princess ere she was a priestess, and she shall have the company of a grave dame. Now you have my leave to depart."

I looked at Right Doer as I turned from the royal chair, and he raised his eyebrows in a sign I knew. A quick glance of the King's Companions and others in the stately chamber showed all their faces bearing a cynical expression, for rarely had they heard, even from Eurytus, always windy and often grandiloquent, such an extravagant excuse for some trick. Obviously he wanted to part me from my companions during the coming trial, perhaps only to decrease my chances of success. Perhaps he had divined that while I did the heaving, Right Doer accomplished the necessary thinking; and of course Actaeon was a skilled hunter, especially useful on the chase of a great stag. But why he contrived for Iole to go with me balked my imagination.

Indeed not only his fishy pretexts but the labor itself had a spurious aspect. While a widespread legend existed of a huge stag roaming the borders of Arcadia and Achaia, no man of sense believed in his having golden horns or at most other than gold-colored horns by some accident of nature. Certainly he did no harm and was not an enemy of the folk such as the Nemean Lion, the Lernaean Hydra, and the Erymanthian Boar. I confessed a tingling excitement at the prospect of Iole's company. Its very mystery, as well as vistas pictured by sensuous imagination, would thrill any adventurer. Still I was curiously frightened by the whole undertaking, mainly perhaps because of the prophecy of Seer of Wonders.

And then it seemed I was not alone in the weird foreboding. As I left the chamber with Right Doer, I caught a glimpse of Megara. Her face appeared pale and greatly strained, and her great black eyes as wild as a black cat's.

Time sped; and my fears, dim and intangible to start with, faded to no more than a vague uneasiness, such as one feels on entering the Acre of the Dead under a wasted moon. Meanwhile the King's minions were putting together equipment for a journey somewhat more lordly than I had ever undertaken—of course because one of the journeyers was to be Iole, his favorite daughter, and the Priestess of Artemis. Never before had I set forth with one mule cart, let alone two. The foremost, in which she and I would ride when we did not wish to stretch our legs walking, was of as fine workmanship as a chariot of war, and rigged somewhat the same, so it could be drawn by two fast mules, driven by a slave. In this we could arrive at our night's lodging well ahead of the baggage wain, drawn by one mule, and have time for pleasant leisure before supper and sleep. I assumed that, in addition to the driver, the grave dame who Eurytus had proclaimed would escort Iole would ride in the rear wagon. It so chanced, or at least it so happened, that she did not come at all. There was no sign of her when we were ready to set forth, Iole did not mention her, and I was glad enough to let the little mystery go unsolved.

Or, possibly, the solution was merely that Iole needed no escort, which no one knew better than the King, unless it was Iole herself. I knew it quite well as she stepped on the hub of the cart and lightly swung aboard, with the grace of a tern in flight. Even without the protection of her Goddess, which would seem to everyone completely real, indeed which her every word and action appeared to reflect, she would still give the impression of being inviolable as well as competent to look after herself in all situations. Surely she was the archetype of Greek maidens.

In all my previous conversations with Iole, we had both been under tension. I wondered what I would say to her when we were jogging along in the cart, especially after we had said all that was worth saying, at present, about the Cerynean Stag. Moreover our journey would be long. To travel by cart from Orchomenus to Corinth would take five days; from the latter town to the Cerynean Mountains there were mule

paths but almost nothing resembling a road; and if we had to use
pack beasts, as I suspected, we would have to leg it for from three to
five days more. Still, after the first hour passed with Iole, my fear of
being a tongue-tied lout and driving her to exasperation with cowherd
clumsiness abruptly passed away.

My companion was a different Iole from any I had met. It was as
though she had put by her priestly office and the goddess-like air that
was at once so beautiful and impressive, and had become my hail-
fellow-well-met. Indeed her exuberance was so marked that I began to
suspect a secret exultation, of which I could not dream the cause, although I found signs of it in the toss of her head, the joyful bells of
her laugh, and in the shine of her blue eyes. There was always something along the road to waken her mirth or prompt her to a rush of
happy speech. When I had nothing to say, she had dozens of things
that demanded saying.

"Why did the King choose the capture of the Cerynean Stag for my
next labor?" I asked, when we both felt warm and close from laughter
and gay talk, although at this moment she was mute, having been
moved by the beauty of the vast sunlit expanse of Lake Comais. "Always before he has given me labors that might benefit folk."

"Heracles, the only answer is pure vanity. I suppose you know the
story of the stag. He was very old and heavy, and senility had set in,
and the first sign, as usual in deer, was short, thick, misshapen antlers,
instead of the tall, sweeping, many-tined antlers he had worn in the
breeding season in his prime. You know, of course, that a stag's
antlers fall off in the late winter or early spring, then regrow throughout
the summer until early fall, when they become hard and solid horn.
In his wandering he came upon a lost shrine to Artemis. I am going
to visit it on this journey, if I can—it stands in a dim hollow in the
mountain, perhaps once the crater of a volcano, near the upper waters
of the Ladon River. The tale is told by an old woodcutter that the
stag had been wounded in a fight with a younger beast over a beautiful
snow-white hind, and that he knelt before the shrine and prayed that
his strength be returned to him along with a magnificent crown never
to fall from his head. To the woodsman's wonder, the beast changed
shape before his eyes, remaining as tall as ever but once more splendid
and lithe, and his misshapen horns turned to a mighty spread of antlers
that appeared to be gold. Ever since Eurytus heard the story he has
pined to put the stag in a pen, feed him rich water plants gathered in

the lake, give him plenty of hinds to cover, and make him his pet. Of course he wants to show him off to his royal guests. More than that, if the stag can be taught to lick his hand, my father believes he will borrow some of his essence—eternal youth and never-failing potency. I tell him that Artemis would give him these, if he made her great offerings. But he fears to ask her, for she is the sister of Apollo, who prophesied his doom."

"Has the stag a name?"

Somewhat to my surprise, Iole seemed startled by the question. "Yes. How did you know?"

"I did not know. I thought it likely because the Nemean Lion had a name."

"So has our stag. A beautiful, fitting name—Bounder. A charcoal burner from that region told the King that he had bounded over a pile of logs twelve feet high when one night he had wandered into their camp. Heracles, how are you going to capture him—alive? The country he has made his own, the upper watershed of the Ladon, must comprise one hundred square miles."

"Actaeon told me to learn his footprint; he said it would certainly be larger and cut deeper than any other stag's in the region. Then I must learn his ways, where he uses, as the hunters say—his drinking pools, his favorite meadows, the thickets where he sleeps. Then I am to bait him with hard salt, of which I have a big cake in the baggage wagon. When he begins to come for it regularly—and Actaeon says he will lick it in preference to the salty ground of natural salt licks—I will dig a pit and screen it well, one from which even Bounder cannot bound free."

"All that will take weeks and months. The budding leaves will be painted with frost before you are done. And if Artemis does not bless the hunt it will all come to nothing. If she does bless it, which I will entreat at her knees, all that will be unnecessary. The great stag will walk proudly into your camp and let you halter him."

I believed Iole, with all my heart and half my mind, yet caught myself yearning for the company of Right Doer, Actaeon, and Nessus. So often our Gods and Goddesses pay so little attention to the prayers of their very priests, even less to our offerings, and truly I knew of but very few incidents, by my own knowledge, where they interfered with what Rhadamanthus had called the course of nature. To turn the horny antlers of a stag into gold had been such an interference on a major scale. For any wild stag to enter a hunter's camp and with docility submit to the rope would be another. If Megara had made any such prophecy I would have laughed at her; in all truth she would laugh at Iole, despite the solemnity of her voice, the transfiguration of her face, and her priestess mien which, for the moment at least, she had resumed.

Then the inkling came to me that despite her mirth and gay talk, and despite the little storms of earthy passion I had seen envelope her, Iole was forever the priestess. Once in a while she rested from the office, but deepmost in her heart remained her dedication. We were enjoying each other's company. Sometimes I took her long slim white hand into my broad, thick, weathered hand, and she let it lie there awhile, although never very long. And now I might as well put by any wish-thinking that in the wild, mountainous country north of Arcadia, when we would share a rude camp with two slaves and three mules, we two might capture, long before I caught a deer with golden horns, the bliss of love. It might be that Iole knew her own fires, their intense pale flame, and she had dared let them leap a little in her sanctuary, where at most we could only dally with each other. In the wild wood, where solitude and the dim light and the mossy banks all breathed temptation, she would be as circumspect as when conducting stately service before the shrine.

This dismal prediction proved only too true. She remained my gay, often exuberant, always enchanting companion whether on the road, at our bivouacs, or in the few walled towns where the King's Companions gave us lodging for the night. At dangerous fords and on heart-stopping steeps she was imperturbable; but the lewd-minded rustics who sometimes gathered by the road to gape at our equipage never for a moment pictured her as my beloved. Facing the facts, I supposed they could not: I was too plain-looking, with my rough hair, stocky body, and farmer's face, to win a maiden so tall, beautiful, brilliant to the eyes, and lithe; and all these charms were added to an attraction far more subtle, felt rather than seen, which was the mien of an immortal nymph, if not a mighty Goddess.

At ancient Corinth we were guests of the King, and here I was bathed and anointed by his handmaidens; we both feasted and drank sea-dark wine in the light of silver braziers, and a lyrist of the ilk of Linus played music fit for the Olympians' halls, and maidens of surpassing beauty danced for our pleasure. Thereafter the road worsened.

Since we were making into a country peopled mainly by drovers and shepherds, woodcutters and charcoal burners, bereft of cities and citadels, it became a common thing to see deer cross or wolves dash away, and to hear eagles scream. Once a huge shaggy bear stood his ground, growling at us, and I feared he would attack our mules.

"Do not be alarmed," Iole told me. "All bears are sacred to Artemis, and he knows that I am likewise, and he will peacefully go his way."

In truth the bear looked at Iole steadily a few seconds, then gave a mighty grunt of surprise, or recognition, or perhaps apology, and turned tail, and trotted awkwardly into the forest. Shortly after this, our course abandoned all pretense of being a road, and became a mule path, so we stowed the carts in a farmer's barn, the two slaves loaded the backs of the three beasts and their own backs as well, and with these Iole and I prepared to leg it. Then I saw that some fifty pounds of gear had been left over, unable to find room on other backs, and since it would be useful to me, especially if the chase lasted as long as my fancies pictured, I loaded it on mine.

We pushed on, Iole caring naught how rough the path, climbing steeps with peaceful breathing where I panted and blew, wading through bogs with bare feet to save muddying her sandals, washing them in the first brook, gracefully skirting the sheer edge of dizzy cliffs, sometimes stopping to pick spring flowers, then running to overtake me, herself like the white hind that Bounder had loved and lost and which, perhaps, by the restoration of his youth, he had regained. Iole never failed to help pitch camp, whether to raise shelters of oiled cloth against the rain, lug water, or to cut fuel for our cooking and watch fire. Often on clear nights she and I made our beds in ten paces of each other, under the peerless starry sky of Greece, and often I lay awake awhile, hoping to hear her cough or see her toss, or pass some signal that she would welcome my attentions, but I had as well wait for the sky to fall; so I must turn with a big sigh and fall to sleep.

The change I noticed in Iole when we had gained the foothills of the Cerynean Mountains boded me no good. Her laughter was more scant, her merriment reduced, her intervals of silence lasted longer, her red eyebrows met more often as she pondered something, and the lines of her face were subtly changed as though from strain. What in the name of Calypso the Witch, I wondered, was her trouble? Why had she come with me in the first place?—a question I asked myself bluntly, from having to confess that I could not quite swallow her ready explanation that Eurytus wanted the great stag Bounder to lend him an essence whereby he himself could bound more nimbly into his slave girls' beds, and that without her present help I could not capture the beast.

The nearer we came to his lofty pastures, the less likely it seemed that I could capture him at all. Not merely Iole's championing me, but the hearty efforts of the Goddess herself would hardly weight the scales of Fate in my favor. More puzzling and troubling, we had heard more about him from the folk of the valleys, far from his haunts, than from weathered mountaineers in his very environs. The former had brothers or cousins or close friends who were thick with him as thieves, knowing him better than their own ewe lambs. The latter were strangely vague in their replies to our questions. One old and grizzled charcoal burner was more voluble than the rest, when Iole's brilliant eyes shone into his faded eyes, but his eagerness to please her was so apparent that I spoke to him later, out of her hearing.

"How long since you have yourself laid eyes on a great stag with golden horns?" I asked. "And in the name of Apollo I bid you speak truth."

"I love Apollo," the gaffer answered. "Without him, and his respect for truth and justice, Gods and men would turn to one great pack of wolves. I love him more for his songs, which I hear just before I come wide awake in the dewy dawns, when I have made my bivouac close to the roof of Heaven. When you invoke him, Stout Fellow who looks more like a drover than a fit companion for a princess, I must speak truth. I have never in my life seen a stag with golden antlers, or a wench cut crosswise instead of up and down, and when I have seen one, I will expect to behold the other."

"Do you know anyone who has seen such a stag?"

"Not one who has ever been wet by mountain dew."

"Is there a big stag hereabouts, with somewhat yellow-looking horns, known as Bounder?"

"There are several large stags, but their antlers look alike to me except for size, and only one that I know of, a big bay who stole our donkeys' barley, had a name. It was 'that red-haired son of a bitch wolf.' And, my lord, when you are capturing Bounder with the Golden Horns, will you do me the slight favor of catching me a white crow? I become lonesome of evenings, and wish to teach him to sing."

Here was a typical Greek, I thought, as I trudged off. At one moment eloquent of a manly bond with great Apollo, causing my heart to glow, and the next, deriding me with sarcasm. And after a few moments' brooding I came to the conclusion that his evidence was impossible to dispute, and there never was, nor ever had been, and I doubted greatly if there ever would be, a stag named Bounder with horns of solid gold. I had been sent to find a mare's nest. And in the name of the Gods, why?

2

As I was falling to sleep, a question vague in my mind at first, then becoming sharp and commanding, demanded an answer. Did Iole herself believe in the giant stag and his miraculous transformation? True, she never spoke of him except in a buoyant tone, her expression animated, her eyes alight. The fact remained that the deepest feeling that her face and manner betrayed appeared when she spoke of the Cerynean Artemis, that very ancient statue of the Goddess that she had said she intended to visit, and which was now in easy walking distance.

Lately she had spoken of the image on a good many occasions. She said it was hewn out of iron-hard volcanic rock, roughly, rather than delicately worked, and that below the breasts, which were not multiple as in the broken relic in the sanctuary, and not especially accented, the stone was not much more than a slab of stone vaguely suggesting the female form. She thought that its presence in the very bottom of a crater-like pit had indicated that at the time of its carving Artemis was probably better known as Callisto (Most Beautiful) and had some connection with the Underworld. This was quite reasonable, Iole thought, since her arrows sent so many aged and sick people down to that world. Possibly mourners who wished to communicate with the dead visited this particular shrine. It was to be remembered that nowhere in Greece was the cult of Artemis older than in Arcadia, on the northern border of which stood this very ancient idol.

Megara had spoken of Iole's capacity for wile. Could it be she who had put it into Eurytus' head to assign me, as my fourth labor, the capturing of the Cerynean Stag because she herself wished to perform some rite before the ancient Artemis? If this was her aim, what part did I have in the singular affair? As a priestess she had free access to all Greece: she could cross any frontier; her person was inviolate; she had already shown her fearlessness in traveling without armed escort. Another puzzling factor was that, although she spoke frequently of the image, and tonight's bivouac was on the banks of the Ladon River, not more than an hour's rough walk from the shrine, she had shown no inclination to pay it an early visit.

Baffled by these mysteries, I was drifting off into slumber when I was summoned wide awake by a medium-loud sound a short distance beyond the dying cooking fire. Because it was followed by heavy silence, as though the sound maker was waiting and watching to see if it had wakened me, I made no movement except to half open my heavy eyelids. Almost at once I identified Iole's tall, lithe form close to the stake where she had picketed a small ewe, whose fancy she had taken, and who hence had taken her fancy, at the camp of the old charcoal burner who had spoken to me so bluntly about Bounder, the stag of the golden horns. She had given the gaffer a woolen cloth for the puny beast, who had trotted after our pack mules over many a rough mile. At present Iole was crouching in the shadows, holding the ewe by a leather collar I had made for her. The noise I had heard might have been the upsetting of a wooden bucket of water that Iole had stood in her pet's reach.

She remained motionless a long minute to see if I was asleep. Then she greatly compounded the questions in my mind by two very curious acts. The notion had already struck me that she was taking this hushed and hallowed hour to visit the ancient shrine of Artemis. The moon was only one night waned from her full frontal splendor, not in the least wasted in my sight, only slightly bulged from her perfect round; and she hung only three hands' breadth over the mountain pines and her face of polished silver had a faintly purple tint. Her beauty in these windless heights, as well as the hush that overlaid all, had no doubt moved Iole to the zenith of the priestess fervor that was never quite lost in her and was so readily inflamed. Truly I could understand her making her pilgrimage at this hour, to be alone with the ancient representation of her Goddess in her strange, deep abode. What really startled me, however, was her tying a thong on the leathern collar of the ewe and, when she started off, carrying the wooden bucket in the other hand.

As far as I knew she went unarmed, although my eye had caught a pale flash that might have been the moon's beams on some instrument of bronze. Also I instantly perceived that the ewe's company, although pleasant to her, actually added to her danger. Pards of great size that we call leopards, meaning they were somewhat like lions in might, ranged these heights, and lions too were far from unknown, and numerous wolves, although usually skulking at this time of year, became desperately bold when hungry. Almost always these beasts, unless habitual man hunters, durst not attack their fellow night wanderers who stood so tall, or else the idea had never struck their beast minds that man was good to eat. But walking behind Iole, or at her side, would be one of their common prey. They would see the ewe in the bright moonlight, possibly smell her too, and their blood would come up, and their fever to kill waken, and in that fever they might strike right and left. It would be quite like Iole to attempt to defend her charge, to her own dire harm.

Truly I needed no prompting other than this thought to make me spring out of bed, put on my sandals and a loincloth, and grasp my spear. The fact remained, and it would be useless to deny it even to myself, that I rejoiced at the need of following her in her defense, because I was already devoured by curiosity about her mission. Because of her office, no one, even her father Eurytus, could properly question her comings and goings. Still, I, Heracles, felt fully justified in trailing her, out of her sight and sound, so I could protect her in a brabble with night roamers who did not know a Priestess of Artemis from a woodcutter's daughter.

Such moonlight as this only appears bright. Actually, as I had long ago discovered, its seeming luminance was a cheat. Most objects begin to dim away at fifty feet and become almost invisible at about a hundred paces. By taking care to cause no stone to clack against its fellow, I had no trouble avoiding discovery. We climbed a long hill, crossed a valley, and then began to mount a considerable steep, which I surmised by its vague shape blotting out moonlight was the cone of an extinct volcano, thrust up long ages ago by fire and violence far underground. I trudged up, puffing a little in my wont. Iole seemed to rise up as though on wings. But to my somewhat alarm, the ewe began to hang back, indeed to try to break from her leash, and I could think of no reason other than her smelling some beast of the mountain which wakened her wild alarm.

What was at least a fourth of the rim of the once volcano had weathered away, and through this gap the moonlight poured in magic flood. Having passed through this, Iole began a somewhat perilous descent into the crater itself. There were numerous crags and low weathered cliffs over which she must pick her way, and soon the moon no longer gave her a gray guidance, because of riding too low in the eastern sky. And then what a country bumpkin could take for a priestly miracle came to pass in the dimness of reflected moonlight before my eyes.

Perceiving that Iole had stopped, I too stopped. She was busying herself with something in her bucket, to judge by its knock against a stone, and suddenly I saw what was not much more than a spark of light, yet almost beyond credence in this dark pit. It looked exactly like a bit of dry moss, such as we use for tinder, smoldering a little after being ignited by a fire drill. Then I perceived the faintest outline of her face as she brought the tinder close to her lips and blew on it. In a few seconds it burst into tiny, yet unmistakable, flame, which she quickly fed. From this she ignited what I thought was a short torch of oil-soaked reeds bound together.

I myself was a country bumpkin. My neck hairs too would have stirred if I had not known aforetime that the priests of our Olympian Gods knew a quick way of making fire, Right Doer having told me so. It was his opinion that the method was employed at the Elysian mysteries to awe neophites, and that it had been brought from Egypt. The device was an ivory cylinder containing a close-fitting plunger, such as he had once seen in the possession of a sailor. In any case the fire kindled was perfectly real, for I heard it pop softly as the ends of the reeds burned with a low, steady flame, which flickered against the rock, dimmed the surrounding gloom, and cast wild-looking shadows.

Now Iole continued her descent, the sure-footed ewe resisting every step. The fall was no less steep, although not long, for in a few minutes the distant beams of the torch picked up what was surely the ancient image of Artemis. It was not a rounded image, rather a work in bold relief, as though some sculptor long ago had taken advantage of a narrow projection, perhaps eight feet tall, in the wall of the crater. Because Iole, on what could be called the floor of the pit, held her torch high for a close inspection of the carving, I could see it well at a distance of fifty feet. The lower part of the body was unworked volcanic rock, as Iole had told me. However, the bosom was beautifully shaped, part of the arms well worked, with the rest blending into the wall, and the face one I would never forget.

Actually the Cerynean Artemis had almost no facial resemblance to the Orchomenus Artemis or to any other statue of the Goddess that I had seen. I fancied her countenance was more like that of some Oriental deity than any Greek. Its beauty was past denial. The planes of her cheeks were austerely chiseled, the lips very full, the long eyes half closed. The whole expression seemed one of great impassivity except for a hint of sadness beyond human. And then my neck hairs did rise and prickle, because Iole dropped on her knees before the image and began an impassioned prayer.

"Artemis! Nay, I will call you Callisto, Most Beautiful, as did your worshipers in the long ago when the hills were young. The folk came often in those days to pray that you give messages to their beloved in dim and silent Hades, and to bring back messages from them; and some sent down their deathless curse to one they hated, or word of their gloatings over an enemy's fall! If the shades were given blood, you brought up their answers sometimes pitiful, but sometimes defiant still. You were the great intermediary between the living and dead. Sometimes, when the offering was great enough, or the pilgrimage most long, and when your power waxed greatest, as on the first night of the waning moon, you could balk Cerberus and open the Adamantine Gate, and could bring back certain shades whom earth dwellers loved or hated, so they could again meet face to face before your shrine. My pilgrimage was long. My offering is as great as I could bring to you down these steep rocks, for no one else must know of communion between you, Callisto, and me, Iole, Priestess of Artemis, who is your aspect in these latter days. Hear my plea. Grant my prayers. And now accept my offering, given with my heart's love and my soul's faith."

Then, it seemed, the common torchlight changed somehow, and became utterly baleful, and my eyes rounded and popped. Yet the thing that happened was common enough too, occurring at every shrine in Greece; perhaps it was only the naked rock, the remoteness from everything of this black pit under the earth, and other factors my brain could not identify, that gave the event a terrible aspect. With one stout tug of the strap, Iole drew close the struggling ewe and the firelight danced along the blade of a bronze knife. In the very next second, the little beast lay on her back, kicking feebly as her beast soul passed, her throat gaped open, and Iole was catching the gushing blood in her wooden bucket.

"Behold!" the priestess cried. "The little ewe that followed me in the pastures and became my pet lies dead at your feet. Now will you answer one question, which I dare ask because of my love of my Goddess, who was very you in the long ago, and who is still bound with you. Her, I have asked a hundred times, but to taunt me, or for some reason I do not know, she will not answer me. As Artemis, did you visit the giant Antaeus in love? You are ever chaste, or are called so in men's speech. He boasted of such a visit. His death alone does not content me. It can never content me as long as this doubt hangs over me, harpy-like, to gnaw my heart. You need not answer in words, Callisto, my beloved. Only answer me in your thoughts, and I will read the thought in your beautiful face. My gaze is locked there. The torchlight shows its every lineament. I pray you, answer."

There came a long moment of waiting. My gaze too was fixed on the strange face of the image, and perhaps I half expected it to give sign, but as far as my eyes could tell, it remained unchanged. Then I knew that Iole's eyes saw no more than mine, for her head, on which the torchlight glimmered, its hair itself like very low, red flame, bowed on her breast. But almost instantly it rose again.

"Artemis! Callisto! If you will not answer, will you bring up Antaeus, so I may ask him in your very hearing? For, if he lied, which is my dearest prayer, he will not dare do so in your divine presence. See, I pour the ewe's blood in this crack in the floor. Thus blood was ever poured by your worshipers, ere you called up the dead, and thereby their silence was broken, their darkened memories revived, and they could speak. . . . I wait for him, Callisto! Do not decree that I wait in vain. Goddess, I implore you on my knees. If you will not, I cannot help—Iole, your priestess, can do naught else—I have no other choice but weep."

Then, after a long, strange, forever haunting moment of silence, Iole did weep, her head falling upon her extended arms, her body racked with sobs. I moved from my place. Perhaps I should have called her name, for that would have changed everything. It might be that I did not think of it, or my lips could not utter sound; in any case I came down the steep slope toward her, my sandals shuffling softly on the rock. Perhaps I thought she heard me, or in some way perceived my presence, but unless all signs failed she did not. My intention was to put my arm about her shoulders, not to comfort her, only to establish our fellow humanity and relieve her great solitude. I was but a few feet from her when she saw my shadow, cast by the burning torch she had dropped on the floor.

She sprang to her feet fast as a wakened panther and sprang at me. In her hand was not the sacrificial knife but what looked like a spike, not as red as polished bronze; instead, it was of the hue of gold. It was an unbelievably swift and deadly thrust, and I would never know quite how my outstretched hand swept sideways in time to seize her wrist. At the same instant she gave forth a shrill yell, and in that wild sound I heard a name.

"Antaeus!"

Then she saw I was not Antaeus and fell fainting in my arms.

3

When Iole had recovered, I picked her up, intending to carry her to the rim of the crater, saving her a sharp climb. Rather sharply, with rancor in her voice against me or something unknown, she at once bade me set her down.

When I had done so, she began at once to collect her belongings, the bloody bucket, the strap with which she had led the ewe, an ivory cylinder half as long as my hand with a plunger at one end, and, her greatest prize, the golden spike, about ten inches long, with which she had attacked me. On her putting this carefully away in the fold of her toga, I half expected her to make some embarrassed explanation, perhaps an apology, for her frantic onslaught. She did not, and her only remark was a request that I bind the feet of the offering and carry it to the rim, since she wished to offer it to the Goddess in votive flame and there was no fuel here in the heart of the mountain.

So we began our journey upward, as strange in light of memory as our descent in the light of expectation. She spoke only rarely on the climb, once to warn me of a loose boulder, once of a slippery place on the shale no doubt wetted by an underground spring. Over the rim, and perhaps two hundred paces down its slope, she came on a mountain oak, long dead, that had toppled and had conveniently broken itself into a hundred pieces of suitable length for a bonfire. Now her torch had burned out, so again she loaded the cylinder with a pinch or two of tinder, which I took for dried moss. With a hard slap of her hand she compressed the extended, tight-fitting plunger.

To my amazement, when she withdrew the tinder, it was smoldering. A little hard blowing of her breath caused it to break into flame.

"What is the principle of the device?" I asked, as might old Rhadamanthus.

"I haven't the slightest notion," she answered, the wonted warmth of her voice still absent.

While Iole fed the fire, I skinned the ewe, and then could do nothing but stand about, feeling uncommonly sheepish, awaiting her instruction. My anticipations that her protestations to the Goddess, followed by her rash act, would sooner or later give me the upper hand, at least briefly, had so far come to naught. Presently she asked me if I wanted to spit one quarter of the ewe for a late supper. With such dignity as I could muster, I told her I did not. Then she bade me lay the whole carcass on the fire.

"To you, Artemis beloved, who tonight I worshiped in your ancient manifestation as Callisto, and unto that manifestation if she can hear me now, I make this offering," Iole murmured, as the first smell of burned meat came rich and strong to my nostrils. Then, after standing a moment in thought, the priestess sat down on a little patch of grass, wonderfully soft and green to be found growing on this volcanic rock, the only such patch visible either in the firelight or the dim flood of moonlight, and I had no doubt that Iole believed, and I myself had trouble not believing, that it had been provided for her comfort. Then she made a courteous gesture, by no means warm, that I might sit beside her.

"Why did you spy on me, Heracles?" she asked, in civil tones but with a cold, impassive countenance.

"I was not spying on you. I was trying to protect you."

"From what? A mountain lion? Knowing I was making for the shrine of Callisto, he would slink away as I came nigh. I suppose you thought the ewe's smell might draw prowling wolves. Don't you know that no beast ever chosen for offering to a great God or Goddess has ever been attacked by a beast of prey? Now you have seen me in my devotions, you have guessed part of my secret, and I have no choice but to tell you the rest of it. Heracles, you are a clumsy fool! By and large, that is, but sometimes you move as quickly as a cat, and for that I can thank Artemis, who shaped you in the womb, and the being, mortal or divine, who begot you. Except for that quickness, my thrust with the golden spike would have gone home. I struck in fury and hatred and the spike is very sharp. I suppose—and no doubt you are entitled to it—you expect an explanation."

"Yes, I do expect it," was all I could say.

"To give it, I have to confide some mysteries I am not supposed to tell except to others in the service of Artemis. You understand that Gods and Goddesses often share secrets with their mortal servants that they keep from the ears of other immortals. I'll tell you first why, apart from the pleasure of your company that I have never tried to conceal, I was compelled to come with you on this expedition. It was not to help you capture Bounder, the Cerynean Stag. It was to prevent you from capturing him."

"I don't think I needed any help in the prevention. It is a well-nigh impossible undertaking."

"I am not so sure. You returned to Orchomenus in triumph after three well-nigh impossible—so Eurytus believed—undertakings. Before that, you killed Antaeus in a wrestling bout—manifestly impossible for any human. Why must I interfere with the capture of the stag? Because he is not just a stag, he is a manifestation of Artemis herself, a whimsy as great perhaps as Zeus' disguise as a bull when he wooed Europa. Who ever heard of a real stag's having golden horns? The reason he is rarely seen is that Artemis takes this form, changing her appearance, her sex, her very nature, only on rather rare occasions. I think she does so mainly in the way of sport. I believe in the body of a stag she enjoys courting and begetting fawns by beautiful hinds. Certainly she enjoys running and bounding in the wilderness.

"But I had a double game to play when I persuaded Eurytus to appoint you the labor of capturing the Cerynean Stag," Iole went on. "You must understand first that Artemis and I cannot speak freely to each other about this manifestation. In fact she has never told me that she took it, and I can think of no reason other than that she herself forgets it, as an idle dream of the night, mainly because before she can assume that form, she first must return to her ancient manifestation as Callisto, who had occult powers that the present-day Artemis does not possess. How then did I guess the secret? Mainly by hearing reports of a great stag with golden horns never seen but in the vicinity of Callisto's shrine; also, perhaps, from perceiving a certain wildness in Artemis' nature. But perhaps she had a much greater secret that she could have told me but never did. It was one that my whole heart yearned to know. At last something occurred that appeared to offer me a great opportunity to learn the truth.

"Heracles, this truth concerned the virginity of Artemis, whether true or false," Iole went on in deep earnestness, a passion I could not identify in her beautiful face. "Mark you, I am only her priestess, yet I am pledged to virginity as long as I serve her. She, Artemis, is considered the essence of virginity, plighted to it forever; our people think and speak of her as the Virgin Goddess. Yet I suspected that in her usual manifestation—the beautiful being whom I worshiped at Orchomenus—once—perhaps many times—she shared Antaeus' couch. Until she confessed it, there was a cloud over my adoration of her. Perhaps a dreadful jealousy, unnatural perhaps, entered in—certainly I yearned for his death and rejoiced beyond all measure when you gave it to him. And at last there came into my hand a thing with which I believed I could buy the truth from Artemis' own lips. Tell me, Heracles, what is this?"

Reaching in her toga she handed me the gold spike with which she had stabbed at me.

"I can't answer," I told her. "It is like no dagger I have ever seen. A little longer than my hand—perhaps an inch and a half thick at the base—tapering to a point and, yes, it is not quite straight. There is a little bend in it. Still it makes a very handy dagger."

"Have you ever examined closely the horns of a great stag?"

"Why, yes——"

"Don't you see that this could very well be a tine broken off from such horns, provided they were made of solid gold?"

"I see it perfectly clearly, now that you point it out."

"It was found by a goat herder at the foot of a steep in the Cerynean Mountains. Nearby were the tracks of an enormous stag, and signs of where he had fallen while bounding down the steep. In that fall he must have struck his horns against volcanic rock. This piece broke off."

"I can well believe it." For the moon was shining in a way I had never seen, a great outpouring of purplish-gray beams, and the firelight, too, flung on Iole's face, rapt now in mystery I could not plumb, and beautiful beyond telling.

"The stag deeply mourned the loss. And truly I can say Callisto mourned it too, although I could not be sure that Artemis knew of it at all, if it was true that she had to become Callisto, Most Beautiful, before she could romp in the mountains as a great beast of the wild. So I had to come and speak to Callisto of the bargain I wished to make. It was simply that if she would tell me, provided she knew, whether Artemis had been despoiled by Antaeus, or, if she did not know, to call him up so I could learn the truth from his own lips, I would return the lost tine of gold. True, in the long wait I had begun to believe that calling up was beyond her power, and I gave way to tears. Still, I was just about to make the offer when a great shadow fell over me—and whose could it be but Antaeus', called back from Hades in answer to my prayer? As I told you I struck in fury and hatred and—I fear I must confess—in horrible jealousy. Thank all the Gods, you caught my wrist."

"Is that all?" I asked, after a long silence. For I hoped so, for although her diction had been lucid, one thought following logically another, still the tale was too unearthly, too remote in the realms of the supernatural for my thick head to grasp without heavy aching.

"There is one little favor you can do me," Iole answered. "I brought up from the shrine the golden tine partly to show it to you, partly because I still held the wild belief I could somehow use it to find out what I wanted to know. Now I realize it is useless. The Artemis I love will keep her secret; I must put it out of my mind and heart. I ask you to throw the tine down into the crater where Callisto can find it and have Hephaestus forge it back upon the golden antler. In return I will tell the King a barefaced lie, yet one that I count justified. It will be that you indeed captured Bounder in a pit, but that Artemis rose before us, in such radiance that our eyes were half blinded so we did not see her face that no mortal may gaze upon, and commanded you turn the stag loose, and by my persuasions too, you did so."

So I trudged up to the rim of the Cerynean crater with the golden tine in my hand, and then gave it a strong pitch into the dim pit. It fell in silence a few seconds, clattered against rock, again fell free, then rang almost like a bell against a stone far down the steep. Once more I heard it clang, very faintly, as it fell near or at the actual bottom of the crater. If Callisto, who in these days had become Artemis, could change herself into a stag with golden horns and bound up mountainsides, surely she would have no trouble retrieving it for later escapades.

So it came about that I made an inglorious and, on the whole, pleasant return to Orchomenus, Iole having regained her blithe spirits. She was true to her word as far as explaining the failure of the mission to King Eurytus; in any case he took it in good part, neither rewarded or punished me, and assigned me, as my next labor, the cleansing of the Augean Stables. I did not speak to Megara during my short stay at the citadel. I yearned to do so, because I felt sure that she believed I had played the satyr with Iole during the trip, and I wished to assure her—but not to tell her that continence had been enforced upon me— that I had not. Actually the only remarks of note in regard to the expedition were made by Right Doer.

"It is a very strange story," he said, when I had recounted the events at the Callisto shrine and what Iole had told me by the votive fire, "but there's something wrong with it."

"What?"

"That I can't answer. I only feel the wrongness in my bones."

"You grant that it holds together well?"

"Almost too well. True stories of any complication rarely hold together well—almost always they contain passages that insult credulity. A question rises in my mind. What story would Iole have to tell if you had been a second slower in seizing her wrist?"

"None. And no one would have ever known what happened to me."

"You are wrong about that, Heracles. The daughters and wives of herdsmen and drovers descend frequently to make entreaties to Callisto. What they ask for, I know not. Perhaps merely, if female, they ask to be beautiful, if male, to be brave, bravery being the left hand of beauty. Your body would be found in a day or two before the shrine that, in a way of speaking, is to Artemis. The Priestess of Artemis would have a hard time persuading hardheaded elders that she stabbed you on the supposition that you were Antaeus' ghost. Why should anyone stab a ghost? He can die no more than he has already died. Yet, I repeat, any theories we may put forward to explain the facts would be even more fantastic than Iole's tale. Perhaps we must merely take for granted that the doings of Gods and Goddesses are beyond mortal ken, and those mortals who have part in them become themselves unearthly. They live in a half world neither with their feet on the ground nor their heads in heaven. Their behavior becomes inexplicable."

Right Doer spoke with a pedantic air that caused me to recall Rhadamanthus. And thinking of that old man, I thought of another

—Seer of Wonders. By and large his prophecy had come true. Unless all signs failed, all the pining I did for Iole would be forever in vain. My heart had taken some sort of wound, and my soul did not ascend with such splendid wings as before; and only great adventures, and perhaps great danger, followed by great victory, could restore the innocent happiness I had once known.

CHAPTER TWELVE

THE GLORY THAT WAS GREECE

1

King Eurytus had not forbidden Right Doer and Actaeon to lend me what help they could in cleansing the Augean Stables. His son Nessus could accompany me also, provided he returned in time from Ithaca. I could hire gangs of workmen, as I had done in taming the Erymanthian Boar, but the actual labor must be accomplished on what we called Midsummer Day, which was the day of the summer solstice, the day preceding it, and the day after.

Megara told me that a petty king of Elis had put the notion in his head, saying that the stables had long stood empty except for their filth, and he wished to use them to stall and fatten a thousand cattle that were being driven into his pastures from Acrorea, at present parched and barren from scanty rainfall. Eurytus wished to please the feudal lord of Elis—no doubt he had been promised a goodly share of the fatted kine—so by appointing me the labor actually he could lose nothing, whether I succeeded or failed. The limited time which he had allowed me was simply an outcropping of his native meanness. The cleansing of the stables would probably be a perfectly feasible feat, Megara thought, if it could occupy half a year. But Eurytus would rather deprive himself of two hundred or more Acrorean cattle than have me win five times in succession—or four times, if the truth were known of my hunt of the Cerynean Stag.

Yet Right Doer, Actaeon, and I started forth on our journey to Elis with open minds and by no means heavy hearts, these lifted by a token sent to us by Nessus, no less than a scroll showing a picture of the temple to Hermes, under the phallic symbol, that had stood since time out of mind at Cyllene on the seacoast. Also he sent a drawing of Nessus himself, making great haste, a pack on his back, and a large phallic symbol emerging from his breechcloth; all in all his pledge that he would meet us at that fishy-smelling town as soon as he could fetch it. So we three entered the wondrous champaign country of Elis, and beheld the countless cattle, horses, and sheep grazing on its verdant grass; and on the hillsides groves of olives and luxuriant vineyards that filled so many of our ewers of oil and cups of purple wine.

At the temple at Cyllene we found not Nessus, but a runner, who informed us he would join us on the morrow. When we saw him approaching us, his great grin found ample echo on our own faces, and all our hearts had the same fierce glow. That evening, at the camp of the caravans, he told us of his meeting with far-journeying Odysseus; and after hearing a brief report of some of his adventures, I thought that Megara had not missed it far in the lively word picture she had painted of the famous hoaryheaded hero. In the morning we set forth for the site of the Augean Stables, between the Peneus and the Alpheus rivers.

We arrived where they were believed to stand, and found no sight of them. There was only a thick deposit not of cowdung, but of black mud, that apparently had washed in from the great bog just under the ridge, carried by countless small, mud-colored rivulets. Indeed, the bog reminded me of the home of the Hydra, although luckily it offered better footing. When we had seen all that was possible to see on first inspection of the site, Nessus brought forth an earthen jug, protected from breaking by woven reeds. When we had sat down in the cordial sunlight, and the wine had been passed and our throats wetted, we could bend our minds more cheerfully to our problem.

"Heracles, how long since King Augeas stalled his cattle at this place?" Right Doer asked.

"Ask the Delphic pythoness. I know not."

"Do you know, Actaeon?"

"Not in any time that my father's father, a windy old fellow, ever recalled." It was quite like Actaeon not to mention that his mother's father had been great Cadmus, King of Thebes.

"I can tell you a little," Nessus broke in. "I think he was reported to be the son of Helios, God of the Sun. That might mean that he lived a good while ago. You have noticed, perhaps, that divine ancestors have a way of retreating in time—pardon me, Heracles, for I mean no offense; I mean with every new generation they withdraw a generation, so that they rarely get closer than great-grandfathers. I am quite certain that the Elieans had no king named Augeas in the last hundred years. As an urchin I had to learn the genealogies of the great families—to which my father did not belong—and I never heard the name Augeas except in connection with dirty stables."

"You know, Heracles, I wish we had talked to Rhadamanthus before we set out. Although ninety and upward, his mind is still broader and better stocked than those of most men of forty."

"An equally wise man lives within a day's march of where we sit."

"Who?"

"None other than Nestor. You had forgotten, Right Doer, that he is native to Elis."

"Heaven above us! Great Nestor, who did most of the thinking for the whole Greek Army in our war with Troy! How old do you think he is?"

"Over eighty. He was snowy-bearded twenty years ago, according to the songs of the blind poet, although still a great warrior and charioteer. Actaeon, you descend from Cadmus, Nessus is the son of a powerful king, Right Doer is the son of Wrathful Leader. Wouldn't it be proper for you three to pay him a visit, and fetch me along?"

"And you, Heracles, are Heracles," Actaeon said quietly. "I think I know who would be handed the first pouring of the wine."

I blushed like a booby at the compliment, and then we busied ourselves washing our feet in the cleanest rivulet we could find. By starting at once we could reach Nestor's citadel in the cool of the evening, when old men love to tell tales of the long ago, a winecup at their elbow. Soon we were setting forth, and soon thereafter—or so it seemed, so greatly we enjoyed one another's company—we were being ushered by a bowing slave into Nestor's palace of sun-baked brick.

The old man soon appeared, herding a bevy of housemaids with washbasins and ewers of aromatic oil and woolen cloths. Most of them were pretty damsels, no wonder to us when we looked into the face of the old warrior and wise man, for although it was weathered by the winds of Troy, and deeply lined, and marvelously chiseled, it was the face of a man yet dominant, unafraid, intensely alive, and virile.

Had I not known that he must be eighty, I would have guessed his age at sixty-five.

When the initial guest rites had been observed and we visitors were washed, scented, seated, and robed in snowy cloth, it came true that the first cup of wine following the libation was poured for me, and by Nestor's still steady hand into a wondrous gold cup that had been part of his spoils of victory from the ravished palace of Priam in Troy. The honor abashed me somewhat, considering that Actaeon certainly, and Right Doer and Nessus probably, were better born than I. However, he spoke with such warmth of the labors I had done in Nemea, in Lernaea, and in the Erymanthian Mountains, serving all the folk, high and low, of our beloved Greece, that my heart glowed; and out of the corners of my eyes I saw glowing the three faces of my friends; so I did not make a donkey of myself by protesting the honor. Then, when all had drunk, the time had come to tell of our business here. This I left to Right Doer, who, like almost all men of deep mind, was adept at speech.

"Godlike Nestor, will you tell us how long a time has passed since Augeas, King of the Elieans, stabled his cattle on the banks of the Peneus River?" Right Doer asked.

"Nay, I cannot, son of Amphitryon. In truth, I cannot say with any confidence that he ever did so, because there is no proof thereof, or even a well-bolstered legend. If Augeas lived at all, and is himself not a myth, it was about five centuries ago. If any great stables have been covered by the mud washed in from the swamp above, they were the stables not of cattle but of centaurs."

All our ears were startled, for somehow none of us had ever thought of centaurs, those strange monsters, half man, half horse, being confined in stalls.

"It is barely possible," the old man went on, "that a considerable herd of centaurs were stabled there under the spell of some powerful king or revengeful God. As for me, I don't believe a word of it. Others have told me of beholding centaurs, but I have never laid eyes on one, let alone a herd of the horrible brutes. Yet there is a legend of long survival and fixed form that under the mud is some kind of edifice in stone called the Hall of the Centaurs. The folk believe it was more like a temple than a barn. And that is all I know."

"Yet my brother Heracles implores your help still further, great King of Pylos!" Right Doer said in his wonderfully rich voice, and as ever with the utmost courtesy that yet rang with power. "King Eurytus has appointed him the labor of cleaning the so-called Augean Stables on Midsummer Day. He cannot report that there are no such stables under the mud until he has ascertained the fact with his own eyes. In the Erymanthian Mountains he was able, by the employment of many villagers, to direct the waters of the Erymanthus River from the bed she then occupied to her former and rightful bed. It was inevitable that some such idea would occur to him and to us, his companions, in regard to the Peneus: the forcing of her waters through the silt and washing it away. That immediate region has no human habitations and I know of no harm to be done, since, to judge from the lay of the land, the deflected waters would, after a short flow, return to their former channel. If, with the help of gangs of workmen we could raise some sort of dam——"

"Curiously enough," Nestor broke in, "I myself have often pondered the problem of deflecting the waters of the Peneus and satisfying my own curiosity as to the Augean Stables, or the Hall of the Centaurs, or whatever may lay under the silt to give rise to legend. For years it has been a whim of mine, but I have been too busy with war and government to indulge it. This was despite the fact that natural conditions would seem to make the erection of a temporary dam no great feat of engineering. The bank on the far side from the 'Stables' is solid rock and rather high. On the near side it is low and marshy; and is commonly flooded after heavy rain, but there is almost no fall just there, the floodwater stands almost stagnant, and very little of the mud is washed downstream. As you have noted, the Peneus is at present a small river compared to the Alpheus, which has captured most of the waters from the Erymanthus Mountains. Perhaps you did not note that, directly above the mudbank that covers the ancient edifice and below a sharp fall, there is a short reach of the river as still as a pond in the woods. Also, on both sides there stands, opposite from each other, a small, thick copse of very tall and ancient trees, swamp maples and water oaks on the mucky ground, cottonwoods and white oaks on the higher ground opposite. In plain words, if I were a peculiarly ambitious beaver, and wished to build the biggest beaver dam in the history of my tribe, I would choose that spot."

"The trees could be felled both ways across the river," I said, "and their leafy tops would greatly impede the almost slack waters. But unless there were sacks of dirt——"

"That would be my part," Nestor broke in. "I told you of an old man's almost lifelong curiosity as to what lies under the mud. I can assemble a thousand stout fellows, some of them woodsmen, all used to delving in the ground, each with one or several cowhide bags; also a fleet of about fifty rowboats used by fishermen. They can build your dam in a single day and I'll warrant that almost the whole of the Peneus will be diverted around the near end of the dam, flow through the bed of silt, and wash it out. But you must understand the dam will burst in the first fair-sized freshet, which usually occurs from heavy thundershowers in the mountains in late summer or early fall."

"Godlike Nestor, I cannot express my gratitude," I stammered.

"Nor I mine, Heracles, for this chance for a lively undertaking to occupy a few of my long-drawn and graying days. Midsummer Day is only a month distant. We shall start the cart wheels turning at once."

When the five of us were sharing a parting bowl of delicious Thessalian wine, all of us flushed and bright-eyed from our excitement, Nestor laid a friendly hand on my shoulder.

"Do you know, Heracles, you remind me of someone I knew well, and I wish in the name of the Titan Memory I could think who it was."

"Is he living or dead?" I asked.

"I know not, although I have a feeling he is dead. The memory hangs, and in fact dances, on the brink of the abyss of utter forgetfulness. If I could just catch hold of it by a single finger I could capture the whole, but ever it eludes me. Was he someone of more than common strength, such as Odysseus? Was he plain-looking like Agamemnon, who would stick to his convictions with the stubbornness of a mule, and who sired the fiery and strangely beautiful Electra? Not Peleus, my good friend and companion, the most handsome, the most fleet of foot, the father of great Achilles by—so we are told—the beautiful Thetis, daughter of Nereus. True, there is a little something— no, it is not Peleus. I will have to give it up. I assure you, if I did not have the mystery of the Hall of the Centaurs for my thoughts to churn in, I would toss the whole night through, like a drunkard denied his cup. Now I see that our bowl is empty. The Gods go with you!"

2

There could be no question about the old man's keeping his word. Nestor had been a doughty warrior in the last days of the Trojan

War, ending twelve years ago, he was ever a great counselor to captains and kings, and he alone of the Grecian host had had the manhood to tell its leader, King Agamemnon, that he must return to Achilles the beautiful Briseis, his female captive, whom the King had seized, which seizure had caused the peerless warrior to sulk in his tent.

On the day before Midsummer Day, all the fields and vineyards of that countryside, flocks and herds, were tended by gaffers, women, and children, for the men of might had gathered at the site with carts, barrows, shovels, and big skin bags. Also, today and for two days to come, the nets and lines in the lagoons and the river mouths would be mended and dried instead of set, because moored to our shore were nearly fifty boats, brought mainly by fishermen dwelling at Cyllene. Finally the charcoal fires of the Upper River would be damped by women almost as wild-looking as the wolves that prowled their kitchen middens, because in our number were thirty or more woodsmen, men adept at tree felling, and to my great joy I knew three of them, fellows from the village on the Erymanthus River who had helped me tame the Boar, and who had crossed the divide to be with me today.

As soon as the men and their equipage were assembled, Nestor put them all under my command. This was fair enough, since I must bear the responsibility of the job's success or botching, before the throne of Eurytus. Truly I took no fright at the office, being a man of my hands and having an elementary knowledge of engineering, or at least of its practical laws. Being a good foreman was what I was good for, I thought, that and lifting and carrying heavy loads, and other feats of strength, not being endowed by Apollo as was Right Doer. All of us set to, which made me think of a great colony of beavers, especially since the dam we proposed to build was not essentially different from a beaver dam, such as stemmed many a little brook in our mountain meadows.

The fishermen and woodsmen first helped the drovers and field workers fill their seemingly countless skin bags with dirt, except for about a hundred which I had filled with rocks from the opposite bank of the river. These were the first to be laid down across the bed, giving a more solid base for our dam of felled trees and earth. Then the woodcutters wielded their keen bronze axes, making long strokes that caused chips to fly, and the teams vied with each other in felling the giant trees, meanwhile taking the utmost care that these toppled into the river at the very spot we had picked. Truly they sent them crashing down, and not a single tree fell out of line, and as each struck with a great splash and the waters flew high, not a mother's son of our whole crew could withhold a mighty yell of triumph. Surely at least one drowsy God on not far distant Olympus rose from his golden chair, or at least craned his neck, to find out the cause of the wondrous uproar.

When all the trees in reach of our dam site had been felled, their innumerable boughs, branches, twigs, and leafage, and of course their mighty trunks already caused a strong obstruction to the slowly moving waters, and we saw it backing up, almost to the top of the mudbank on one side and lapping higher the steep rocky margin on the other. Then the boats came swarming, back and forth, and the bags of earth were heaved in. Had a naiad dwelt in some underwater cave upstream, she might have wondered what was happening to the ancient Peleus to cause this unseasonable rise, and have been half minded to take off to Olympus and complain to the assembly of the Gods. When about two thirds of our skin sacks had been dumped, the river's flow had been virtually checked, and already the waters were breaking over and through the bank above the dam. Already a dozen rivulets, all of them increasing, were feeling their way through the muck to find a way around the obstruction so that they could pass on to their mother, the sea.

As we heaved the remaining bags, the rivulets began to join with one another into considerable brooks; and although each was limpid when it began its flanking movement, all turned black with the silt that they had eaten as they flowed. And now all the bags were down, and the strong force of the river was completely balked against the interbound obstruction of rock, timber, and earth. Suddenly the brooks that meandered through the mud flat swelled in size, then joined with one another with great rapidity, and as we workers gazed, our necks prickling, all at once the whole of the Peleus flowed full and wide before our eyes, black as ink. Gazing down, below the burial ground we meant to excavate, we saw the river turn slowly to its bed, now almost dry, find the lowest entrance, and spill through.

Still our hearts beat wildly, for we could not help but see with what rapidity the river was demolishing the mud flat. Not only where it flowed, ever narrowing and eating out a deeper path, was the muck swept down. On both sides it was sifting and sliding into the river, sometimes by gradual disintegration, often in big fragments that tumbled in with a dirty splash. The bed had been firm enough that, walking on it, we had sunk barely to our ankles; yet it was falling apart before our eyes.

We had completed the dam in midafternoon. Before sunset the region close to the river, suffering the most rapid washing, was from three to six feet lower than at first. Then, just as the sun dipped behind Erymanthian Mountains, the men began to point at something. Nessus looked at me with wild wonder in his eyes, and Actaeon grunted, as he always did, when deeply startled, and Right Doer slipped his hand into mine. I looked, and above the muck I could see the abacus of a marble pillar, and half-see the ovolo and the neck. As the mud sifted away, a good two feet of its beautiful shape was revealed, and then the top of another, and then of a third. No one could speak. Even the rustics gazed in wide-eyed silence, for most of them knew that the land of Greece, thrusting like an eager hand into the wine-dark sea, had been peopled time out of mind by beauty-loving people of great prowess and almost illimitable vision, for every child had seen vestiges of great works, the history and the meaning of which were lost.

I could not speak until the tops of thirty or so pillars were revealed, and now I could perceive that when all were uncovered they would form a rectangle, perhaps sixty feet long and forty wide. With a frog in my throat, I spoke to Right Doer.

"It's either a temple or a palace. But why should an intelligent people build such a noble monument where it would be swamped in muck?"

"Who can foresee the future? Perhaps the pythoness at Delphi and Tiresias can catch glimpses of it now and then, but at most their vision casts forward a generation or two, then the mists of distance intervene. No, perhaps drunken Seer of Wonders saw further than any. You remember his saying that Iniquity was the precursor of another conqueror how many centuries hence?

"Heracles," my brother went on, "no doubt the erectors of this monument meant it to stand, a glory to men's eyes, forever. There is no such quality as everlasting; I doubt not that at last our sun and our moon may die. When this temple, or palace as it may prove, was built, perhaps the river flowed in some other bed, and the bog that brought about its ruin had not been formed. Look! The light fades swiftly, but I think I can see the head of a manlike image, larger than life-size, bearded, most strange. It is just outside the enclosure with no pillars immediately behind it. Could it be at the opening of the edifice? Could it be the head—and now the shoulders—of a centaur? If so, he would be taller than any standing or seated figures within the rectangle. And now something is emerging from the mud, equally tall, on its left side, at a distance of about twenty feet. If it is another centaur, which I cannot doubt—two of them standing in guard at the entrance—we know now how the name that Nestor told us, heard in his boyhood, came into being."

Then Right Doer spoke with an intensity of feeling I had rarely sensed in him before.

"I can see no more, the shadows are too deep, but I can make a prophecy, to be proven true or false when the sun comes up. Instead of cleansing the cattle byres of a king named Augeas of their century-old deposits of cowdung, we have unearthed the Hall of the Centaurs, raised perhaps by a people quite like ourselves, whatever their complexion, five centuries gone. How did such a wonderful name become changed in men's speech to the Augean Stables? The centaur is half horse, half man. But the dwellers of the countryside had never seen one—I never have; I would bet my new toga against one of your sandals that none exists—but the people had seen cows without number. They almost always turn to what is familiar from what is strange and marvelous. Now let us go to supper and to bed. If the dam should break during the night, all four of us, and Nestor too, would go raving mad. But there is nothing we can do but pass the time, wait, and see."

Then in due course we four comrades supped and drank wine with Nestor, but his maids could have mistaken it for a funeral feast, we spoke so little. I wished I had put five hundred skin bags of stone, instead of one hundred, into the river bed. If the latter were silt, these would have sunk through it, and lent great support to our dirt-and-timber dam, and possibly given it many more days of life. And I could have achieved the labor, if I had set my heart on it; the white-haired king, rich and powerful, crammed with Greek curiosity which, when all is said and done, may be our most important mental gift, would have backed me. Now our beds were being made on the pillared porch. Little sleep would I catch, I thought, and my companions the like, in the long and aching hours before the dawn broke. Eos, can you hasten it a little? You are young and forever beautiful, and Tithonus is too old to know when you come and go, and he can only dream of the days when you were both young, and both knew the beauty of life and love!

One prophecy that I thought was a surety failed. Although I wakened now and then, desperately worried about the dam, I soon drifted back to sleep. The truth was, as I had long suspected, my nature was such it would not permit me to go against nature, to commit any dissipation injurious to myself, and surely lying awake is the quickest and surest way to dissipate strength. The same was true of food. When I hungered, I ate whatever food was at hand, stuffed it in until I was satisfied. When I thirsted, I drank, never obeying the folk belief in parching one's self to prevent sweating, which they thought weakened a man when doing heavy labor. There were other appetites that I indulged. I took it that they had not been put in me if their indulgence, in reason, was not beneficial. Megara had compared me to a raw force of nature. At least I was a child of nature. Although I dreamed wildly about the Hall of the Centaurs and could almost see it, whole and beautiful, as when first erected, and the night seemed longer than any I could remember, still I wakened refreshed.

We broke fast with no unseemly haste, and the maidens poured warm water on our hands, and Nestor poured a solemn libation to the Gods. Then we set out, still half afraid to speak, and there was a great craning of necks when at last we came to a hillside that overlooked the scene of yesterday's labor. Truly our luck had held with marvelous staunchness. The whole temple, for we saw it could be nothing else, had been unearthed, and now stood on what appeared to be a gravel bank above the river that had scoured out a bed between the temple and its ancient bed, and which reflected the blue sky with a beauty that could mean only that it flowed with virgin purity. The dam appeared staunch as ever. And even if it broke this minute, Nestor remarked, our temple would take no harm, for the channel would merely resume its former course; and the inundation of the temple had been by mud, not water.

Even so, one fact worried me, because I was a dunce. We could plainly make out all the pillars that still stood, by far the greater portion of the original number, the images of two centaurs at the entrance, and seated and standing figures within the rectangle, but all these forms and the pillars too were an ugly brown color.

"It's merely dried mud," Nestor said quickly, in the voice kind-hearted men use to a troubled child. "The men encamped on the high ground can wash it off with buckets in a few minutes."

It warmed my heart that none of our helpers had gone home. All had waited to explore and examine our fabulous find, although none had ventured there ahead of us, which was again the Greek sense of fairness, even sometimes of propriety and a wonderful social feeling. And then old Nestor revealed to us his own greatness in a little thing. He bade us four companions wait on the hillside while he went forward and had his liegemen wash every statue and pillar of its mud-stains.

"I want you to see the temple in its pristine beauty," he told us, "as it was before the mud washed down."

The time of waiting soon passed. When we came to the temple entrance all was shimmering white—every pillar, every worked stone of its floor, every carved figure. For a long time we stood gazing at the centaurs, and this was a kind of carving I had never seen, not in the least delicate and lovely such as the carving of the Artemis, but bold in the extreme, and ineffably strong. True, there was a certain lack of naturalness in the structure, both of the human-like part of the images, as well as the horselike part. Still I felt that if centaurs had ever really lived, this was their true depiction, as perceived by the soul—monsters of unity, not half man, half horse.

We went in, and here stood or sat the Olympian Gods, as our forebears had conceived them centuries gone. Each was an individual force, and we seemed to see the essence of each rather than its anthropomorphic form. On every face was the same fixed smile. There was no suppleness in the limbs—they looked stiff compared to human limbs, but immortal. In the center sat Zeus, with a great square beard, a queenly and imperious Hera, untroubled by jealousy, at his side. At one end of the hall sat his mighty brother Poseidon, his trident in his hand; at the opposite end sat another brother, Hades, his gaze implacable, his lips stern, his helmet on his head, a three-headed monstrous dog at his heels. Standing about were younger Gods, and only Apollo's image openly portrayed the beauty Greeks associated with him. Ares was there, a vulture perched on his arm, wearing a shield and bearing a broken sword; Pallas Athene was roughly shaped and presented an aspect awesome, if not terrifying, bearing the aegis of Zeus and what I took for a thunderbolt in her left hand. Artemis was very like the image I had seen in the crater in the mountain heights of Erymanthia.

I identified Demeter by a sheath of corn she carried in one arm, and by a strong and yet benign look, not commonly seen in the faces of her fellow deities. Lame Hephaestus was absent, so was Dionysus, and to my amazement so was beautiful Hermes, and unless these were late-comers to Olympus, I could not guess the reason. There was no Goddess that suggested Aphrodite. In what might have been her place, close to Ares, was the only image in the hall that struck me at first sight as ugly, and even so, my soul told me that it possessed a beauty I had come too late upon the earth to understand. It was an almost unworked block of marble. Its only humanoid features were huge and unnatural-looking breasts, a greatly swollen belly, and short, stout legs blending into the stone, between which was a crude representation of the genitals. Her eyes were closed, her mouth immense, the whole figure one of enormous energy and power. Yet I thought if our lovely, golden Aphrodite had derived in the long centuries from this monstrous form, we had come a long way.

We had roamed about, staring, perhaps an hour, when something on the floor caught sharp-eyed Nestor's attention. I gazed, and as far as I could see, it was only a little snakelike streak of mud.

"Where did it come from?" he demanded. "It wasn't here when we washed the floor, two hours ago."

"It must have washed in with a little trickle of water," Right Doer answered. And I knew from his voice and his countenance that this was not the trifle I first supposed.

"Where from? Obviously from the great swamp under the ridge. And here comes another, making its sinister way to the stone floor. Heracles, we may have to move quickly."

"I don't know what you mean."

"It should be a slow process, the reburying of the Hall of the Centaurs, but no power this side of the Gods can prevent it," Nestor went on after a long silence. "That is my guess. I can post men here, and they can wash out the mud as fast as it sifts in—for a month, three months, perhaps a year—unless there comes a great flood of rainwater into the swamp and it slides down in vast quantity. That might happen any day. We must provide for the Greek people to see the Hall of the Centaurs before it is again swallowed up. They must know what glory they inherit. Tomorrow I will send runners to all my great companions who are still alive, those who fought before Troy. We will choose a day not far off—only distant enough for them to travel comfortably from any part of Greece—and on that day they may see this marvel, and so may all the kings, and all whom we call great, such as aged Rhadamanthus, and Tiresias. On the following day, and for a fortnight—that long will I essay to keep out the insidious foe; anyone who can make the journey may come to this incomparable shrine and pay his due in wonder and awe. Then—what then?"

"Sir, I know not."

"Nor do I. But I fear the worst. Now let us invite our good helpers of yesterday. And from this moment forward I will set free every child born to one of my slaves. That is my act of gratitude to Apollo, who was beautiful and learned even when this temple was raised, and who has let me live to behold it, ere my eyes are darkened by desolate death."

3

About two weeks after we had unearthed the Hall of the Centaurs, Zeus gathered a great herd of clouds, filling the whole sky, and they surged and heaved a few minutes, then broke in rain. All that day it pelted down, and all that night, and at noon of the next day our flimsy dam began to disintegrate, passing more and more of the impounded waters, and the trees we had felled broke out of their mesh and rushed down-river until quiet water calmed them, after which they quietly drifted down. What would have seemed a cataclysm to a colony of beavers mattered hardly at all to us journeymen engineers, for the only consequence was the river's returning to its ancient bed, without washing one stone of our great find. However, the seepage of muck from the moor under the ridge onto the temple floor was increased by the heavy rain. The labors of Nestor's gang of slaves to keep it clean were doubled and redoubled; a morning bath no longer sufficed; and on the day of the showing of the wondrous Pantheon, crews had to stand duty with buckets and mops from sunrise to sunset.

On the preceding evening the power and the glory of our times began to gather at Nestor's palace or at pavilions erected by the brooks and springs nearby. So great was his name that all frontiers had been opened for the period of the showing, even those whose masters were presently at war; and the kings came down from utmost Thessaly, up from southmost Laconia, and in from islands as remote as Ios and Lemnos, and they brought their queens and sons and daughters, not so much to pay honor to the Gods and Goddesses represented in stone, but to satisfy an itch that was peculiarly and wonderfully Greek. Nestor had sent word that the images had captured astounding beauty. No Greek from king to beggar ever heard of a truly beautiful thing without wanting to feast his eyes upon it. Also, I think we are all preoccupied with the long ago, in love with it somehow; and overweening national pride had something to do with it, for although Greeks might rant of the wonders of Hyperbore or the Land of the Lotus Eaters, they would not trade one acre for a whole kingdom on the Nile, or one flea-bitten town for all of Babylon. When Greek meets Greek—the saying was as old as our hills. Beyond those hills dwelt not Greeks, not Hellenes, as we sometimes called ourselves, but barbarians.

King Eurytus did not miss this chance to show off. He came with a great train, and he appointed himself a kind of master of ceremonies because it was he who had appointed his bondsman Heracles to cleanse the Augean Stables; and the hand of his son Nessus had loomed large in the labor. When I had heard him boasting to the King of Sparta, I asked Megara if it did not bode well for my receiving a great mead of victory, perhaps the forgiveness of the tribute of slaves he had demanded of Thebes for about five years, if not forever.

"My guess is," she answered, "you will receive no mead at all for uncovering this wonder. The Augean Stables had become a byword in Greece for filth and confusion, but every man of good learning knew that they belonged to the realm of myth. My father did not know. A spiteful man, he will resent his own ignorance the more he contemplates it. And you will be his scapegoat."

Iole roamed about the temple with a dreamy beauty on her face, and I could not doubt that she was deeply moved. Oddly enough, the image that attracted her most was the monstrous big-bellied, big-bosomed statue representing fertility, but if she saw in this the beginning of the cult of her adored Artemis she did not confide the fact to anyone.

A greater experience than to see the galaxy of kings was for me to watch the reunion of twenty or more of Nestor's old companions, who had fought beside him at beaten, buried, burned, but deathless Troy. The strange thought struck me that they looked alike somehow, these grizzled veterans, or at least their countenances had one common quality which might be their having fought with Gods. Hector to them was not just a heroic name; it was the flame of his glancing helm, the flash of his great sword, the wild catastrophic rush of his chariot; and himself the living symbol of valor, chivalry, and of invincibility save from the godlike thrust of Achilles. They recalled the great battle before the ships. In those days they had been young, warriors almost without peer; and together they had weathered a storm, Gods against giants, the like of which the world had never seen and, I believe, would never see again.

Great Odysseus was not in their number. He had been away from Ithaca in one of his ships, perhaps on some petty business, perhaps on a great emprise, when Nestor's invitation had arrived, and had not come home in time to join the assembly of his comrades. But I saw Penelope, almost as famed as her godlike mate. Her name was becoming a byword for wifely fidelity, at which Megara had snorted; and from the look of her, I too thought that the horde of her suitors, devouring her husband's substance, had not been too strictly rebuffed. An old woman now, she still had winsome ways. There was a gleam in her eyes which, once born, never dies until they are darkened by dread Death. She shone it upon beautiful Right Doer, upon magnificent Actaeon, upon the great horseman Nessus, but not on Heracles, the heavy heaver. Megara observed the fact and threw me a mocking smile.

To the strange awe of everyone, Electra came in her litter—perhaps it was because she was Agamemnon's daughter, and it was her obligation to behold the great works of her ancestors before they again disappeared under the muck. Certainly she spoke to no one; she moved dimly through the little crowd, looking into one marble face after another; and I had the strange notion that she cast no shadow, in this like a ghost of the dead. Her beautiful long hands were almost always clasped. I wondered if she could not forget, even for one moment, asleep or awake, that they had committed matricide. The old soldiers moved aside to let her pass.

Just after noon, a hope of which I had almost despaired came true. A woman entered the temple, and no man could call himself a fool if, for a moment, he thought she was one of the Goddesses, down from Olympus to see a representation of herself, as perceived by stoneworkers five centuries gone. A light appeared to sift into the room.

I would swear it fell on the floor where she walked. She was no longer young, indeed well past middle age, but her beauty was as timeless as that of the deep underground Callisto I had seen, an aspect of Artemis, and indeed she looked somewhat like her, although far more beautiful. The most dramatic aspect of her arrival was the way that the white-haired warriors, companions of Nestor, and of Achilles, looked at her and then at one another, in utter understanding, congratulating one another, I would almost say, and the mysterious light moved from one weathered face to another, and to me they seemed all to be like Gods, for they had been equal to the great challenge, its like never before given to a whole people, and never to be given again. Suddenly I knew that the Greeks were a chosen people, beloved of the Gods or of Fate greater than Gods, that only they, not the monster-worshiping Egyptians, not the voluptuous Babylonians, not even the bold mariners of Tyre, had been given a chance to accept or refuse the gauge of war over one woman's beauty.

And as suddenly, the greatest moment of my life came to me, without announcement, in the stream of common moments, and the wondrous light shone upon my face, because the woman spoke to me.

"Heracles, I thank you in the name of all Greeks."

My throat filled, and I could not answer.

"Do you yet know who your father was?" she asked, her miraculous eyes full on mine.

"No, Helen, I do not."

"If I knew, I would tell you. If Apollo knows he has never confided in me, although he loves me still. Aphrodite knows, of course, but the only honor that she observes is not to tell the secrets of lovers. But do not despair. I think that you will know while you are still young and lusty and able to understand. For Alcmene was the most beautiful woman in Thebes."

She bowed her head slightly and walked away and I, somewhat the same as the old men who fought at Troy, would be forever changed.

She stayed about an hour, during which hardly a word was spoken by anyone; then she said farewell to Nestor and a few other old friends of her husband, Menelaus, and went her strange and shining way. The rest of the great folk left before sundown, and on the next day came common folk, with whom I belonged, or at least with whom my soul had the deepest sharing. And for subsequent days came countless others, from all over Greece, but every day now the muck took more labor to remove, and on the last days that Nestor's slaves fought it, with buckets of water and shovels instead of brooms, it became ankle-deep on the stone floor. A few days thereafter there came another great rain, and tons of mud washed down, and it began to climb the pillars and up to the knees of the images. And then there came the day that we founders could no longer endure the sight of the wondrous statues, half immersed in mud, and the whole temple giving the effect of sinking into earth out of men's sight; and we were left no choice but to turn away.

Thus the great Hall of the Centaurs was once more buried. It might be that after this generation, and perhaps one more, men would no longer speak of it; then the generations to come would not know of its existence, and only a misshaped legend of some sort would be told, instead of truth. Still I dreamed that, in some far-off time, centuries beyond my reckoning, the earth itself would move to reveal its jewel, or else the river would be dammed up for some useful purpose, and her waters deflected through the bed of muck, and once again the god-like edifice would emerge, shining-white and beautiful. Or perhaps some scholar, like Rhadamanthus, would read certain signs and postulate that a great treasure lay hereabouts, and seek it with common tools, and find it.

The river would still flow, in this bed or some other. The River of Time would likewise never rest, swallowing here, upspewing there, building hills and wearing them away, and even the deathlessness of the Gods would be proven false, for change itself was endless. But still a woman would grow great with child, and then give the baby suck, and then a man would toil to provide it bread, and the generations would not fail, no matter the vast horde who had come and gone. This was the only meaning of immortality, the only breachless bargain between man and eternal Cronos, and the most we need ever ask.

CHAPTER THIRTEEN

THE LITTLE BIRDS OF DEATH

1

From the Europus River in Thessaly to Cythera in the Ionian Sea only a deaf and dumb Greek had never heard or spoken of the birds supposed to dwell in a dark and swampy woodland in Stymphalus. These birds were not like our larks and robins and wrens and sparrows; of no resemblance to the cranes, swans, ducks, geese, bitterns, and plovers that inhabited other watery regions. They had become synonymous with beings of malignance, monstrous, foul as harpies, attacking those who ventured into the fastnesses of the forests, often maiming, sometimes killing, frequently devouring their human prey.

The sixth labor appointed me by King Eurytus was driving away the Stymphalian Birds so that woodsmen could fell and haul for shipbuilding the valuable hardwoods of the swamp, and so that travelers on the footpaths and boatmen traversing its waterways would be safe from attack. Remembering the outcries of Ismene the Shepherdess in the agony of brooked desire, I could not say that the appointment took me wholly by surprise. But the birds were not likely to be as dangerous as rumor pictured them, and since their dispersal would benefit the folk, I could ask Eurytus for a handsome mead of honor.

My three companions and I set out for Stymphalus, and there we talked with plain-speaking rustics. Not one of them had ever laid eyes on the fabulous fowls, although a few thought they had heard them croak. A real curse upon the district was violent chills and fevers, gotten by entering the swampy woodland after sundown and before sunrise, and these lingered in the body for days and weeks, sometimes for months and years. Often their victims wasted away, and no few found untimely death. Sharp-eyed Actaeon noticed what at first he thought was a sign of unusual fecundity in the wives and daughters of the dwellers hereabouts, so many of them having swollen bellies as if three or four months with child, but on inquiry he was told that almost always this was a sign, as surely as wasting, of the same strange malady.

"It is caused by bad air," Right Doer said decisively in one of his seeming bursts of brilliance, which was rarely more than sound common sense. "The bad air is caused by stagnant waters. Drain the woods, dry up the pools, and I'll wager you a cask of the finest Thessalian that the so-called Birds of Stymphalus, that eat people alive from the inside out, will disappear." Still I was not quite convinced, no doubt because Ismene had foretold that "little birds that kill men in the swampy woods cannot make their nests." No prophecy of the Pythoness could have rung more true.

All of us knew of various swamp districts that had been drained, whereby corn could grow and beasts find better pasturage. Almost always the method was the digging of ditches to carry off the water, or the widening and deepening of the brooks. In this case the lay of the land seemed to favor the former method.

It happened that Nessus was one of a number of the sons of Greek kings who had been invited by Minos, King of Crete, to lend a light hand to the erection of his newest palace, more of an honor than a labor. Eager of mind, aware that the Minoans had been once the greatest builders in the whole of our seas and still retained knowledge of many crafts connected with building, Nessus had sailed there, and there had become acquainted with what was called a mason's level. This was a narrow, shallow box about six feet long, containing water and covered with a top of Egyptian glass. A cork floating on the water responded to its lightest movement, either toward one end or the other. Without the slightest difficulty he made one of the contraptions, lacking only a glass top, for which he substituted light, easily removed board.

We were already aware, because of its stagnant waters, that the dank forest lay almost level. However, Nessus' instrument revealed beyond question that the land had a very slow decline toward the river, perhaps two feet in its total length of four miles. But its lower end terminated on the riverbank, a good five feet above high-water mark, and a great deal of seepage through it showed the dissipation of surplus water from heavy rains. Now we could do no more than report our findings to King Diamenes, whose citadel at the river mouth was little better than a nest of pirates.

Happily he had an itching palm and his shipwrights would pay well for the hardwood timber of the watery forest. Also, besides his household staff, he had about sixty slaves, a polyglot lot of every color of skin from creamy white to ebony black that had been recently captured in piratical raids. These we could work in two gangs every day from about the second hour after sunrise to the second hour before sunset, when for some reason the air was not as noxious as at dawn, dusk, and at night. So we began a prolonged and grueling labor. Its aim was to build a ditch through the lowest part of the woods, about six feet wide and gradually deepening as it neared the river, and lesser ditches connecting this with various ponds and sloughs.

Right Doer commanded one gang, I the other. Nessus remained our engineer; Actaeon spent most of his days hunting deer, countless in the woods, to supply meat for the crews, King Diamenes' rations being too scanty for jewel carvers and weavers, let alone for hard shovelers never with dry feet, often up to their waists in cold water, unsheltered from rain and frost. I had no doubt that the abundant eating the men did was the great factor in their being content with the heavy toil, never fighting among themselves; and not once in the whole siege taking the desperate chance to escape. Only four were "eaten" by the Stymphalian Birds—attacked by chills and fever—and of these, two wasted away, their water turning black, and died; and two recovered after a short seizure.

We took utmost pains in one safeguard: not to try to make water run uphill. Because of this we made many small mistakes, sometimes backing and filling, but never went wholly wrong. A full year after we had begun digging, we broke open the last wall of dirt between our big ditch and the river. It happened that the latter was in freshet, we had no fall to spare, but a child could see the swamp waters moving slowly but steadily into the flood, and the latter muddied by the addition. When the freshet receded and the sun beamed down and skies were blue again, it was a wonder how quickly the sloughs and the ponds in the wood emptied into our ditch, and how manfully the ugly rift in the earth carried away its load, and poured it harmlessly into the river.

After a fortnight of drying out, the wood no longer smelled dank; it was like summer woods anywhere, and one night when Actaeon and Nessus were away, reporting to the King, Right Doer and I made our beds in its quiet midst, under the big trees. Not only did we fail to see any monstrous birds, we were not even bitten by mosquitoes, which from low sun to high sun had harried visitors and travelers there.

After waiting fourteen days, the utmost time visitors to the region must allow before they are out of danger of attack, my brother and I had no ague, no fits of weakness with fingernails turning white, or any other symptom of the malady caused by the legendary Stymphalian Birds. Along with legendary, could I not say nonexistent as well? No, because of a thoughtful remark made by Right Doer.

"You know, Heracles, we Greeks like fanciful names but rather often there is solid fact behind the fancy."

"I don't see any, in this case."

"Because perhaps we were looking for big birds, not little ones. Take mosquitoes, with which we have done away in a large part from this watery region because there is no longer any stagnant water in which the wrigglers may breed. Could you call a mosquito a bird? Not truly, but certainly he has wings and something like a beak. Please note the interesting fact that travelers and woodsmen in this region were fairly safe in the daylight hours. It was at night and in dusk when something happened that, in a few days, caused them to come down with a dread disease. At night and in dusk is when mosquitoes fly and bite. Could their tiny fangs introduce a slow poison?"

"Right Doer, that is claptrap. If mosquito bites were poisoned, the whole population of Cyllene would have long ago been wiped out. In the summer months the people are driven out of their minds by mosquitoes."

"They may be of a different variety than the Stymphalian Birds," Right Doer remarked imperturbably. "In fact, I believe those mosquitoes breed in salt lagoons instead of wood ponds. Well, let it go. It was only a wild surmise. No doubt the malady was caused by bad night air."

If we four comrades had been in haste to return to Orchomenus, we had as well cool our heels. King Diamenes was not easy to convince that his pestilent woodland had been made wholesome by rough-and-ready drainage. He sent word by Nessus and Actaeon that we must linger another month, putting finishing touches on our works, whereupon the lot of us, all sixty slaves as well, must spend a night in the part most dreaded by travelers. Then, after two weeks wait, if not a mother's son of us came down with the dread chill, he would declare himself satisfied and I could properly ask him for a mead of honor, in addition to what I expected from King Eurytus. Truly the delay irked us not at all, and rejoiced the two gangs of slaves. We smoothed the heaped-up banks of our ditches until they could do for the mounds over honored dead; we stuffed ourselves on venison; and we marked with pleasure that although most of the waterfowl dwelling hereabouts had taken themselves off, birds of other feather were taking their place, chirping away in the trees with the blitheness of proprietors; and even pheasants of gorgeous hue, never seen here previously, began to inhabit the woods. To judge from the swirls, no few fish ventured from the river into our ditch, along with an otter to keep them wise and wary.

We two foremen, our engineer, and our meat hunter, along with both crews, bivouacked in the forest on the night appointed, which proved uneventful except for our merriment over a big cask of wine that some grateful woodcutters presented to us. Later, my comrades and I came to a decision over what I should ask for my mead of honor from the petty king, and the idea presented by highborn Actaeon delighted us all, increased our delight in him, and was unanimously adopted. So when we sat at meat with Diamenes, and finally, after great and patent perturbation, he asked what I desired as a mead of honor, I was ready with a handsome answer.

"King Diamenes, we visitors to your kingdom have become friends and good companions of the sixty laborers you lent us from your slavepens. As my mead of honor, I ask that all of these who wish to return to their homes be allowed to do so, on your own ships, and those who wish to settle here be set free, take up occupations they are fit for, choose wives suitable to their stations, and become your loyal subjects."

The King heaved a sigh of relief. No doubt he had feared I would ask for a talent of gold.

"Heracles, your petition is granted. I will give that and no more. But to satisfy my curiosity, why, instead of favors for a pack of ditchdiggers, not even Greeks, did you not ask something for yourself?"

"The Gods gave me enough for myself and many others," I answered, looking him in the eyes. And if this was a boast, I could not help it; and if, instead, I had caught a glimpse of some great truth, which Right Doer and Megara both perceived more clearly than I—indeed it had evolved suddenly, from a muddle in my head, and probably would rarely seem so plain and true as at this present moment—I felt vastly proud.

"Nessus," the King remarked, to put an end to a moment of unexplainable emotion touching us all, "I will give you a word of advice in case you ever become King of Orchomenus. You will have household thralls and field thralls, born to what we call slavery in Greece, actually your henchmen, if not your sons, bound to you by a hundred ties. But do not let slave traders bilk you into buying captured slaves from across the seas, thinking you will profit from their labor. I can assure you they are the costliest possession you can maintain, not only their constant eating and the necessary watching, and the gray hairs they will bring to your head. I can assure you I am only too happy to be rid of that batch of sixty, who speak in tongues I do not know, and hence whom I suspect of plotting my murder. Now, Heracles, I will have my scribe draw a picture of a monstrous bird, lying dead with an arrow through his gizzard, his feet in the air, and under it I will put my royal seal. That you may bear to my cousin King Eurytus in testimony that the labor he has assigned you has been performed. Also I will send him a silver cup, inlaid with gold, and a beautiful maiden that one of my crews captured on the Island of Ogygia. By the Gods, I would think her very Calypso, who the yarn spinner Odysseus says kept him spellbound for something like seven years, if, in the first place, she were not literally a maiden, and if she could speak Greek. When you present her, give him this message. If he wishes to cut her throat, he will have my full consent if not my congratulations."

"If you please," I replied, after brief thought, "I will bear the cup to King Eurytus in pride and pleasure. But I petition you to send the maiden in one of your ships, under due protection, for we four intend to travel fast and light, and if an accident should occur to her maidenhood during the journey, the King would take it amiss."

"Perhaps that would be the better plan," the King concurred. "Not that I fear her maidenhood would suffer . . . but you have all served me well, and I wish you all a safe journey, hardly possible with this latter-day Medusa, with sunlit, silky tresses, in your company. So let us empty our cups, pour a libation to Hermes, God of Travelers, salute one another, and go our ways."

2

King Eurytus would certainly hold court on the autumn equinox, a day of thanksgiving to Demeter for the ripened corn, the ruddy apples, the stored and aging wine, the oil pressed from olives, and the fatted beasts. Also it was the priestly view that on this day Persephone went down to Hades to rejoin her pining husband, although every layman of sense knew that in the lowlands of Southern Greece she lingered for something like another month, and atop Parnassus and in the highlands of Macedonia her scant blessings began to fade away two weeks before. According to travelers, she never forsook the warm valley of the Nile. I doubted greatly if old Rhadamanthus put the least faith in her comings and goings, and instead believed the changing seasons were a matter of natural law.

So I chose this day to present the parchment from Diamenes, along with the gift of the silver cup inlaid with gold. Before his Companions and many of his greater liegemen, and with Megara's big eyes fixed on my face I made the offering, which he received in a nervous and irritable manner, as though he had been sorely tried.

"A gift from my cousin Diamenes has already reached me," he remarked acidly, "along with news of your dispersal of the Stymphalian Birds. Although he lent you great assistance, as you had also from my son Nessus and your other companions, yet I will not deny you have served well, and hence will award you a mead of honor. What do you desire?"

It was on my tongue to say what Right Doer had proposed—again a request that all Thebans forfeit to Eurytus by the terms of our surrender be set free. This he would not grant, but it would din in the ears of all present the fact of our harsh and cruel bondage, that of one Greek state, among the noblest, oldest, and most honored, to another Greek state not nearly as famous and ruled by an upstart king. Hence that greedy king would be well-nigh forced to make some sort of concession, probably an added year of reprieve for the young manhood of Thebes.

With the same breath he would no doubt appoint me my seventh labor, more difficult than any previous one if he had his way, as near the impossible as he dared command in the hearing of nobly born subjects. Also it would be as dangerous as the Greek people, in whose eyes I had gained heroic stature, would tolerate. For such I had been fated. Truly one of the Sisters, Lachesis, had gone out of her way to cast for me a lot unique, I believed, among mortals. Thereby I had been given a giant's strength and gone into bondage to a puny king, who in fear of the Gods or in some wild hope of his own escape from the doom spoken at Delphi had assigned me tasks that a truly great king would himself essay, most of them beneficial to the folk, and one, the capture alive of the Cerynean Stag, fantastic in the extreme. Could it be that I was his son? Fate that had gone this far would not stop him from visiting Thebes, unknown, the year of the departure of the ships; and he might well have been captured by Alcmene's beauty and she by his ruthless ambition. If so, he might be reliving his youth in me—vicariously winning the victories that I won—and the mark on my shoulder had been only my identification, not the foreshadowing of his death at my hands.

I did not believe it. I had time to come to that decision before answering his question, through the accident of an underling bringing him a picture writing to which he must give immediate attention. Rather I believed that my cutting off of his Right Hand, the giant Antaeus, had put us two in juxtaposition whereby his somewhat disordered mind lighted on me as the possible realizer of strange ambitions, desires, and not always natural dreams.

No, I did not believe he was my father. The fact remained I no longer craved his death, except as it might benefit Thebes. Suddenly I perceived him not as a hateful figure, but one to be at once admired and pitied. Once before I had glimpsed his vanity. It might be overweening—the moving force of his complex personality. And again I rejoiced that I had fallen into his power, for thereby I had found myself and realized my own powers, impossible elsewhere. Would I have slain the Nemean Lion, destroyed the Lernaean Hydra, tamed the Erymanthian Boar, driven away the Stymphalian Birds, and unearthed that wondrous treasure of our forefathers, the Hall of the Centaurs, which rude yokels had come to call the Augean Stables, except that I had been forced to do so by an eccentric tyrant? No, I would have thrown away the glory of my youth stuffing my stomach and draining cups, as well as covering wenches with the indiscrimination of a stag tupping hinds in heat.

The able mind of Right Doer had been strictly tried. Actaeon and Nessus both found life more exciting helping me than, in one case, taming horses, and, in the other, hunting wild beasts. As for myself I had been marvelously happy, by and large, although I had always known, and in this moment in hard introspection knew better than ever, that something vital to me was missing, some great need had gone unfulfilled. I glanced at Iole in her chair of state. Her long legs were crossed. I thought in a sudden frenzy of what softness lay between them, inviolate and inaccessible, the mysterious channel I ached to open and explore, forbidden me—and then, with much greater ease than before, the frantic yearning ceased and my heart longed not; and I looked at her pensive and lovely goddess-like face, and my soul confided I would never see it close to mine upon a pillow, and that I had been wishing for the moon. Still my soul would not have spoken, instead keeping silent at my command, leaving me free to dream, except for the dreadful happening in the crater of the Cerynean Mountains. Perhaps in jealousy, certainly in hate, she had struck at what she believed was a spirit, up out of the Abyss, but the hate too had been abysmal, beyond human it had seemed to me, and I could deal with no one capable of its like. Then and there, Iole had been lost to me forever. What a fool I was to think of it in this way, considering I had never had her in one iota! Her kisses had left nothing in my mouth but hunger. She had wakened my pinings but she had only briefly pined for me.

From her countenance, second in beauty only to Helen's of all I had seen, flawless except for a tiny black circle of pigment that called attention to its otherwise flawlessness, I looked up into the face of Megara. She had been gazing at me, and when my sudden glance caught her in the act, she did not turn away her great dark eyes, and instead she called up something into their depths in direct intercourse with mine, although I knew not what it was. Even so, I did know something new, and with perfect wholeness and clarity I knew whom I longed for most, throughout my remaining days on earth. And at this very instant the minion in low talk with Eurytus went back to his place, and the King was ready to hear my reply to his question.

"King of the Minyae!" I answered with some pomp. "You have asked me what I desire in the way of a mead of honor for my dispersal of the Stymphalian Birds. First, I desire that all Thebans forfeit to you by your decree be set free forever. Second, I desire the hand of your daughter Megara in marriage. If I can have both, I will endeavor to show my gratitude in services to your throne and person. But if I must make a choice between the two, I choose freedom for my countrymen of Thebes."

My gaze could not help but leap to Megara's face, to ask if she favored, or was adverse, to my second petition and if, woman-like, or like woman in common report, she would be angry at my putting the freedom of a thousand Thebans ahead of my love for her. She gave her head a lively little toss and made no reply to my questions. On the other hand, a smile curled Iole's beautifully chiseled lips, such a smile as I had seen once before on her face so like that of her Goddess. It was a solitary smile. It was not meant as a message or a token to anyone. It was dreamy and my soul seemed to tell me that it was divine, that no mere mortal could smile like that, that only Gods and Goddesses, assured by Heaven of their godhead, never to meet Death in this world or any world to come, forever safe from the reach of his icy hand, could thus curl their lips in secret, in assurance more sure than the hill's of his heart of stone, in carelessness of all the world because the rivers of their own lives were fated to flow forever in a serene and majestic flood.

"I will grant neither," King Eurytus answered with spirit, now that he had caught his breath. "As for your second wish, I do not deny it to you, but Megara herself, a free woman of Greece before she is a princess, shall decide whether to take you for her husband or to refuse your hand. As for your first wish, I am of a mind to be generous. The periods of parole which I have already granted to Theban manhood forfeit to me may be extended for two more years. Throughout this period you are to remain in bondage to me and perform such labors as I appoint you and which are in your strength to do."

Most of his hearers, including his Companions, shouted their approval; and truly he appeared to stand higher with the great folk of his realm than ever in my observance. With no little vainglory he quaffed from his cup.

"Your last labor, Heracles, was a tedious one—a matter of digging ditches and draining poisonous fens," the King went on. "In the labor I now appoint you, you are only to satisfy my curiosity as to what folk regard as myth, but which I do not doubt was sober fact, and your

affording me that satisfaction should supply a lively adventure for my
son Nessus, the great hunter Actaeon, your brother Right Doer, and
of course yourself. All of you have heard of the Minotaur, that dwelt
in the labyrinth in Crete, to whom beautiful youth and maidens of the
Minoan people were yearly sacrificed. You know too the tale of his
slaying by the great hero Theseus, who found his way through the
maze by the aid of the King's daughter, Ariadne. But do all of you
know how the Minotaur came into being in the first place? Perhaps
not; so soon are the great tales of our fathers forgotten by our sons.
Know, then, that Poseidon once gave to King Minos a beautiful bull,
snow-white, with pink eyes, on the agreement that Minos would sacrifice the beast to the Sea God's shrine. This the king failed to do.
Perhaps in punishment for breaking his vow, or perhaps because of a
certain strangeness of her nature, the King's own Queen, beautiful
Pasiphaë, fell madly in love with the bull and bore him a son, who
was the man-eating Minotaur. Does this end the tale? No, for although
the monster, half bull, half man, perished before most of us were born,
the white bull that sired him, Poseidon's gift, still roams the forests
and the wild heaths of Crete. I have a curiosity to see him. So have
many Greeks, I doubt not—to behold a common beast so beautiful
that he could win the love and passion of a queen. Your next labor,
Heracles, is to go with your companions to Crete, capture the bull,
bind him fast, and bring him unharmed to Orchomenus. You have my
leave to go."

It made me grin to see the King's wide-eyed hearers start and return
to their everyday world. Truly no people that ever lived loved a strange
tale more than do we Greeks; and yet in one way it is a paradox, for
I would be hard put to it to name a people more rational of mind or as
free from thought-clouding superstition. Perhaps I could lump it off
with saying that the Greeks were childlike in imagination, but never
let their imaginings interfere with having a full meal and deep, health-
ful sleep, making delicious love, shaping a beautiful vase, raising a good
crop, or turning a good trade.

I thanked all the Gods of Olympus that my unknown sire, seeking
a delectable adventure in the year the heroes sailed for Troy, chose a
Greek lady for his couchmate. This soil was my very own.

CHAPTER FOURTEEN

AN APPOINTMENT

1

Throughout my boyhood I had supposed that Amphitryon, Alc-mene's husband, was likewise a native of Thebes. I was almost grown when I had learned that he was an exile from Toryne, a rock-girt citadel on the plain of Argos. It happened that as I was leaving Eurytus' court, an aged Torynian stopped me to speak of my foster father, whom he had known as a youth. This delay interfered with my encountering Megara, as I had hoped, and walking with her into the cypress woods for what might happen there.

It so chanced that Iole was likewise delayed in leaving the pillared porch, and fell in with me. The secretive, somehow unearthly smile was no longer on her face; nor was the mien of a Goddess in her person; indeed she seemed as carefree and vivacious as on our first day in the mule cart on our journey to the Cerynean Mountains.

"Megara will be greatly flattered that you, Heracles, already named in the same breath with Theseus, has asked for her hand in marriage," the priestess told me, slipping her silky hand into mine.

"Theseus was a king. I am a cowherd, and lately a ditchdigger, of unknown heritage. Still, I hope she will consent."

"I think there's a fair chance that she will." And Iole's pure forehead furrowed a little, as though from deep thought.

"A fair chance, you say. Do you mean by that an equal chance, or a little more than equal, or a little less?" I tried not to let Iole know how I hung on her answer.

"A little more than equal, I should judge. After all, she can't keep

on living in the past. As you know, her great love was never returned.
It was not because of any lack in her—her beloved perceived her worth
and beauty and was greatly attracted to her, and he has never taken
any other woman for his wife. But he had another passion that ex-
cluded marriage—what I mean is, a man of his nobility would think
it unfair for him to marry, because he could not give enough. Do you
not agree with him?"

Iole had said to me, "as you know." For a moment my pride almost
made me pretend that I did know. Then I thought of the greatness
of the issue, perceived more clearly than ever now, and I cried down
my pride, and spoke.

"Iole, I have lately come to Orchomenus and I do not know whom
you mean."

"Are you trying to tell me that you never knew that Megara and
one of your dearest friends were once lovers of a sort, and a great
many people thought it a settled thing?"

"I had never heard it."

"I shouldn't have mentioned it. Still, you would have had to face it
in the end—Megara would certainly tell you all about it before you
both plighted troth. You still don't know?"

"I have very few friends. I haven't the gift of making many, so it
must have been Actaeon, who loves hunting almost as much as
breathing."

"Of course it was Actaeon of the royal house of Cadmus. In all
truth, if Megara had won him for a husband she would have married
far above her, for you know her lineage and my own, compared to his
descent from great Cadmus. What of it? Don't stand there like an ox
struck by a butcher's cudgel. If she still pines for him, you wouldn't
want her anyway. If she has gotten over it, it will make no difference
between you and her."

It had already made a difference, I was thinking. I remembered too
well my discovery when Megara and I had made our bed on a sheepskin robe beside the Pool of Truth. I had given little thought to it
then; Greek girls of the highest class as well as the most humble were
under no great restriction before marriage; indeed at some of our festivals, especially those honoring Pan, beloved Dionysus, or in memory
of beautiful Adonis, license was almost unbridled. Yet now it seemed
to me that I would rather have any Greek for my precursor than magnificent Actaeon; and the fact that, of all young men, I admired him

only second to Right Doer, did not erase the unworthy thought and instead made it burn deeply.

Then some impulse that I was never to explain caused me to gaze deeply into the lovely face of Iole. Perhaps I was hoping to find there a trace of malice, even of jealousy, or some sign of deceit. Megara had told me her sister was a liar, although her lies were invariably political. All that I found in her face, besides its deathless beauty, was trouble, reflecting the trouble she saw in mine. Plainly she was regretting she had mentioned what the whole city knew, which Thebes knew too, I supposed; and suddenly I was ashamed of that reflection, ashamed of myself for my moment of weakness, and it must be that I remembered that I was Heracles, who must live and die unweakened, or some great destiny would fail. A muscle throbbed in my arm. Although it did not appear so, even on close examination, it was a mighty muscle, capable of great workings. So was I, myself.

"I love Megara, and want her to love me, and whom she loved before me was worthy of it, or she would have not have done it, and that settles it," I told Iole, as quietly as I could speak.

She looked at me with an expression in her eyes the meaning of which I did not know, although I could not mistake its intensity, almost a wildness, which I had seen there once before, and I wished I could remember when and where. When we had made our pleasant parting, it seemed to me I had performed another labor worthy of men's remembrance, certainly of my own if I lived to grow old, although I could not perceive exactly what it was. And certainly it would not be numbered among those assigned me by Eurytus. I had the irrational feeling that it was somehow related to my strangling of the giant Antaeus.

2

When I overtook Megara she was walking into the cypress woods with Actaeon, her hand slipped into his. If I had found them thus before Iole had told me of their once love affair, I would not have given the matter a second's thought. So I resolved not to give it a second's thought now; and by and large I kept to it, although my soul knew that doing so required a slight firming of my will, which feat I had to repeat when the two passed what was meant to seem an empty glance, but which was really a token of some kind of understanding between them. Actaeon was a great prince of the realm of Thebes. Of heavier build than Right Doer, he had the same clean carving. He was not godlike but wonderfully human, and people of keen vision who did not know he was a great hunter would have perceived his fitness for all the manly sports, being lithe of limb, broad and deep of chest, quick and precise of movement, and with eyes magnificently alive. Aye, he was a man to focus instantly a woman's sharp and speculative attention and for fellow men to admire. I, Heracles, if I lived to fulfill Linus' prophecy, was not a man but a monster.

"I'm glad you caught up with us," Megara said. "Actaeon and I have been discussing the Minoan Bull. We have some notions about his pursuit we would like to present to you."

"That statement, Heracles, is typical of every lovely lady's studied disrespect for truth," my friend broke in. "I had no notions about the bull. Those we discussed were Megara's notions. To be more precise, instead of a discussion between us, she spoke and I listened. And since I can say nothing of any value at this point, I'll take myself off."

He did so, in his graceful fashion, modest and yet princely. Megara led me to a wooden bench I had not seen before, merely a hewn slab of oak wood pegged to two stumps, yet pleasant enough for sitting, it being somewhat secluded and safe from eavesdroppers and presenting a distant view of the glimmering white shrine.

"Heracles, I don't want you to go to Crete," she told me after a moment's gathering of her thoughts.

"I've been sent there by my master."

"There are many ways, the people say, to pluck a goose. I am going to hear a rumor, which I will repeat to the King, that the Minoan Bull, who begat the Minotaur, left the island in grief and madness at the death of Queen Pasiphaë, his beloved, was seen in Ios, then in Nexos, then in Andros, and finally in Attica. Plainly he had swum the whole distance, no feat for a bull that once belonged to Poseidon, God of the Sea."

"Then what?"

"He has roamed the Pernes Mountain region ever since. You, having also heard the rumors, will hunt for him there, and find him. Tell me, are white bulls extremely rare in the droves of cattle you have seen?"

"I should say that one bull in forty is snow-white."

"Attica has a thousand bulls. An ingot of silver, which Nessus can supply, will buy the finest. He won't have pink eyes——"

"He might. They're not rare in what Right Doer calls albinos."*

"The bull can be led to Orchomenus with a nose ring. But perhaps even that won't be necessary. All my life I have played on my father's superstitions—although Iole has beat me at it tenfold—and I think he will want you to turn the animal loose in his own grounds. This labor, Heracles, is child's play. But it might have a very serious aspect if you went to Crete."

"I don't know what you mean."

"The present King of Crete, a real son of Queen Pasiphaë—in this case by her husband—is too close to Eurytus. At least they both want favors from each other—and will grant favors. If you went there, you might never come back to Greece. And you will be greatly needed here, perhaps more than ever, by the young men of Thebes . . . and by me."

When I was away from Megara I was always wishing I could resound in my ears the warmth and depth and earnestness of her voice when she was telling me something close to her heart. I succeeded much better in calling back the appearance of her face, particularly her deep, dark eyes, although at best my imagining of these brought only pale ghosts of their reality.

"Megara," I told her, "the King refused to give me your hand in marriage, and very properly, since it is for you to say, not him, as he was a great enough king to admit. Here and now I ask you. Will you marry me, Megara?"

"I would love to marry you, Heracles—when you are ready."

"I am ready now. I have waited too long already to find out what I wanted."

"You have found out what you wanted, perhaps, but not yet what you do not want. I surmised that something happened—some happening of great importance—when Iole went with you to pursue the Cerynean Stag, which of course does not exist. Whatever happened, I am positive that it had a far different meaning and motive than you suppose—or than she told you. Still, I think she lost ground. I think she was not quite as clever as usual, or as adept, and all your dreams

---

* This is of course an anachronism of the most patent sort. The Greeks must have had a word, translatable into English, for albino, but I do not know where to find it.—E.M.

about her are clouded. I do not think her power over you is as great as it was, although she might be able to re-establish it. That is only one of the reasons you are not yet ready for marriage to me, if you will ever be. The other is the labors to be imposed on you in the next two or three years. In dealing with Eurytus, you are dealing with a man whose mind is clouded by superstition. I think he broods about death—fears it will strike soon unless he has some miraculous weapon against it. He still fears that you are the fatal figure of the prophecy; at the same time you are the only one who can win him some sort of control over the Gods, either by propitiating them, especially Zeus, or bribing them, or applying some sort of pressure upon them."

"I wish you would make that a little clearer for my thick head."

"The slaying of the Lernaean Hydra and the Nemean Lion, the taming of the Boar, and the driving out of the Stymphalian Birds all were intended first to please Zeus, who the folk believe cares for the folk—and I wish to my soul that he does and it might be so. Also, these labors brought Eurytus reflected glory throughout Greece. His wanting you to capture the Stag with the Golden Horns was to put a weapon in his hands against Artemis and perhaps against Iole, who he thinks may be an avatar of Artemis. Your capture of the Cretan Bull is to give him a weapon against Zeus' brother, Poseidon, who can be expected to put pressure on his other brother, Hades. As for the following labor—I am going to appoint you that, although Eurytus will never know it was not his own choosing. That labor will put you into direct conflict with evil, the very essence of evil, not a mere natural enemy of man, such as you fought in the Nemean Lion. Heracles, you must understand that Evil is not merely the absence of Good; it is the Dark Powers as opposed to the Bright Powers, and these are only too real, only too powerful, and you must destroy one focal point, one festering abscess on the body of mankind, of which I know. That labor will take you all the way to Thrace."

"Why can't you go with me? You are not afraid."

"Because I am needed here. Now let me speak of the labors. You will be assigned two—perhaps four—more. I know how Eurytus' mind works: very likely there will be ten or twelve, ten because it is regarded as a magic number—he has ten fingers and ten toes—or perhaps twelve because there are twelve signs of the zodiac. His motives will be the same—power over the Gods. Tonight I will see Nessus. In the morning I will tell you how you may cope with the King's wild fantasy of your capturing a bull that does not exist. Thereafter steel yourself for as great, and almost as strange a battle with Evil as Perseus fought when he killed some female monster—probably born of woman—that we call Medusa."

With tears in her eyes Megara took my big, rough hand and kissed it. I knelt and kissed her sandaled feet.

CHAPTER FIFTEEN

THE DARK TOWER

1

It so happened that a runner from the Pernes Mountain region in Attica brought to King Eurytus what was purported to be a message from me. It was that I had found the snow-white Cretan Bull without the least difficulty, that he had charged down the mountain, bellowing, on catching the first whiff of me, and although I might have killed him with my spear, it was impossible, at this first meeting, to capture him alive. In ensuing days he had maintained his belligerent stand, and it was now possible to snare him with thongs or in a pit, but for two reasons I thought best to ask the King's approval before I did so. One was that he bore on his flank a birthmark, appearing like a scar, in the shape of a trident, unmistakable proof that he belonged to Poseidon, God of the Sea. The other was that every time he bellowed in rage, a peal of thunder sounded in the hills above, not an echo, and beyond question the voice of an angry God. But I, Heracles, was prepared to do my utmost to carry out any command that the King might send me.

I had certain reasons to believe the device might work. One was it was invented by Megara, who knew her father's mind. The other arose from my observation that many cunning and hardheaded people, able in their earthly pursuits, swiftly penetrating ordinary plots, often skeptical of what was solid truth, would swallow whole the wildest fantasy if it were dressed in the trappings of religion. Eurytus sent me word by the runner that I was to leave two bushels of the choicest barley in the bull's path, pluck a great bouquet of asphodel for him to smell or eat, according to his desire, then depart speedily from that region, and to return to Orchomenus with all dispatch.

There I hung about for a matter of about three weeks, seeing little of Megara and nothing of Iole, until Eurytus summoned me into his presence. The only others present in the chamber were two of his old counselors, his musician, a priest from the great temple of Zeus in nearby Elatea, a wild-eyed soothsayer of some sort, a grave dame, and two serving wenches. When I had given him the salutation, one of the girls poured me wine in a silver cup.

"You will need its warmth when you are gone to the land of the labor I now assign you," he told me. "That land is said to be the home of the North Wind, yet at this my common sense rebels, for traders have told me of lands yet nearer the pilot star, even more wintry, where Boreas howls like a hundred wolves. Yet it is cold enough, and far distant truly, in the northeast of the sacred land of the Greek-speaking people, almost to the border of the realms of the barbarians. It is no other than Western Thrace, a fortnight's journey with pack mules. Needless to say, it would be much swifter and more comfortable by ship, but our hardy captains do not like to approach that coast."

He paused, and I bowed my head as Rhadamanthus had taught me.

"On a region of the coast known as Abdera stands the citadel of King Diomedes, bearing the same name as the hero of the Trojan War, but of another line," Eurytus went on. "In the harbor lie his ships with yellow sails, the business of which is usually told in whispers. Also he has pastures where mares feed and foal, and stables for them when Boreas blows shrill."

At his signal a handmaiden refilled his golden cup and then mine.

"The labor appointed you is not of my own choosing," Eurytus told me. "Rather it was the prompting of a dream sent to me by some God. The words were these; I seemed to hear them spoken in the voice of an immortal, not merely to dream them. 'Bid Heracles teach the mares of Diomedes to eat grass.' Then and there the dream ended. I know no more what it means than you do. I would not have known who Diomedes was, except that a priest of a temple to Dionysus nigh that region brought here his filly to be covered by Nessus' stallion Earth Shaker; and he told me that the King, Diomedes, had heard of the Sons of Poseidon, the society that Nessus founded, and he had been greatly taken with the idea of men riding horses, although he himself used them to draw chariots of war. So you will set forth as soon as possible, and on this enterprise you shall have two pack mules and some ingots of lead of my providing. Right Doer may go with you, but my son Nessus and Actaeon the Great Hunter must remain here."

He raised his hand to indicate my dismissal.

As I emerged from the arch, Megara met me and, saying not a word, slipped a long index finger into my hand. By this she led me to the open air, and then through a gate in the wall to the cypress wood, and there we found a short, solidly built woman, young and comely, with a great richness of russet-colored hair. Although her countenance had been changed somewhat since I had seen her last, I instantly recognized her as Daphne, the wife of Dyctus, my great comrade in the pastures above the Nemean Plain.

"What a joy you are to my eyes," I told her, when she had kissed my hands and head.

"And you to mine. More than that, what hope you give to my heart!"

"What has happened, Daphne? Is Dyctus well?"

"Dyctus is in the Land of Shades."

I wished I could disbelieve her and believe he had merely disappeared awhile, and one day soon would reappear, but her tone spoke more plainly than her words, and her eyes plainer than either. She showed none of the usual signs of grief, her self-control was so strict that people who did not know her might mistake it for callousness, and it was a world removed from resignation to the will of the Gods and to the dread shears of Atropos. Then I perceived that beneath her calm demeanor she harbored a mighty passion.

I could not speak at once, from dwelling on Dyctus, and how he had volunteered to stand behind me when, hidden in a bull's hide, I met Iniquity, and how he had never quailed, did his part with unfaltering hands, and, when the last green glare had died in the Beast's eyes, he had wept, and then I had wept with him.

"Tell Heracles," came Megara's soft voice, "what Dyctus' companion, Draces the Sailor, told you."

"Our master sent his tall ship on a trading voyage to the towns on the Chalcidicean Coast," Daphne said in level tones. "It chanced that Dyctus had a longing to see that distant land, so he asked permission to join her crew, and since he was not needed at the pastures, our master consented. Off Acrathoum their ship spoke to another that had the guise of a peaceful trader, and when by a stratagem she drew alongside our master's ship, from under her gunwhales sprang a hundred armed men who swarmed aboard, killing some of our men and capturing the rest. Among those captured were Draces and my husband Dyctus. Then our ship was manned by the capturers, and both ships were brought into a harbor called Abdera, above which stands the citadel of King Diomedes. And there Dyctus was slain in a way unspeakable, but Draces seized an opportunity to flee, and by hiding in a tidal marsh and then by long night marches he gained Gigonus, from whence a fishing vessel brought him to Eurymense, in Eastern Thessaly. In due course he came to Nemea, to tell me of my husband's fate, and that is all my tale."

"But you have not told Heracles how your husband died."

"Nay, and I cannot. The words will not form on my lips."

"Nor on mine," Megara said with a deep gasp. "But Heracles, you can find out, when you make your way by stealth to the pastures of Diomedes. And you know now that it must be by stealth, for there will be only you and Right Doer to do what must be done, two against —how many? Even so, say to Daphne what you can to comfort her."

So I said what came to my tongue, without thought.

"Daphne, never have I been appointed to a labor as close to my heart as this."

"That is all I need to know," the woman answered. Then she turned to my companion. "Megara of Orchomenus, girl of the great eyes, my mission has been fulfilled, and now I will return to the flocks and herds."

In a moment she had gone. Megara and I stood hand in hand and for a while neither of us had anything to say, and although I ached to tell of the surging within my soul, I knew that I could not, even with the tongue of Apollo. But Megara spoke at last.

"You won't forget how we bathed in the Pool of Truth?"

"As long as I live."

"Or how we made our bed and were flea-bitten, in Snag Tooth's sheepskins, but even so were blessed by Demeter of the corn, and Pan of the wild mountains, and perhaps by the nymph who had loved Snag Tooth in his youth."

"That too I'll remember. And I will remember that Snag Tooth was slain by Iniquity before Dyctus and I darkened his baleful eyes,

and now the eyes of Dyctus are darkened, and thus the debt laid upon
me is beyond measure."

"Return to me, Heracles, if you can, in your present shape and
substance, but return to me if only a shadow at my bedside, pausing
briefly on its journey to the Land of Shadows, that I may know that
the debt is paid."

2

Right Doer and I journeyed comfortably enough across the fertile
lowlands flanking the Strymon River. Only when we were approaching Antisara and the frontier of the Diomedes' domains need we present ourselves as shipwrights, freemen looking for work, after the closing of the yards at Triton Lake. Then, after entering the wild coastal
region about Pistyrus, we traveled at night and in secret.

I do not know why the region that the people called Abdera seemed
so minatory both to Right Doer and me. The cape offered havens for
ships both to the east and to the west; although at fiery sundown,
when we first viewed their waters, they looked bloodstained, the ships
riding at anchor were pretty enough to see and gave no sign of their
black hearts. The seven small hills were clothed in rank greenery almost to their tops, which were curiously naked. It must be that through
some accident of nature this immediate region received superabun-
dant rains. All growth was rank, whether the grass, the thickets, or the
gaudy flowers.

The region had a peculiar smell. It was faint, but horrible. I thought
I had imagined it until I questioned Right Doer; a slight pinching of
his nostrils answered me. Then we both looked up to Diomedes' citadel on the naked top of the highest of the seven hills. It was not large,
although stout, and it stood black against the sun. In a hollow between
this hill and another lay a pasture, rankly green, and what appeared
to be stalls built of stone. We could see no more tonight, and when
we had made secret bivouac and gone to bed, I thought the night
would never end.

In early morning Right Doer and I climbed one of the hills, following a goat path. Often the rank growth would hardly let us through,
and tendrils, slimy with the wet, clung to our clothes and skin, and the
smell of decay thickened. With great caution we stood at the edge of
the hill's bald pate, and gazed almost straight across the hollow to

the citadel, and down a little into a pasture with a stone wall. Now we discovered another building, quite large, likewise of stone, that we had not seen before. It had no openings to the air, and had what we thought was a strongly barred door. Except for minute, sporadically moving figures on the ships in the harbor, we saw no human being. The absence of the usual bustle about the gates of a king's palace gave us both a dreamy feeling of unreality. The moisture of the heavy air mixed with sweat on our foreheads, for we were already aware of menace, brooding and flagitious, and of what might be the weird and unnatural. Our comfort was that surely the fortress was lightly manned.

"Do you see the big bronze bell over the roof of the pillared porch?" Right Doer asked, his eyes glimmering.

"Yes."

"How can it be rung without someone climbing to the housetop? I imagine by a rope running through an aperture. I can't quite see it —a cobweb seems to appear and disappear—but there's the answer to our question why we see no men-at-arms guarding the gates or strolling about the courtyard. King Diomedes keeps no dogs that do not hunt. His hunting dogs live aboard his ships, and the ships go back and forth to the sea lanes and bring back captive ships—and captive cargoes—and captive men—and captive women. I'm going to make the wild guess that no male human being old enough to wear a loincloth occupies the palace other than the King himself. There may be old crones to mend fires, spin, weave, carry water, sweep, empty pots, and cook; otherwise the King dwells alone with his handmaidens. And if an enemy force should appear on the horizon, some sharp-eyed wench would ring the bell, and the crews of all the ships then in harbor would rush to defend the citadel."

"Truly it is a wild guess, Right Doer," I answered. "I grant that his pirates serve as his guards in times of need, but as for his living alone, without companions, without musicians or minions, with only captive women for his service and his entertainment—that I find hard to believe."

"You are a lusty fellow, Heracles, without being lecherous in a fine-haired way. To possess the only prong of pleasure available to a whole flock of maidens is the secret daydream of many a man. That dream accounts for the haremlik of Oriental potentates—women beyond count, helpless eunuchs, and the king's weak maleness worshiped for uniqueness' sake alone. To tell you the truth—but that I had better not confess. But I will still wager you a cup of honey mead that my guess is right."

"I can attach no importance to it, except that it makes his citadel more vulnerable to surprise attack. Nor was it his piracies, which are a common thing in these seas, going back to the youth of Dionysus, that aroused Megara. It was something much worse. She spoke of the Dark Powers. How bad can men go, Right Doer? Piracy, murder of helpless captives, selling prisoners into slavery—are these only the beginning? And what causes that faint, horrible smell?"

"Evil."

"Do you know what form it takes?"

"I think I do. Heracles, I see visions. They are unspeakable and I wish——"

"A man is coming through the door of the stone outbuilding and he carries a whip with a short handle and a very long lash."

"My brother, it may be that King Diomedes has his captives whipped to death. I wish it were only that, for a nobly born Greek threw Hector's baby over the wall to his death. Perhaps Diomedes wields the whip himself, with a hideous rapture. Surely there is nothing much worse within human capability. And now we will see something—what? The fellow is making toward the stalls."

Presently he vanished within the building and all we saw was a drove of perhaps a dozen horses dash through a wide-open door. The man followed them and locked the door behind him; meanwhile the animals began to frolic. Truly their mettle was the highest I had ever seen, exceeding that of the great chariot horses that Nestor still kept, which lapped barley from his palm and which grazed in his pasture but no longer drew the thundering car into the red field of battle. The morning sun glossed the hides of Diomedes' horses; and he must keep skillful grooms, I thought, to cause them to be as beautiful as red deer stags in the mating season. In another way they resembled stags —their high, vivacious boundings. They could not stop their romping to nibble the rank grass.

"I take it they are all mares," Right Doer said.

"You can't tell at this distance."

"Not for certain. But mark their light build, their narrow heads and slender necks and small, pointed ears."

"I too believe they are mares."

"Diomedes must be a great breeder. But we knew that, aforetime, by his sending a filly all the way to Orchomenus to get a foal from Earth Shaker, Nessus' stallion. Heracles, forgive me if my tongue wags, if I talk nonsense. We have heard the tale of a queen in love with a bull—a tale at which both of us scoff but which the Greek folk believe. Could a king who has shut himself up in a fortress with what I cannot doubt are a score or more of beautiful young women, captured on the coastal raids by his pirate ships, love not them and instead love mares?"

"I forgive you for talking nonsense."

"Heracles, do you ever dream about horses?"

"Rarely, perhaps—why?"

"I often do—and always when my loins ache. Remember that in our myth the lecherous centaurs are half horse, half human. What does Diomedes do with those beautiful beasts? He breeds them to stallions, of course, but what other use does he make of them? We have seen no track or sign of a chariot; there are no tales of his horsemanship. Heracles, a horrid pattern of thought is forming in my mind. Now the man with the whip has returned to the other building. What will happen now?"

"Only the Gods know."

"We must find out. We must see with our own eyes, or you will fail to perform the labor appointed you. I think that if you do see, there will be little danger of your failing, if I know my Heracles. Can we find a path to lead us through the dense growth down to the pasture wall? That wall is high but it appears to be made of rough-cut stones set in plaster, and surely there will be chinks through which we can watch."

"There must be deer paths. I saw where many deer, the small, pale-colored kind that love thick woods, crossed the goat path."

"I think we should start at once, Heracles. A long day lies ahead; still I feel you will be pressed for time to do all that you must do."

"We will start at once."

We met with no great difficulty in descending the hill and making our way to the wall of Diomedes' pasture. There were numerous narrow deer paths which met and parted, and wild boars had paced and eaten out and packed down what looked like narrow cart roads. Our garments became soaking wet and slimy-feeling from the rain-drenched rotting herbage, and when we could, we held our noses to stifle the horrid smell that poisoned every breath of air. It was a smell of pollution and decay, with an added taint of sickish sweetness. Once I saw the pallor of nausea in Right Doer's face; but I handed him a piece of the dried venison that I carried, and he ate it staunchly, and his strength returned.

There were many small openings between the rocks of the wall. We were able to post ourselves within reach of each other and still view the whole pasture. The next scene in the drama I felt developing and deeply feared and still could not forecast bulged our eyes a little. By looking up over the wall, we saw a red-bearded man emerge from the citadel and start down a steep path toward the pasture. He wore a coronet with golden plumes that glimmered in the midmorning sun and a blue-and-white robe, doubtless of wondrous weave, and fastened with what I thought must be clasps, richly bejeweled to judge from their twinkling gleamings. That this was King Diomedes neither of us could doubt.

His sole companion would have made me laugh, had I watched his antics at the festival, but my brother and I were worlds away from laughter now. It was an ape of some sort, not large or savage-looking, rufous in hue and resembling those sometimes brought from Barbary by our seafarers. It walked sedately on all fours in the King's wake.

We lost sight of the strange pair in a few seconds, as his descent brought him behind the opposite wall. To our amazement, when we saw them again both were atop the wall. There the ape sat himself down on what appeared to be a big rock that had been set there, but a kind of throne had been provided for the King, for by looking closely we saw stone armrests, roughly carved, while his legs hung over the edge. That both had gained their seats by some kind of ladder back of the wall, Right Doer and I could not doubt.

"What now, Right Doer?" I heard myself ask, my throat tight.

"I do not know, Heracles, but I fear the worst. I bid you steel your heart for a dreadful sight, one you can never forget and which will visit you in many a dream of sleep. I have pity on your eyes as I have on my own. I may be wrong, but every sign is prophetic of ineffable evil—and after that, of the awful vengeance you must take. As great Tiresias told you the night of my father's funeral pyre, it is not good to be great."

We need not wait long in this almost unbearable suspense. No doubt the King was impatient, and his minions that had their lodgings in the stone building made haste. We had already noticed a slit in the wall about a foot wide, only a short distance from the King's seat, and closed with what might be a slab of wood on the far side. This slab was drawn back. The figure of a man standing sideways appeared in the slit, and in an instant he was thrust through into the pasture, and the barrier restored behind him. He gazed once into the field and screamed. It was the most blood-chilling outcry I had ever heard from a human throat.

As his breath gave out, the King shouted in stentorious command: "Fall to!"

The mares stopped their romping and every neck turned and they stood and stared at the prisoner in their pasture. One of them neighed shrilly, and then the whole drove began to gallop toward him. He hurled himself against the wooden barrier, only to fall down, then he began to run along the inside of the wall. The mares changed their course to intercept him. Their necks were extended now, their bared teeth gleamed white, white glimmered their eyes, they rushed with a ferocity which no charioteer had ever seen, or, at least, that their tales disclosed. The first mare to come up to the prisoner struck at him with her forelegs, but missed, and he dashed into the field, yelling hoarsely in horror.

There was only one mercy granted the doomed man, once no doubt a sunburned, happy-hearted sailor on a gallant ship, and that was the actual brevity of the chase, although it seemed endless to Right Doer and to me, and only the Gods knew all of its aspects in the brain and heart and soul of the victim. Why did the Gods not stop the horrid happening? Because they do not make a practice of such use of their godheads. No thunderbolt was hurled at the tensely watching King. Poseidon, who gave horses unto men, according to the tale, did not strike dead the screaming mares. The Olympians may have glanced up with lackluster eyes, then gone back to their godlike pursuits, watching the Graces dance, eating ambrosia, drinking nectar.

The victim ran and dodged with marvelous swiftness and agility. It caused the ape to leap up and down, and in between the frantic cries of the man and the frenzied neighing of the horses I heard his shrill chatter. The King reached down and clasped his groin with both hands, his body rigid. And now the runner stumbled. He leaped up and started to run on, but a mare's neck stretched long and her gleaming bared teeth closed in his shoulder. She lifted him off the ground, shook him as a terrier shakes a rat, and threw him to the ground. Then all her band rushed to his prostrate form and ringed it, every neck stretched, every head lowered—every set of gleaming teeth sank and tugged, and then hideously chewed.

In hardly a moment the uproar ceased. A great stillness came to pass, and one by one the beasts made off, with strange sedateness, perhaps in surfeit, from the little scattering of red bones.

The King stretched his arms, the ape grew quiet, and in a moment both disappeared. I turned my head to find Right Doer's wondrous eyes gazing into mine, asking a question. I nodded my head.

3

As though to get in tune with the hearts of Right Doer and me, the south wind began to rise. In Thebes the wind from this direction is usually warmed by the Libyan deserts and is rarely very strong, perhaps because it is broken by the highlands of Peloponnesus. Here it had the immensity of the Aegean Sea over which to sweep and gather strength ere it smote the Thracian coast.

Within an hour sailors could call it half a gale, and no doubt a good many ships setting forth on brave voyages from our countless havens turned back to port, or else took refuge in ports other than those toward which they had been making. It would not impede Right Doer and me in any ventures we might attempt tonight, any at all seeming impossible. Were any possible, it might help us somewhat with its rushing noise and occasional low howls, because these would swallow up our own accidental noise.

So far we had only one fixed goal. It was so surely and so implacably imposed upon us that it seemed more like the dictate of the Fates than the decision of two men's minds. Neither of us spoke of it directly; we discussed only ways and means to achieve it with as little danger to ourselves as we could manage. Both of us took for granted that it had three phases, two of them preparatory to the final phase. One was, under cover of darkness one of us must gain the roof of the citadel and cut the rope by which the alarm bell could be rung to summon up Diomedes' warriors from their berths on the moored ships. The other was to breach its heavy gates.

The first task would be difficult, the second needed ingenuity or might that I did not at present see any way to command. Right Doer too, was stumped; his little ways that I knew so well told me so. Common sense told us both that only by long waiting and watching, with patient search for some weakness in his guard, could we hope for success. This seeming certainty was a dismal, hateful thing within our bosoms, so deeply we had been moved, and so consuming our desire. Still, I knew we would be equal to any delay circumstance imposed. We could dwell undiscovered in these thick and slimy woods for many an aching week. Both of us had been drovers; we knew how to bivouac comfortably when possible, livably always. With my bow and arrows I could supply our belly timber. The horrid thing was to contemplate what would occur daily in the King's pasture in the meantime.

"From our loopholes to Diomedes' seat on the opposite wall is a long cast," Right Doer remarked. "But I've seen your shafts fly farther."

"One miss, and we would face defeat," I answered. "Anyway, we would be selling too cheap."

Right Doer returned to his thoughts. I went back to mine, and again with the sick horror of delay, and while I listened to the wind, my belly sickened and my spit turned bitter in my mouth that there seemed no way to take advantage of it. Could it have been sent to us by very Aeolus, God of the Winds? Surely he loved mariners, who rarely touched shore without making him offerings, and surely then he would hate Diomedes with a mighty hate. If so, why had he not sent his servant Boreas, the North Wind, which would cause bluster and bring biting cold and likely rain, whereby the King would hover by his braziers, and the guard of all his henchwomen would be down, and we would have a far better chance to act unseen?

Just then the back of my neck prickled fiercely. My usually slow-wheeling brain began to turn over at a dizzy pace. It seemed to visit a dozen doors, and if one were barred the neck prickling and the wild beating of my heart would be in vain, but all opened to admit my thoughts and seemed to make them welcome. I was sitting on a great half-rotted log when Right Doer's idle glance fell upon me, and at once it was startled, and he stared.

"What in the great name of Hades, Heracles, has come over you?" he demanded.

"Right Doer, you have noted the pirates have brought their boats into a little cove, more secure from the South Wind than either the east harbor or the west harbor?"

"I do notice it."

"They have moored them short, for lack of room, whereby they sit like a flock of ducks."

"I perceive that also."

"At the southern end in more shallow water lies a barge of some sort, very strongly secured fore and aft. Will you tell me its direction from the fleet?"

Right Doer glanced at the sun, then back to the ships. "I would say exactly south."

"You notice the barge is loaded with wooden casks, of the kind made at Messene. What do you suppose they contain?"

"I cannot doubt they contain olive oil. Another style of cask is used for wine."

"It comes to me, Right Doer, that we may not have to cut the bell rope on the citadel roof or break down its strongly bolted doors. I think that the strong South Wind, which stirs the water even in the cove, will give us complete victory in one stroke. It is such a wind—I know not the direction of the other—that gave victory to the fleet of Tyre against the ships of hook-nosed, dark-skinned people from the Euxine Sea. Rhadamanthus told us of the battle, and we had cause to speak of it when we dispatched a ship to the lair of the Hydra."

Right Doer gave me a great, intense glance, his eyes ashine with joy.

"Heracles, you are beside yourself! Have you forgotten that I, the clever brother with the weaker back, not the thickheaded brother with the strong back, am supposed to be the tactician of our endeavors?" Then he turned deeply grave. "If the wind persists, and the barge's anchor ropes are cut, I see no power this side of Heaven to keep her from drifting slowly but surely into the moored ships. I take it by the time she strikes she will be garmented in fierce flame, and with her casks that we have not spilled to feed it——"

"Say no more, Right Doer, lest you tempt some God who loves Diomedes—there may be such a monster—to prevail upon Aeolus to change the wind."

He and I went about out lesser chores, such as spying, measuring distances, choosing paths for quick maneuver, and, with a deal of labor in wet woods, gathering kindling and rosin from a few long fallen scattered pine trees. Ever we had our ears cocked for the noise of the wind and cast a hundred anxious glances at the waving foilage. It did not abate in the least or vary a point. In the afternoon there fell into our hands another piece of good luck, as if no God loved Diomedes and one of no small power must hate him. I was about to boast that this deity must have cordial feelings toward Right Doer and me, when suddenly I remembered that this whole affair had been born in Megara's heart, most potent to love and hate, and if any deity had moved in our behalf, it was in regard for her.

The new and sweet smile of Fortune was that the King had chosen this night to feast his whole pack of pirates. We could deduce that only lately they had pillaged some rich argosies and delivered him the spoil, and he had looked at it and been well pleased; and the barge of olive oil had been part of the corsair's share, not yet distributed among the various ships.

We began to glimpse the glorious truth when male slaves, who were no doubt quartered in the stables or the compound, came down to the beach with donkeys bearing twenty-gallon skins that doubtless contained wine. The mariners threw overboard their skiffs, and truly the King was generous with his booty, for every ship received one of the skins. And right glad were Right Doer and I that his generosity stopped with feasting his henchmen on their own ships, that he did not invite them into the citadel where, when his back was turned, they might make free with some of his other treasure.

The feasting began at sundown; and by deep dark, as stars burned dimly in the murky sky, it was in full gorge. At our hiding place, as close as we dared draw to the barge, Right Doer and I heard first lively talk and coarse laughter, then shouts, raucous singing, cursings as fights set to, and then a big splash as one sot fell overboard, only to be fished up by his yelling shipmates. The uproar lasted about an hour, then very gradually began to subside. We heard sporadic noise for perhaps an hour more, then none was left but the noise of the wind and of lapping waters. There was not one outcry, not even the gagging of a sick man, not a stir of any kind. Every single seaman was deep in dark and drunken slumber.

"Now is the time to strike," I told Right Doer.

Together we worked the bung from one of the casks of oil and poured it over the afterhalf of the vessel. Three more we breached slightly, so the contents would ooze out. Then while Right Doer was setting fire under the foredeck, I cut one of the two mooring cables with my well-whetted bronze knife. The blaze had begun to leap, unquenchable in the oil-drenched ship, when I left Right Doer to cut the

other cable and set off at a jog trot toward the citadel. All the way
I kept glancing over my shoulder. When trees did not hide the cove, I
saw a low, soft, slowly moving glimmer, that at my every glance appeared to grow and brighten.

I was walking up a mule path, no doubt used to convey booty to the
King's treasury, when what seemed a crawling glowworm broke into
violent flame and revealed, for a single instant, the shape of a barge.
I think that at the same instant it collided with one of the ships, for
her too I saw immediately enveloped in the crescendant fire. And now
I must run to the recess in the wall of the citadel, close to the entrance way, that Right Doer and I had chosen for my ambush, for the
sky was lighting up, and the whole harbor, most brilliantly, beautifully,
and terribly, and it would not be long before some sleepless inmate
saw the holocaust through her loophole and waked the King.

Then I doubted that he would need an arouser other than his ears,
for the casks began to explode, hurling the flaming oil in all directions.
Some of it shot high; some overflowed onto the sea, forming spreading pools of fire in which the moored ships were captive; some flew in
wondrous sheets halfway across the cove, only to fall in incandescent
rain. Hardly a moment had passed, it seemed, before the entire fleet
was fiercely ablaze, utterly destroyed, the drunken pirates waking in
agony only to quickly die. Nor were any warned of their fiery doom in
time to escape, for although the now glaring light gave me brief
glimpses of tiny black forms between one wall of flame and another,
these were almost instantly swallowed, and not a single ship moved
from its fatal mooring.

I had been hoping that Right Doer, who I believed would come
hard on my heels, would arrive before the King could arouse himself,
gaze through a loop, marvel at this destruction—worse than being
struck by a whole quiver of Zeus' thunderbolts—and come to his porch
to gape, hoping that he was still in the midst of a nightmare and would
presently waken, to behold his fleet safe in his haven, and not his whole
power annihilated in one stroke. Even this fond wish, in no way vital
to our victory, was granted by Fate or by the Gods. Although my
brother took a little longer than I had thought to reach my ambush,
Diomedes was even later in opening the barred door, no doubt because he had run about the rooms in a daze, unable to believe what
had occurred.

Braziers behind him threw his shadow in the doorway. Then it emerged, and behind it the red-bearded King, and behind him were a flock of women, too frightened to make a sound. Right Doer and I stepped briskly to either side of the King. My spear point barely pricked his side; my brother's bronze knife lay along his throat.

"Who are you?" he stammered.

"Seekers of revenge," I answered.

"Let me go. I'll give you anything you want."

"We will take what we want. Now lead the way back through the door and bar it well. Do not startle me by sudden movements, for my spear thirsts."

Diomedes obeyed me promptly. Urged on by my spear, he walked with a reeling gait through the great hall and at my command sat himself on a wondrous throne, inlaid with gold and silver that I thought had come from Egypt. Meanwhile Right Doer kept his knife ready for any maiden, or more likely a hag, who so loved the King that she would attack us. Not one did so, and all only stood and stared as though the world were ending, but it so chanced that my brother must use his knife.

There rose a horrid noise, close to the floor, behind the crowd of women, and then there emerged into view a hideous foe, chattering with fury as he rushed to the attack. Happily Right Doer was wondrous quick of foot and hand. He dodged the gaping teeth and at the same time struck with his long blade. At once the ape toppled, shuddering in the agony of death, and then one of the women broke her stunned silence with a long scream. Whether she loved the little beast or hated it, or perhaps believed it was some sort of demon that could not die, we never thought to ask.

"My brother, will you give orders for the night?" I asked. "I have done no heaving, but have worked my head harder than usual, and I feel weary."

"Gladly, Heracles." And then, turning to the King, "You may doze in your chair, if you please. I beheld the belt of Orion as I climbed the hill, and the dawn is yet distant."

"What will happen then?" the King gasped. "Tell me, for the love of the Gods. Your brother spoke of revenge. I have never harmed either of you. For the love of the Gods——"

"What Gods? Poseidon? He was the giver of horses to men, but he had provided that they eat grass, and I doubt that he loves you. Ares, the God of War? No doubt you made him many offerings, but if he should try to help you, my brother, Heracles, would impale him on his own spear. Faugh, I am a windbag." Then he turned with his usual grace and civility to the crowd of women. "Which of you grave dames presides over the King's cook fire?"

"I do, my lord," a tall, lean woman, once a great beauty, replied. "And none here can match my skill."

"That I doubt not. But we ask no display of your skill tonight. Bring at once a newly plucked goose, and roast him the best you can over a brazier, and after you have eaten a fair share, my brother and I will eat."

"I go at once."

"Do not be gone long. I yearn to hear him sizzle. And another of your company may bring an ewer of unwatered wine, of which she will be the first to drink."

As the two women sped away I looked at the rest of the lot, about two score in all, and truly my gaze seemed to make a journey across the known world, and ventured into the world unknown to us Greeks, so diverse they were in lineaments, form, and complexion. Two or three were certainly Egyptians, with a wondrous refinement of feature; one with a hooked nose I thought to be Hittite, and several had the voluptuous darkness and facial molding that we Greeks ascribed to Babylonian maids. These and some other beauties had begun to recover from their shock enough to take thought of their own survival, and so threw sidelong glances at Right Doer. When he did not deign a response, two or three, perhaps not the most choice, gave me somewhat the same.

Meanwhile I was gazing at the King, hoping that his countenance would appear as evil as his heart was proven. Actually, it did not; instead he was a coarse-faced dog, brutal-looking rather than fiendish, about forty, tall, and powerfully made. His pallor was not as marked as when we had first captured him. No doubt he had begun to scheme, or at least to persuade himself that all was not lost, to remember that he was Diomedes, a great king of Thrace, and that the Gods that had appeared ever to befriend him would save him now; and truly it was not Atropos whose shadow seemed to glide in the corners of the room.

Although the crone took almost an hour cooking the goose, it was still half burned and half raw when she served it up. We watched her eat a yoeman's portion before Right Doer and I fell to, and then we had no appetite and must wash down the mouthfuls with wine, for we had never been so shaken by any event as by these of today and to-night. While we were eating, someone knocked, first quietly and then loudly, on the door—perhaps beating it with the handle of some weapon, meanwhile making an outcry in some alien tongue. Right Doer quietly took a bow that hung on the wall, along with a sheath of arrows, and went searching for a ladder that might lead to the parapet.

He was gone not more than five minutes, then made a quiet entrance. I looked into his eyes and spoke.

"Who was it?"

"The fellow who let Diomedes' mares out of their stables. He was carrying a torch and I recognized him."

"What has become of him?"

"He is lying on the porch with an arrow through his chest."

The quiet announcement had little effect on me, so many souls had sped already on this awful day, but it put a quick end to Diomedes' reassuring fancies. His face uncovered by beard became wet with sweat, which gleamed in the beams of the braziers. Soon after this Right Doer told the King's women that they could lie down on the floor and seek what sleep they might find. He and I sat in chairs which his favorites must sometimes occupy, and took turns keeping watch according to our custom, and if neither of us slept, still we rid ourselves of the worst of our strain, and rallied strength for the morrow.

Through an aperture I saw darkness fade. The dawn that rose over Propontis had no lovely tints, only grayness and dankness and chill. Bidding Right Doer keep an arrow nocked on his bow, I went out the little door, called the Needle's Eye, and picked up what had fallen from the hand of our last night's visitor, a hand cold now and stiff. It was exactly what I had expected to find, a whip strongly made with a stout handle and a long lash. It was then that I came to a resolve regarding Right Doer, which in no large sense concerned King Diomedes.

When I returned, I took the string from another bow, and looped it in a way I knew about the wrists of the pale and panting King.

"My brother, Diomedes and I are going on an errand," I said.

"Am I not to go with you?"

"No, because I do not need your help and I wish to give you mine, in a way you will always remember, and in proof of a love greater than love of woman."

"I do not think I can stand it not to go. I know there is no danger for you, but would not this blanket of evil enfolding us both be lighter on your soul——?"

"No, it will be lighter if you stay. I entreat you to say no more."

"I will say no more."

I turned to the now wakened, wildly staring crowd of women.

"Will one of you bring me a little carded wool?"

A grave dame sped away at my command. When she returned, I took the soft stuff and gave it to Right Doer, and bid him stuff his ears with it until I returned. By now the King was all but insensible with terror. As I led him forth, he whimpered a little, and his copious sweat had an evil smell, his lips twitched now and then, and his nose curiously twisted, but he made no manner of struggle and spoke not a word. I tied him to a tree, as though he were a beast, as I attended to a matter in the stables. I need crack my whip only once.

Then I returned to Diomedes, and stuffed him through the narrow slit in the stone wall of the pasture, and replaced the slab of wood and fastened its bolts. And now wild turmoil rose, and what part of it issued from a human throat and what part from the gaping mouths of mares, I could not tell. Yet as I waited until it died away, the air seemed to sweeten a little, and a kind of horrid fog seemed to engulf all, but perhaps it was only on my eyes or within my brain. Then I again removed the plank and went into the pasture, armed only with the whip, and when the mares came rushing, white of eye, lips curled back from their long teeth, I laid on the lash with all my strength. Every blow brought blood from a long slit in the skin, and soon they were standing their distance, neighing in fury, and when I moved toward one of them, brandishing my whip, she fled. In only a few minutes all were cowed, and with ease I forced them back into their stalls.

Thus ended the heaviest of my labors until now, although I dared not believe, or dare ask the Gods to grant, it would be heavier than any yet to be laid upon me. The aftermath was a simpler matter than my worried brain had hoped. One of the women told us that Diomedes had a son dwelling at Antalante on the Axios River, a fugitive from the court. To him we sent tidings of his father's death, carried by one of the prisoners we released from the compound. We did not kill the man-eating mares, for their hearts were no more evil than that of a goose-killing fox, and instead, by simply starving them until they learned their lesson, I taught them to eat grass.

Before the arrival of the King's son to sit on Diomedes' throne, neither Right Doer nor I frolicked even once with his beautiful slave girls. We thought that Diomedes might have done so now and then, and his taint would be on them, and it would wear away only when the new King had sent them to their native lands, as he swore before Apollo he would do, and they found lovers who did not know their history. Like Right Doer and me, in time they might forget their days in the Dark Tower, or recall them lightly only in troubled dreams.

CHAPTER SIXTEEN

THE GREAT MAGUS

1

On our journey to Orchomenus, when only a day's march distant, Right Doer and I tarried at the little fishing town of Opus so we might eat what we had long craved, young squids cooked in a metal dish. While my brother was visiting a nearby wharf to buy the little sea creatures, I fell into talk with an old sailor who had voyaged as far as Egypt, to the land of the Hittites, and to the most easterly waters of the Euxine Sea. When I marveled over some of his narrow escapes from tempestuous wind and wave, he told me something that caused my ears to prick up.

"Why, my lord, you don't have to go to the deep sea to fetch a drowning," he told me. "You can drown in a woods pond, or, for that matter, in a well. I reckon you haven't heard how the daughter of King Eurytus and the grandson of great Cadmus came nigh to drowning on Lake Comais only a fortnight gone."

"No, I hadn't heard of it."

"They had been fishing for eels, and stayed out after moonrise, and a light wind came up, not enough to blow spray, and of a sudden their boat broke up as though it were made of rotted bark. Some God must have loved them, because two swains, going out to spear carp on the shoals, chanced along to see them spill, and hauled them in. Maybe the pair wouldn't have drowned, since they're said to be good swimmers, but they would have been sucked into the bogs and floundered, and that's as good as a drowning for a quick trip to Hades."

"Why, it might be I know them," I told the ancient mariner in a guarded voice. "Was the lady named Megara?"

"That she was. And the folk would have grieved to lose her, for they've loved her mightily ever since she stood forth against the sacrifice to Artemis of the daughter of my old friend Bromius, when the Goddess herself demanded it, and I believe those people would have torn down the holy image to back up the Princess."

"I dare say her companion was Actaeon, the great hunter."

"You're right again."

When Right Doer brought the squids, cooked them over a beach fire, and both of us fell to, I could hardly relish the feast. Moreover, away down under my casual remarks to him, and sometimes under my laughter, an undertow was running in my mind. Nor did I dwell on Megara's narrow escape from pitiless Death. I did not think of her in the water in peril of quicksand but as seated in the boat with godlike Actaeon, my friend and helper, in gay or grave talk, their hands often clasping, their excitement when their floats disappeared from sight, the thrill of a writhing eel on the line, their perfect fellowship. Once they had been lovers. They knew each other's bodies so much better than Megara and I knew each other's, and perhaps each other's souls. The moon had risen, and swains did not come to spear carp until after dark. And at last the dark thought came to me that I had lost Megara, the greatest prize ever dangled before my eyes, and what dim eyes these were not to have perceived that so patent fact; and although I had performed, with the help of my companions, eight sturdy labors, what a sluggard I was at winning riches for myself!

Well, it had been foretold me that I could never have and keep a woman's love, that any woman that I loved would turn away from me at last. Why should they not, when I had cracked Linus' skull by a little angry knock of his own lyre? Also I had broken the lyre and it would never sing for me.

Right Doer and I went on to Orchomenus and before long entered the citadel of my master Eurytus. There I begged audience with him, and in the presence of his Companions and a few minions, I told in as few words as possible, speaking softly, that the labor he had assigned me had been performed. This news he heard with princely calm, but I was not done yet; I had other news to tell as soon as he gave me the opportunity, as I felt sure that he would do, will I, nill I, for his Companions were waiting and watching in sharp attention, their eyes alight, and he could not wave me away with a royal gesture.

"My seafarers in the region have reported to me that they have not in the past month run even once from Diomedes' pirates," the King remarked, not quite as though it were choked out of him, but as though he had a sore tongue. "Did you see anything of them?"

"Yes, my lord," I answered with a modest mien which was a far cry from my feelings. "My brother and I destroyed his entire fleet with fire."

Every face flushed, including the King's, and every man sat or stood a little straighter, and his chest swelled as the greatness of my moment became his own; and truly it was the greatest moment of my life, except for a very few. One, when I had heaved a stone into a glen to frighten a deer and thereby knew my strength; one, when I had felt the last throb in Antaeus' throat between my hands; one, when I had wept with Dyctus at the sight of a mighty lion lying dead; and one when I had seen Helen.

A deep silence ensued. I was watching the King's face, turned a little from me, and I divined rather than saw that he was coming to a new feeling toward me, breaking not without struggle with his old feelings. I think he saw the hand of Fate in my becoming his thrall, and in the events of the past few years arising therefrom; and that, after all, they had turned out to his advantage, which was always his first care if not his only care. He might still fear me in some devious way, but he was more fearful of the Gods and he must not risk their anger by ingratitude. He could never be a great king or even a good king, but he was far from a dullard, and it was light enough now that he could see his hand before his face.

"Heracles, the pirate fleet of the tyrant Diomedes was the single greatest threat to the ships of our countrymen trading east of Hellene and north of Lemnos," he said in deep earnestness. "Now they need not skulk at night to enter the Helles Pont, and from thence the way is open to the vastness of the Euxine Sea. So I pledge you, that if you are slain in the further labors I appoint you, I will free the Theban youth forfeit to me by their defeat in rebellious war."

He paused, a little bit shaken by what he had said. I saw in his face his self-question whether, carried away by the good news, he had said too much. Also I perceived, not by any sign that I can describe, the edging inward of his old cupidity, once more to take possession of his soul. His great moment had passed. He had not been capable of storing it and drawing from it happiness and glory and generosity all his days.

"These labors I believe will be either two or four," he went on. "Ten was the sum that came to me in a dream, although Tiresias has foretold there would be twelve. When these are performed, you shall receive mead of honor. If the Theban youth are not set free, at least their bondage unto me shall be greatly lightened." And I thought of a rich man bringing forth from his purse a ring of gold to give beggars for them to sell and buy golden fruit and purple wine and baked ox and wheat cakes, then replacing it, and giving instead a ring of silver to buy watered wine and ewe mutton and barley bread.

"In the same dream I saw wide waters, which I think you must cross to perform the labors assigned," he went on. "And its truth is hinted by the visit lately to my court of an ambassador from Hippolyta, Queen of Cimmeria, sometimes called Queen of the Ambozad, because her citadel stands on the river of that name," the King went on. "She has a wondrous girdle, woven and once worn by Pallas Athene in deadly battle. It is set with gleaming jewels. Now it chances that she had heard from a traveler a tale of the slaying of the Lernaean Hydra and the taming of the Erymanthian Boar, and she has a curiosity to see the doer of these deeds. Also, she wishes the promotion of trade between her kingdom and mine, especially the exchange of her furs, salt, gold, and tallow for our wine, olive oil, and especially the handicraft of our artisans. So she beseeched me to dispatch a noble ship bearing you and fifty stout companions to amplify her crew of twenty-five, many hands being needed in those broad, windy waters. Moreover she asked that my ship be allowed to linger in the port while shipwrights studied her design and rigging, all of you being well entertained the while. Then on your return she would send me her wondrous girdle as a token of her love, and thereafter favor trade with the ships of Greece over those of Tyre and Egypt. Her kingdom lies as far from here as the mouth of the Nile, but my ship will have been precoursed by many others, and at this season the Euxine Sea is truly the friendly sea to mariners—except for occasional gales. So when you have rested from your journey into Thrace, and visited your loves in Thebes, I bid you undertake the journey; of course with your valiant brother. If my son Nessus and noble Actaeon would care to go also, so much the better. And in due course I wish you to recite the burning of the tyrant's fleet to some noble poet, that he may sing of it in many cities and in distant days."

As I came on the porch, Megara, with great eyes of glimmering jet, was waiting for me and took my hand. She led me to a retreat she knew, where grave dames were wont to dye cloth, and there we found a rough bench that overlooked a loop in the walls, through which we could look down on Lake Comais. She had searched my eyes on their first meeting with hers. Now she searched them again before she spoke.

"I have one question. Is Diomedes dead?"

"It's a simple one, isn't it?" I replied. "A live man and a dead man pose such a striking difference; I know of no greater contrast. In this case, the answer is yes."

"Heracles, you are more thoughtful than you used to be. Did you catch it from Right Doer?"

"Partly, and partly from head-scratching."

"Do you realize that you are becoming as famous in your own lifetime as was Theseus?"

"No, and I don't believe it."

"Take my word for it. In ages to come you may be more famous. Of course if three thousand years from now you heard a poet sing of your adventures, provided there are any poets in the far-off day, you wouldn't recognize them. They will be exaggerated utterly beyond belief. They will be packed with miraculous happenings, monsters, every kind of marvel, the help or the enmity of Gods and Goddesses—because that's what the listeners want to hear, forgetting that the greatest marvel ever seen on earth is man himself. Still I don't think you will lose all human shape. It would be hard to take humanity away from a man who eats, drinks, and makes love as gustily as you do, who looks rather ordinary, who has not the brilliance of Right Doer but perhaps more common sense, and yet whose achievements, although easy for you to recount and explain, have a superhuman aspect. I don't know what to make of you, Heracles. I rejoice I was born in your times, saw you with my own eyes, lay with you between lousy sheepskins. But by that involvement, I have got myself into trouble. People who are close to you cannot escape from having great or at least very unusual experiences. Have you heard of my narrow escape from the mud bogs of Lake Comais?"

"Yes—I heard it a full day's journey from Orchomenus."

"Most of the calking had been worked out of the boat's seams. Actaeon was with me that night—this is his theory and I have no doubt it's true: the boat literally came to pieces. Somebody wanted to kill both of us. The person I would naturally blame has no conceivable motive, unless it was my defiance of Artemis the day before you went into bondage. The person seen tampering with the boat has only a remote connection with her—he was the servant of the man for whom she had a terrible jealous hatred. I am speaking of a fisherman from Delium who was once servant to Antaeus."

"I thank the Gods that the plot failed. If I had lost both of you, beautiful Megara and godlike Actaeon, I truly believe I would have been greatly weakened."

"You say, 'thank the Gods.' I doubt if the Gods had anything to do with those two yokels coming by on their way to spear carp. Also you say 'godlike' Actaeon. He is not in the least bit godlike, any more than you, Right Doer, or Nessus. Greedy Eurytus is more godlike than all four of you put together—according to our concept of the Gods. Eurytus lives for nothing but his own pleasure and gain and exaltation —you understand that in comparing him to the deities I leave out Demeter, Apollo, and a few more; maybe even Zeus cares for the folk. I will go with you if you say 'goddess-like Iole.' She couldn't manage to have a gale swamp us but she could get calking taken out of a boat's seams—but why? The Goddesses have often played dirty tricks like that, if we can believe the stories. As for Actaeon, he is manlike, not godlike."

The thought came to me that Megara spoke with authority—she had known his manhood too well for the peace of my heart, perhaps ever its peace again. But although my mouth tasted bitter I said not a word.

"Heracles, you didn't seem to have finished off the giant Antaeus as completely as I would have wished," was the next darting of Megara's thought.

"He does seem to haunt these scenes."

"Iole made an offering to an image in the bowels of a mountain, praying to hear that Antaeus had never visited Artemis' bed. She tried to call him up and mistook you for him and stabbed at you with a golden spike, mistaking your great shadow for his shadow's shadow. Now his faithful servant, who has never ceased to grieve for his mighty master, tries to kill Actaeon and me, or at least one of us. Perhaps he *was* the son of Ares and hence was neither mortal or immortal, but in some strange realm between. Again our talk reverts to Iole. I wish she would be swept off her feet some night by a wooer—let's say she had drunk too much unaged wine, and he would break that maidenhead that keeps her from being human. How foolishly I speak! She could drink a quart of love philter and still stay the stainless virgin who kneels with mist in her eyes at Artemis' shrine. Heracles, you are far from a stainless virgin!"

It came to me to say, "Megara, so are you," but I held my tongue. "You have certain resemblances to a bull. Not one of whom Zeus might take the form, but a common one, with good beef, in a pasture. So I am wondering what will happen when you get to the court of Hippolyta, Queen of the Ambozad. I hear she is a very beautiful woman, somewhat older than you. The whole enterprise has a fishy smell. She dwells far to the East—and you know the symbolism of the girdle."

"No, I don't know it."

"When our ships were able to dodge Diomedes' ships and enter the Euxine Sea, the captains would trade at her capital, Cimmeria, but not let their sailors, especially if they were sturdy fellows, go farther than the docks. You see, a good many who had gone into the town failed to return."

"Do you think they were murdered?"

"Very slowly and pleasantly, perhaps. I've heard the manhood of Cimmeria are a sick-looking lot; perhaps that point should be considered. On the contrary, the women are robust in the extreme, do the heavy work, and, it is said, sometimes bear arms against invaders. Before you traffic with the Queen, get her solemn pledge, before the God of the Tartars, and the Celts—I think she is a mixture of both—that you and all your shipmates will be allowed to take ship and depart at a given time."

"She wants trade between her realm and yours, not captives. The King said so."

"Women can get along without luxuries from Greece. There are other things that they cannot do without. Will you do what I ask?"

"Yes, because—so far—you have always advised me well."

"Good. I will sleep sounder of nights, and have sweeter dreams. Now I shall say something that would be unseemly in a proper maid— but I am neither maid nor proper. Heracles, on this adventure, you will not be stabbed by a horn. But you may stab with a horn."

With her eyes glinting with ribald mirth, she hastened away.

2

It chanced that I saw Iole before I left the citadel. We met in the hall and she walked with me as far as the porch. Megara had expressed the belief that her strange effect upon me, perhaps her power over me, had been somewhat lessened by that strange, dark hour in the abyss of the crater, yet it was still great. Her beauty, I could swear, was greater than ever. She was not a Helen or near it, I thought, but she was an Atalanta. Was she an avatar of very Artemis?

She put her long white hand in mine and, as we stood nigh a pillar, she swayed and kissed me, her lips moving hungrily against mine.

"Heracles, when I heard of the labor appointed you I went to my Goddess to ask if you would return safely."

"Was she of a humor to reply?"

"Yes, while you and Megara were whispering together in the dyers' room, Artemis whispered to me. She, daughter of Zeus by Leda, with the beauty of the swan whose form Zeus took when he wooed Leda, whispered to even me, Iole, her servant. You will return, and so will Right Doer, and so will Nessus. When she did not speak of Actaeon, I feared for him, so I asked about him, too. I understood her to say that Actaeon will not be with you on this journey."

"I don't believe it. He was grieved when Eurytus forbade his going with me to the Court of Diomedes. True, I haven't seen him since my return——"

"And true, I could be mistaken in Artemis' tidings. Her whisper had become very soft; I could barely hear it. You see, she does not love Actaeon—he has killed too many of her charges, stags, lions, and bears. Still, I believe she said he would not be with you, and perhaps that is a good thing."

"Will you tell me why?"

"Only two of our great Gods or Goddesses are worshiped in Krim— that is the name of the whole land of which Cimmeria is the main port—Artemis and her brother Apollo. Although both were born in Delos, they were conceived, so Artemis has confided to me, far to the eastward, on the summit of Demir-Kapu, where Zeus flew with Leda on his swan's wings to escape Hera's wrath. Certainly there is a temple to her crowning Cape Parthenium in Krim. It was there that the beautiful Iphigeneia served as priestess, reborn after her sacrifice by her father Agamemnon, until Artemis took her to Heaven. Certainly too, Artemis' power in Krim is beyond measure; Zeus would not interfere with her as he might in Thebes, and her sullen rage against Actaeon might burst into flame. No, it is better that he stay here."

It would be better for Megara, I thought. Still, I would not believe Iole.

When the chance came for me to speak to Actaeon, he told me that his mother was old and sickly. Even so, he was making every plan to board our ship when she sailed for Krim. As for the remainder of the crew, Bromius, her Captain, ever memorable as the father of little Arne, had his pick from the best and sturdiest young men of the kingdom. Indeed, they vied with one another for the places, knowing well that these demanded the roughest sort of labor with their hands, calking seams, scrubbing down the deck, heaving and taking in the big bronze anchors, manning the oars when winds were contrary, as well as perilous tasks such as shortening sail in sudden gales. The fare would be of the roughest sort. The water in the casks would turn foul if we were blown off our course and could not touch friendly coasts and islands. Yet, if they were princes' sons, they would take their share of hardship with the rest because first of all, they were Greeks, not soft and luxury-steeped Egyptians.

The ship was one of the largest and most seaworthy in Eurytus' fleet. I found fault with it only when at last Bromius sounded the call to cast off her mooring ropes and put to sea without my great friend Actaeon aboard. Almost at the last moment I received a message from him that his aged dam had taken a turn for the worse, and he durst not leave her lest he never see her again this side of the River of Woe.

In terms of sea miles our journey would be three times as long as that of the Heroes to Troy. Indeed we had made only a fair beginning when, after stopping at Lemnos, we touched the very shore where Hector harried the Greeks back to their tall ships. This was an experience that we young men could never forget. Our business here was to take on fresh water and dried goat flesh from Greek colonists who had built hamlets almost on the ashes of the divine city; when the prosaic chore was done, we walked about the very strands paced by Achilles, tall and shining, and we looked into one another's faces and could not speak. What other names re-echoed in our ears—incomparable Helen, her craven lover Paris, old Priam the King, tender Andromache, the aged Hecuba, Agamemnon, across whose glory fell the awful shadow of Clytemnestra, Cassandra, whose wild prophetic outcries no one would believe, and scores of others. But ever our thoughts wheeled back to Hector of the Glancing Helm, defending the doomed wall, only to fall before the spear of Achilles, who was unconquerable save by dark Death.

3

We sailed into the Helles Pont, then the great widening called the Propontis, and when we had traversed it to the mouth of the Bosphorus, where Io wandered pursued by jealous Hera, again we found a Greek colony, small and poor, but we reckoned that some day a great, rich city might stand here, for it was such a natural place for trade between dwellers of the lands fronting the Euxine Sea and mariners from the west. To us this mighty water was indeed the friendly sea, and we made our way half across its seeming immeasurable expanse—and truly it could have swallowed the Aegean—with Zephyr swelling our sails with gentle strength, and with never a need to out-oars or seek a haven.

The harbor of Cimmeria was the finest I had ever seen. Indeed old mariners aboard proclaimed it the best in the known world. The town, built on the estuary known as Ambozad, was in no way equal to its magnificent setting, being built entirely of wood, and the so-called citadel of the Queen was nothing more than a wooden fort, although her own lodging there was said to be luxurious. Anyway there was much more at which to gape. Bumboats that came alongside to sell victuals and drink were manned by women; and when we had moored, crews of women put ashore our cargo. I cannot say they were beautiful—only the young could be called pretty, and the delicate features of our Greek girls appeared wholly lacking. Still there was a strange attractiveness in their sharply slanted foreheads, long, narrow eyes, high cheekbones, rather broad noses, and wide mouths. In coloring they were a bewildering mixture. Many had black tresses but no few red or golden; many eyes were brilliant black but some sunny blue. Megara had told me that Queen Hippolyta was herself a mixture of Celt and Tartar, one a fair race, the other a yellow race, and I took it that most of her subjects were the same.

The most admirable quality of these women was their magnificent bodies, tall, shapely, and surely muscular, to judge by their handling of heavy casks and bales. An old mariner aboard had foretold us that the Cimmerian men were in sorry contrast with the women; Megara had said the same; still, when we beheld the difference, we could hardly believe our eyes.

If these were men, they hardly looked the part. Truly they looked like eunuchs, one of which I had seen on a ship from Tyre. Their sides, rather than their bellies, were fat; they had fat jowls, and very soft-looking, scant hair. They did not stand like men, upright, ready to pivot quickly, instinctively bellicose. They stood with their shoulders sagged and their bellies thrust out. They wore manly costumes, shirts that I thought were buckskin tucked into woolen pants, and horsehide boots, all at odds with their rolling gait. Their faces looked soft and their eyes large and dull.

And we sightseers could not help but wonder if there was some connection between the lax appearance of the men and the conspicuous lack of children in the doorways and on the streets.

We soon learned that these males did all the women's work about the homesteads, such as cooking, cleaning, and weaving, and that some prided themselves on beautiful needlework, while the tall women tilled fields, slaughtered and butchered beasts for the spits, attended flocks and herds, felled trees and sawed lumber, and built houses and byres. Indeed, some of the males crushed grapes with their white feet in the place of laughing maids. A very few played musical instruments and composed poetry, but their music and their odes were thin and pretty, without memorable strength.

The Master of the Queen's Household, an old but manly man, brought me word that Hippolyta would receive me for supper at her quarters this very evening. Garbed in my best raiment, with the King's gift ready to hand—apparently a cup of solid gold, but I durst not scratch it, lest base lead be revealed under gold plate—I was waiting when at sundown the captain of my escort came to our ship. She was a fine-looking young woman, with military bearing; and the guard of honor were sixteen strapping girls, none over twenty, all garbed alike in knee-length tunics that appeared to be astrakhan, the black furlike hide of unborn lambs widely seen in Krim. All carried what were ostensible spindles on their right shoulders, but these were never used in spinning unless I missed my guess, and their ends appeared whetted to needle point.

I was brought to the Queen's quarters in the wooden citadel, and these were indeed luxurious in a way new to me, since they appeared and smelled more Oriental than Greek. The Gods knew I had never seen censers burning incense, or sniffed its heavy, sweet scent, or beheld such a wealth of draperies, rugs, and cushions, silver and gold platters and urns. I had been somewhat afeared that flaccid-looking men would pay me the courtesy of washing and anointing me; happily it was done by muscular, though engaging, young girls. They skipped out, laughing, in a bevy, not at me but from sheer high spirits, so I was alone in the warm, fragrant chamber when the Queen entered.

She was a woman of about thirty, as tall as I, very solidly but not heavily built, womanly in outline, and truly queenly in demeanor. Her hair was almost flaxen, her long eyes a dark brown, with the high cheekbones and flat cheeks characteristic of the Krims, and a wide, but by no means gross, mouth. This last she used amply to kiss me, and her lips were soft and warm like any woman's good for kissing. Then she had me sit on a great heap of rugs, while she sat opposite me with a foot-high table of gold and ivory between us, and on this her maids of honor set fruits, some fresh, some preserved in honey or syrups of flavors and content unknown to me; also honeycakes filled with spices, a small pitcher of aromatic wine, and a big bowl of a tart beverage that did not please my taste, which she explained was fermented mares' milk and the favorite drink in her kingdom. Of this she downed something like a quart.

Seeing that I was not making a full meal of any of these dainties, she sent for a baked wild duck of a large species, such as she said was commonly served, along with other meats, at the midday meal. With this I filled my craw to plenitude, and then wiped my chin and hands on a silken cloth handed me by a serving wench.

Meanwhile I could not keep from glancing at her girdle, worn ostensibly to keep closed her robe, although actually the long garment, of some light, snow-white fur and fringed with a very rich, dark-brown fur, had been fastened with gold clasps. The sash was about a foot wide, apparently of some very light, soft leather, edged its whole length, bottom and top, with what I supposed were jewels of many colors, none of them larger than a pea but of great brilliance. The ends had long tassels in front and back somewhat like the rag of modesty worn by the young maids in barbarian lands of torrid climate. The leather band was dyed in various colors and designs. It tightly embraced the Queen's narrow waist, calling attention to the slight curve of the belly that all well-shaped women show, and was pleasant to gaze upon and vaguely exciting to the gazer.

When we had both put by the desire for food and drink, the Queen made a remark intended to appear casual; yet I knew from some little change in her countenance it was her first move in getting down to business.

"Heracles, I suppose I should have delayed serving you the duck until after a game which would give me great pleasure to see you play. Perhaps it was too heavy fare to precede exercise."

"I am not aware of any discomfort, my lady."

"Well, then, you must know that I have a gymnasium adjacent to my chambers. It is copied after the Greek gymnasiums, although, of course, on a much smaller scale. I exercise there on first waking, and my serving maids practice there an hour every day, the games being some of those played at holy festivals in Greece. Now I ask a question. Did you have regular exercise aboard the ship on your long journey hither?"

"No, Royal Lady. But I helped with the sailing and the chores, and sometimes sweated freely."

"Even so, if wrestling is your favorite sport—which I have heard—you must have been deprived of it on the deck of a vessel."

"There was no wrestling aboard. To speak truly, I do not wrestle often, nor am I greatly skilled in the sport. However, I have enjoyed it on various occasions."

"All Krim knows of your victory over the giant wrestler, Antaeus. Many of my ladies are expert wrestlers—of course in the upright style, not the deadly pancratium. And it so happens that the son of a great Khan of far-away Kazak is visiting me here. His name is Kamal, and truly he is a man of mighty strength. He has taken to the style of wrestling that Greece has given to the world. He offered, for your entertainment, to challenge you to a bout, one, or two, or three throws as you desire, and truly I would rejoice to see his prowess matched against yours, if you are in the humor for it."

"Your wish is my command." This was the conventional reply of courtiers to any whim expressed by a king, and which I had learned to prattle. "But by your consent, the match will be for only one throw. On giving thought to it, I realize that I have dined heartily and well."

"Then we will proceed at once to my gymnasium."

My brief glance showed it well laid out and equipped, and I had no doubt that a Greek once connected with the great gymnasium at Elis was its architect. Then I must look at my opponent, waiting for me in his loincloth. He was very little taller than I, no more than an inch, but a great deal more massive, immensely broad of shoulder, and of muscular development startling to see. Very patently he was from the remote East. His head was of a different shape from those of my countrymen and his blond hair had been clipped so close that it looked bald. His body grew less hair than my own, which was almost as bald as an egg. As soon as he had greeted me—and I could see in his face a great satisfaction with my common-looking body—he put his big hands at the Queen's waist and gave her a playful toss high above his head.

I stripped to my loincloth and then let him get the hold he wanted, which was an arm grip for a shoulder throw. This I broke in brief seconds, and instead of my being thrown I caught him by one leg and one arm and tossed him lightly over my back. This was the whole bout, over in half a minute, and I had never seen a man more crestfallen than this Cossack champion when he picked himself up, shaking his head in astonishment. As for the Queen, I thought she would be at least mildly surprised by the brevity of the affair and my placidity, but she was not placid in the least, and I could sense the wild excitement surging through her, which she did her best to hide but which her long, gleaming eyes betrayed.

"Thank you both," she said as I was putting on my tunic. "I wish my ladies could have been here to watch. Heracles, I wish you to meet now not a great athlete but a great scholar, and I will not be present at your conversation, for my poor wits would be unable to comprehend it. Kamal, a supper has been laid for you, and a couch made on the porch, and in the morning a caravan is setting out for Astrakhan, and from thence other caravans will soon make for the steppes of Kazak. Please carry my obeisance to the Khan."

The Queen took my arm as we walked out of the gymnasium to our supper room. The wine bowl and the pitcher of mares' milk had been refilled, but she paused only briefly by the entrance.

"Heracles, it is customary for visitors to compliment my girdle, which legend has it was fashioned by an immortal Goddess."

"Please pardon my laggard tongue. I admire it greatly."

"In that case, I hope you will in due course untie its knots—they are

most intricate and will challenge your wits—and convey it as a token
of my love and reverence to King Eurytus."

4

She left me, and presently an odd-looking little man with a large
head, bald of crown, and a virile-looking black square beard entered
the room. I took him for a Persian, and was sure of it when he gave his
name, Artamanya.

"It is a difficult name, so will you please and honor me by calling
me Magus, my address in my native land?"

"Gladly."

"Pray understand that I am a Mede by birth, although my mother
was a Cimmerian from Krim," he told me. Then with a manner I
could not call formal, yet dignified in the extreme, he began a discourse utterly astonishing to me and which I did not interrupt except
when he paused for breath, with polite but otherwise meaningless remarks.

"To be with my mother, who is a widow, I have made Cimmeria
my home," he began. "And at this point I feel I should name briefly
my credentials, whereby I presume to speak to you on the grave matter toward, and act as an adviser to Queen Hippolyta. My main studies
were in Egypt. In Memphis, at the temple unto Ptah, who is identifiable with the Greek God of the Forge, I was admitted into a society
of savants of the third grade. Our studies were in mathematics and
astronomy, with particular accent on astrology. My degree in scholar-
ship would compare roughly with the Greek letters Mu Alpha, and so
will I call it. At Thebes I was invited into another learned society, this
of the second grade. It delved into all the intellectual relations between man and man, man and the Pharaohs, man and the Gods. Using
the same rough comparison with Greek, I will call my degree Phi
Delta. Finally, at Cairo, I was received in the foremost of all learned
societies in the known world, dealing mainly with the so-called occult
sciences, the esoteric sciences would be a better term, picking up
where Phi Delta leaves off. My degree in this society could be freely
translated as Delta Delta; its members are called by the title Magus.
That is enough of my scholastic history. I need not mention uses I
have made of my learning, such as my inquiry, under the auspices of
Shelmaneser First, into the phenomenon of water boiling at a lower

temperature in the high mountains than on the lowland plains. Little did I dream that my most difficult study, and most important to mankind, lay still before me in my mother's native city of Cimmeria."

"Is it possible?"

"The seeming impossible proved true. And mark you, Heracles, I had no profound grasp of biology, the science necessary to its success. For instance, I had made inquiry into the metamorphosis of the frog, cataloguing and sketching every phase of its life from the egg to the mature egg-laying or sperm-producing amphibian, and postulating much that was yet unknown, but whether rightly or wrongly only time will tell. In all truth I knew little more of the mysteries of progeneration than, say, the average initiate into what I called Phi Delta. Hence I blanched at the task before me and almost turned away from it in intellectual cowardice."

"Wonderful," I muttered.

"You must understand, Heracles, that Hippolyta married her own brother. That was the custom in the royal families of the Ambozad country, the same as in Egypt. Happily, the unworthy husband died of some disease of malnutrition. And sad to say, this royal custom had spread first to the noble families and then to the humble, with what I believe was a dreadful consequence. Certain scholars—I will call them that—give other reasons, many colored by superstition, but I would stake my reputation that these incestuous matings, widely practiced, resulted in the terrible infliction of impotence, complete or partial, upon the vast majority of our men."

"It did not seem to affect the women," I remarked.

"No, it did not. Thus my hypothesis would appear open to challenge. Truly our women remained marvels of strength and vigor; indeed these two virtues seemed to wax under the vicious system, and their fertility, or at least their concupiscence, seemed to increase. The Queen has now forbidden, on pain of death, marriage between closer kin than first cousins, but the damage has been done. In the last fifty years the number of legitimate births per thousand citizens steadily fell; in the last ten years these have almost disappeared. Except for union between mistresses and their Caucasian slaves, or of female slaves with aliens, our city would soon be an empty shell.

"I agreed to undertake an inquiry into the disaster, and to make recommendations, no matter how drastic, for its alleviation," the Magus went on. "Obviously my first concern was to conserve what fertile seed remained available, meaning that it must not be wasted in mere pleasurable conjunction, and distribute it as widely and as usefully as possible. Thus it was necessary that I discover at what times in the menstrual cycle the womb was most open to fertilization. Do you follow me?"

"Yes, Magus, I think I do."

"Egyptian scholars had already determined that parturition—childbirth, to use plain Greek—almost invariably occurred 280 days after the first day of the last menstruation. But at what day, between that date and the first miss, did the actual conception occur? There was a spread of twenty-seven to thirty days in which it *might* have occurred as far as the mother knew. Still I hoped and dreamed—always with the idea of the conservation of seed—that the womb was not open all of those days, and that the period of openness might be only seven days, corresponding to one phase of the moon. How could I discover the truth? Only by the most patient, unremitting investigation.

"This, my young friend, I undertook. I enlisted the help of nearly five hundred women of more than average intelligence and public spirit, and bade them keep an exact record of their connubial and extraconnubial experience. Yet, despite my dedication, I met with terrible difficulties in establishing these histories. You may not know that the Egyptians safeguard their methods of making paper, and its export is virtually forbidden. Yet I induced a fellow savant to send me a supply, only to learn that he had been bilked by a dealer, and on its arrival it proved of an inferior grade, worse than useless. The writing fluid soaked in and so blurred my entries that they became illegible! So I had recourse to writing the dates and the names with chalk on especially prepared boards. And then, when I had accumulated a large stack in a rainproof shed, the building caught fire. I rushed from my chamber in my loincloth to try to save the precious records. As I was bending over, picking up an armful of the boards, the cloth caught fire. I had no choice but to tear it from my limbs, and even so I was painfully burned on my posterior parts. Did my neighbors sympathize with my misfortune and revere the dedication of my endeavors? No, I, Artamanya, Mu Alpha, Phi Delta, and finally Delta Delta, an accredited Magus from the Egyptian temples of learning, became a laughingstock."

The Magus paused in his recital to wipe the sweat from his brow, to sigh deeply, and to wipe his eyes.

"I trust that all turned out well," I said.

"By diligence I will not attempt to describe, by unflagging devotion to my cause, I finally accumulated enough data to draw a conclusion. Since then it has been virtually proven by further data. My conclusion was that the womb was open for fertilization on the twelfth, the thirteenth, and, especially, the fourteenth day after the onset of menstruation, and at *no other times*. True, I could not find corroborating evidence by physical examination. I had had fashioned twenty probes, of perfect workmanship, varying in diameter by one one-hundredth of an inch—and I will not take your time by explaining the ingenious method employed to achieve exquisite accuracy. These probes did not show the slightest increase in that sacred orifice through which every human soul finds its way to the mystic chamber where it grows flesh. But by encouraging the mating of mistresses with their male slaves on those very days, and comparing unions on all other days, and by tabulating consequences, I may boldly say that my hypothesis has been shown to be solid fact."

"I congratulate you, Magus."

"I have recorded the findings in Egyptian script and sent them to every savant worthy of the name in my mother temples. And now the time has come to tell you, Heracles, how, by your co-operation, these findings can lose their until now somewhat academic aspect and become the saviors of a people. I beg you to hear me out before you answer. If you answer as I passionately hope you will, I can truly believe your coming here was by the will of some beneficent God. First you must know that Captain Bromius, by the King's prior-given consent, has agreed to linger three months in our harbor, and sail on the full moon of the fourth month, one hundred days in all. This is to enable our shipwrights, skillful women with the exception of a few aliens, to study the design, rigging, and the operation of your vessel, so the Queen, too, may have a merchant fleet worthy of her crown. But what, I ask, is the good of ships in a not too distant future, without crews to sail them?"

"None whatever, Magus," I answered, eager to please the passionately earnest little man.

"Yet that is the fated outcome if my enterprise fails. Heracles, it must not fail! To further its success, as far as is in my power, not only I but my agents have been tireless. Fifty young women volunteered their services at my latest call. These and myself have spoken to over five thousand women in the city and the immediate countryside, none dwelling more than two hours' ride from the harbor. From this number we have picked two and one half thousand to be beneficiaries of our undertaking—choosing them by their health records, their visible womanliness, menstrual regularity, and, I must add, comeliness. None is over thirty. All are cleanly and pay due reverence to our Gods and Queen. Needless to say, the exact dates of their lunar periods have been tabulated. We can already calculate, with little margin of error, the three days in the next twenty-eight days when Nature will, to use an inexact expression, open their wombs in readiness for fertilization.

"Hear me out," the Magus pleaded, as I stared. "You, Heracles, are the head of a band of fifty young men. All are athletes, all under thirty; they represent the best young manhood of great Greece. May I say, with no intent to flatter, that we choose the Greek manhood above that of Egypt and Tyre and of other kingdoms fronting the Euxine Sea. We have noted the astounding vigor of the Greek race, how today there is planted a small colony, how tomorrow, or so it seems, the hamlet has become a busy town, how the day after tomorrow it is a bustling city. Besides your fifty companions there are perhaps twenty members of the crew who are upstanding virile fellows in the prime of life. To allow for accidents and hidden weaknesses, this gives us a task force of sixty-five."

The Magus' voice dropped a little and became indescribably solemn.

"Our plan is, Heracles, that these seventy men visit seventy different homes every night of their stay in port. They will be escorted to the right doors; the frail husbands would not dare raise a hand but, to prevent any embarrassment, they will be locked out during the stay of the guests. Pray you, hear me out!" he cried, when I started to speak. "A suitable, I may say a scientific diet will be provided your companions to prevent any danger of debility. It will consist of our excellent steppe mutton and beef, in abundant quantity, both fresh-water and salt-water fish of known nutritive value, the roe of the sturgeon, clam buttons, oysters, eels, a leaven of fat fowls, and the hardy northern wheat. Need I say again that every beneficiary has been carefully chosen? Her couch will be clean and covered by her best Astrakhan robe. The guests will arrive at sundown and remain until sunrise, but they are to be instructed that only two plantings may be made in any one womb; the remaining time to be spent in restful sleep. If, after two opportunities, the hostess does not kindle on one of the days nature has provided, we have done all we can to remedy her loss. I point out that sixty-five times one hundred is six thousand five hundred. A conservative estimate, considering the virility of the Greek manhood and the womanliness of those chosen to receive them, would be six thousand healthy offspring, three thousand of which would be males. In due course those three thousand males could repopulate our wasted kingdom and the curse upon us be forever lifted. Now, Heracles, speak. Give me your answer! Will you agree and your companions follow your example? Keep me no longer in this dread suspense. Say yes or no."

"Yes!" I shouted, almost to raise the roof.

The Magus almost collapsed on the couch, then wiped his eyes.

"This is a great moment in the history of the ancient Kingdom of Cimmeria," he told me presently, in a faltering voice.

"Mayhap the Gods smile down," I answered, somewhat carried away.

"As for yourself, you are free to choose, but I cannot resist expressing the hope that you will choose none other than Hippolyta, Queen of the Ambozads as she is popularly known, and Guard of the Folk. Now I must leave you, because I am overwrought; also I wish to bring the glorious news to my lieutenants. I wish you a happy night! A beautiful night!"

5

The Magus departed; and event followed very closely in the order and direction he desired. When, in bright day, I told my followers of the hospitality to be given them, they gaped a little in astonishment but none uttered a complaint. In the following weeks and months, the thought often struck me that if the Magus had chosen a military career instead of that of a humanitarian, and scholastic, he would have been most successful. His arrangements proved almost flawless, and his lieutenants, a bevy of about fifty of the best girls of the kingdom, were apt in their duties, cheerful as larks, escorting my shipmates to the various rendezvous with the efficiency and lack of muddle that I have noted in Greek damosels when they are appointed to gather flowers and prepare feasts in honor of our Gods. All were better riders of the steppe ponies than most of my followers, winning Nessus' praise;

and I am not at all sure that some of the most winsome did not receive extra favors.

Although the Magus met with his lieutenants every day and no doubt studied their reports, strangely enough he also met daily with Right Doer, in a privacy so strict that I, as well as all of our party, could not invade it. They were together nearly an hour in the recesses of the temple to Apollo; and the only explanation my brother would give me left me but little wiser than before. His eyes twinkled as he talked, but very plainly he did not intend at present to divulge the secret.

"Heracles, the Magus is instructing me in what may be called an occult science, one that has been known in the Temples at Memphis since time out of mind."

"I am glad you are the scholar, not I. It would be over my head."

"It is a fascinating and quite wonderful thing. There are certain practices connected with it which I am learning, and with unusual swiftness, according to my teacher. However, I had to give my oath, before Apollo, that I would teach them to no other person. But so you won't feel you have been shut out, the reason I am undertaking the study is to prepare myself to help you on what will be the final labor appointed you by Eurytus, whether the tenth, which will be the next, or the twelfth. You see, I had asked the Magus something about rare and powerful drugs used in Egypt, and it chanced that he told me of this science. Also it happens that by the confiding of Megara, I think I know what that final labor will be. The King has boasted of it when in his cups. He believes its performance is impossible, and at the same time the folk, whom he must appease, will not think so, nor think he has taken base advantage of you, and will expect you to succeed as before, and hence your failure would be all the more conspicuous. My brother, you appointed me the thinker, you the heaver, and although we have sometimes changed roles, pray put your trust in the old relationship! I ask you to trust me, Iphicles, your brother. And we may yet clog the wheels for the King."

I grinned, and we patted each other's backs.

I myself was closeted with the Magus only once after our momentous meeting at the palace, and this at the close of our stay in Krim—indeed the day before we were to set sail for Greece. He asked to see the girdle which Hippolyta was sending to King Eurytus in my care; and although he expressed doubt that it had been woven and adorned by the hand of a Goddess, he thought it was the handicraft of some greatly gifted queen in far-off Hind.

Meanwhile I had observed that his countenance was somewhat leaner than when we had first met, no doubt from overwork. Yet there was a shine in his dark, splendid eyes that emboldened me to ask a question.

"Magus, do you regard the operation as a success?"

"I rejoice that you made that kind inquiry. Now I may speak without fear of boasting. Heracles, there is no longer the slightest doubt of glorious success. The returns began to trickle in within two weeks after the operation got under way. Now they are arriving in a flood, and the number of failures is, I must say, trifling. And that is not the only good news I have for you."

"I will be glad to hear it," I said, in complete truth, for I was feeling a little saddened by our soon departure from these shores, although at the same time I longed for the rough coast of my native land.

"Holding the position of Magus, I am empowered to invite you to a Society of the Fourth Grade in Egypt, its name roughly comparable to the Greek letters Beta Alpha. It is given to hardy young men of good family, adventurers, hunters, and a few of middle station who display facility in trade, men who have little scholastic ambition but who are vital to a nation's welfare. It entitles you, among other privileges and honors, to wear a three-cornered hat, of silk or fur, on holy days and at festivals in honor of the Gods. Hoping that you will accept, I have brought a hat of the proper shape made of astrakhan, to which Hippolyta has affixed a diamond pin, in form and representation of a sword."

"I will thank you kindly."

"Also I have passed the word to my fellow Magi that you deserve still another honor, which I have no doubt they will grant. Thereby the upright cylindrical stones seen everywhere, erected by our forefathers, shall no longer be known as phallic symbols, but as the Pillars of Heracles. Thereby your name will live when the names of most of the Pharaohs are forgotten."

"Truly it is a great honor."

We parted shortly and on the morrow set sail. No less than five thousand of the young womanhood of Krim crowded the banks of the estuary to see us on our way, and quite a wail rose when the sails filled and the brave ship started to move, and then there was a great

waving of girdles, which I fancied gave no pleasure to a handful of
Cimmerian males, sickly-looking as the most, standing about.

"Heracles, this is one of your labors in which I had no part but
amiable compliance with your arrangements," Right Doer told me as
we stood by the rail and watched the shore recede.

"I wouldn't call it a labor," I answered.

"There will be people in various lands and times, that would call
it a disgraceful escapade. Happily, I am not among the number. I
doubt if any Olympic God, even chaste Artemis, would complain,
unless it be bloody Ares, who seems to prefer dead men to live men.
The other deities have more level heads. They know that without
people, no temples would be raised to them and no fat cattle offered
in votive fires. And who would see the beauty of that blue sky, and
sense the power of this wine-dark sea? Let us be thankful, Heracles,
that we were among those chosen to live and breath awhile on this
remarkable planet, and let us deny the privilege to as few as possible."

"Right Doer, you too should be appointed a Magus, the head of
the lot."

CHAPTER SEVENTEEN

ACROSS THE RIVER

1

The day came, two hundred days after my departure thence, that I stood in the council chamber of the citadel of Eurytus and put in his hand the famed girdle of Hippolyta. He barely glanced at its wondrous weaving but scanned avidly its border of small, multicolored jewels, and his eyes had the same hardness and almost the same shine. Suddenly I knew that Right Doer and Megara had both misjudged the King, indeed they had underestimated the capacities that had won him his high seat, when they had reckoned that my next labor, the tenth, might be the last he would lay on my broad back. The grim truth was he meant for me never to escape his dominion. For enriching his coffers and enhancing his fame, I was his most valuable thrall; and these gains were over and above the favor of certain Gods and Goddesses that this cunning, crass, vain man supposed that I, laboring mightily at his command, might curry in his behalf.

Yet I meant to escape his bondage before long. To take him by the throat and kill him only seemed the easy answer, such a thought as a chained bear might hold, when truly it was no answer at all, and would give some greedy leaders of his hosts another excuse to ravage Thebes. Instead I must trust as ever to my own heavy heaving, Right Doer's hard thinking, and the strange force of Megara. And these three, I thought fondly, would never fail me.

"I am pleased with the gift," Eurytus said pompously for the ears of his Companions. "Also I rejoice at the word brought me by Captain Bromius that if I would dispatch argosies of our wine, oil, and handicraft to Cimmeria they would return laden with furs, salt, the peerless horse leather of the Tartar, dense wool of the north, hard grains, and porphyry for our temples. Now I give thought to a worthy mead of honor to bestow upon you. Heracles, you will recall asking for the hand in marriage of my daughter Megara."

"I remember it well."

"I said I would not deny it you, but that the maiden must speak for herself. While she has not said so in plain words, she has caused me to believe that she would welcome the alliance. So instead of the neutral stand that I first took, I now give not only my consent, but express my hearty approval and pleasure at the prospect."

"Sir, I cannot express my gratitude." And I stammered and flushed from a surge of feeling.

"What greater mead of honor could you ask than marriage, you the son of the Noble Lady Alcmene by an unknown father, to the beloved daughter of the King of Orchomenus? Nor will she come dowerless to your door. At the wedding feast I will endow her with wide domain and a talent of gold. As for the Theban youth forfeit to me, I will prolong their parole for one year, following your successful return from two ventures on foreign shores which I command that you undertake. I assign them both at the same time, for I believe you can accomplish both in a single journey. The first is to bring hence the so-called cattle of Geryon, who is believed to be a three-headed monster living on Erythia, one of the islands of the Hesperides. The other is to fetch me seven of the golden apples found on an adjacent island. It is said these are identical with those Atalanta's wooer used in winning his amorous race, although hardly as beautiful or as precious as the prize that Priam's son, Paris, awarded our Golden Goddess at the ineffable contest on Mount Ida. Now all present except Heracles have my leave to go. To him I wish to give instruction, suggested by my seer, that may assist him in these endeavors."

When the chamber was empty except for the King and me and I was wondering what trick he was up to now, he gave me a sly smile, somewhat winning in spite of all that I knew about him—and about myself.

"The people must not be deprived of their monsters and miracles and imaginings so dear to their childish hearts," he remarked sententiously.

"Sir, I don't follow you."

"You will not go to the Hesperides, but to Oenotria, in the instep of what mariners call the Boot, the southern part of the great land westward of the Ionian Sea. There in the realm of a king named Geryon are herded cattle of great size and good beef. Their reddish color is explained by their living so close to the sunset that they have absorbed its tints. I want a shipload of the best bulls, whereby we Greeks may improve our own herds. The golden apples I desire are silver apples. More precisely, they are iron apples, iron ingots from the mountains of that region which produce the best iron ever traded by the crafty mariners of Tyre. You and your brother and companions are to learn the miners' ways of melting the metal out of red rock, the like of which is found in our own mountains. You are to bring back seven of the ingots as proof that you have fulfilled the mission; then we will see what may come to pass. And for this undertaking I will furnish a stout ship and a good crew, and ingots of tin and copper with which to buy the cattle and the iron. You will come to great fame, Heracles, as the slayer of a three-headed monster and a gleaner of golden apples. And I—I may become the most powerful king in Greece."

2

Megara was waiting for me on the porch, and with a quizzical look I could not interpret she led me to the same plank bench on which we had sat before. I offered nothing in the way of a remark. Somehow I had got it through my thick head that there lay an advantage in letting others, not me, start conversation.

"I hear the King has been beforehand with me," she observed, quiet mirth in her dark eyes.

"He spoke of giving me your hand in marriage, if that is what you mean."

"It is my business, not his. He made it his business to get out of giving you a noble mead of honor for doing so well in Cimmeria. And take note he only spoke of the marriage and did not promise it. The prolonging of the further parole of Theban manhood begins with that marriage, not before. In all my father's dealings I have never known him to get so much for nothing. The other kings of Greece had better look to their laurels. After a few more labors by his bonds-man, Heracles, the upstart Eurytus will outshine them all."

"In plain words, if you reject the upstart Heracles, I will have no reward at all for my long journey to Krim."

"There will be no skin off the King's back. Still, I think you have been rewarded, Heracles, in a fashion. Hasn't Queen Hippolyta been beforehand with me too?"

"She presented me with a diamond pin, representing a sword, to wear on my Cap of Honor."

"A sword! A fitting symbol, or I miss my guess. And what have your fifty young companions been up to? Of course ship fare is not very good; it is hard to make a full meal on the rolling wave—still they shouldn't have that gaunt, wasted look——"

"They worked very hard in the Queen's service, to combat a public calamity." And I could almost think it was Right Doer, the clever brother, who had made the pat reply, "My companions will soon fatten up from the good beef, barley, oil, fish, and wholesome wine of home. Pray you mention the matter no more, and instead tell me whether you are in the least agreement with what I took for the King's wish."

"I believe it is really his wish—if he can get off fairly cheaply. You see, if his daughter should marry Actaeon, grandson of Cadmus, it would be a great triumph for the grandson of a slave, but he would certainly have to free the Theban manhood and give a princely dower. On the other hand, if I marry you, it will please the folk and he will expect you to continue to serve him. You see, the pattern of his thinking—or rather feeling—has changed greatly since that strange and awful beginning. You have proven more valuable to him than the giant Antaeus ever was. I believe that he has almost—not quite—put by the idea that you are the fatal figure of the Delphic prophecy. And, Heracles, I am in full agreement with that wish. The question is—when?"

"Why not today?"

"Heracles, it is not a good thing barely to warm the bridal bed before the husband departs on a journey of three months or more likely half a year. If the wife can remain continent, she can hardly expect it of her mate. If we marry, I want you for myself alone—at least until you catch a Cassandra or a Briseis, in the way of Greek heroes, and over these I would still have precedence. Do you know that I have sometimes thought I would be happier married to a rude drover, far from a hero, than to a prince with his bevy of handmaidens?"

"I am a rude drover."

"You never were. You were ever Heracles. Perhaps when you return from your tenth and eleventh labor, I will think the risk worth taking. There will remain a twelfth labor, and I think I know what it is. I will not tell you my thought—it would burden your mind on your journey. It is one that the King believes, never doubts, will fail; but Right Doer has a trick in his bag—he and I talked while you were with the King—and it might not fail. This labor will not entail a journey of long duration, although the distances to be covered are unthinkable. I have spoken too much in riddles. I want to say that before or immediately after your return from the Hesperides, I'll marry you."

"On these few days before I go . . . in these few nights . . . can't we——?"

"I think not, Heracles. It would be hard to tell you why not. So you and Right Doer go to Crisa, below which lies Captain Bromius' ship, and Nessus will join you there, and so will Actaeon, and many of his crew who sailed with you to Krim. You four will have three nights of revelry before you set forth on the broad and lonely sea."

By and large, this was the course Right Doer and I followed. At Crisa we four companions reveled amply, if not grossly, while the ship was being laden; and one night they dared challenge me to a drinking bout, each of them taking turns in draining a cup with me, whereby my total stowage of unwatered wine would be equal to all of theirs combined. Even so I carted all three off to bed just when I had felt inspired to sing a song, a ribald and sacrilegious ditty dealing with Zeus' courtship of Leda in the guise of the Swan, and of various mishaps the lovers met, which I had learned as a swain from a gusty old shepherd at the pasturage under Parnassus. Truly, I thought, if I ever drank enough to down me, a vintner could sell me for a wineskin, I would be that full.

On the evening our captain reckoned to set sail, Megara, with a grave dame in attendance, came down-river in an oyster boat apparently to bid her former lover, her brother, Right Doer, and her present wooer a fond farewell ere we put out on the wine-dark sea. Then it proved that she bore tidings, too, especially to Actaeon, and these last were woeful—that the priest of the temple to Hermes had sent him word that his dam was so weakened by old age and a congestion in the breast that she could not live until his return from the far West, and if he wished to hold her wasted hand when she set forth on the last and loneliest journey to dim Hades, he must return now to her bedside.

I know that my plain face fell at the news. Actaeon bore his bow and quiver, in which I put great trust in case we were attacked by pirates out of their chimaerean nests; and over his shoulder, on the strap, was the wine flask he invariably carried; and on his feet were the sandals that I knew well and he peculiarly loved, for they had belonged to Snag Tooth, fashioned and beautifully dressed by his skillful ancient hands. On the sole of one was a patch in which Actaeon took especial pride and, indeed, showed to all comers. It was the same that had left markings in the path up the Hill of Olives that we had seen when we had searched for him on the day of Iniquity's return, only to find Snag Tooth in dire ruin, but ruin most momentous because it had sealed the beast's fate. All these were part of the costume Actaeon wore when he went forth with me on great adventure, all the more poignant to my sight since I knew the call he now received could not be denied, and he would turn back, and we three friends must explore the rose-colored, unknown West without his sustenance to our hearts and souls.

When Megara saw my eyes dim, she gave me a quick glance, and her eyes filled with tears, and as soon as chance offered, she called me aside.

"I have news for you, too," she said. "Or rather, I have a proffer to make, which you may accept or reject as your heart bids."

"I do not think I will reject it."

"I have been thinking, Heracles, what a long, rough way it is across the Ionian Sea. You traveled farther, in sea miles, to Krim, but the Aegean Sea offers a thousand havens, and the Euxine is the friendly sea, while on the Ionian, Aeolus blows his angry breath, and if your ship is storm-driven into its vast wastes, which way can you turn? You and I are betrothed. It is not good that I should let you go from me without a token of my love. The captain of the oyster boat that brought me here has a snug house, not far from here, and it so chances that his son is at sea, and his bed is turning cold in his absence. Let us warm it tonight, Heracles, you and I. I fear you will not find me the like of Ismene the Shepherdess—Iole, who hears everything, told me of her tribute—still you know what you will find, my enfolding arms and my soft breast and tender yielding rather than fierce conflict. Do you want to, Heracles? Look me in the eyes and tell me."

"I want to more than any words can tell."

"Then we will. And it comes to me that in this I am no longer second choice to Iole, and I need never fear her again."

3

When five moons had waxed and waned, when the verdure had changed with the changing seasons, when certain planets had journeyed an allotted distance in the vastness of the sky, watchers on our homeward-bound vessel sighted the Capes of Corcyra. From henceforth we would have safe sailing off shores peopled by Greek-speaking folk, with no fear of pirates and with scores of havens in which to run in case of suddenly breaking gales. In seven days we pushed into the Calydonian Gulf; in three more we were midway westward in the great Gulf of Corinth; and in one more day we moored at Articyra, about twenty miles by gull flight from Orchomenus.

Our crew disembarked ten bulls broader of back, deeper of brisket, shorter of leg, yet fully as tall as the largest Nemean bulls that had fought Iniquity, and red of color. Also, in my pack bag, carefully wrapped in cloth, were seven very heavy objects roughly the size of apples, resembling silver when polished with an abrasive. And in my head, fully as fixed as in the heads of Right Doer and Nessus, was the lore of how to take a certain red, crumbling rock, put it to intense heat in charcoal fires, and draw forth what looked like molten silver, but which hardened to almost pure, malleable when white-hot, unutterably useful iron.

Before I entered the citadel to answer to King Eurytus, Right Doer gave me a word of advice; and a chill ran down my spine when I marked the intensity of his gaze and of his voice.

"I would not count on any great mead of honor. He will speak again of marriage between you and Megara, rich dowers, and princely office. But most of his promises will have strings on them—he can take them back if you fail to perform the next labor he assigns you. The assignment will appall you. You will think, indeed know, its performance is impossible. But it is a tribute to the man's cunning that it will not seem so to the folk—myth is their meat and drink; he will not have to contend with their indignation at what the few will know is an outrageous tyranny to a bondsman that has served them well."

"Why not tell me what it is? I'd like to know before I face him."

"I can tell you what I believe, what I'm almost sure it is. It is to go down to Hades and bring back Cerberus, the three-headed dog that guards the gate."

"Right Doer, that is beyond the power of any man, living or dead."

"Of course it is," my brother replied with some acerbity. "Don't be any more thickheaded than you were born. Still, take the order calmly. That may shake him a little, and I want him severely shaken before we're done with him. And above all, do not despair. His knife may be so whetted that it will cut both ways. Like the fabled woodcock, he might pitch into his own deadfall. You may, if you like, speak of the deep caves on the coasts of the capes of Messenia and Laconia. They are popularly supposed to be openings into Hades. And be sure to tell him you will need a full month to make the journey."

"What would I do without you, Right Doer?"

"So far I have barely filled my office—sometimes not that. This time I will. And without you, Heracles, I would be a vain dreamer of dreams, a thinker without a goal. It is a good thing for mankind that a hero comes along now and then, otherwise we would all sink in the muck, as did the Hall of the Centaurs. Only the hero can lead our purposeless swarms to the mountaintops—even to the stars. Enough of this babble! Go in, confront the King, and come back to me. All will be well."

No oracle in Greece, even the exalted pythoness at Delphi, squatting on her stool over the mist-filled rift, could have foretold more accurately what would happen at my audience with the King than had Right Doer. In this case, I met with him alone; even so, his promises of preferment held many an "if" and "when," and the most I got out of him of worth was a reaffirmation of the pledge he had made me before I set sail, that my performance would win for Theban manhood an additional year's parole. Then his expression changed to one of frank cupidity, as though inviting my admiration of his craft, as he told me of the use he intended to make of the so-called cattle of Geryon. The bulls would be branded by his seal and kept in his own pastures, and there any Greek, high or low, could bring his amorous cows, and the King could yield the heifer calves and keep the bull calves. As for the iron eggs and the knowledge of how they were laid, they presented such prospects for the prosperity of Greece,

especially Orchomenus, and particularly its King, that the imagination of a miser must fall short.

"Heracles, do you think you can capture, and bring hence, Cerberus,
guard of the Gate of Hades?" he asked, his whole manner swiftly
changing.

"I can try, master, if it is your command."

"If you can, my soothsayers and seers can bargain with Hades the
King, and preferment be won for our loved ones that go down, and
for all my host who fall in battle. Therefore I assign you the labor,
and if you achieve it, your mead of honor will be all you ask, in reason.
The young moon will wear her silver bow five nights from now. When
she wears her burnished shield, full-rounded, return hence with your
captive, and you shall be warmly welcomed. I charge you, do not fail!
Now you may kiss my hand and take your leave."

4

"Be as a little child in my care."

So Right Doer told me, as he started to lead the way down a goat
path fronting the sea in southernmost Laconia. I had never been here
before, but my brother appeared to know the region well, and I surmised that he had visited it in the past fortnight, when he had absented
himself from Orchomenus, and in the company of a slave and two
pack mules had made one or more considerable journeys. The slave
Thoas, whom Right Doer had inherited at the death of Wrathful
Leader, was with us now. On his broad back he had strapped a box
made of boards, not very heavy to judge from his light sweat, but
awkward, it being nearly three feet square. Our leader carried a sheepskin robe, bound with cord, an empty bucket with a metal cup, a
flask of wine, some dried meat and barley cakes, but no visible weapon.
The hour was barely sunrise.

Some distance above the beach we came to what appeared to be a
long, deep cavern, well lighted near the mouth by a flood of sunlight
but receding into darkness. On its floor, as level as that of the grotto
at the ever memorable Pool of Truth, Right Doer and Thoas spread
the robe and on it laid a pillow which had been concealed in its folds.
Then Thoas took his departure and the sound of his ascending foot-
steps died away.

"Heracles, I want you to lie on this robe with your head on the

pillow," Right Doer told me. "I entreat that you remember my studies
under the Magus, and this is the procedure when the soul of a living
man undertakes a long journey into some weird, unearthly realm.
You must understand that his carnal body cannot enter such realms;
only his spirit may do so, but by certain ceremonies I have learned,
his spirit obtains strength beyond mortal, and can work wonders."

"It sounds like trumpery to me, but I will do what you say."

"I have here a needle of polished silver, attached to a thread. This
I am going to swing slowly back and forth in the shaft of sunlight. I
ask that you follow it with your gaze. As you see, it looks very bright
and pretty."

"Yes."

"Your eyes may tire in a brief space; at least they will soon feel
heavy. As I continue, you will become sleepy. Have no fear of that.
In fact, go to sleep, and then your spirit will go forth from you, but
what you are to see is not like vistas of ordinary dreams. You are to
remember everything, be able to recount everything that happens.
Hear me, Heracles? I am to be your guide on a most strange journey;
but have no fear, in due course you will return to the world you
know. Ah, you are getting drowsy. . . . You yawn. . . . Your eyes
can scarcely keep open. . . . Sleep, my brother . . . sleep, sleep."

It must be I did sleep awhile, I know not how long, before I again
heard Right Doer's voice.

"Yes, I have the bucket and the cup. The bucket is filled with calf
blood, the blood of an unblemished calf sacrificed to the Gods of the
Underworld. . . . Now you are making your way into the recesses of
the cave. But a faint light beats up from below, and you will not trip
and fall. See, the light grows as you descend these stone steps, cut
ages gone in the rock. . . . Heracles, you are far below the level of
the earth. You are deeper than in any pit, below the bottom of the
sea, and still you descend. . . . And what is that sound? Is it not the
lapping of water against reeds? Yes, it is a deep, wide river, across
which your vision will not reach. But fear not, you will cross in safety.
You will float across, because you are rid of your body for a space, and
your soul has no weight. What river is it? Yes, the River of Woe, that
separates the Kingdom of the Living from the Kingdom of the Dead.

"And now you approach the Adamant Gate. Aye, and dread Cerberus, three-headed, dragon-tailed, most monstrous, stands on guard.
But you will not now make him your captive. That you must do when

you come forth from the Kingdom, for now you must enter, and give blood to those who have precoursed you here, those you knew on earth, that they may again recall the sun and the rain, and may speak to you. Do you remember when the ghost of Linus visited your bedside? He told you that when he who sent him to you spoke a command to Cerberus, the monster crouched, whimpering. It will be the same when you speak your command. Do so, Heracles."

"Down, Cerberus," I said.

"See how he fawns, in fear of your voice. Pass on, Heracles, into the dim halls beyond. How dim, how gray, how utterly forlorn. But now the shades have seen us, and come crowding, but wave back all of these except the Noble Lady Alcmene, who stands in their van. To her you may speak. But first, pour a little of blood in the cup and offer it to her. Until she drinks it she cannot answer you, or remember your lips on her teat."

So I did as my brother bade me, and the shade of the beautiful woman sipped at the cup, and her lips moved.

"Alcmene, who was my father?" I asked.

"She is answering you," spoke the voice that I thought must be Right Doer's. "'That I could not reveal in life, nor may I reveal it in death. But he was worthy to be your sire, as you are to be his son.' And now her eyes are again vacant, her lips are still, and she draws back among the horde of shades. And who comes now? It is an old man, toothless except for one snag in his lower jaw. With awesome hunger he eyes the cup, yet he may not ask for it; he cannot speak, only you may offer it.

"Pour a little in the cup. He drinks it more greedily than more than once the wine you shared with him. He takes your hand and kisses it and now he speaks.

"What is this, Heracles, he is saying? That Iniquity came through the gate not long or far behind him, but Snag Tooth knew him not, but now he remembers that the Beast Soul snarled at him, and now he knows why, for they were implacable foes. 'Heracles, I could not rejoice then, for there is no rejoicing in Hades, except a little thrill that comes and goes and we know not its cause, but now that there is blood in me again I rejoice like the maids who follow Dionysus in their mountain revels. And I bid you, when you return to earth, to speak to great Actaeon, who schooled you at the camps, and who sometimes wears my sandals, and wish him a long absence from this dim Hell. And do you know who comes now, pushing his way through the thirsting throng? Is it not Dyctus?

" 'Aye, Heracles, it is Dyctus, who hid with you in the bull's hide and with whom, next to you, my heart is the most bound. My heart died under the lion's stroke, and it you burned in fire, and that was a mighty serving to my soul, for thus you cheated the grisly birds of death on the Hill of Olives. Now my strength wanes, master. I must soon withdraw into the dim horde. Call to Dyctus, Heracles, my lord. Otherwise he will not dare draw nigh, for he met death most horrid, and only his mangled and gnawed bones were thrown into a stinking pit without honored burial. Save for me, who stand high in this bleak realm because I thrust an arrow into Iniquity's great shoulder even as my soul sped, Dyctus would never have come here out of the half world that lies between the Living and the Dead. Aye, I, Snag Tooth, held out my hands to Dyctus as he struggled in the River of Woe, about to be swept back across the flood. Thus I pulled him to the dismal shore, and saved him from forever lurking, wailing, a homeless ghost, about the pastures of Diomedes. And I walked beside him through the gate, and Cerberus dared not bite him, or even snarl, because I had made my mark on Iniquity, the mighty. Still Dyctus walks with his head lowered in shame, so call to him, I pray you, and give him blood in the sight of all the shades. And now I depart from you and from the warm glow that your living soul gives forth.' "

"Dyctus, Dyctus!" I called.

"See, he hastens toward you," spoke the guiding voice that ever filled the air softly but insistently, issuing from an invisible throat. "Offer him the cup. . . . See, his dim eyes brighten, and then dim again with tears, for he remembers his loathsome end. Yet he gropes for your hands, Heracles, the hands that gave him vengeance that until this moment he did not know had blessed him, even here, in this gray, chill, silent land of shadows. And he will never again walk with his head hung, because he remembers now how he stood with you in the bull's hide, and never quailed.

"What does he say? 'Heracles, when you come down, I will be your servant. That I will not forget; I will not know who you are or why I serve you, yet so great is my intent that it will not fail. I will break a path for you through the throng when blood is poured down as an offering to the dead. Remember my sturdy shoulders! They can still thrust. And if you go to the Elysian Fields, I will find my way through the barrier, and pluck asphodel for your fragrant bed. And there stands Antaeus with hollow eyes. Little does he know that the hands that bent his neckbones until they broke are now held in mine. Once, when he got a little blood that was poured down, he entreated Hades the King to be sent to the sweet fields, but Hades laughed loudly. But thence have gone most of the heroes—Theseus, Perseus, Hector, and all the rest save one. Him you may see. Even as a shade, somehow he gives forth light. But now my own light is burning out. Remember me, Heracles, I pray. Do not forget. . . .'

"See, he withdraws. In the throng you see the strong face of Agamemnon, but he does not push forward; some memory of a memory bids him forego memory forever. And the beauty that still lingers as in a fading dream is the beauty of Andromache, for her last memory was of the glancing helm worn by the warrior second to only one, and she wants no other memory. But why does the throng part? Who comes with a long stride? Who stands taller than almost all? Is it the very King? No, or you would see his cap. Is he an immortal God who fought with Zeus and was cast below? No, he was mortal, yet a man forever marked among men, now a shade forever marked among shades. Yet when you offer him the cup, an offering you cannot choose but make, he shakes his head.

"He draws nigh, and as again you offer the cup, he dips his finger in it only, and draws it across his lips. What is he saying? Pay close heed, for the message will be brief, but of forever moment. 'Nay, I will not drink. Nor will I go to the Elysian Fields, where went my great companions. For I, who conquered mighty Hector, was slain by a craven's weak and falling arrow that struck me in the heel. Farewell!' "

"Farewell, Achilles," I heard myself cry out.

"He withdraws," came the voice. "And soon you too must go, back across the river—still, a little blood is left, and there is one, foremost in the throng, who aches to speak with such aches as the living know, for you can see the agony in his face. You never knew him, but a stone image of him stands in Eurytus' citadel, for he was once Zetes the Well Beloved, Eurytus' cousin, who would have inherited the crown of Orchomenus if he had not been crushed by his own chariot on the Thitherean Plain. Ah, you hand him the cup. He drinks with awful greed. And you will mark well what he tells you, and remember it, word for word, when you have returned to the Upper World, and when the need comes, you will speak.

"Oh, hear him! 'I am Zetes, and my mother and Eurytus' mother were sisters. Heracles, I was not alone in the chariot, as was told. My cousin that I thought my dearest friend was with me, none other than Eurytus. As I stood before him, driving, he crushed my skull with the hilt of his sword, then leaped down and let the team run unreined until the chariot overturned in a watercourse, wrecking itself and pinning down my corpse. I do not ask that you dispatch him here, for Atropos will cut the thread of his life soon enough, but see that his sword no longer hangs over noble Thebes, where I, too, was schooled by great Rhadamanthus. Mark me well, visitor from the Upper World. Remember me in that world.'

"Once more his eyes grow dim. He retires into the shadowy horde." Then I felt a hand on my elbow, and soon heard the voice close to my ear. "You must go now. And when you come to the gate, grasp Cerberus with one hand at his throat, the other by his dragon tail, and hold him fast until we can put him in a box, to carry to the King. Beware of his three heads, each with three jaws, and every jaw set with fearful fangs. He can strike in front and right and left at once."

The voice went on to warn me that attack by the grisly monster was virtually certain. While he admitted most comers into the gate, he almost always tore down those who attempted to leave, inflicting hideous pain from which their chill, shadow-like being did not spare them, although a few had cowed him, and a greater number had slipped by him, emboldened by some deathless passion, and had haunted for a brief time familiar scenes on the Upper World.

"Yet confront him boldly," my monitor advised. "Although he is Cerberus, you are Heracles. . . . See, he eyes us even now. He crouches and his lips curl back and white teeth glimmer even in this dimness, in contrast with his black and horrid shape— Now he rushes to the attack. But Cerberus! What now? Heracles has sent you spinning back to your portals with a kick that nigh broke your bones, and you are slow to resume the battle. . . . Now Heracles has seized you in gigantic grasp. You snarl fiercely and snap your jaws, and your tapering tail grasps at his left arm like the coils of a serpent I saw him slay, but you are his prisoner, and you had best make no further struggle, lest his rage flame and he tear you in twain. . . . Now, Heracles, through the gate and down to the bank of the river. A herd of poor shades follow us, seizing this chance to revisit the sunlight, and to-night they will walk many an old path or parapet, and linger at forgotten tombs, and rattle doors, and gibber like Diomedes' ape in closets and corners, but they cannot linger long unless given blood, and must return to the shadowy, silent halls. . . .

"Now your captive lies supine and quivering in the box, and you make your way up the carven steps of stone. Ever you ascend, high above the dark river and the black gate, and you see a pale, distant gleam of light that was born in the goodly sun and blesses the orifice into the Living World. It brightens slowly. You pass through the opening. But on the shelf of the cliff stand four black horses with wildly waving manes and tails, and they are harnessed to a black chariot, and down from it steps a manlike form, although mightier than any man's, and half concealed in black, swirling clouds.

"Be thankful, Heracles, you cannot see his face. You can be sure that it too is black, black with rage, black as his cap, for if mortal eyes beheld it they would be straightway darkened by dire death. In fury he strides to the box and breaks it open, but the mists thicken and you cannot see what follows. Now he departs. No word of doom does he pronounce, no rage he vents on you, no punishment he inflicts for your invasion of his kingdom; and it must be that he fears your sinewy hands, and belike he fears too some great lord within his halls who might avenge a stroke against you; aye, taking vengeance against the darkling King for the sake of some lost love.

"And now, Heracles, your soul that has wandered deep and far returns to its old home. You can feel its sinuous entrance into the doors of your body, eyes, ears, nose, and mouth; your dim eyes brighten, you breathe familiar air, the strange scents of the distant realms fade in your nostrils, the sound you hear is of the breaking of the gentle surf of your native seas. You are sitting on the sheepskin robe. You feel a little drowsy but you stretch your arms and yawn, and once more your heart throbs in familiar beat and you know the glow of life. Welcome home, Heracles, my brother. And now you will eat of the good meat I have brought and drink purple wine."

But before I did either of these things, I went to the box and looked in. There, quietly lying on a bed of straw, was a marvel of nature I had not seen before, a two-headed calf.

5

"What is this, Right Doer, my brother, and how did it get in the box in place of Cerberus?"

"Can we not suppose that King Hades, in taking from you what you had seized in his domain, left it as a mockery to Eurytus for appointing you a labor of such affront to a mighty God?"

"We can suppose it, but not believe it. You put some kind of spell upon me, which the Magus taught you how to cast. I remember all that seemed to have happened but know it did not really happen; and the sun is hardly an hour higher than when I lay down on the robe and you swung the bright needle on a thread."

"You need not tell Eurytus that it did not really happen."

"How would I dare say otherwise? I have no proof."

"You have what he will think is proof. That and all the rest that seemed to have happened will be so clear in your mind, so like actual experience, that old Rhadamanthus himself would well nigh believe it. Heracles, how do you think the calf got in the box?"

"You heard of its being born in some remote pasture, and you went to buy it in those days you were making preparations for my journey into the Underworld. You put it in the box, and it never left there, and the visit of King Hades was a figment of my trance, along with all the rest."

"Thank the Gods! The one fear I harbored is now lifted from me. You see, Heracles, what you call your trance is truly a spell of great power. The Egyptian priesthood call it what in Greek would mean the transport of the soul. They maintain that the experiences of the transported soul have a kind of ghostly reality, much more substantial than the dreams of sleep, although they are born in the brain or soul of the guide, he who casts the spell. I could not quite dispel the fear that I could never again bring you back wholly to yourself, to the plain, good earth, although the Magus assured me a score of times this would be the case. Your instant penetration of my hoax with the calf proves it has been the case. Truly I did not need the trappings; an empty box or an imaginary box would have served as well in persuading you of the phantom. But I wanted some kind of monster for you to show Eurytus. It will lend color to your account of King Hades' wrath."

"Give me a drink from your flask and, for the love of great Pan and sweet Demeter, find milk for the calf."

"I fed her at dawn. And I still have some milk in a jug in my pack sack, along with a cloth teat I can fit over the neck. I fear the poor little monster will not live long—the best we can do, and just now her need is not as great as our need for the mellowed juice of the grape. Let us both drink, Heracles, and strengthen ourselves with meat, and then we will feed little Cerbera—that will do as a name for a female Cerberus—and happily her double head has only one mouth. Then we will pursue our most curious adventure."

That pursuit was short. In two days we were in Sparta, where we lay as guests of the King; on the third morning following we caught a fishing vessel at Cynuria; and in four days' pleasant sail passed the dangerous straits into the Euboean Sea. From thence we made our leisured way to Orchomenus, arriving at the citadel with many other travelers, for this was the King's birthday. I had a present for him in a wooden box strapped on a mule. I could not help but grin at the prospect of its presentation before the eyes of his court and his Companions; yet my heart was wildly beating, as though it knew of some march of event upon this moment that I could not see.

Presently I stood in the presence of the King. I felt a sense of strangeness in finding it so familiar, so little changed since last I stood here, considering how far and wide I had journeyed in the meantime—and then I remembered my actual journey had been no farther than a cave overhanging the sea on a headland in Laconia. The court stood in full array, with Nessus, Iole, and Megara in attendance. A trifling difference was that a group of artisans were about to erect a newly carven image of the King, life-size, amazingly lifelike, although the expression of the countenance was somewhat more royal than his wont. They had already placed the pedestal behind the King's chair and a little to the left. Rhadamanthus had told me it was a common thing for the Pharaohs to have images of themselves everywhere about their palaces and especially in their throne rooms, some of them of giant size, but it was a new thing in Greece. I supposed Eurytus had been shrewd enough to have his image of the same proportions as himself, so he would not appear dwarfed.

A great shrewdness was in his face this morning, more truly a triumphant cunning, for he had me where he wanted me, he thought, forced to admit defeat or to tell a fantastic lie, whereby he could sentence me to lifelong bondage and perhaps shorten or renounce the promised probation of Theban manhood. True, he gave one startled glance at my big box, only to decide it was still too small to contain Cerberus the Monstrous, nor was there any prodigious growling or snarling from within, which a three-headed dog of such fierce repute would surely give forth.

"Heracles, you may stand before my chair," he said.

"Aye, master."

"Have you returned from the mission on which I sent you, to the Gate of Hades?"

"Aye, master, and far beyond the gate." And I was astonished at the ring of truth in my voice, some liking to utter conviction, which I had not forced; and the King was startled too and, for a moment, dismayed.

"I suppose you saw Hades, Zeus' very brother, King of Hades," he remarked with a twisted lip, when he had recovered his majestic manner.

"Not within his own realm, Eurytus, but I saw him when I had returned to the Upper World."

"You looked into his face, and lived?" And he meant to put great scorn into the question, but he sounded only peevish and his eyes were more round than before.

"No, master. That and most of his body were wreathed in cloud. But I knew him by his darkness, and his cap, and his black chariot and his four black horses."

"Why should he come to the Upper World? His visits here have been most rare, since he seized Persephone. Why should he appear before you? What was his mien? Was it benign?"

"My lord, it was most wrathful. But I did not feel that his rage was against me. He came to the ledge of rock at the mouth of the cave that leads down to his domain. He did not speak to me or look at me; he only went to the box in which I had imprisoned Cerberus, and took him forth, and put something in his place that I did not see then, because of the black clouds, but which I looked at later. And this I have brought for you to see, since I knew it was the wish of the great God, or he would not have put it there."

"Open the box that I too may see."

I did so, and the King rose from his chair to look. He stared, and the sweat came out on his pale face, and then he remembered his

Companions, watching him with narrowed eyes, and made sturdy recovery, and even managed a mocking smile.

"That box would never have held Cerberus the Monstrous. Did you expect to cheat me with a freak of nature? I myself have seen a two-headed colt, and a two-headed infant was born in Corinth in my father's time. Heracles, it may be you have undone many of your winnings until now. But if you will confess——"

"My lord, Cerberus was not a large monster, and by my pressing him into the box, his tail coiling under him, I was able to close the lid."

"Tell us more of the wonders you saw in Hades."

"I laid eyes on great Achilles."

"Now that cannot be. A child would not believe it. Achilles is in Elysia——"

"Master, he chose to live in the chill, dim realms of Hades, along with common soldiers, because he had been felled by a falling arrow, shot by a craven and striking him in the heel. Those were his very words, when he had wet his lips with calf blood which I had brought down."

Eurytus made no immediate answer. He must have felt, as I did, a change of air in the room, a different mood in those who listened, a slowly increasing excitement. His Companions stood very quiet, looking into his face, then into mine. I caught a glimpse of Megara's brilliant eyes; Iole's beautiful face had an expression I could only call forlorn, for it was utterly lonely and strangely sad, as the face of a great commander when the tide of battle turns against him, and his captains stand apart from him and no one speaks.

Only the workmen raising the stone image of the King went on with their labors with unconcern. The only sound was the scraping of stone on stone.

"We have heard how great Theseus sits in a chair, speechless, devoid of memory," the King remarked at last, with a courtesy intended to be subtle mockery. "Did you see him?"

"No, master, nor great Perseus. I saw Cassandra, whom Agamemnon seized as his mead of honor, and whom Clytemnestra killed. I saw my mother Alcmene, and I saw your cousin, Zetes the Well Beloved."

"You saw Zetes?" Eurytus asked in a brave voice.

"Yes, master. I gave him blood, and he spoke to me at length. He told me of the chariot ride on the Thitherean Plain. He spoke of all that happened on the ride, ending in his pitiful death."

Quick-witted though he was, Eurytus needed a little time to frame his reply. He stood at the brink of a precipice, and he needed a moment to recover his balance that he had almost lost. So he rubbed the back of his neck, then pretended a little sound made by the workmen had attracted his attention, so he turned and gazed critically at the statue now in place.

"The pedestal is not tall enough," he remarked to the foreman. "It gives the effect of diminishing my stature, which the Gods did not make great. I see that the feet rest on a disk of marble. Have you one at hand of greater thickness?"

"Aye, master. My fellows will fetch it. It will raise the image nearly a hand's breadth."

"That will do." Again the King turned to me, and now his manner was open, his eyes appeared lighted from within, his expression was happy, his voice had a manly ring.

"Heracles, the eyes of my cousin, Zetes the Well Beloved, were darkened by dire death when you were an infant, dwelling in Thebes. You could not possibly have heard of the fateful chariot ride on the Thitherean Plain if you had not, indeed, spoken to him in Hades. I have no doubt now that you did. I doubt not that you captured Cerberus, and his dread master, angered that I dared send my servant on such a mission, rebuked my insolence in this way, and truly he showed mercy in not hurling me into darkest Erebus. I count it that you have done the labor appointed you, its complete fulfillment prevented only by the vast hand of a God. What do you ask as a mead of honor? Speak boldly."

"Eurytus, I ask first that you renounce all claim on Theban manhood and swear brotherhood with the King of Thebes, neither of you less nor greater than the other. Also I ask that I be freed of bondage to you. Finally I ask a house and domain suitable for a faithful vassal and his wife, your daughter Megara. For this I will pledge my hand and heart in honorable fealty as long as you reign."

"All this I grant. Hear me, my son Nessus, my daughters, my great Companions, and all in sound of my voice. This is a great day in Orchomenus. The Gods have moved——"

He paused, perhaps to speak a warning to the foreman, who had thrust a bronze pry under the marble disk on which the image stood, no doubt to try to insert the thicker disk that his fellows had just brought.

The King's warning came too late. The statue started to topple forward—very slowly, so it appeared to me, and with a kind of grace, related to that grace with which great men die. There was only one force in the room that could have prevented its fall, and that force was mine, to use when opportunity permitted and need demanded. The opportunity presented itself—I saw it as with the eye of my mind —because I was standing close to the King, and by leaping forward, I would have enough time to grasp the tumbling statue in my arms and thrust against it with my chest—no plenitude of time, but enough.

I did not utilize it. I resisted a powerful instinct and did not move. I was not aware just now of desiring the King's death, since I had just won a crushing victory over him. I cannot say that I foresaw further tyrannies in the future, quite possibly betrayal of our pact, either schemes costly to those I loved, for the furthering of his ambitions. Instead, I left the outcome to Fate.

Eurytus was making a frantic effort to get out of his chair, out of the way of the great sledge of death. I watched him, wondering if he would succeed; and this period might have been a second, perhaps two or even three. Meanwhile I heard Iole scream, an outcry not unlike that she had uttered as Antaeus died. I had decided that Eurytus would escape to safety, when the foreman's desperate attempt to thrust the missile to one side changed the outcome of the accident; and Atropos, whose shears never fail to cut a thread of life once she has decreed its severance—which decree supersedes all chance, all circumstance—moved upon the scene.

The foreman did succeed in changing the direction of the image's fall, but in the wrong direction to save Eurytus—indeed, in the same direction he had sprung. His head was not struck squarely by its imitator; the blow appeared to fall on his right shoulder and against his neck, away from which his head had tilted. But it was all one to Atropos, to any Olympian God who might take interest in the deaths of kings, and to Hades, waiting on his throne beyond the Adamant Gate. The King's neck was broken. I knew it by the way his head lolled as he lay on the floor and he gave forth a long sigh and the light in his eyes dimmed. No other harm was done him, nor was the image broken or even scratched. The two lay side by side, equally lifeless, but looking almost as good as new.

Nessus came forward and took the foreman by the arm, but in no fierce grip, only to hold his attention, and the terror in the man's face faded as he saw Nessus' manly face.

"Friend, you did what you could, but you must answer a question."

"Sir, I will, and in the hearing of Apollo, whom I love and serve."

"Have you some mark on your body—say, a birthmark—that might have been put there by a God?"

"Sir, I have this. My mother thought it was put on when she was frightened by lightning, as she carried me in the seventh month."

He pulled his tunic enough to show us a flame-colored mark on his side. In shape it was like that which our sculptors portray in the hands of Zeus or sometimes of Pallas Athene his daughter, a very short arrow with a deeply barbed head and with lines running down at an angle at the base to represent fletching.

And then Iole's voice rose again, ringing through the room, a full-throated shout, and we must look at her with our hearts beating in our throats, and truly she was never more beautiful than in this moment of what she deemed her revelation and her glory.

"It is the thunderbolt, the mark of Zeus," she cried. "The oracle never fails. The Gods and Goddesses are above all, and their wills be done forever, and I am the Priestess of great Artemis, and I will be Queen, reigning alone in Orchomenus with absolute power."

She ran, then, and flung herself into the chair Eurytus had warmed and so lately vacated. Nessus had one moment in which to act, and I saw it emerge to its brief existence, wondering what it would bring or take away, and Nessus seized that moment.

He grasped Iole's hand and yanked her from her seat and flung her halfway across the room to strike and fall against the wall.

"My sister Iole suffered a disordered mind from seeing our father die," Nessus said quietly to the big-eyed court. "Doubtless she will make a quick recovery. I am the son of Eurytus, and I proclaim myself King, and all of you may put your hands in mine in honored fealty. My great Companion Heracles, soon to be my brother, may come up first of all, and his brother Right Doer and highborn Actaeon, like-wise my Companions, shall come in second and third place. And when the pact is made, we shall build a funeral pyre to consume the body of the King, and games will be played in his honor, and a feast spread."

When Nessus and I had kissed each other's hands and heads, I watched my brother and my great friend plight their troths likewise, but I did not watch the pledging of fealty by the lords of the realm, crowding each other a little for places in the line. Instead my gaze went quietly to Eurytus' cooling corpse, and to his counterpart in cold marble, and I seemed to see a fitness in his destruction by his own image, as though ever just Apollo, not a foreman's blunder, had brought about the terrible but strangely beautiful end.

CHAPTER EIGHTEEN

THE THIRTEENTH LABOR

1

When Megara and I had been married about three months, dwelling in a house fully as worthy as the house of Amphitryon where I was born, I had a hankering to revisit the pasturages under Parnassus. There I could look again upon the face of Fold Watcher and other drovers and shepherds I had known as a youth, and behold the lovely highlands crowned by the holy mountain; the rough, brambly steeps in a riot of summer bloom, when the spring-born lambs were playful from the warmth and strength of their mother's milk; and calves pretty as red deer fawns.

If I had any business there, it would be to speak privately with Fold Watcher, to ask him to recount to me a tale he had told Amphitryon of going forth in the deep tide of night, of seeing in the pale downpour from the moon a godlike figure making toward the arch of absent Amphitryon's house, and of hearing him laugh softly—this occurring at the time the Grecian host was gathering for its vengeful voyage to Troy, some nine months before I was born.

As Megara had slept in my arms, I had dreamed of this old telling and had been awakened by the moon, and the thought had struck me that perhaps Fold Watcher had seen more than he had told his master, and might even have recognized the visitor. But the shepherd's love of him, or of beautiful Alcmene, had locked the door of his lips. Both Amphitryon and Alcmene were now shadows of their once warm substances in shadowy Hades. In all likelihood the trespasser by night was a like shadow, unless he was an immortal God, which I did not believe. In any case, no one would be harmed by my knowing all that could be known of my begetting; and my mind, which sometimes despite myself busied itself with this mystery, would be set at ease.

It chanced that Megara could not go with me on the journey, she being needed at home to direct the cleaning and carding of some sacks of wool stored from the last shearing of the homestead sheep. Nor was Right Doer at my right hand, where I loved to have him be, and in all truth he was often absent there of late, since my marriage and his appointment as third in command of Nessus' host. So I had set forth with one thrall from our fields, more truly one companion, and a single pack mule. And before the sunset I had ingloriously turned homeward, from an accident of our mule going lame from a sharp stone deep buried in his hoof. Indeed I turned back at full stride, leaving the thrall to lead the limping beast, I being in haste to rejoin Megara, to have her cuddled against my back between midnight and the soft and beautiful summer dawn, and having not the slightest fear of mishap on the dim path, of which I knew every stick and stone.

My torch had burned out as I neared the homestead, an incident that mattered not at all under this effulgent moon. I came up quietly, intending to waken an old watchman who slept on the porch, and then to take Megara by surprise in the midst of some lovely dream. Then, as I stood over the old man, I heard a postern door, ordinarily at night bolted from within, creak on its bronze hinges, and softly close. Darting quickly around the corner, I caught a glimpse of a tall man, running lightly and quickly in the gray moonlight and swiftly melting into darkness.

My heart was dark, almost my eyes were darkened as I entered the door that the intruder had just fled. Still some light deep within my brain and soul warned me with implacable sternness to take care, not to speak until I had pondered what to say, by no means to act until I could be sure of acting rightly, or at least not with irredeemable folly, and in accordance with my manhood as I conceived it, or longed for it to be. It seemed that, deep and cool in the storm swirling in my brain, I remembered Linus, and how I cracked his skull with his own lyre because I could not pluck music from its magic strings with my blunt fingers.

I went to a blazing oil lamp set on a pillar in the hall, and by shortening my torch, relighted it. Now I heard Megara's voice from her chamber, frantic with alarm. First she wakened a grave dame sleeping in a nearby anteroom, and then called from the curtained arch.

"Who is it?"

"Only I, Heracles. I have come home because of a trifling accident, and now must go forth again for a short space. Go back to sleep, my best beloved. I will be with you soon."

Then I went again into the moonlight and, holding my torch close to the ground, I looked for the footprints of the intruder in the path recently wetted by rain. I need not look long. At first I found only old prints made by barefoot folk of the homestead, overtrodden and smeared; but a little farther on, where the ground was somewhat softer as it sloped to a brook, I found the fresh track of a man wearing sandals. And I need hold the torch close only once, twice, three times, to make certain that the sandal of the right foot had a patched sole—a patch I knew too well.

Still my actions remained unhurried, and as well considered as my bestormed brain could manage. I went into an empty fold nearby, stoutly walled against prowling wolves, closed its door, and sat down against the wall. At first I could think of nothing to do but affix the string of my bow, which I had carried unstrung, not to weaken its tension in time of need. Then the wild thought came to me to take only one arrow when I went forth to do what some God or some unknown and unnatural being of Subterranean Darkness seemed to din in my ears that I must do. I had had in my quiver one especially fine arrow. I had taken great pains with its making, of straight-grained ash, shaping it straight as a shaft of sunlight, and fletching it with falcon feathers; and a skilled metal worker, worthy to be the son of Hephaestus of the Forge, had affixed a bronze barb, beautifully planed and of perfect balance. I had intended it for a birthday gift to Actaeon who, shortly after the feast, had planned to hunt for the so-named King of the Wolves, a very large, old, cunning, and savage heifer- and sheep-killer that ravaged the herds in the highlands above Elatea.

Yet when I searched my sheath, I could not find it. Having given it no thought when starting forth to Parnassus, certainly I had noticed it among the others only three days ago. I knew not what to think. My brain became dreadfully weary from even trying; and perhaps I did not try, perhaps I never wanted to think again; I wanted only darkness and long rest and shadowy dreams which my soul would tell me were not real. So I laid down against a wall. A stone was on the earthen floor, and I drew it toward me, and lay on it my aching head. It must be I did sleep, or at least time passed without my measuring it, for when I came to myself there was grayness between the boards on the eastern side.

I went to the door and gazed eastward. Eos was half awake, I thought, rubbing her beautiful eyes, while aged Tithonus slept on, sleep being the nearest he could come to death because of her fatal gift given in love, the dreadful gift of immortality that only changeless Gods and Goddesses have strength to bear. To Megara I had given love, and it too was an immortal thing, imperishable in this world or in any world to come; and I had loved brave and ever princely Actaeon, and whatever I must do I loved him still. I took some dried meat from my pack bag, which I had worn when I lay down but had taken off, unknowing, in the night. This I ate, and I drank from my flask of watered wine. Then, thinking that our drovers and shepherds would soon come into the meadow with their droves, I rose hastily, again slung my pack, and started to pick up my bow and sheath of arrows. But I had no need of these, I thought. Heracles had no need of weapons to commit any great and irresistible wickedness against man and the Gods who might love man. So I let them lie.

I went forth from the shed, and in the gray light I met our thralls, and they shrank back at sight of me and were tempted to run, yet they stood their ground with their heads drawn close to their shoulders, as if in the first movement to crouch, and they looked at me with round eyes and their mouths open.

"Don't be afraid. I have come to bid you only to leave your beasts, which will take no harm, and go forth separately, on separate paths, to seek my great companion Actaeon. And the first of you that finds him give him this word. 'Meet me at the Pool of Truth nigh the pastures above the Nemean Plain, where I slew Iniquity.'"

"Master, we will," an old drover said in a faltering voice when all the rest were silent. In a moment, all were gone.

I walked about a little while, and looked at the grazing beasts, and watched the glorious break of morning, until finally the blood-red sun heaved up over the broad shoulders of Parnassus. Then I too set out, tramping steadily but not fast, seeing so much that I loved as I went along—man and beasts, children who ran from me, birds, flowers, little brooks that had a charmed, immortal life that never hurt them, pastures, woods in summer greenery, the hills and dales of my beloved country; and it seemed to my soul that I was saying to all of these, "Farewell."

2

I had gone about five miles from the homestead when I saw a man behind me, running to overtake me. He ran as did Right Doer when he wishes to cover a medium long distance, say half a mile, in the shortest possible time—not dashing, instead in a seemingly effortless long stride and with a wondrous suppleness; and half of my heart hoped fiercely it might be he; and the other half prayed it would not because, since there was no way that either of us could help the other, in no jot or tittle, we would be as strangers; which would finish breaking both halves of my heart. Of course it was not he, as I knew full well; for only yesterday he had set out for Thebes to see to matters of his inheritance. The fact remained he might have turned back by now, not knowing why except for an uneasiness that came and went, like a dim ache of a dying tooth, across his forehead.

The runner was a man fully fifty years old, trim and lithe like to many Greeks of middle age. His face was troubled; but he spoke to me with untroubled breath.

"You are Heracles?"

"Aye."

"My master sent me in search of you, to ask that you meet him at the Pool of Truth above the Nemean Plain."

"I think you mean to say that he had received the message which I sent to him by many couriers, to meet me at the Pool of Truth."

This messenger seemed confused by my remark.

"My lord, I do not understand," he answered. "My master, Actaeon, received no message from you, unless it was brought by the Lady Megara, who came to his house two hours after midnight and had him wakened, and spoke to him in privacy. Soon after, he summoned me. I must search for you, and make the entreaty I just made. I had trouble finding you or I would have spoken with you long ere now."

"It must be that his mind moved with mine. Now I resume my journey."

I could, if I dared, take hope from the courier's words; but I dared not, because of doubting their truth. I was no good at unmasking lies.

A little yellow bird warbled wondrously about summer and the world, of her snug nest of strands interwoven with a skill outmatching Penelope's, and of peeping fledglings; but she had better hasten home, lest she find the babies eaten by a jackdaw; and if he came then she could only flutter about the nest, twittering her impotence to defend it. A squirrel frisked in a treetop, leaping vast distances, as measured by a squirrel's yardstick, taking gallant hazards, performing feats worthy of a tumbler at a festival, all from unalloyed joy and trust in life; but she had best watch yonder mist that might overspread the sky and fling down a cloudburst that would drown her sucklings. And should her store of acorns fail in the bleak of winter, her line would be wiped out.

At the end of the second day's march I camped with shepherds in the pastures of Corinthia, and ate with them a great breakfast of baked lamb before the light cleared. The sun was not yet high when I gained the familiar scenes, the upward slopes of the plain heaving suddenly into knolls, hills, and dales; and I saw in a distance the butte from whose top Iniquity had roared defiance, and, crowning the pastures that Snag Tooth had once guarded, the verdure-clad Hill of Olives. The grazing beasts knew naught of the great marauder, he did not even trouble their dreams when they slept in the sun; and of two strangers who watched them, one, the younger, fled from me, I knew not why, and the other, much older, came forth to meet me with a lagging step, but with his eyes on mine.

"Friend, I am making for the Pool of Truth," I told him, "and there I shall wait for Actaeon, the mighty hunter, who has an appointment with me there."

"My lord, he arrived an hour gone, and he waits for you."

So I followed a new worn path around the base of the hill, and soon saw at a distance the dark mouth of the grotto, and then the pool in which Megara and I had bathed; and a little mist ever formed and floated away over its beautiful waters, because the morning was cool. But I saw no sign of Actaeon and heard no sound but the continuous murmur, with its little changes, of the brook.

Then I went to look in the grotto itself, and at its mouth lay Actaeon in dread death. There was enough light to see his tunic stained with blood, and a little pool of blood had formed on the rock beside him. On one of his feet was a dusty sandal of a common kind, and half on, half off the other was one of Snag Tooth's sandals, its mate and the mate of the first lying close by, and I knew that whoever had tried to change his everyday sandals to the pair that he especially loved and wore on great occasions had been interrupted at the task.

And by looking close at what thrust up from his broad and manly chest, I found my lost arrow.

3

I know not how long I would have stood there, gazing down, more lost to myself than in the dim realms of Hades that my soul had visited, if I had not heard a dead twig crack in the thickets close by. I ran toward it, and someone ran ahead of me, someone with light feet. The fugitive was more fleet of foot than I, and might have escaped me except that the thickets thinned, and I caught a glimpse of a head with flaming hair, and then of a whole form, tall and beautiful, and then a side view of a face as beautiful as a Goddess'.

"Iole!" I called, but that was the only breath I wasted. For there was some likelihood of her escaping me yet, and the chance had been greatly increased as she made for the mountain, the one direction from which I could not intercept her flight, although on its rough steeps I could follow fast. And now I marked that she carried no visible weapon, the beautiful bow of bone and ivory with which she often hunted in the way and almost the likeness of her Goddess being nowhere in sight. Perhaps she had hidden it, I thought, when she first discovered my approach.

She outdistanced me a little as we both toiled up the steep, but I cared naught for that, because she could not maintain the pace for long, and the turtle would surely gain upon the hare. And so began the strange chase. Now and then she looked over her shoulder, and at first she laughed at my plodding gait, perhaps because she believed I could never overtake her, or else that her Goddess would snatch her to safety out of my hands. As the sun beat down, and still the mountaintop looked tall and distant, I grunted, as was my wont, and sweated freely, but still I saw no gleam of sweat on her white arms or any heaving of her chest from scant breath. The fact remained that her laughter changed to only a smile of mockery, of infinite disdain, and after a while it seemed to me to become fixed, and then, as the distance between us ceased to widen and remained for a long time unchanged, to vanish altogether.

Not long after this, one of her backward glances showed me a little nearer than before. She tried to hasten her pace, and succeeded a brief while, and again the distance between us widened, for my steady gait remained unchanged. Even so, she paid no little price for the transient advantage, for soon her skin was drenched in sweat, and in the silence of the mountain I heard her racked breath. And now, perhaps because she knew that the path lying westward was nearby, and not as steep and rough as this one, she set off across the mountainside. Sometimes she stumbled and once she fell, and I remembered with vividness and great wonder her strange fall when she had left the ring of death where Antaeus and I had wrestled, as she sped to the shrine of her Goddess. She got up quickly and hastened on, and when she struck the westward path, she paused for one deep breath as she gazed quickly upward to the mountaintop, and then downward to the pastures. An instant later she began her descent and for a space she again gained, for it was my plodding way to descend steep slopes at the same pace I mounted them, thus sparing my lower legs and ankles as much weight as possible.

And if she thought that her downward flight would restore her breath and strength she had reckoned wrongly. I saw signs of her growing weakness, such as her reeling a little at times, often tripping, and I believed the time to be not too distant when I would have her in my hands. What then? With those hands I had killed Antaeus, and had thrust Diomedes through a slit in a wall, where horrid Death was waiting, but by and large I was not fitted to be an executioner of my fellow humans. So I thought to tie her wrists with a thong I carried, and bring her pinioned before Nessus the King. How she would fare there, I knew not, but I did know that Nessus loved her not at all, and no mortal did or ever could, I thought, and Nessus had loved Actaeon with the same kind and strength of love that I had given that princely man.

And now a thought most strange stole into my mind, fled before a force of resisting thoughts, and then in guilty strength retraced its steps and entrenched itself. I thought to take from her her greatest treasure, whereby she could no longer be the darling of Artemis, the Virgin Goddess, no longer prate of her, no longer ape her if not image her; and whether she lived or died at Nessus' hands, she would not be turned into an eternal star. Still, perhaps the dark intent could not have become fixed in my mind if it were not in accordance with a dark desire that I had often confessed, which lately I had thought had died, but which had hidden away, and somehow fed and breathed in the deep realms of my soul. And it might be that her very flight had caused it to quicken and revive.

Whatever I was going to do was not far off. Weak and reeling, Iole had reached the last steep of the mountain, and ahead of her was a brush-grown valley, and beyond that the Hill of Olives, whose gentle slope she must ascend in order to descend to the open pastures for which she yearned. There she believed her grace and lightness and fleet limbs would at last prevail. She gained the foot of the mountain. Instead of trying to break through the thickets, where I would surely catch her, she took up the well-worn path. Since her mien was now a little changed, as though new hope had quickened her weary heart, the thought struck me that she had concealed her bow in some thicket close to the course she was taking, and an arrow was nearby, and that she meant to snatch up both, and launch quickly with deadly aim.

Still she toiled upward, and she had gained almost the crest without the slightest belligerent action. Yet the change in her that I felt rather than saw, a rallying of her spirits and, in some measure, of her strength, did not pass off. She reached the hilltop from which she could take a well-worn goat path to the pastures, so steep that I would be handicapped by my own weight in making swift descent, while her light, sure feet could swiftly outdistance mine if she would take the risk of running and leaping. Instead of darting down this path, she took me by surprise by making a quick turn toward a big crag crowning the hill. It was a favorite pedestal for goats and venturesome rams, sometimes a perch for eagles, as its flat top loomed more than twenty feet above the highest ground.

This action bewildered me as I turned tardily in her pursuit. Did she not know that only one face of the crag offered footholds, that the other faces were naked cliff, and that she could not descend the big granite outcropping except by the way she went? It looked as though she were deliberately trapping herself on the lofty summit. Confusing me still more was her violently swift ascent. As the runner in a foot race appears to hurl himself forward by a final agonizing lurch to the finish line, she was exerting her whole remaining strength to widen the distance between her and me and thus gain a little time for some as yet unknown action.

As she gained the top and whirled to face me, I knew what the action was, but not what it meant. It appeared to have no meaning.

From under her tunic she drew what looked like the toy bow of a child, not much over a foot long, and a short, weak arrow. The head of the latter was wrapped in a cloth, which she tore off with one jerk of her hand, disclosing an odd-shaped although undoubtedly sharp barb, so discolored that I could not tell whether it was silver, bronze, or gold. Swiftly she nocked the little shaft, aimed it at my breast as I started up the steep pitch of the crag, and at about twenty feet range, her eyes wildly bright, she sped it on its way. It flew weakly toward me; even so I tried to dodge it, not because it could reach my vitals or hardly scratch my bone; rather because of the expression on her face, infinitely confident of victory, heavenly serene.

She had shot as I came between two rocks, where I could not leap to one side, and could only turn sideways. Thus I was hit on my bared upper arm, and the barb broke the skin, its point entered no more than half an inch, and the little arrow clung there dangling till I plucked it out. Only a few drops of blood oozed from the trifling wound and trickled down to my elbow, leaving little winding trails of dark red.

Yet as I gazed at the weak missile at my feet, my head swam a little, and when I lifted my foot for another upward step, it did not obey the command of my will. It was as though a God or Goddess had mysteriously intervened in my pursuit of a priestess. Rejecting the thought, but still unable to doubt an attack of dizziness, not unlike that which comes with the first chill of fever, I acted on an impulse not to let Iole know of the debility, to conceal it from her now dreamy-looking, but no doubt probing eyes, until my familiar strength surged back into my thews. It would not take long, I thought. Heracles could not long be weakened by the prick of a toy arrow. It might have struck some master nerve, I thought. For I remembered seeing a stout playmate faint when stung by a wasp.

So I took my facecloth from under my tunic and rubbed off the thin streaks of blood from my arm, as if it were unfamiliar and unseemly stuff. Then, wiping sweat from my face, as if it too were not a verity of my being, I leaned against the rock.

"Iole, was the casting of that little stick a piece of priestly ritual, representing something or other, that you truly believed would save you from my visiting the death of my great companion Actaeon upon your murderous soul?" I asked with a great show of scorn.

After making herself comfortable on the flat top of the rock, one leg under the other which overhung the brink, one hand under her chin, and her face pensive, she spoke in a soft, melodious voice.

"First things first. Let us consider the death of Actaeon. Do you not think it likely that when he came to the Pool of Truth he happened on Artemis bathing there? She often goes there. It is one of her favorite resorts when she is heated from hunting. If so, he saw her divine form unclothed and looked into the face of an Olympian Goddess, for which the price is death. Although he had fled wildly to hide himself in the grotto, he had gained only its entrance when she took up her bow. Then, as he turned to entreat mercy, she shot him through the heart."

"I do not think it likely that a great Goddess would steal one of my arrows in advance to use at the execution."

"Why Heracles, you are not nearly as dense as usual. Why should your brain work so well, when your body is so weak?"

"I am only pausing here a moment as I decide what will be your first punishment—and your last."

"You had chosen the first punishment when you were chasing me up the mountain. I saw it in your face and I smelled it in your sweat. You intended to ravish me, always your secret desire; then to kill me or to lead me, your captive, to my brother the King. Why not do so, Heracles? Why do you hesitate when the quarry is almost in your grasp? Why do you lean against the rock? Your sweat has a different smell than before. Now it smells like death."

"Death? From the prick of a child's arrow?" Yet I must cling to the rock to keep from falling.

"Yes, from the prick of a child's arrow—shot by one you call Iole. But no one will know it was the instrument. You have wiped off what little blood there was—there were only a few drops—the little puncture in your arm will not be found. All Greece will believe that a God who loved the house of Cadmus struck you down for killing your wife's illustrious lover with your own arrow. No one who knows you could mistake its fine workmanship. I will continue my visit to earth. I will remain priestess of my own shrine—the shrine to me!"

"I understood the first part, not the last part. It has a fantastic sound."

"Heracles, I was initiated into the priesthood at sixteen. Voices I heard in dreams had bidden me offer myself to Artemis. For a year I marveled why she never showed herself to me when I loved her so passionately and served her so well. Suddenly I knew the answer. I had seen her face every day in a silver mirror, often her whole form in a woodland pool. But why speak of mysteries you cannot grasp? Instead I will tell you what is to come. That will be easy to get through your thick head. I will be Queen of Orchomenus. Nessus will have pricked his thumb on a little thorn; I will take the seat he has briefly warmed; it is a trifle but will make good sport. What will you be doing, Heracles? Even now you have turned pale. You sway. You had better sit down, lest you fall. Could the conqueror of Iniquity be sickened by a prick in the arm? It must be so, so I had better hasten with these tidings."

"I still do not know what you mean."

"Knowledge will soon be obtained, Heracles. It would not have mattered had you caught me on the mountain. It would not have mattered had you ravished me, for I would have hardly known you were there. Once I had a lover whose presence I did know. He was the son of Ares the Bloody, so it was no shame for an immortal Goddess to be the slave of his great loins. His name was Antaeus. By some trick I know not even now, perhaps worked through your hands by some Goddess jealous of me, you killed him. For that you will die a horrid death before Helios dips to his rest in the red West. That death was fated you. If you had caught me on the mountain I would have seized my chance to prick you with the child's arrow. But I chose to taunt you by a long race, then let you die in agony on the Hill of Olives, a place sacred to you because here died an old drover whom you loved, and here leaped high the flames of his funeral pyre.

"But no pyre will blaze to consume your rotted flesh and bone, Heracles, slayer of Antaeus my beloved," Iole went on in her beautiful limpid voice, a pensive beauty on her face. "Only doting Iphicles will dump your stinking corpse into a shallow grave; all others will abjure it because you slew in stupid jealousy your true friend. Megara will hate your memory because you did not trust her love. Heracles, what I have done to you I did from implacable hatred, and all the punishments that my father's brother, the King of the Dead, visits upon you in Hades will never balm that hatred. I hate you as much as I love great Antaeus, which is Heaven-wide, Hell-deep, and everlasting."

I heard her as in a horrid dream, yet marked every word. And now

I drew my breath in pain, darting and ineffable, to ask a stammered question.

"You say, 'my father's brother.' Your father was Eurytus, the grandson of a slave, not an immortal God."

"I tried to tell you at first, but your brain was cloudy. Now it is being cleared by pain. My earthly father was Eurytus. I had chosen to dwell awhile on earth; what did it matter in whose seed was instilled my divinity? You know me as Iole. In truth, I am Artemis, the Huntress; daughter of Zeus. When I am done with these adventures, I will return to my true place and office. And then I will lift up Antaeus out of Hades and seat him at my side. There will be a new deity in my golden house."

My brain dizzied even more, but I drove off its mists and got a flask of wine from my pack bag, the sea-dark, incomparable wine of my native land, and drew from it deep draughts. When I spoke again the issuing voice was my own.

"You are no more Artemis than I am Zeus. You are Nessus' sister Iole, whom he hurled against the wall; and you will be hurled against another wall, and crushed. Still, I cannot doubt my soon death at your hands by a subtle poison. Before I go down to Hades, bereft of speech or thought or memory, there remain puzzles that I long to solve, other than those of your inborn evil, grandiose lies, and perhaps madness. Will you answer my questions as to some of your doings that I do not yet understand?"

"Why not? Being of unusual strength, you have two or three hours, perhaps four, maybe even five before your soul passes in a last agony. I mean to stay with you to the last. I will watch your every writhing; when you faint I will wait in patience till once more the pain wakes you. Your brain will be the last part of you to die—it is a property of the poison, one reason that I chose it from among many that I know. To converse with you will make the time pass even more pleasantly—for me. This is the hour of my victory, second only to my going home, above the clouds of Olympus, and that is still far off. This hour I wish to savor in all its delectable bliss."

4

Of the tides of pain in which I drowned, some were higher than others. The lowest I could bear without giving much sign; they were not much worse than a heavy ache in my back, loins, and limbs; the highest caused darting torments like tongues of fire, and then I must pant or bite my tongue to stave off yelling. Now my mouth was often filled with blood from the crushed or severed vessels, and this I swallowed in a last pride rather than have my torturer perceive her triumph. There was no surcease ever, for under the lowest tide, what might be called slack tide, a surf of pain was beating slowly and incessantly.

In Babylon stand hollow images of bronze representing the God Baal, and these are appeased by putting people inside them and building a fire under them until the metal glows dull red, and the fiery eyes of the God shows his satisfaction. In other barbarian countries there is a device called a rack, to which the victim is bound, and there his body is stretched by pulleys until one by one his bones rip apart and break. And on far-off deserts, or so I was told in Krim, men condemned to death by chiefs or priests are fastened to giant anthills, where their flesh is slowly eaten off their bones by the myriad of ferocious inmates.

My torture seemed intended to partake of the nature of all three: roasting, destruction of my skeleton, and the slow eating away of my flesh. Worst of all, I thought that what Iole had promised me was coming true, and my flesh was rotting and would soon slough off.

"Since I have no antidote," I said to her with my thickening tongue, "will you tell me the source of such a potent poison?"

"Gladly," she answered. "It was discovered by so-called witch doctors in the deserts about Egypt; and the priests of Osiris, the God of Death in the temples of Memphis, have learned its lore and use. First, the liver is removed from a carcass, preferably that of a newly slaughtered slave, but the liver of certain beasts will do almost as well. This is lowered into a pit of serpents, these being long, black and slender, with short fangs instead of the long fangs of the viper, and after it has been bitten many times by the angry snakes, it is removed and allowed to rot in the sun. Then in due course it is boiled in the blood of a slave dying of the bites of many vipers, whose poison is of a different sort than that of the long, black, slender snakes. When the meat disintegrates, some of it becomes spongy matter of no use. The residue is a viscid and pale-yellow liquid. The tiniest drop on a knife blade or an arrowhead scratching the skin will corrupt and cause dissolution of the whole body, whether that of a puny man or the great tusked elephant of Ethiopia. When you say you have no antidote, you put yourself with the greatest physicians and priests. There is none. If you could bring Antaeus back to me, beautiful and whole, still I could not save you from loathsome death ere tonight the Belt of Orion blazes in the eastern sky." And Iole spoke with great beauty of tone.

"It was an evil day for me, a darkling moment, when I first caught a glimpse of you in the forest under Parnassus. Will you tell me your business there, so far from home? It could not have concerned me then."

"No, I did not know of your existence. I had been sent there by my lover Antaeus to observe the cattle, and see if they were worth taking by the Sons of Poseidon, the band of horsemen that he commanded, and who, to delude the louts guarding the herds, pretended to be centaurs. But when Antaeus' lieutenant, Nessus, came to drive off a few head, he talked to you, and did not obey his master's orders—indeed, his disaffection began then and there, I believe, and although he still feared Antaeus with a deadly fear—and why not?—still, he moved against him in secret. And thus a seed of hate was planted in my heart, hate of you, Heracles, and it grew slowly but with great strength; and then suddenly, when you slew him, it was a growth rank and poisonous, and today you know its consummation."

"Why, since you had no doubt of Antaeus' killing me in the wrestling bout, did you invent a device whereby I could turn tail?"

"By then, a faint but horrid doubt had begun to torture me. I had looked at the carcass of the great stallion Erebus, and when I saw how he had bled under his hide, and had run my hand over the broken rib bones, I did not believe Nessus' story of the beast dying of heart failure, and perceived that you were indeed of mighty thew. Not nearly the giant among men that Antaeus was, of that I was certain, and am certain yet, still you might know some trick to win; and to think of my dwelling on this earth with Antaeus gone, never enfolding me in his mighty arms, never in the black hollow of night pressing upon me, almost crushing the life out of me with his great weight as he hurled into me his own gigantic life, chilled my heart with terror. My trick was clumsy. Still it might have postponed the perilous issue, and given me time to wipe you from his path and mine before you did harm. Then I saw him die in your cowherd hands. I know not how I refrained from some swift and rash revenge, unless it were fear of Megara. Even I, an immortal Goddess, feared that black-eyed Medea. Aye, I confess it to you. What does it matter on this glorious day?"

As she spoke, a wondrous and almost unearthly beauty in her face, I became aware of a change within myself, holding out no hope for tomorrow but a faint, wan hope of some last stroke, of comfort to my soul even as it sped, that I might deal today. My pain was no less, the presage of a horrid sloughing of my flesh from my bones was more distinct, yet the first stunning attack of the poison had passed as it penetrated my vitals, and I felt a surge of returning strength, perhaps my body's last and vain resistance to its destruction, like a quiet hollow between two tempest-driven waves. To conserve it and to conceal it from Iole, I slid down the rock against which I leaned, and thus sat then at its very base, my back at rest.

"Just before Eurytus took Theban youth into bondage, you prayed fervently for his death," I said, my voice a little stronger. "Nessus heard you. Megara thought it was for love of Thebes or for some Theban. I know now you had some other reason. Will you tell me what it was?"

"Gladly. It was so Antaeus could become King and I his Queen."

"Your prayer went unanswered—Antaeus is in Hades and Nessus is King. And your plans failed again when you persuaded Eurytus to send me to capture the Stag of Artemis with golden horns. Still I cannot penetrate their intricacies and your extravagant behavior. Did you not trust too much to chance—perhaps to the help of Callisto the Beautiful, whom you believed an earlier manifestation of your own godhead?"

"You must understand, Heracles, that then I did not possess the poison known as the Fang of Mamba. I knew of it, but it was exceedingly rare as well as costly. You need not remind me that my plans failed, I know it only too well; yet they were soundly conceived. I meant for you to be found beside the image of Callisto deep in the crater, with what looked like a tine broken from a golden antler deep in your breast. The folk would believe that Artemis was enraged by your chase of her stag, and in his form she had gone down to the ancient shrine, and there she had impaled you on his horn, which had broken off. My actions before I struck were well considered. Ever in my mind was the teaching of Eurytus, my father, the King, which had been taught him by dire battle, and with the help of which he gained his throne. It was, simply, ever to keep open a line of retreat in case an attack fails. I had great respect for your combative

powers, and I laid the ground for my preservation in case I struck and
missed.

"I had wakened you from sleep by tipping over a bucket of water,"
Iole went on, her face radiant with self-worship. "I knew you were
watching me as I stole out of camp and knew you would follow me.
You heard me invoke the soul of Antaeus, and utter before the image
of the Goddess those monstrous lies, but in her heart she knew my
motive, for she and I were one. I did strike and miss. You could not
deny that I had mistaken you for a ghost you believed I hated. And
since then, Heracles, I failed once more in the matter of the boat on
Comais Lake. Evil chance brought those two carp fishermen in the
fateful moment—otherwise two mouths hateful to me would have
been stopped with mud. Yet I have lived to rejoice in that failure. By
one stroke I have taken full measure of revenge against all those whom
I hated with the deathless hate of a Goddess. I have surpassed in divine revenge my slaughter of Niobe's children, ere I came to earth."

Again I felt a surge of strength, greater than before, perhaps the
last that I would feel before my dissolution.

"Iole, why did you hate Actaeon? Had he ever harmed you?"

"Once he mocked what he called my pretensions to divinity. This
he will remember and repent when he is given blood in the bleak and
dusky realms of Hades. Anyway he was your great companion. But the
main reason that I sped your arrow into his noble breast was that in
death you will be dishonored as a murderer of a true friend. Megara
has blocked my plans more times than I can count, mocked me also,
and today my vengeance will be fulfilled when she gazes on the rotting
carcass of her true love. What glorious fulfillment! All is well with
me, Heracles. How is it with you? There is more color in your face,
but doubtless that is fever. Your eyes look feverish; you seem very
frail. Perhaps the time of our parting is nearer than we thought."

"It may be so." Meanwhile I was testing the strength in my stubborn body by pressing with my palms against the rock, and I felt
tension in the muscles of my arms, a thrill of might despite the poison. "It was you, Iole, who caused my mule to go lame, I care not how,
so I would turn homeward and in the dead of night, hear a door
open and find in the moist ground the track of a patched sandal
which you had imprinted. Still, there were countless chances that the
scheme would go wrong. I might have delayed my return until
morning——"

"I thought not. You would too greatly miss Megara's warmth as she lay in your arms. If it had gone wrong, I was protected against shame or loss. I told you how I always kept open a line of retreat. Even on that day unspeakable, with the abhorred shears of Atropos already reaching toward my lover, no premonition of their true aim dulled my wits. Recall the children's performance of the Ritual of the Bears, led by little Arne. I had considered the possibility of the throng's taking a wicked, rebellious stand against her being sacrificed. True, it was Megara who led them in that stand. Do you wonder that I hate her? Yet I was saved from defeat by having the kid ready, with a faithful minion to release him at my signal and let him run in search of his dam in sight of the people."

"Why should you want to sacrifice little Arne?" I asked with a strange quietness.

"She was pretty, and charming, indeed a joy to my eyes, and I wanted her for my attendant, in her joyous childhood, when I resumed my place on Olympus."

"Well, you may now ask your fellow deities at Olympus to come to your help—your father Zeus, your brother Apollo, although I think both will scorn your plea." And I rose in my place and started to climb the crag to Iole's place.

"You are mad! I am an immortal Goddess. What do you mean to do?"

"You will know, and then you will cease to know." And I climbed sturdily, my members sustaining me well, my heart fluttering weakly yet faithful to me still.

Iole had turned marble-white as she saw my steady advance, and retreated to the edge of the flat summit of the crag, and I saw her look down, hoping perhaps that some fellow deity would lend her wings; but none did so, and by stretching out my arms I prevented her slipping by me to the one avenue of escape. In a moment I had cornered her and my hands had clasped her arms. It would take a mighty God to save her now. None such appeared. There was no blast of thunder, no bolt cast from on high, no arrow of death; there were only the rock and the wooded hill and the peaceful pastures below, all wondrously quiet under the noonday sun. I flung Iole across my shoulders.

"Let me go, Heracles," she pleaded. "I cannot save you from death —the poison is implacable—but I will see that your corpse is honored on a great pyre, and that a feast is spread, and games are played, and your soul will pass swiftly to Elysia and forever bliss. This I pledge you, in the name of Artemis. If I am not she, if some jealous Goddess has lied to me, at least she loves me with a great love, and her father is very Zeus, and her uncle the King of Hades. Let me go. Do not harm me. If you do, you will suffer agonies in hell worse than those of Tantalus."

"I will harm you, Iole, do not doubt."

"Gods, come to my help. Zeus, let your thunders peal, and hurl down the dread lightning against this monster, lest he shake your throne. Apollo, brother of Artemis, speed your fatal arrow. Artemis! If I am not your manifestation upon earth, at least I am your priestess. I served your shrine in unfailing duty and love. Cast your deadly shaft before it is too late."

"It is already too late."

For I had carried her down the broken rock, and around to its sheer side, and before this I took my stand at a distance of about six feet. Then I raised my captive high in my arms and, as she screamed as shrilly as when she watched Antaeus die between my hands, with a great surge of strength surpassing any I had ever known, I hurled her against the rock wall.

Her whole body made a long crackling sound as she hit. Then she dropped to the ground, the ends of her broken bones thrusting through the flesh, and of her goddess-like beauty no sign could be seen in this bloody blob that was her shattered body. Her wide-open eyes stared at the sun, but reflected no light.

This was my third killing of an earth dweller in human shape, and the last ere I departed from the earth; but in all these killings I had destroyed inhuman evil; and I would go down to Hades with my head high.

5

Presently I fainted, falling in the grass and knowing naught how long I lay like a poled ox, then was aroused by pain. Yet my head cleared quickly, and well I remembered that from the moment I left my seat to climb the crag until this moment I had felt very little pain, only a throbbing ache throughout my body, no stabbings of pain's knife or burning within my vitals. The idea struck me that my great exertions had somehow moved contrary to pain, and partly blocked its passage.

And if this was true, it was an added reason for setting to my last great labor. By my mother's labor I was born; for twelve great labors had I been fated and these I had performed. Labor was my element; through labor I had realized my being as some men realize their beings through deep thought. One more remained, worthy of Heracles. In the glory of her fickle victory Iole had told me that no one would erect a funeral pyre on which my racked and blackened corpse could be consumed; and she had been wrong to start with, because Right Doer would have raised this last edifice to me, if with his last breath. And now she was proven doubly wrong, for there came to me the strong intent, not shakable by pain, hardly to be balked by any God or Goddess, rising above weakness, to build my own pyre, set it alight, and to die in flame instead of from vile poison eating me from within, and let my soul be cast upward along with sparks and red smoke and floating brands. Then when the weight of my once humanity caused it to sink, it would have crossed the River of Woe and fall to its final abode in the Land of Shades.

It so chanced that since great Snag Tooth's body had been burned, along with that of his great enemy Iniquity, a wind of heavy force had smote the east side of the Hill of Olives, doubtless a whirlwind born in a great black cloud and reaping destruction in a narrow path. It had uprooted many ancient wild olive trees that had formed a labyrinthal tangle of broken trunks and boughs. This lay only a little below the summit, so I put aside my backpack, clambered down the brief distance, heaved to my shoulder one of the pieces of wreckage, about my own length and weighing no more than two hundred pounds, and bore it to the very site of the holocaust that had consumed my great friend and foe. And from the instant that I picked it up until I laid it down in its due place I felt very little pain.

So I began my labor, all alone on the hilltop, and ever my spirit strengthened, and I bore increasingly heavy loads. Ever I panted, as I toiled, and often spat blood, and sometimes it oozed from my ears and nostrils, and frequently I fainted; yet the work went forward, one log laid in place, and then five, and then ten laid crisscross, and in moments of great weakness I carried up boughs of no weight to lay down as kindling. In a little while a drover came running across the grass, then walking swiftly, and then very slowly, and he ached to speak to me, I thought, but I shook my head and he went away. In a little while he returned, bearing a bronze ax, and this he brought nearly to the tangle, then leaned it against a log and again departed. And I went and got it, to cut away obstructing boughs, thus hurrying my task.

The sun dipped from his zenith, the short shadows slowly lengthened, the stillness of late afternoon lay on the land, and by now I had laid down twenty logs, making a pyre six or eight feet broad or long, and six feet high—nothing to compare with the high pyre of a king, yet adequate to consume my body and the body of my friend, the grandson of great Cadmus, Actaeon. I would build it higher for his sake, if given the time; but this I could not reckon on with any surety, for my body had begun to give forth a smell most loathsome—the smell of decay, I thought. I would get used to it and hardly notice it until some little puff of the sweet pure evening air was defiled by it, and blew it again into my nostrils. Thus I could not trust Atropos not to bring her shears in sudden haste—in sudden mercy I would almost say, for pain devoured me if I stopped a single moment to blow my fetid breath—before I had finished my most urgent preparations. So I lumbered down the hill, frequently falling, once lying in a faint, arousing to find the sun wearing great plumes of red and gold that gloried every western cloud and shot high into the sky. Onward I made my way to the grotto by the Pool of Truth; and never it lay so beautiful and serene, symbolic of some final truth beyond my dreams. There I put Actaeon's stiffening body across my shoulder and it seemed a light burden, and one of love, as I bore him upward.

I fainted during the climb and we lay side by side awhile until I again restored the body to my shoulder; and night was falling swiftly as I lay it by the pyre. And then the need of haste seemed greater than before, but this was an illusion, for the dread Sister did not glide in the gliding shadows, her shears did not reflect a glimmer of the dying day, and what had spurred me was the sight of two comers here, a man and a woman, approaching swiftly in a mule cart on the track winding upward from the Nemean Plain. They were yet far off, and I ran stumbling and reeling to the nearest supper fire built by frightened drovers, almost at the very spot where Snag Tooth had raised his tent when he was young. And the folk drew back, into the shadows, at sight of me, and when I asked them if I could take a firebrand to ignite my pyre, none dared answer but a little girl, born since the marauder's death, and she spoke in a voice as clear as a flute.

"Yes, Heracles, you may."

So I took the brand and, holding it downward, brought it safely to the place of burning, and there I lighted a little brush under and at one end of the edifice. From hence the light evening breeze would slowly but surely waft the flame to the other kindling which would ignite the logs. And now I picked up Actaeon's body for the last time. Clambering halfway up the pyre, I laid it on the top, moving the half-stiffened limbs until they gave the appearance of repose. And then I climbed up beside him, for night was falling; the stars had begun to burn in deep recesses of the cobalt sky. This was my proper place as I spoke to visitors, the two on earth that I most loved, who now were hastening up the footpath and already in sound of my voice.

"Heracles, come back to me," Megara said quietly.

"I cannot, my beloved," I answered. "Already my flesh is stinking from decay, and my bones rot from a most potent poison."

"Then come down and put your hands in ours as you cast your soul, Heracles, my brother," cried Right Doer. "And I pledge you, in the name of our long love, that when your eyes are darkened, I and the men of the pastures will build another pyre, greater than this, to consume your body and the body of godlike Actaeon, our true friend."

"Nay, Right Doer, for the first time in my remembrance I refuse your prayer. This pyre I have raised with my own hands, a last labor not for a king, not for the folk, not for the Gods, only for the solace of my own soul. I am Heracles. My soul is about to take wing in flame of my own making. What else is fit? Pray you, watch beside the flame until our bodies are utterly consumed, and then eat meat to sustain your breaking hearts, and in due time, when your tears are dried, each of you take the other, partly to fill my place, and so you may miss me less, and be bound in love and marriage, until you come down to me."

"Come down to you?" Megara asked in quiet wonder. "No, I will go with you."

"And so will I, Heracles, my brother," Right Doer told me in a ringing voice. "Drear and gray the realm where we three will go, even so it will be more welcome to my soul than this beautiful earth, under the bright sun by day, the myriad of gleaming stars by night, after your departure. Make room for me, Heracles. I come to join you."

"And make room for me," Megara cried, as she mounted the first tier of logs.

They were climbing swiftly, and what could I do but descend, and in each hand take one of them, and gently as I could, thrust them back? But it so chanced that I was too gentle, and both of them clung to me, and I fell with them to the ground. And before I could break their desperate grasp and resume my place, the Gods moved, or mere chance intervened to interrupt the grim and steadfast movement of event. The kindling at one end was flaming fiercely now, and a sudden gust of wind drove the flame through all the rest. It all caught fire at once, and the thickening walls of darkness were thrust back, and the most daring shadow darted away, and we saw one another's faces as under the noonday sun.

Megara's eyes, fixed on my face, began slowly to widen, and her mouth dropped open as she drew an unbelieving breath, and at first she could not speak, and only her hands groped to clutch my garments, as though these could speak what her tongue could not. But finally her breath came back to her cramped throat and she cried out with great vehemence and illimitable wonder.

"Heracles! You are well!"

"That cannot be——"

"I tell you it is true. Do I not know your face? If the taint of death were there would I not see it? It must be you have sweated out the poison. The stink is not of decaying flesh but of the vile venom that has oozed out your open pores. Right Doer! Do I tell the truth? Find your breath, man, and speak."

"Aye, speak," I bade him, "remembering I have never told you a lie, nor have you ever told me a lie. My brother, do not love and vain hope dazzle Megara's eyes?"

"No, they do not," Right Doer answered in a ringing voice, and it seemed to re-echo from the distant mountain. "Heracles, I too know your face, so plain and beautiful, and your common form that hides a giant's strength, and I swear to you before the Gods, all that ever were or ever will be, more than that I vow it by my love, that you are well."

And then we could only stand with interbound hands, watching through the blurs of tears the beautiful upward-leaping flame.

6

It came to pass that Megara asked me to pick up the shattered body of her sister and give it to the clean fire.

This I did, and then we three stood watching the fire mount to its zenith, roaring and crackling in the silence of the night despite its meager feeding compared to the pyres of Snag Tooth, Amphitryon, and Eurytus. Before long we heard murmured voices behind us, and then perceived that all the dwellers of the pastures were gathering, still timid but no longer fearful of me, for no longer hateful Death looked out of my eyes. Some were toddlers and little children born since the dread days of the marauder's raids and the great days of his death, and some were youths and maidens, and the most were men and women in their prime, who had helped dig Iniquity's grave or had brought spitted meats for his funeral feast; and a few were old. And these few might be warming their wrinkled hands at a great funeral fire, watched by the Gods, for the last time before they themselves lay down in humble graves.

And we three drank of the wine the people brought, and ate of the meat.

"Orion's belt, gleaming in the high sky, tells us it is midnight," Megara said as the fire was burning down. "Tomorrow the sun will heave up at his appointed hour. But it is not good that we three go back to common living. What shall we do ere we grow old and weary? Where may we go to hear Apollo sing?"

"I can answer that," rose Right Doer's ringing voice. "Nessus the King will give us a ship, and stout Bromius and his crew will sail her, for they have drunk of adventure and crave more of the heady brew, and we will point her prow toward the Ionian Sea, and Hesper shall be our guiding star. Heracles and I have touched the great land beyond the sea, but other lands lie farther on, and if we can believe the legends, by a long sail we may reach the River of Ocean. Who can swear that the Hesperides are only a myth? Of a certain we shall see new shores, eat fruits unknown in Greece, drink unimagined wine, behold new peoples. If we turn southward after we have passed the mountainous gates of our sea, we may see a river as great as the Nile; if we turn northward we may look upon mountains higher than Olympus. Heracles will find labors to ease his restless arms. I may acquire a little knowledge, which somehow I have come to love. Megara, you may bring forth babes with the hearts of eagles. We will make good use of glorious youth. The Gods in their golden seats, denied adventure because they are immortal, will envy us."

When we had sipped from one another's cups in forever troth, and poured libations to Hermes, God of Travelers, and to great Pan lest he deny us the wild music of his pipes, I caught myself speaking of a matter on which ordinarily I kept silent.

"There is one old shepherd I would like to see before we sail. I want to ask him a question."

"He is called Fold Watcher," was Right Doer's quick reply. "As Megara and I were leaving Orchomenus, the thought struck me that what he might tell you could have great bearing on coming events. So I sent a slave, famed as a fast runner, to my pastures under Parnassus, and bade him come in all haste. I think you will see him here before dawn."

Speak of Zeus, and you will hear the rattle of his thunder!

Fold Watcher's coming was not as pat as the adage would have it, yet he arrived in a little more than an hour, and we three sat with him about a low fire, when the herders and drovers had gone to their houses and only dark-red coals remained of the funeral pyre. And then, rallying my breath, I spoke my great question.

"On the night that I was conceived, you were wakened by a bear threatening the fold, and you rose, and you chanced to see a visitor approaching the arch of the house where my mother slept. You heard him laugh lightly, and you told Amphitryon that you thought he was an immortal God. Did you think so?"

"Heracles, I did not tell Amphitryon I thought so. I said he looked to me like an immortal God—but I had never seen a God and I doubt if I ever will, except black-capped Hades. In all truth, I did not think he was a God. I thought he was a young warrior, going out of his way to visit Thebes ere he took ship for Troy."

"Did you know who he was?"

"No, my lord."

"Have you any notion?"

"What worth an old shepherd's notion? They are not proof. And Alcmene's and Althea's believing the visitor was a God—at least pretending to that belief—made me close my mouth. Still, Alcmene, my mistress, is long gone, and Althea is an old woman, no longer frightened of the truth if the truth I tell; and you, Heracles, are alive and young, and it comes to me I have no right to withhold from you my thought, my guess, my inkling true or false. I make bold to tell you that I think that the tall visitor I saw approaching the arch, his helmet and his sword and his very being shining in the moonlight, was the great Achilles."

I was struck dumb. Right Doer turned fiery red in the face. Then he asked, in a low murmur:

"Fold Watcher, did you say *Achilles?*"

"Aye, master, I said that very name."

"What fools we are! Why did we not surmise it long ago? Linus gave you the first hint, Heracles, when he came to your bedside and said that he had been sent to tell you my father had done wisely to keep both of us from the war until you had gained your full strength. You asked how he had passed out of the Adamant Gate. Linus answered that when he who sent him to you raised his voice to Cerberus, the monster crouched down. Amphitryon, on his death bed, sensed in you some illustrious heritage. Aged Nestor said you reminded him of Achilles' father, then knew he was not quite right. Do you remember my saying that King Hades would never punish you for the invasion of his realm, lest some inmate whom he greatly feared would take vengeance on him for the sake of some lost love? The visit of the Death King to the ledge was a figment of the spell I had cast, but the spell was real to me, too, and my soul spoke through my lips. Heracles, let your own soul speak forth its truth to us who love you."

"My soul speaks only unto me, Heracles, myself alone, apart even from you in this, Iphicles, my brother, and my lips are dumb."

"Then I will speak it for you. There was no mortal other than Achilles to whom my mother, the pure and beautiful Alcmene, would have yielded, and to him only on his maiden passage, ere he set forth for Troy where he was doomed to be slain; and only because thereby she might bear a son as great as he, who might in the fullness of time serve Greece better than Achilles was fated to serve the Grecian hosts in ruinous war. Lift your head, man! Do not stand with your gaze fixed on the ground. Look your fate in the face, as you have always done."

"Aye, raise your head, Heracles, my husband," Megara said.

So I did, and looked on the two faces I loved most. And then the common world was returned to all three of us by Fold Watcher's stammered entreaty.

"Will your honors please pour me a cup of wine? I am deeply shaken."

We made haste to grant his plea, and Megara wiped his chin when a little of the purple wine spilled from his trembling lips. Soon after, when I had bathed in the Pool of Truth, we four made our beds at what was once Snag Tooth's camp, and the trailing curtains of the night vanished behind the western highlands, and the dawn broke.

As I lay wakeful, Megara still asleep in my arms, I pondered the revelation for a little while, ere I dismissed the matter forever from my mind. And I was glad that doomed Achilles had lived to fight his peers, the horse-taming Trojans, in a war to be remembered when the pyramids of Egypt had crumbled into desert grit. And most of all I was glad that he had lived to beget a son in a glorious age. I deemed that there had never been, or ever would be, an age to equal it in splendor, an age in which common men were as proud as kings in meaner ages—swift to avenge a slight, fearless of dark death, haughty of soul, loving beauty with deathless love, honoring bravery as a peer of beauty, fierce in defending honor, never cringing, even before a God. I rejoiced that I walked the ground on which Achilles had towered. I would never see the first golden ray of the rising sun leap over the eastern hills without visioning the fiery glance of Hector's helm.

I would journey far, but if I lived, I would return to walk the hallowed paths of my native land. Beautiful, brave Greece, I love you.

The hero of this imaginative and powerful novel is Heracles, who in Roman myth was Hercules—born in the first year of the Trojan War, fated to become the greatest figure of the heroic age when Greece was ruled by scores of jealous kings, when weapons were made of gleaming bronze and diadems made of gold.

At the age of five, Heracles crushed in his chubby fists the spade-shaped heads of two messengers of death that had invaded his bed of sheepskins. Who was this child? What was the source of his seemingly supernatural strength? Here Edison Marshall searches for the man behind the myth, as he sought for the real King Arthur in his recent novel, *The Pagan King*. Here the reader divines Heracles as a force compared to nature's, yet one who worshiped beauty with the typical passion of the ancient Greek, whose strength and greatness stemmed from the vital earth he loved.

The twelve great labors Heracles undertook in order to free his countrymen from the yoke of a tyrant king are portrayed as entirely believable, none transcending the humanly possible, despite their strangeness. They are labors which embrace high adventure, feats of primitive engineer-

(continued on back flap)